Donald Harstad is a veteran of the Clayton
County Sheriff's Department in northeastern Iowa.
A former deputy sheriff, Harstad lives with his wife,
Mary, in Elkader, Iowa. Fourth Estate also
publish his other novels, *Eleven Days*
and *The Known Dead*.

The Kronen Dead
Freven Dead

ALSO BY DONN   OVERSAL

H   STAL

The Big Thaw

Donald Harstad

F/H86836

FOURTH ESTATE • *London*

This paperback edition published in 2001
First published in Great Britain in 2000 by
Fourth Estate
A Division of HarperCollins*Publishers*
77–85 Fulham Palace Road
London W6 8JB
www.4thestate.co.uk

Copyright © Donald Harstad 2000

1 3 5 7 9 10 8 6 4 2

The right of Donald Harstad to be identified as the author of
this work has been asserted by him in accordance with the
Copyright, Designs and Patents Act 1988

A catalogue record for this book is available from the
British Library

ISBN 1–84115–395–8

Printed in Great Britain by Clays Ltd, St Ives plc

To Rae and Nick Anderson

Thank you for your encouragement, support, and confidence that good things were going to happen. Most of all, thank you for prying open some doors.

Acknowledgments

To Dr. Peter Stevens, I wish to express my great appreciation for his great knowledge of pathology, his enthusiastic advice, and his support of my efforts. I would like to express my gratitude to the Officers, Dispatchers, and Staff of the Clayton County Sheriff's Department, for their continued cooperation and assistance, and for the work they do every day and every night. I would like to thank my friends "on the boat," who explained some complex things to me. I thank my wife, Mary, without whose support and encouragement I would not be able to write; and my daughter, Erica, who provides honest and constructive criticism in the early stages of each book.

The Big Thaw

One

About a minute after I got settled in bed, I heard a faint scratching sound. It took me a second to realize that I'd left my police walkie-talkie on. It was sitting in its charger, about fifteen feet from the bed. I thought about getting up and turning it off, but there were several reasons I didn't. First, Sue was already asleep beside me, and I didn't want to wake her by moving around some more. Second, the intermittent transmissions by the bored dispatcher were kind of soothing, in a distant way. I could hear her talk, but the volume was set so low, I couldn't make out the words. Perfect. Third, I was just too damned tired to get up.

I was getting to that presleep stage, when the pitch of the dispatcher's voice began to rise. After a moment, she began to speak rapidly, excitedly to cars that were apparently too far away for me to hear. I sat up, and listened for a moment. Still couldn't make out the content, and now I just had to find out. I swung my legs off the bed, got up, and padded over to the little radio. Just in time to be able to make out the Maitland car, which was within a quarter mile of me, asking a question.

"Comm, Twenty-five, what's going on?"

"Twenty-five, Five and Nine are in pursuit of a burglary suspect, out on the old Grange road."

I knew what was coming, and was reaching for the phone when it rang.

"They want some assistance, and Lamar said to call you, since it might involve a burglary investigation. They started the chase about five minutes ago down by Hellman's curve, and they've been going up . . ."

"Okay . . ." I interrupted, "just let me get dressed . . . give me directions after I'm in the car . . ."

"Ten-four . . ." She was new, and newbies had a tendency to use ten codes over the phone.

"Wear your long johns, it's getting really cold."

"Yeah . . ." as I hung up the phone.

"Who was that?" mumbled Sue.

"Gotta go . . . they're chasing a guy and need help." I reached into my drawer and pulled out my long underwear. I pulled it on, and put on two pair of socks.

"Dress warm . . ." came a mumbled caution from Sue, who was going back to sleep.

"Yep . . ." I pulled on my uniform trousers, which had the utility belt attached, and were hanging next to the bed. On with the laced Gor-Tex boots, stand, slip on the turtlenecked jersey shirt, grab the uniform shirt, pull the pants up, tuck everything in, pull the "woolly-pully" sweater over my head, and I was heading down stairs less than three minutes after the phone had rung. On the way to the back door, I grabbed my handgun out of the drawer, and inserted a magazine. I pulled back the slide to chamber a round, pressed the hammer drop, and shoved it into my holster. I pulled my little walkie-talkie out of its charger, and grabbed my recharging flashlight from the shelf by the door as I left the house. When I opened the door, it was like walking into a wall of cold air.

"Boy," I breathed to myself. Marsha's "really cold" hadn't done it justice.

I used my sweater sleeve to protect my hand as I opened the car door. Even in the garage, it wasn't smart to touch metal in this weather. I turned the key, and the engine took right off. Back out of the car, unplugging the engine heater, then hit the button to open the door.

In the car, turned on the defroster, set the temperature to high, turned on the headlights, dropped the rechargeable flashlight into its charger on the dash, rear-window defroster to "on." I turned on my flashing headlights and red dash and rear-window lights as I backed out. Then the police car radio.

". . . onto Willims road, but not sure . . ." came blasting over the speaker. Sounded like Five's voice.

I waited a beat to make sure the radio traffic was clear, then picked up the mike and told the office that I was back at work. "Three's ten-eight. Comm," I said, "where you want me?" Hopefully I would be able to get ahead of the chase from here in Maitland, and not end up following the pack.

"Stand by, Three," crackled the voice.

She had no choice, but I was already at the main intersection leading out of Maitland, so I had to stop and wait to be told which way to turn. Frustrating, but not a lot could be done about it. I fastened my seat belt and shoulder harness.

"Five," she asked, "where do you want Three to go?"

As luck would have it, he was close enough for me to hear his transmissions, so Marsha wasn't going to have to rebroadcast everything we said.

"Tell him to head north, toward the Whiskey 6 Victor intersection, then west toward the County Line road . . ."

"Three's direct," I snapped, saving Marsha and the rest of us a little time.

"Three, Five, I've been behind this idiot for almost eight miles. New snow, can't see him anymore, but I'm following the tracks and the cloud of snow." Nine struggled.

"Ten-four." Been there. With new snow, the first thing you lose in a chase is the taillights of the vehicle you're chasing. Snow packs up on the rear of the suspect vehicle, and they just fade out. Quickly. Then, if the car you're chasing is moving fairly fast, they throw up a rooster tail of snow, and you don't even get to see the reflections from their headlights. The good news is that the tracks they leave make it virtually impossible to lose their direction of travel. It's just that you can't be sure how far ahead they actually are. So, to avoid running into the back of them at a high rate of speed, you tend to get a little cautious. Because of that, they tend to lengthen their lead.

"Any idea how far up he is on you?" I asked.

Five answered. "Probably not more than a mile. I'm doing about sixty, and it's really hard to stay on the road. His tracks look like he's fishtailing a lot on the curves, so he's probably about sixty too."

"Ten-four, and where's Nine at?"

"Ah just tried to cut 'em off and missed . . ." came Nine's familiar drawl. "Ah'm behind Five somewhere, I think . . ."

Out of the picture, in other words. Damn.

"You think I can get to the intersection by Ullan's farm, Five, before the suspect gets there?"

"Close . . ." he said. "Could be close."

I was still on paved roads, as opposed to the gravels the chase was on, so I was able to take a few more chances. I pushed it up to about 75 on the straight stretches . . . but had to back off pretty far on the downhill curves.

I figured I could cut the chase off. I hate that. No lonelier feeling in the world than to have a pursuit coming right at you. It had to be done. If not, the suspect would be in Ossain County in two minutes after turning onto the paving.

"Comm, Three," I said, after switching the radio to the INFO channel, "you might see if Ossian County has a car anywhere near this area."

A few seconds later, as I descended a long, straight hill, I could see the intersection by Ullan's farm. No lights visible except the golden glow of the yard light near Ullan's house.

"Three's comin' down the hill to Ullan's, and nothing yet . . ."

"Three, Five . . . he's gotta be close, because I just passed the quarry . . ."

The quarry was less than three miles from the highway.

"Ten-four, Five." I slid to a halt with my car across the gravel road at the intersection. "Uh, you got anything good on this guy, or what?" I had to know if there was any sort of a confirmation of a crime, hopefully a felony.

"No, negative, Three. Uh, I just saw him and, uh, tried to stop him and he took off . . ." The "uhs" told me that he was really concentrating on his driving.

Damn. I backed my car up, being sure I was leaving enough room for the suspect to get safely by. You aren't allowed to really get serious about blocking a road unless there's a felony charge on the oncoming driver. I got out of my car, taking my shotgun with me. I deliberately didn't take time for my parka, because I felt the suspect should be there within a few minutes or less. I did, however, put on my down-filled vest. God, it was cold. I pulled my gloves on, and jacked a round into the chamber of the 12-gauge pump. I stood well off to the side and rear of my car. No point in getting run over if he lost control. I pulled my turtleneck up to cover my face.

The only sound was the purring of the engine on my car. Dead quiet. There was either no moon, or it wasn't up yet. I looked up, and the stars were just everywhere. No twinkling, just millions of little steady points. The way it gets in Iowa when it's so cold the moisture freezes and precipitates out of the atmosphere.

I became aware of a faint whining sound, growing louder. Then the squeaking of tires on fresh snow, and faint headlights coming right toward the intersection. He'd been traveling so fast, and busting through drifts, the snow had covered his headlights. He probably couldn't see much of anything except my headlights. I could barely see him as he slid past me, disoriented by the sudden appearance of my car's bright and flashing lights, lost control, and shot off the road and the shoulder and straight into the ditch on the other side of the paved road, disappearing in a cloud of snow.

"Uh, Three's got him stopped at the intersection!" I said into my walkie-talkie, as I walked quickly toward the suspect's car. Through the snow piled up on the roof and the snow stuck to the windows, I could just barely see someone inside trying to get the

door open. The depth of the snow was making that pretty difficult, as it was piled up nearly window high in the furrow he'd
made through the drifts.

I stopped at the edge of the ditch, and watched the driver's
door being opened, closed, slammed open an inch farther into
the snow, closed . . . After five or six repetitions, I just pointed my
shotgun at the struggling driver, and yelled, "Hold it right
there!"

The door stopped moving instantly. Then, after banging on
it a couple of times to loosen the ice, the suspect rolled the window down. "I surrender!" he yelled. "Don't shoot! I surrender!"

I got my first good look at him. "Fred?" I looked at the thin,
frightened face. "Is that you, Fred?"

"Mr. Houseman?"

Two

I was sitting in my patrol car with Fred Grothler, a.k.a. Goober; the driver of the car that now sat comfortably in the ditch. I had Fred in the front passenger seat. He was no threat, and seemed sober. I was filling out the officer's section of a state motor vehicle accident report. I had to do it instead of Five, Mike Connors, as Mike had been involved in a chase with the vehicle in the ditch. He would be assumed to be biased, and unable to be objective in his assessment of the cause of the accident. I, on the other hand, the proximate cause of the accident, was assumed to be emotionally uninvolved. Attorneys. But having to fill out the accident report was just another reason I hated assisting with chases. I had unzipped my down vest, and had donned my gold-rimmed reading glasses. I turned to Fred/Goober.

"You wanna tell me what the hell you were doin'?"

Goober just sat there, shivering. Nerves, I thought. It was cold, and he was a bit damp, but it was warm enough in my car. He shouldn't have been shaking from the cold.

"I, I, I dddon't know," he said.

"You don't know if you want to tell me, or you don't know what you were doing?"

Goober looked at me. "I ddon't kn, kn, know."

I'd talked with Deputy Mike, and he'd told me that he'd been doing routine patrol in the area where we'd been having some residential burglaries, and he'd seen a car sitting on the side of the road, honking its horn. He turned on his top lights, and was just getting out of his patrol car to see if the occupant needed help, when the suspect vehicle had turned on its lights and taken off, scattering snow clogs all over him.

He'd very reasonably gotten back into his patrol car and started the pursuit.

Mike and Nine, John Willis, were still across the road, sitting in Mike's car, and waiting for a wrecker. When we'd taken Fred out of his car, I'd noticed several tools on the floor of the front seat. Whether they were carpenter's tools, or auto repair tools, or burglar's tools was open to question. That was the trouble with tools . . . they were pretty much described by whatever you wanted them for. We did have several area burglaries that had used a half-inch pry, and that could be just about any screwdriver. On the other hand, just looking at Fred's car led me to believe that most of the tools on the floor could easily have been used just to get the ugly thing started. Mike leaned toward charging Goober with Possession of Burglary Tools. I disagreed, but we'd left it kind of dangling, ready to be used if we could prove Goober had been about to go into a place. But any way you cut it, all we had was traffic on him at this point . . . and minor traffic at that.

We couldn't even get him for "eluding pursuit," because in Iowa you had to be doing at least 15 mph over the posted limit for that to come into effect. The limit on gravel roads was 55, just like rural highways. None of us thought we could prove 70 mph, because Mike was pretty well keeping up with him at 60. And 70 on those roads was just about out of the question.

The other problem was that, out of the three possible rural residence burglary targets in the area where Mike had made the first contact with the horn blowing Fred, there were no tracks in the farm drives. The snow had some down a couple of days ago, and any movement into those drives would have been immediately noticeable. After we saw the tools in Goober's car, Mike had driven back up the course of the chase and had checked himself. No tracks. No evidence of any crime. Well, not yet, anyway.

"So, Fred," I said. "What were you doin' out on a night like this?"

"De, de, deer," he said, still shaking.

"Deer?" I asked. "What deer?"

"The ones I was honkin' at," he replied. "I was hon, hon, honkin' at deer."

"Honkin' at deer . . ."

"Well," he said in a whiny voice, ". . . yeah. I heh-heh hit one a year ago, and I stop and honk at 'em nuh, nuh, now. That's all." He looked so serious and honest in such a studied way, it was almost painfully obvious he was lying through his teeth.

"Fred . . . you really expect me to believe that?"

There was a long pause. Then he said the most honest thing he'd said all night. "Well, it'd bu, bu, bu, be nice if you di, di, di, did . . ."

We had nothing, we couldn't hold him much longer than the time it would take to do an accident report and get his car out of the ditch, and I was very, very tired. "Tell you what, Fred . . . You think about it, and we'll talk again in a minute or two." I looked at him for a long moment. "Just don't lie to me, Fred. You know how I hate that."

He nodded. "Okay."

I picked up my mike. "Comm, Three. I'll be bringing the driver into the department as soon as the wrecker gets here. Any idea on an ETA for that?"

"Just a few minutes," she replied. "I called him about fifteen minutes ago, and he said he'd go right out."

"Ten-four," I said. I felt sorry for the wrecker driver. Bundling up, going out to an ice cold garage and getting into an ice cold wrecker, just to come out here and pull out some idiot's car that shouldn't have been here in the first place . . .

"No!"

I looked at Goober. "What?"

"No, no, don't take me in there. We can't go in to Maitland."

"We can't?" I looked at him over the top of my reading glasses. "And just why would that be?"

Suddenly, he looked as if he were about to cry. "They, they, they need me there . . ."

" 'They,' Fred? Who are 'they'?"

I'd known Fred for about five years, since the time I'd busted him for DWI when he was sixteen. We'd always gotten along fairly well, really, and had met officially three or four times since his DWI. Minor stuff, a small theft, a couple of vandalism charges. Fred wasn't exactly what you'd call a career criminal. Just a bored kid in a very small Iowa town, who honked his horn at deer.

He opened his mouth, and made a tiny choking sound. He didn't look directly at me.

"You know, Mr. Houseman, those break-ins you beh, beh, been having around the county, in the farmhouses?"

"Yeah," I said, being noncommittal. I knew them, all right. Eleven burglaries at rural residences in the last sixteen days. That was just as far as we knew. One of the problems was that the burglaries were at a select number of farmhouses that were empty for the winter, the owners being elsewhere. Elsewhere as in warmer. Most of the burglaries were reported by whoever was looking after the place, when they showed up to check the furnace and the water pipes. Usually once a week or so. The main problem was, we had no idea if, or how many, more would be discovered. Neither did we have much of an idea of when they'd been done, except after the date the owners had left. We only knew the date when they'd been found.

"Well, uh, do you have a, a, a list, like, of the places that have been robbed?"

"Yeah." We had two lists, actually. The first was a simple listing of the known burglaries, in chronological order. The other was a list of residence check requests, filed with the department by the owners before they left, and giving information like the dates they'd be gone, who was going to check on their property for them, and asking us to have a car drive by every night. We were beginning to regard the second list as an indicator of the next burglaries. It was also very painful for Lamar, our sheriff. Many of the people who were on the list were his supporters.

He'd gotten their support, at least in part, by having the residence check program in the first place. Simply being able to be the first to tell them they'd been burglarized, however, wasn't his idea of a positive result coming from the RC program. As a direct consequence of Lamar's pain, it was becoming a particularly painful experience for the officers on the night shift, who were supposed to do the actual checking.

"Uh, well, do you have anything about that Bohr, Bohr, Borglan place, out on W4G, down by the Church crossroads?" asked Fred.

"Cletus Borglan's, you mean?" A perfect target. Borglan and his family wintered in Florida, usually leaving right after Christmas. And about a half mile from where Mike had come upon Fred about an hour ago. I began to feel a glimmer of hope.

"Yeah, that's it." Goober began to rock back and forth, just a little twitchy movement, but noticeable.

"No." Not unless somebody had forgotten to tell me, I thought.

"Oh, boy. Oh, boy." He sat holding on to the front edge of the seat with both hands, looking down. "I wish you had, Mr. Houseman. Oh, boy." He sounded like he was going to cry. He began to rock a bit harder.

I figured that he was about to snitch somebody off, and that he was hoping that we had a report of the burglary already, so that he wouldn't be telling me something that only he and the burglar would know. A hazardous practice, without a doubt.

"If you're worried about us 'finding it,' Fred, we can always come up with something that'll keep you out of that part." I tried to be helpful.

"No, it's not that. Thanks, though."

"Sure." I waited a second. "Come on, Goober. Spit it out."

"It's just that, well, meh, meh, me and my cousins from Oelwein . . . we been the ones doing those break-ins, you know?"

"Just a second, Fred. Are you saying that you've been directly involved with some of them?" A confession? Could I be that lucky?

"Mostly all, I suspect," he answered, in a soft voice. The rocking increased, perceptibly.

Thank you, God. Thank you, thank you. Up to now, we hadn't had a single clue as to who had been doing the burglaries. I took a breath, to slow myself down, and to try to appear matter-of-fact. "I'm going to have to advise you of your rights, Fred."

"Sure, but that ain't what it's about. Not why I was out here . . . not directly, Mr. Houseman."

I told him to hang on a second, and very quickly recited his Miranda rights to him. To be safe. "There, Fred. Now, do you understand those rights?"

"Yeah. But, Mr. Houseman, you gotta understand. Dirk and Royce, my cousins, they had me driving the car, you know?"

"While they did the burglaries, you mean?"

"I just drive 'em out to the place, you know, and they get out and sneak in, and then I go away for a while, and I come back and pick 'em up."

"You pick 'em up? They go in on foot?"

"Yeah."

He looked up beseechingly. "Am I gonna get charged with manslaughter, or something, if they're dead?"

I must have given him my dumb look.

"If they're dead, are you gonna send me away? I just gotta know."

Fred leaned forward, terribly earnest. "You gotta understand, Mr. Houseman. That's what I been trying to tell you. I dropped 'em off Sunday night. Two nights ago. On the other side of the hill back of the place. I saw 'em go over the hill, to go into the place." He stared at me with wide eyes. "They never came back out."

Three

Fred kept talking. "I came back two hours later, like I was supposed to, and they wasn't there. I came back again after an hour, and they wasn't there. I honked the horn, even if I wasn't supposed to do that. I waited right there. I wasn't supposed to do that, neither. I waited fifteen minutes or so. Nobody. I drove all the way to Vickerton, and came back. Nothin'. Nobody there. Then it got light, and I had to go." He was speaking in a rush. "Yesterday morning, I got scared they'd really be wantin' to get back at me for missin' 'em like that, and them havin' to walk and all, and I called Aunt Nora, and she said they wasn't home. I called again at suppertime. They still ain't home!" He looked at me, worried he wouldn't find them, and sort of afraid that he would. "I went back last night, and they wasn't there then, either. That's why I was honkin' the horn. It wasn't no deer. And I was afraid to go in, 'cause I figured you'd be there by then, and waitin' for me." He drew a deep breath. "And they ain't come home." He looked up at me, his face all screwed up. "They still ain't come home, and I think maybe they froze to death!"

I hate to admit it, but my thinking was running quickly along these lines: I had a confession, albeit a tentative one regarding details, to a string of very irritating burglaries. I was virtually certain that the two cousins who had been dropped off were lying low somewhere else, having, for reasons of their own, ditched

Fred. I was in a position of having good reason to check the Borglan place, based on Fred's statements. I certainly didn't need a warrant. But, to make the case as good as possible, I wanted to have Fred with me when I went to Borglan's, so he could show me where he'd let them off, and where he would pick them up. So far so good. But to take Fred with me, and to talk with him any more, I really should have him talk with his attorney first. Except . . . The lateness of the hour helped. But the biggest boon of all was Fred's genuine concern for the safety and welfare of his two dumb cousins. Exigent circumstances, as they say.

I picked up a pen. "What are your cousins' names, again?"

"Dirk Colson and Royce Colson. They would be brothers. Both of 'em."

"Okay, Fred." I wrote the names down. "And how old?"

"My age or so," he said. "Are you gonna help 'em, Mr. Houseman?"

"Of course."

Mike followed Goober and me as we drove back along the track of the chase toward the Borglan farm. We left John at the accident scene, to help the wrecker with any possible traffic control as they pulled Goober's car out of the ditch.

About a quarter mile from Borglan's farm drive, just around a curve screened from the farm by a low, tree-covered hill, Goober told me to stop.

"Here's where I let 'em off," he said.

"Look here on the right," I said to Mike, over the radio.

Mike turned on his right alley light, and I squinted through the window on Goober's side. Although the ditch was filled, you could just make out faint depressions in the snow, from inside the barbed-wire fence line, up and over the hillside. Filled in almost completely by the new snow, the tracks would have escaped all notice if they hadn't been pointed out to us. There could have been two sets. It was hard to tell.

"Right there?" I asked Fred.

"Yeah . . . ooh, shit, I wish they'd come back . . ."

"And you were to pick 'em up here, too?"

He began to rock again. "I didn't, I didn't screw it up. I was here!"

I picked up my mike. "Delivery and pickup point," I said. I began to move down the road, toward Borglan's lane. "Let's just go on in, Five," I said.

It took us about three minutes to negotiate the lane at the Borglan place. It wound to the right, then back to the left, among the stark and leafless trees. The branches were outlined with fresh white snow, which proved to be a distraction in my headlights. I nearly slipped off the lane and into a small ditch on the right. As I concentrated on the lane, though, I noticed that there were absolutely no indications of any tracks. None. Given the faint tracks where Fred had told me he let them off, I thought there surely would have been some indication if his cousins had left by this, the easiest route.

Fred was becoming more and more frightened and nervous the closer we got to the Borglan house. He was tapping the heel of his left foot on the floorboard so vigorously his left knee was jumping in and out of my peripheral vision.

"Fred! Knock off that foot-stompin' shit! It's bothering me."

He stopped abruptly. "I don't like this. I sh, sh, shouldn't be here . . ."

"Why not?" I asked, distractedly.

"I don't know. I just sh, sh, shouldn't be . . ."

"Don't worry," I said, as we pulled into the Borglan farmyard. I stopped, and rolled down my window to obtain a totally un-fogged view. No tracks here, either. Not even faint.

It was a nice place. Nice house and large garage. Fresh paint on the outbuildings. Bright orangish light provided by a sodium vapor streetlamp on a high pole. Really looked homey.

There were no lights on inside, except the faint glow of what I assumed was a night-light in the kitchen.

I walked back to Mike, who was rolling his window down at my approach.

"You want to get Fred back here to your car? I'll have a look around, but I don't want to leave him alone in my car too long."

"In the cage?" asked Mike.

"Naw. He isn't in custody. If we need to secure him, though, I'll let you know."

"How we gonna know that?" asked Mike.

"If I have signs here of forcible entry, we just pop him for suspicion of burglary. He drove 'em in, according to him."

"Suits me," said Mike, with a wide grin. "From those tracks, you mean?"

I grinned back. "Yep. It's beginning to sound like he and his cousins have done the whole series over the last month or so. Cool."

I went back to my car, instructed Fred to get in with Mike, and grabbed my winter coat and flashlight. It was terribly cold.

I crunched and squeaked my way around to the left of the house, where the ground sloped away to reveal a limestone basement wall. I swept my flashlight back and forth on the slope. No signs of any tracks down there, so I stayed up top, not sure I'd be able to keep upright if I tried to walk the slope. I retraced my steps toward the right side, and newer section, of the house, looking for a point of entry. As I passed close to the sliding glass door, I flicked the beam of my flashlight toward the lock and handle. I noticed it seemed to be open just a crack. There was also a very obvious silver metallic mark on the flat black frame, near the lock. I stopped, and squinted in the bright beam of my flashlight. I clumsily took off my glove by holding a finger in my teeth, unzipped my vest, and reached in under my sweater to my shirt pocket, and took out my reading glasses. I looked more closely. Yep. A very small pry mark at the latch, probably from a quarter- or half-inch screwdriver. Not all that big, but in the beam of my light it was like a little mirror. I reached out, and put side pressure on the handle. Sure enough, the door slid to the right. Point of entry, no doubt. I put my glasses back, zipped my coat, and put on my glove, and closed the door again, most of the way. I left a small crack, because, with my luck, although pried, it was still functional, and I didn't want to lock myself out.

I walked back to Mike's car. He unrolled his window again.

"Looks like a forcible entry," I said. "You want to do the honors?"

As I squeaked and crunched back to the Borglan residence, I heard Mike begin to recite a Miranda warning to Fred again, having just placed him under arrest for burglary.

"Not gonna be your day, Fred," I said to myself.

Having been burned a couple of times by assuming one obvious entry point and later finding the real one, I continued around to the right, checking toward the rear of the house. The slope was gentler here, partly illuminated by the headlights of our cars, and I ventured carefully down. I played the beam of my flashlight around, and saw lumps and bumps all over the backyard, probably small bushes, and lawn stuff covered with snow. There was a gazebo sort of structure, all snow and ice. It reminded me of some sort of a Russian village church. A snow and ice gas grille stood on its silver pedestal in what had to be a patio area. There were very slightly depressed tracks, visible only as I looked back up the slope, fairly close to mine. I'd missed them in the glare of the headlights, but now that I was in the shadow, they were easier to see. More were around the rear, and some at the back door, which was recessed and in even deeper shadow than the rest of the place. I checked it. It was protected here, though, and there was almost no snow near the walls. I stood on a narrow concrete walkway, and looked at the door. There appeared to be a fresh dent in the white steel storm door casing, and fresh pry marks on the wooden main door. I tested it with a gentle push, and it stayed firm. I pushed a bit harder. No result. Out with the glasses again, which I dropped in the snow. Made them wet, and very cold, but at least they hadn't broken. I peered at the marks on the door. Looked to be about quarter- or half-inch screwdriver marks. There was also a pretty good footprint near the lock. I grinned. Burglars almost never noticed the print they left when they tried to kick a door in. At night, when it was fresh, it probably just looked wet. But everything outside has a coat of dust, and with snowy boots making wet dust, and with wet dust making very fine mud, you'd frequently get a very fine shoe print.

At least after it froze or dried. I angled my flashlight more, and could even make out a possible section of lettering from the label on the sole. Cool.

I pushed the door once more, very hard. Nothing. Tough door. Most good modern doors were. I noticed the rubber doormat had been pushed away from the door. A couple of drops of white paint on the concrete, and three or four pink ones. Sloppy painters, I thought. I removed my glasses, which were beginning to freeze to my face, and put them back in my pocket. I stepped back, out into the reflected light from the headlights.

Perfect. They'd tried the back door, found it difficult to pry, and had come up to the front, where the sliding door offered much less resistance. Happened often at burglaries. The suspect would go for the obvious entry point, and find it blocked. Proceed to another, hoping it would be easier. It also fit, since it was reasonably likely that the cousins hadn't closely scouted the Borglan place before going in. That brought up another question, which was how they'd know Borglan's was empty in the first place. The answer was, of course, that they probably wouldn't know. Ah, but living within five miles, good old Fred sure would. Grumbling slightly to myself, I struggled back up the slope, breathing hard in the cold air. I was puffing by the time I reached the top. "Better lose some weight," I puffed to myself.

I went to the sliding door, and opened it. I shouted, "Anybody home?" It never hurts to ask. Especially as I was looking for the two lost cousins. Well, ostensibly, anyway. "Police officer, anybody home?" I waved at Mike, stepped inside, and closed the door behind me.

It took several seconds for my eyes to adjust, coming from the brightly lighted snow to the dark room. I fumbled for a moment, located a light switch, and turned on the lights.

The first thing that struck me was the bright blue carpet. Wall to wall, it had a fine nap, and was the same shade of blue I remembered seeing in copper sulfate solutions in high school chemistry. It was a nice place. Matching blue and white recliners close together in sort of random positions in the middle of the room, and a large three-piece couch, with really big pillows. Red and green throw rug in front of a modern fireplace, where a dog might lie in front of a fire. Huge TV set and stereo in a nearly ceiling-high oak entertainment center. Photographs of family-type people all over the walls, with many, many children. Grand-children, I suspected. A large oak gun cabinet with a flying duck etched in the glass door. Every slot was filled with six shotguns, two 9 mm auto pistols, and two .357 revolvers. That was a sur-prise. I stepped closer. No signs of a break, and there simply wasn't an empty slot in the cabinet. That struck me as strange, as the guns were very nice, and in the other burglaries, they'd taken guns and cash.

I was also struck by how warm it was. Well, probably not more than fifty. But quite a contrast with the outside. I slipped off my winter coat, and hung it on a big brass hook just inside the door. Much better. Off with the gloves, sticking them into the pockets of my down vest.

I reached over and turned on an another, adjustable light switch. Track lights came on, flooding the room with light and making my job very much easier. I stepped toward an arched doorway, which obviously led to the older portion of the house. The carpet gave way to yellowish tile at the archway, which con-tinued into a large modern kitchen in the remodeled older part of the house. There was a blond wood island running the length of the room, with hanging cabinets, hanging pots and pans, and hanging glasses with long stems. The stove was countertop, and the oven was a stack of three running up the wall. My. But noth-ing appeared at all disturbed.

I turned, and headed back toward the living room arch, in-tending to head for the basement. As I approached the carpet, I was seeing it from that direction for the first time, and I saw two things that made me stop in the archway.

One: I could plainly see dents in the carpet, which looked to have been made by the bases of the recliners. The dents were in a very reasonable location facing the entertainment center, unlike the rather pointless current arrangement of the chairs. Strange.

Most of the time, if you're going to change the position of a chair like that, you'd vacuum underneath, and restore the nap at the same time.

Two: There were two parallel tracks, connecting the closest recliner and the steel separating band between the carpet and the tile, in the archway. They were faint, but they were there. My first thought was that they'd stolen a third recliner. Right, Carl. Embarrassing, but not the sort of thought I'd have to share with anybody else. It did conjure up a quick image of two burglars struggling over hill and dale in ankle-deep snow, lugging a recliner. I grinned to myself. Best not put that in the report.

I crossed the carpet again, and looked at the end of the tracks, where they disappeared under a recliner. No reason at all for them to be there. None. I squatted down, reached into my shirt pocket again, and took out my reading glasses. I peered very closely at the carpet. There appeared to be a faint discoloration at the edge of the chair base. I pulled my little mini-mag light from my utility belt, and shined it on the carpet. Sure enough. Rusty color, faint and deep into the nap. I stood, and lifted the arm of the chair, tilting it sideways on its base. Underneath was a very large spot, only about two shades darker than the surrounding carpet, that looked like somebody had spilled about half a gallon of water and then dried it the best they could with towels. Still damp-looking, but not too bad a job. I moved the chair aside, and knelt back down, shining the mini-mag and running my fingers against the nap of the carpet. Rusty-looking, penetrating, stains very deep, almost to the base of the carpet. It looked for the world like somebody had tried to clean up a bloodstain, and had done a pretty damned good job of it. I stood, and took the room in again.

Bloodstains are strange. If your imagination gets ahead of you, you can look at a spot of spilled spaghetti sauce and see a bloodstain. With the small reddish stains I was seeing, it was going to take a lab to tell. Great. How was the Borglan family going to feel when a deputy sheriff, having discovered a burglary with nothing missing, cut out a sample of their carpet from the middle of the room . . .

My eye settled on the red and green throw rug near the fireplace. It was at a bit of an angle, and the red didn't go with anything in the room, and the green was jarring against the blue carpet. I walked over and lifted it. Smaller stains, two of them. Just like under the chair. Well, maybe the dog wasn't housebroken.

I stepped to the second chair, tilted it, and sure enough, a bigger stain under there, too. I walked to the middle of the room, and turned slowly through 360 degrees, looking at the pale blue walls. Sure as hell, there was a paler portion, over near the throw rug. I went over and peered closely. A small dot, like a nail hole, near the top of the lighter area. Well, a largish nail, for sure. I couldn't see any stain on the wall, but it looked like somebody had wiped something off, and thoroughly. The "nail hole" was about five and a half feet off the floor, and not quite round. Oblong. Well, it could have been distorted when somebody pulled a nail out of the wall. Swell.

A creepy feeling came over me, like I was being watched. I stopped, and just stood still, listening. The faint sound of Mike's and my cars running outside. The refrigerator way out in the kitchen was humming. Nothing else. No creaks, no bumps. But I felt eyes on me. Not terribly strong, but it was there. I turned and looked out the sliding glass doors. Just the cars, Mike half turned away, talking to Fred, neither of whom was looking my way. After a few seconds, the feeling began to subside.

"Grow up, Carl," I said to myself. But I casually reached down and unsnapped my holster, anyway. Feeling more confident, I tried to pick up where I'd left off.

"So," I said, "let's tell the court . . ." I do talk to myself, occasionally, hopefully when I'm alone. Just to organize my thoughts. Somebody told me once that it was a trait of only children. At least it fit.

When I go through a possible crime scene, I try to imagine describing the evidence to the court. It helps me concentrate, and to evaluate what I've got. In this particular instance, I said to myself, "Your Honor, there was what could have been a tomato sauce stain on the carpet, and there was a lighter mark on the wall, so I assumed it was where blood spatters had been washed off around a nail hole . . ." "And how did you come to discover this evidence, Deputy?" "Uh, well, I was checking on the welfare of two burglars . . ." I smiled to myself. Sounded a little weak.

So, I needed more. Well, for the court, anyway.

The residue of the feeling of being watched lingered, just at the edge of my mind. My first instinct was to call for backup. I didn't, though, for several reasons. First, the only backup available was Mike, and he had to be with Fred. Second, what I had wasn't anything solid, and even if it had been, the evidence indicated the scene had been created a couple of days ago. Third, if we did have a scene of something more than a burglary, then the more people tromping about, the worse it would for a lab team.

I squatted down near the chairs, and looked back toward the kitchen, trying to get a better indication from a lower angle. I could just barely discern the parallel tracks from here, and they didn't head toward the kitchen so much, as off to the right side of the archway. They looked suspiciously like drag marks, to me. There was a sliver of a door frame, just visible, through the arch. I got up, my left knee complaining, and crossed to the door. Descending stairs to the basement. Great. I hate going down stairs into basements, especially when you aren't sure who might be there. You expose 90 percent of your body on the way down the stairs before you can defend yourself.

I turned on the lights at the top of the stairs, rechecked my holster strap and went down slowly. It was one of those basements that's about three-quarters finished, with the area around the furnace and water heater left in concrete floor, studded walls, and unfinished ceiling. The first thing that caught my eye as I descended the stairs was the top of the water heater. White. Clean. Except for a puddle of what looked like a rusty water stain near the middle. The center of the puddle was reddish, and the outer edges were yellowish to almost clear. The problem was, all the pipes seemed to come out the side of the heater, not the top. So much for a rust stain. I peered over the edge of the railing. It looked like the water had dripped from somewhere up under the stairs. I continued down to the basement floor, and walked back to the heater. The puddled stain was dry, but thickish, looking like you could flake off chips from the edges. And there was a similar colored stain on the underside of the basement stairs, right over the heater. I looked a little closer, and saw that this stain, too, was more solid than water stains would be. It had a bit of a convexity at the center, like it had been trying to form into a droplet when it congealed. Stalactite or stalagmite? flickered through my head. I could never remember which was which.

I was virtually certain it was blood. I couldn't "prove" it, not yet. But that's what it was. The lighter edges were a dead give-away. Large stains tend to congeal, leaving the plasma in a ring around the outside, the red cells clumped together in the middle. They begin to clot, while the plasma seems to stay liquid longer, so it spreads a little farther.

Well, so I was sure it was blood. So what?

I was getting really creeped, mostly because the house was so completely quiet. I moved through the partition door and into the finished part of the basement. Nothing remarkable, it was plainly a playroom for the grandkids, with those big plastic tricycles and riding tractors and things parked next to the far wall. Plastic ball, Hula Hoop, and an old couch and a Nintendo on a caterer's cart. Nice room.

The throw rug at the door was bunched up, right where it would've been if the door had been opened and it had been pushed aside. But I'd tested that door from the outside, and it was locked. I snorted to myself. Sure, Carl. But it could be opened from the *inside*, and shut again. Concentrate.

I opened the basement door, and looked out into the blackness of the backyard. I played my flashlight around at the gazebo ice palace. With the light angle, I saw something I hadn't seen when I was out there. There was a gentle depression, kind of like a filled in furrow, in the snow, leading right from the back door to the gazebo, past it, and on toward the largest of the machine sheds. A virtually straight line, in the old snow. Made before Monday noon, when the new snow was laid down deep.

I glanced down, and the pink drops on the concrete took on a more sinister meaning. Frozen blood on concrete looks for the world like drops of Pepto-Bismol. Pink. I'd thought it was paint. Now, I was pretty sure it was blood. If you'd dragged a body down the stairs, and then opened the door, and paused to get your breath, and let the body sit just long enough for blood to drip . . .

Well.

I was going to have to go to the machine shed, to see what was at the end of the furrow. Had to do that. I was now just about certain that the cousins had argued, and that one had killed the other. Just about. Either that, or somebody had been staying at the house after all, and they had been killed by the cousins. Or, that Fred had killed somebody and was trying to place the blame on two noninvolved cousins. That brought me up short.

As soon as I got out the basement door, I pulled my walkie-talkie from my belt, and contacted the office.

"Comm, Three?"

"Three?"

"Could you get somebody else here? We'd like some ten-seventy-eight out here. We'll be ten-six for a while. Not ten-thirty-three, but send him." That meant that I was going to be busy, and it wasn't an emergency. I sure didn't want my favorite sheriff sliding into the ditch, running lights and siren, coming to help me look into a shed. Even though he was a good boss, that sort of thing could adversely affect my career.

"What you got, Three?" asked Mike, from his car in the yard.

"Maybe something on the order of a seventy-nine. Not sure. Wait a couple. I'm gonna be walkin' over to that big machine shed, from the basement back door." 10-79 was the code for coroner notification. A "79" told Mike I might have a body in here someplace.

"Ten-four," he said, crisply. Bodies, even if just suspected, tend to get your attention.

I put my walkie-talkie back on my belt, turned up the collar on my quilted down vest, pulled my stocking cap down over my ears, pulled on my gloves, and headed the fifty yards over to the steel machine shed. God, it was cold. I'd left my coat upstairs in the house. Of course. Well, I wasn't about to go back. I squeaked and crunched through the snow, being very careful to swing widely away from the drag marks. It was remarkable, but looking back toward the house, the different light angle prevented me from seeing the marks at all.

When I got to the machine shed, I found the "walk-in" door stuck with ice. Great. I stepped to the big sliding steel doors, kicked at them a couple of times to break the frost adhesion, and slid it open about five feet. "Never trap a burglar, unless you want a fight." Training turned to habit.

I went into the gloom of the big building, which was designed to hold a couple of tractors, and a combine. There was hay on the concrete floor, as insulation. One tractor off to the other side. A workbench. Those I could see in the light provided by my flashlight. I needed more light. This was a very large building. I reached over to my right side, feeling for a switch. Not likely I'd find one at the machinery entrance, but there should be one over by the walk-in door. I shined my flashlight to my right, and saw the switch at the end of a length of steel conduit, on the other side of the "people" entrance. I moved toward it, stepping over what I thought was some lumber, covered by a tarp. I glanced down to avoid tripping, and in the shadowed gap between the tarp and the wall, I saw a human hand.

Four

I recoiled, moving back so fast I nearly lost my footing.

I caught my breath, and let the effects of the adrenaline rush subside a bit. Okay, Carl. Get it together. This is what you were looking for. Just not quite where you'd expected to find it. Yeah.

Standing there in the large opening at the sliding door, I felt those eyes on me again. Stronger. I turned and looked back toward the house. Nothing. "Just what I need," I said to myself. "You're turning into an old lady, Houseman." But it bothered me.

I fumbled with the microphone for my walkie-talkie with my gloved hand.

"Mike, why don't you get Nine here, and hand your passenger over to him?"

"Ten-four . . . I think he's comin' over here anyway. So what's up?"

"I think we're into a real seventy-nine situation. And . . . uh . . . you might want to get alert here."

"We got company?" He sounded almost happy.

"Not sure, just don't take a chance. You . . . uh . . . might want to hand your passenger over to Nine back up the lane. Out of sight of the residence." I just couldn't shake the feeling of being watched.

"Ten-four." More serious now. It was sinking in with him, too.

I forced myself back into the shed. I hated to do it, but I stepped over the tarp again, and switched on the big fluorescent overhead lights. They flickered a few times, and then came on, casting a bluish light throughout the shed.

"There," I said to myself. "Better . . ."

Cautiously, I shined my flashlight down into the recesses of the mustard-colored tarp. Sure as hell, there was a hand. Pinkish, with the flesh flattened in a way that only the lifeless can manage. And frosted.

I had to know. Hell, I was required to know. Gingerly, I reached down, and pulled at the stiff, frozen tarp. It didn't want to move. I pulled harder. It resisted, and then, suddenly, came away from the wall.

I stepped back, again. I was looking at what appeared to be a human, with the head in a white garbage bag. There was a tear in the bag, and part of the head was exposed, including the right eye. Lying on the floor of the shed, whoever it was was very, very dead.

The tarp was still clinging to the floor. A light edging of ice. In the back of my mind, that told me that the tarp had been placed there before the cold snap. I reached down, to pull it free. As I did so, I noticed booted feet protruding from underneath the tarp, at the other end.

Three of them.

Two bodies? Two? I walked over, and lifted the stiff edge of the canvas sheet. It was really dark under there, but I could see, side by side, frost-covered and stiff, the lower half of two frozen bodies.

Brothers, I was willing to bet. Both of them, as Fred would say.

They were nearly identically "packaged." White plastic bags on the heads. I could barely make out some features, like noses and mouths. The bags didn't appear to have been fastened around the neck. Just placed over the head.

I could see no obvious marks, holes, or bloodstains on the clothes. But, before the medical examiner and the lab got here, it would be most unwise to touch them.

I glanced back around the shed. One tractor. Otherwise, empty. Just a lot of straw-covered concrete floor, and two bodies under a tarp.

"Well, son of a bitch." I took a deep breath, and dropped the stiff canvas. "Son of a bitch. What'd you get me into, Fred?"

I heard the crunch of footsteps behind me. "Who you talkin' to?"

It was Mike.

"These two, here . . ."

He was still just outside the doorway, about eighteen inches behind me. I stepped aside, pointing to my discovery as he stepped over the threshold.

"These dudes," I said, holding up the same corner of the tarp.

"Holy shit," he said, quietly.

"Yeah." I released the corner of the tarp. Being frozen, it very slowly fell back toward its original position. "We better get out of here, before I disturb any more than I have. We're gonna need the crime lab up here on this one."

"Yeah." He stared at the slowly descending tarp. "Any idea what killed 'em?"

"Not the faintest." I pulled my muffler up about my face. "Nobody's in the house, far as I know, but there's some evidence in there. These two might have been done in the house. No idea how. Just remember we don't let anybody in . . ."

"Okay." He looked up toward the house, then back at the shed. "Are these Fred's two cousins?"

"I dunno," I sighed. "Don't let anybody say anything to Fred, yet."

"Sure," said Mike.

"I suppose he's now a murder suspect . . . but don't say that." I doubted that he really was, but we had to be safe.

"Right. Yeah. So, what? Just leave him with John?"

"Yeah. For right now. Just don't talk to him." Fred was officially in custody, and Mirandized, but I didn't want anybody talking to him without him having access to an attorney. I wasn't a raging liberal, it was just that there was absolutely no reason to blow a case at this point. Time to start dotting the *i*'s and cross-ing the *t*'s in earnest. I looked around the shed. "I sure as hell hope there aren't any more in here."

"Shit, don't say that . . ."

Mike and I trudged back up the slope together. I told him I was going to get my camera and do some quick preliminary shots through the door of the shed, and try to get some photos of the tracks in the headlights of our cars. If it was to snow again, or to warm up, all the remaining exterior evidence would be lost.

When I got to my car, I called the office. Radio being so closely listened to on scanners, particularly when everybody was in their homes to escape the terrible cold, I had to be pretty cir-cumspect with my requests, and hope that the dispatcher got the oblique references. I felt secure that my transmissions on the 5 watt walkie-talkie had gone unnoticed, but the 100 watt car radio and the 1,000 watt main base transmitter were a different story. I didn't want anybody to know we had found bodies. Not yet.

"Comm, Three?"

"Go ahead . . ."

"Yeah, look, we have a seventy-nine here, and we're going to need the whole shebang. Ten-four?"

There was a pause. "I, uh, copy the seventy-nine. Could you ten-nine the rest?"

Well, I could repeat it, but I chose instead to try to clarify. "We will need the usual ten-seventy-eight here."

Silence. 10-78 was the code for assistance. There was no code for crime lab, none for requesting a DCI agent. But, at a homicide, we always needed both. But, cagey soul that I am, 10-78 tends to vary depending upon the situation. Of course. All I had told her was that we needed a coroner, and the usual as-sistance.

She was new. "Copy you need ten-seventy-eight?" The edge to her voice told me right away that she thought we needed more cops, and fast.

"Negative. Negative, Comm. Look, I'll ten-twenty-one in a minute." That meant that I would call her on a phone. That would be best, naturally, and I could explain everything in detail. I hated to do it, though, because it meant that I had to reenter the Borglan residence. Each time you do that, a defense attorney will try to make it sound like you strolled through the scene, scattering bogus evidence like they used to scatter garlands in front of Roman emperors.

Never try to clarify with more obscurity, though. Especially on a radio.

Back in the Borglan household, I found a phone in the kitchen, and called the office. I explained that we would need her to contact a medical examiner, the Iowa Division of Criminal Investigation for an assisting agent and the mobil crime lab, and that she would have to call our boss, Nation County Sheriff Lamar Ridgeway, and tell him what was happening.

"Uh, Carl, could I call in another dispatcher to help?"

"Sure. Good idea. Just remember to tell me, 'Ten-sixty-nine' as you get the items done." 10-69 stood for "message received," and would mean that she had completed a call. "Message one will be for the medical examiner, message two will be for DCI, and message three will be Lamar. Got it?"

"Yes."

"Now, I want you to try to get a DL on two subjects . . . a Dirk and a Royce Colson. Should be about twenty or so. Maybe twenty-five. Not from Nation County, but I think maybe from around Oelwein."

"Okay . . ."

"Eventually, I'm going to need height and weight, eye color, and that sort of thing. The physical descriptors."

"Got it."

"Cool. Okay, now I'm gonna be a long way from a phone for a time, taking some photos. Just give me the ten-sixty-nines over the radio. I'll be on portable. If I don't acknowledge, Mike will. He's in his car."

"Okay . . ." She didn't sound quite sure, but I knew she'd do fine. Especially when the other dispatcher arrived.

"And don't give anything, and I mean anything, regarding the Colsons over the radio unless I specifically ask you to do so."

I let myself back out, grabbing my coat this time, and went to Mike's car and told him what had been said. I got my camera out of my car, and crunched my way back down to the shed. I figured I'd better take the photos there first, since the subzero temperature might deplete my camera battery and leave me with no way to take photos.

As I stood in the doorway of the big steel shed, fumbling with the flash attachment in the cold, the feeling of being watched came rushing back with a vengeance.

At the Academy, years ago, one of our instructors told us that, if you ever got a spooky feeling, pay close attention to it. You might be reacting to something you've picked up subconsciously, that just hasn't made it all the way up to awareness. I'd always considered it good advice, although it had only worked for me one out of about ten times, when there was a man hiding in the rafters of an implement store we were searching. I thought that once was pretty good, though. He'd had a gun, and we later found he was just waiting for me to pass before he shot me in the back. I'd stopped, and backed up a step, which had put me out of his line of fire. We all figured I'd glimpsed him in my peripheral vision, but that it hadn't registered. Anyway, it was a distinctive feeling, and that time before it had been very strong. It was back, and this time it was even stronger.

I stopped after I attached the flash, and paused for a moment. Then I looked around, very slowly. Nothing unusual. But I had the solid feeling that I was being watched. I switched the flash off, and did a slow pirouette, snapping a shot about every ten degrees or so. It was just possible that I might catch something with the camera I was overlooking.

The feeling persisted.

I tried to shake it off. "Probably Mike," I said to myself. Could have been. Could have been the residual effect of that frozen eye. Most likely, I thought, it was the result of being alone with the two bodies. Most people seem to get really self-conscious when they're alone with the dead. I was no different.

"Three," crackled my walkie-talkie, "Ten-sixty-nine on message one!"

That startled me out of my thoughts about being watched. Just as well.

"Ten-four" was all I said. All that was necessary. The medical examiner had been notified.

I went back to the residence and took a few shots of the marks on the sliding door. I tried for a wider angle shot of the faint tracks in the snow, leading toward the shed, but didn't really have much hope. As I turned toward my car to get a fresh roll of film, I saw Fred's face in the back of Mike's car. He was just watching, but looked pretty rough. I guess he really began to catch on when he saw my camera flash down by the shed. Mike said later that Fred started to cry about then.

Five

Three . . ." came the familiar voice of my favorite dispatcher, Sally Wells. She was obviously the second dispatcher called in. That made me feel a lot better, as Sally had been with us for years, and was a certified departmental asset.

"Go ahead," I said, turning my head toward the mike mounted on my left shoulder.

"Ten-sixty-nine on items two and three."

"Ten-four."

"Regarding item two, the mobile unit will be ten-seventy-six within ten minutes or so, with the other assistance to be ten-seventy-six shortly." Translated, that meant that the mobil crime lab would be on its way to us within ten minutes, and a DCI agent or two would be coming in shortly. The bad part was that the mobil crime lab was in Des Moines, about three to four hours away. The good part was that the agents were based much closer.

"And . . . uh . . . Three, could you get back to a phone?"

That was unusual, and I really didn't want to do it, because it meant that I'd have to traipse back through part of the house again. But Sally knew what she was about, and she wouldn't ask if it weren't really necessary.

I let myself back in the Borglan house, and called the office.

"Sheriff's Department . . ."

"Better be good," I said, grinning.

"You're not gonna like this one bit," said Sally.

"So . . . ?"

"The assigned agent is Art Meyerman."

Oh, great. Just great. Art Meyerman had been the chief deputy in our department for several years, was a thoroughly unpleasant man, and had left under a bit of a cloud. He's gotten a job with state, with what I suspected was a bit of political assistance, and had become an agent for the Iowa Division of Criminal Investigation. It was rare, but it happened.

I suspected that state wouldn't send Art back into his old county lightly. He'd been with them in Waterloo for almost two years, and as far as I knew, had never set foot in Nation County during that time. There had to be a shortage of available agents, for some reason.

I took a deep breath, and exhaled. "Hokay, Sally. Why don't you get Lamar to stop off in the office on his way through town, and give him the news. Maybe he can make something else happen . . ."

I truly didn't want to be working with Art again. Although he and I could get along if necessary, he hated Mike, Sally, and just about half the rest of the department. With a double homicide, I wanted a really smooth investigation.

"Maybe Hester Gorse is available?" Hester was just about the best General Crim. agent in the state.

"Already checked, she's still on her temporary gambling boat rotation. They won't pull her out. I tried." The *General Beauregard*, a Mississippi River gaming boat was home-ported in our county.

"Right." Well, we'd just have to make the best of it. If there was a best. "Right," I said, again. "Well, as long as I've got you on the phone, get an ETA for the medical examiner, will you? And find out who it is."

"You bet. Sorry about Art."

"Not your fault. Just remember that you secretly love him . . ."

"Yeah," said Sally. "Right." If she could have spit over the phone, she would have.

I got that spooky feeling again, just as I hung up the phone.

I talked to Mike on my way to my own car. "You might want to move your car around over there," I said, pointing in the general direction of the steeper of the slopes leading to the backyard, where his lights would do the most good and he could observe the back door. "I'd feel better, just in case there's still somebody in the house."

He gave me a startled look, and I kind of grinned to myself. Had him spooked, now, too. Misery loves company.

Then I sat in my warm car, and waited for everybody else to arrive.

I could hear the radio traffic begin to pick up as people came to work, or got closer. First, as John Willis, Deputy Number Nine, hit the road, and then as Lamar started out from the office. Shortly afterward, I heard a terse, one-line announcement from State Radio that an agent was *en route* to our county.

It was just warm enough in the car to destroy any adaptation I might have made to the cold. I reloaded my camera, and then began to scratch out a series of notes to myself. And I started to think about Fred.

Could he have done this? Sure. In this business, you learn early on that anybody can do just about anything. The real question was, did he? I didn't think so. If he'd done it, I thought it would be more likely that he simply would have run away, and sure as hell wouldn't have been discovered sitting out on the road, honking his horn. After all, running requires the least, immediate effort. We probably wouldn't even have discovered the bodies until the Borglans came back. Which reminded me . . .

"Comm, you might want to try to get hold of the owner here, wherever they said they could be reached. Not too many details, okay, but I think we might need one of them up here."

"Ten-four."

"And, let me know if you reach them . . ."

"Ten-four," she said, being a bit short. Of course she'd let me know. Telling her something that basic was just a bit of an insult. I was sure I'd hear about that one later. I was wrong. I heard about it right away.

"Comm, One?" That was Lamar.

"One?"

"You want to let him know when you tie his shoes, too?"

"If it makes him feel better," said Sally. She sounded happy.

I could hear Lamar chuckle as he said, "Three, we're already on that."

I grinned, and got back to my notes. Back to Fred. Back to the Borglans' vacation. They were in Florida. Great. Should probably be a day or more before they could get a plane . . . Oh, well. We'd need their permission to search the place, just as a courtesy, and to possibly extend that search over their entire farm. Not only that, but they were the only people who could tell us a lot of things, including whether or not anything was missing. Whether or not Fred knew them. Who would have had access to the place. What was disturbed. All the stuff that I needed to know.

We'd just have to do what we needed to do without them. It occurred to me that I'd be a little irked if I had to come back from Florida into this deep freeze, for something like this. Hell, for any reason, really.

"Three, Comm" jarred me back to reality.

"Comm?"

"Have contacted the subject you requested. They will be ten-seventy-six ASAP."

"The property owner?"

"Ten-four."

Cool. Almost like magic. "They give an ETA, Comm?" I still thought it would be at least forty-eight hours.

"The male subject is already on his way, was coming up for some business things, for a couple of days."

"Well, ten-four, Comm. Excellent!" I just love it when things happen to go smoothly for a change.

"Should be arriving at the Cedar Rapids Airport in an hour or so, according to his wife."

"Ten-four!" Perfect timing. How about that.

"Three, the other subject is ten-six, but will be able to head up in about an hour or so, from the Manchester area."

I thought rapidly. Who was the other subject? Oh.

"Last name end in a nine?" As in 10-79, which would be the M.E.

"That's the one." She was quick, as usual.

"Ten-four." The one I really wanted was based near Cedar Rapids. Manchester threw me. "Comm, did they say which one it was?"

"Negative, Three."

I hung the mike back up. All right. I wasn't sure just how much of a rush we should be in for the M.E., with the bodies in a deep freeze. If they'd gone out to the shed on Sunday, and it was way up in the twenties, would they be frozen through by now? Would it make an appreciable difference? How in hell was the M.E. going to come even close to a time of death? They did have frost on them. Warm when they got out there? I thought for a second. If they'd been covered as soon as they were deposited, would the frost have formed? Or did it mean they were covered afterward? Damn. If they'd been pretty warm, I thought we might just get frost as they froze. And just what did that tell me? Nothing, yet.

We'd need to try for a core temperature, but what would that tell us? With the ambient temperature varying from what . . . room temperature to minus thirty-five degrees, with pauses at the mid-twenties, how would temperature determine time of death? Or, rather, how close could it get us? I didn't have much hope for that approach.

Stomach contents. There was a chance for you. Frozen food, so to speak. We'd have to find out when they'd last eaten.

What other evidence would there be in the house? I was really anxious to do the whole place. There had to be something in there. Then Fred's question about whether or not I'd charge him with manslaughter popped back into my head. Why had he asked that? Just dumb luck? I thought so, but I was far from sure.

I was beginning to be afraid his was going to be an interesting case.

I jotted down the questions, and was just going to pick up my mike when I saw Lamar coming down the lane in his four-wheel-drive SUV, completely marked in the white with blue-outlined gold striping of a normal patrol car. It had the newest set of top lights in the department, as well. "Lamar's Awesome Machine," as Mike called it. I waved, and he pulled up on the left side of my car, motioning me to join him. I did so, grate-fully. My car was a standard-sized Chevy, and bearable; but Lamar's truck was larger, and almost luxurious inside. I'm six feet three, and about 260 or so. I like to be able to stretch out a bit in a vehicle.

I clamored in, and shut the door. Lamar gave me a long look. "I posted Nine at the end of the lane, so the DCI can find this place. You know it's Art who's comin'?"

I nodded. "Can't figure that one out."

"I called his supervisor from the office. They've got a major case down in Washington County, and everybody else is out with the flu." He looked at me for a second. "Art ain't gonna know I called his boss."

"Right."

He sighed, the way only a stressed sheriff can. "So, just what the hell you got here?"

I told him. When I was finished, he only had a couple of questions.

"How were they killed?"

"Dunno, Lamar. Didn't look that close. I didn't move any-thing, and I just raised the tarp enough to see that it was two males. Very, very dead." I grinned. "And no, I didn't recognize ei-ther one of 'em."

"I was gonna ask that," he said. "Okay. Okay." He was think-ing. "You think Fred, over there, did it?" He gestured toward Mike's patrol car.

I took a second before I answered. While doing so, something in the truck caught my eye.

"Is that a thermos of coffee?"

Lamar squinted at me. "We'll have a cup after you answer the last question."

"Okay," I said. "Got any doughnuts? Get a better answer for doughnuts."

He reached down behind my seat, and produced a white paper sack with MAITLAND BAKERY in red letters. He sort of waved it in front of me.

"Well," I said, "I think he's pretty much the only suspect we got." I waited a beat. "But I'd be real surprised if he turns out to be the killer. Mike came up on him as he was sittin' out at the pickup point, honking his horn. That worth a doughnut?"

"Sure," said Lamar. "Yours is pretty much the only opinion we got." He grinned. "So far."

They were chocolate, with chocolate frosting sprinkled with those little multicolored things. I took one bite, and said, "You got another one of those, I'll try to think of another suspect for ya . . ."

Less than thirty minutes later, the assigned DCI agent drove up. Our ex-Chief Deputy Art Meyerman. Art was kind of anal retentive, so much so, he'd been stuck with the nickname of "Anus" I wasn't sure if he'd ever found that out.

I gave him a very brief description of what Fred had told me, and a short walk across the front of the house, pointing out the highlights.

"And they're over in that shed?" asked Art.

"Yep."

"And the M.E. isn't here yet?"

True to form, I thought. He had to ask. There were just four of us standing in the middle of the desolate, frozen yard: Mike, Lamar, Art, and me. With a prisoner in the back of Mike's car. Nobody else, no other car, nada. I felt like looking behind me before answering. "Nope, but he should be here in half an hour or so."

"I'm glad to see you left a couple of uniforms at the end of the lane," said Art. He was trying to be nice, but I found it very irritating that he referred to uniformed officers as "uniforms." The way he said it, it meant "second-class cop," and I thought it was very unfair. Partly since he had been mostly uniformed until a couple of years ago. And mostly since I was in my uniform.

We walked over toward Mike's patrol car. Art wanted to get a look at Fred, to see if he remembered him.

"Mike," he said, "would you contact State Radio and get the mobile lab up here?"

I resented his talking to Mike like that, particularly since he'd left the department to get away from the rest of us, but he didn't seem to mind a bit. "Sure thing, Art." Well, the "Art" did seem to have a thin glaze of sarcasm.

I stepped back with Art. "You recognize Fred, there in the back?"

Art sighed. "Can't tell. I want him out of here, though. Get him back to the office, or something. I don't want him around when we start doing serious stuff."

Fine with me. I told Mike to get him back to the S.O., and to hold him on a burglary charge. I didn't think we had anywhere near enough to do even a Suspicion of Murder on him.

"Let's go do the bodies with the M.E., at least a preliminary," I said, to both Art and Lamar. "As soon as one gets here. I haven't been back to the shed, so I don't have any photos except what I can see with the tarp pretty much in place. We can at least do that."

There was always the question as to who got to do the bodies first . . . the lab folks, who would gather evidence, or the M.E., who would tell everybody what evidence to look for. Since I had absolutely no idea what had caused the death of the two brothers in the shed, I was going for the M.E.

Art didn't look too sure, but Lamar jumped at the chance to have something to do. "Good."

That ended that discussion.

It was understood among us that, while Art and the DCI were the "detectives" on the case, it was our case all the way. They were assisting the Sheriff's Department. Not the other way around. Lamar was going to call the shots. But he was also smart enough to let Art work. Art had always had a nose for certain kinds of crimes, and knew a lot of people in Nation County.

Our job at this point was to protect and preserve the evidence for the M.E. and the lab team. Not that a frozen body was going to decompose or anything. But we did want photos for the M.E.'s later reference as well as ours. I thought I'd better get my camera. I knew that DCI probably had at least one, but I wanted my own shots, too.

On the way I noticed that the light had changed quite a bit with the headlights of the other cars. Some tracks were more noticeable, others had virtually disappeared. Sunlight was going to wash them out completely.

We all got into Lamar's extended cab, and cozied down.

Lamar lifted the air pot. He glanced at Art, who held his hand over his cup. I held my cup out. As he filled it, he said, "Ain't it something. The way that cold air makes your bladder act up?"

LAMAR PASSED THE TIME sweeping the area with his electronically controlled, state-of-the-art spotlight, mounted well forward on the right fender of the "Awesome Machine." The whole farmstead was in a wide valley, with a small stream running along the far side. I had to really look, but then I saw the track. Or, more precisely, tracks. There must have been a dozen separate tracks, some leading clear down the valley, some rising up a hill and disappearing.

"They look like old snowmobile tracks," I said. "I didn't see 'em before. Must have been the lighting."

"Must have," said Lamar, sarcastically, sipping his coffee. "We know how you never miss a thing." He grinned.

He was referring to an incident where I had left my raincoat at a crime scene, and it had later been found and taken in as evidence by the FBI. Art snickered.

My first thought was that the suspect or suspects had gotten away on snowmobiles. Fred had brought his cousins to the farm in a car. Couldn't have been Fred. Unless, of course, Fred had lied about their coming in a car. But the snowmobile track from the rear of the house sure looked like a possibility for a fleeing suspect.

"That could be our suspect," I said. I'd assumed everybody had been thinking along those lines.

"Then," asked Art, "how do we explain the others?"

"Hired man," said Lamar. "He checks the place once in a while, while they're gone. He lives next place down the valley. I know he has a snowmobile."

"I see," said Art, lowering the binoculars. "We may want to talk with him."

"Already had 'em contact his wife," said Lamar. "Before I left the office. She said he's gone, picking the owner, Cletus Borglan, up at the Cedar Rapids Airport. Left about three hours ago. He'll call the office as soon as he gets back." He took another sip of his coffee. "I told the office to let us know when he calls. Didn't know if we wanted him here, or if you would want to talk to him at his place."

Lamar has been around the block.

The M.E. came driving up. Very nice black four-wheel-drive Bronco. Driven by Dr. Steven Peters, my favorite pathologist, and the one I'd hoped we were going to get. He had a forensic ticket, one of very few in the state, and he had a tremendous knowledge of his subject. He was also delightful to work with, and tended to bring his own supply of snack food. I can't begin to tell you how comforting it is to know that your autopsies have been done by a solid M.E., and that regardless what else happens, you always have the firm foundation of the M.E. report to fall back on.

We all got out of Lamar's pickup, as Dr. Peters pulled up. As he got out, he said, "I hope this is in the house! My God, it's cold!"

He knew us all from past cases. Lamar broke the bad news about the bodies being in the machine shed. After a brief consultation, we decided to drive Lamar's pickup and Dr. Peters's Bronco down the slope, and park them right at the edge of the shed. We could use them to warm up in, and to avoid having to walk back and forth for various items of equipment. And, as Dr. Peters said, to keep the doughnuts soft.

We chose a course that would avoid all the visible tracks, and down we went.

Just as we stopped, Lamar picked up his mike and said, "Comm, log the time. 0207."

"Ten-four, One."

"Nine, One?" as Lamar called Deputy Willis.

"One, go . . ."

"Nine, you want to stay put. Nobody gets in without a badge."

ONCE WE GOT to the shed, all the lightness left us, and the somber business of investigating two dead bodies began. Everybody had their heaviest coats on by then, and mufflers or scarves wrapped over their mouth and nose. I couldn't help noticing that Art was rather underdressed for the occasion, with a topcoat instead of a parka.

Lamar and I were able to open the door another couple of feet, letting a bit of light in, and making access easier. We cast about, and finally located a light switch on the wall about ten feet from the walk-in door that was padlocked. Large fluorescent overheads flickered, struggled a bit, and then came on, flooding the entire space with light. Perfect.

I took three photos of the inside of the shed, which looked to be about 60 x 30 feet. The inside wall was a galvanized steel. Then three shots of the bodies as I had left them, with the tarp covering everything but the feet. That tarp was an olive-green-colored canvas, with aluminum eyelets, and stiff as a board. Lamar, Art, and I pulled sharply to unstick the frozen edges from the floor, and then slowly lifted it off the victims, and carried it off to one side, still frozen in the shape it had been when it covered them. I turned, and got my first good look at the two dead men.

The nearest one was on his back with his arms at his side, the other about three-quarters onto his face with his arms folded underneath. Both had white plastic trash bags on their heads. They didn't look to be cinched with cord or anything, just sort of twisted. Yellow pull tabs, integral to the bags, had been tied under the chins. Stains on the outside of the bags showed they hadn't been terribly effective. I figured the blood puddle on the water heater, under the basement stairs, was also indicative of that, but we'd have to check. The white bags were stiff, too, but not as bad as the tarp.

Three shots with each head in the center of the focus, for a total of six. I changed from the 50 mm lens to the 70–210 mm zoom. I fumbled a bit, as my fingers were getting cold. They were dressed in what at first seemed a light fashion. Jackets, blue jeans, and tennis shoes. Not dressed for today, that was certain.

"What was the temperature when they were supposedly dropped off?" asked Dr. Peters.

"Would have been in the middle to upper twenties," said Lamar.

"Hmm. Snow cover at that time?" Dr. Peters was pulling out the shirt from the waistband of the first victim, and sliding his gloved hand up onto the abdomen. Checking for indications of core temperature.

"Not a lot. Maybe, oh, two or three inches?" Lamar glanced at me. "Carl?"

"Yeah, about that." As soon as I spoke, the moisture from my breath froze on my glasses.

"Like ice," said Dr. Peters, mostly to himself, as he pulled his hand away and pulled the sweatshirt of the second victim up, reaching again toward the abdomen. This shirt, too, was stiff, but movable. "Quite a bit of moisture in the clothes, to freeze like this. Not wet . . ." He struggled for another few seconds with the sweatshirt. "Maybe damp, though." He tried to turn the body over to get his hand underneath in the abdominal area, but failed. "Somebody got a hand?"

I reached down, with my own latex-gloved hand, and grabbed the jacket near the right shoulder of the victim. I pulled, hard, and the body rolled about a half turn. They were as stiff as steel. No movement of any joints, whatsoever. Much worse than rigor mortis, where there was at least some possibility of some movement. "Corpse sickles."

Dr. Peters felt the abdomen of the second victim. "Just like a frozen supermarket turkey," he said. He stood. "Was there any reason they might have, oh, maybe sweat a bit before they were killed? That we'd know of at this point . . ."

"They were supposed to have walked in from over the hill," I said, letting go of the body, and watching it roll stiffly back to its original position. Just like a log, I thought. With the arms just like stiff, broken branches. "There are what look like may have been tracks in that direction."

"Good. I think that might do it, especially if they'd stopped in a warm place for a while . . . like the house, for example."

"They sure aren't dressed for snowmobiling, even in the twenties, are they," said Lamar, making a firm point.

"I shouldn't think so," said Dr. Peters. "Not an expert in that, though," he said with a grin. "But if they were to do it, they'd be needing the services of another kind of doctor by now."

"We don't have any injuries yet, do we?" said Lamar.

"Not yet," said Dr. Peters, kneeling at the heads of the victims. "I suspect we'll find something inside the bags, though."

"Asphyxiation," said Art.

Dr. Peters looked up. "Pardon?"

"Asphyxiation," said Art, again. "You think?"

"I shouldn't be betting a large amount," said the Dr. Peters. He began tugging at the bag on the closest victim. "These aren't at all tight."

The white bag was stiff, the way that polyethylene gets when it's really cold. It gave Dr. Peters a rough time for a few seconds, since it also appeared to be stuck to the victim's head by frozen blood. He finally tugged really hard, and as it came off, it suddenly revealed a black-haired male subject, approximately twenty-five or so, unshaven, teeth exposed in a grimace. It was sort of startling, and took us all a second or two to adjust.

There was a lot of clotted blood on the right side of the head, stiffly clumped in with the longish hair, and with a patch of frozen polyethylene adhering to the clumped strands. The right eyeball protruded a bit, with the left appearing sunken, at least in comparison. The complexion was sallow.

"Hmm," said Dr. Peters.

"Blunt object?" asked Art.

"Not going to be your day," said Dr. Peters, gently prodding the matted blood and hair. He tapped the protruding eyeball, producing a clicking sound. "Frozen solid," he said. He felt around to the other side of the head. "I suspect a gunshot wound, I think I feel an exit here." He leaned way over, supporting himself with one arm. "Could someone shine a flashlight over here?"

In the yellowish circle of Lamar's light, he was able to clear the left side of the victim's head. "Yes. Appears to be our exit, and . . . temporal."

Cool. I took four shots of the first victim's face, concentrating in the first two on the clot, the second pair on the protruding eye. Establish, then zoom in. Lamar held a tape measure next to the nose for me. You should have a scale in the shots, whenever possible.

Dr. Peters gingerly removed the white bag from the head of the second victim. This one slipped right off. This fellow had a recently shaved head, and the small goatee I could see from my angle was blondish. There was blood on the second victim, too, but not nearly as much. And what appeared to be a bluish purple spot on the back of the head, to the right of the middle, and about halfway to the top. Above it, about two inches, was a whitish squiggle of what looked like those worms kids squirt from cans. About an inch or so long, it protruded from another purplish spot.

Dr. Peters pointed to the squiggle. "Extruded brain tissue," he said. "Shot twice."

I was working the camera, so Lamar said, "Gunshot wound on both of them, then?"

"Two of them on this one," said Dr. Peters. He pointed to the upper spot, with the extruded matter. "This is the first shot, this is an entrance wound." He pointed to the lower spot. "Entrance wound, second shot. Pressure from it caused the material to squeeze out the first hole."

Aha. Lamar held the tape again, and I got in as tight as I could, showing both wounds. "Think it was a .22?" I asked. It looked about that size.

"I should think so," he said. "Note the facial features."

The young man's face was all compressed and flattened on one side, like he had his face pressed against a pane of glass. Except there was none. The simile apparently occurred to Art, too.

"World's best mime," he said, dryly. He surprised me so much I laughed. The DCI might have done him some good, after all.

The corpse's tongue was protruding through his lips, and his teeth weren't visible. There was a yellowish tinge to him, as well as a purple discoloration to the rounded portion of his face that looked like a huge bruise. Post-mortem lividity. The flattened part of the face, on the other hand, was almost white.

"He was placed here a while after he died," said Dr. Peters. "The face is flattened by this floor, but there is no lividity in the flattened area."

Post-mortem lividity was the purplish color produced by pooling blood in a corpse. Gravity forces the blood to the lower points of the body. The process stops after a time, and if the body is moved to a different position after this time, there will be no liquid blood to pool in the new low spots.

"Affected by temperature, though," said Art.

"Oh, yes," said Dr. Peters. "Very much. But when we defrost

him, if freezing interrupted the clotting process, we may well have continued liquid seepage into low spots . . ."

"Do you think there are two holes in the first one?" asked Art.

Dr. Peters stood again. "Can't say, but I certainly wouldn't be surprised. I want to bag the hands."

He reached into his kit, and pulled out a roll of transparent bags and a roll of tape. I helped him bag the hands. The first victim's hands were easy. The second one required Art and I to heave the body up and onto its right shoulder, so the M.E. could get at the hands. The body was so stiff it was like tilting a statue.

Lamar asked for Art's cell phone. He reached in his inner pocket and handed it to him. He dialed, and said, "Yeah, it's me. Look, get Christiansen in early and have him take Fred up to the clinic and have Doc or a nurse use the gunshot residue kit on his hands. Yeah. No, he doesn't. No. It ain't testimonial evidence. His lawyer isn't necessary. Yeah? Good." He handed the phone back to Art. "Fuckin' attorneys, I tell ya . . ."

"These two gentlemen," said Dr. Peters, "are very thoroughly frozen. I suggest we leave them here until the lab team can see them, too. There's certainly no harm in that, as long as they get here fairly soon."

"They should be here in a couple of hours," said Art.

"That long," said Dr. Peters, pulling off his gloves. "Well, we have to defrost them before we can do much else . . . no matter. That'll take twenty-four to thirty-six hours."

"Damn," I said, pretty much to myself. "That long?"

"Just about the same formula you'd use to thaw a frozen turkey before Thanksgiving." He grinned. "Don't worry, Carl," he said. "I'll X-ray the heads as soon as we get them to a machine. Most of the information you'll need right away should be available then."

"The heads should thaw a little quicker than the rest of them, as well," he said.

"Freezing going to affect the tissues . . . the tests?" asked Lamar.

"Oh, sure. But not in an appreciable fashion. Burst cell walls won't prevent toxicology testing, for instance." Dr. Peters smiled. He looked around. "It's fairly obvious they weren't killed here. Any ideas?"

I told him what I'd seen in the house.

"Very good news," said Dr. Peters. "I'll need to take a look inside, then." He glanced at me. "The heat was on in there?"

"Yes."

"Ah, excellent," said Dr. Peters.

"Let's hurry up," said Art, "I'm freezing to death."

"Next time," said Lamar, dryly, "maybe you could wear a real coat . . ."

We went into the house via the kitchen door, and were very careful not to disturb any evidence. If it had just been a burglary scene, nobody would have gone in again until the lab team got there. But it was important for the homicide investigators to see the scene in the least disturbed state possible. That outweighed the lab requirements.

I walked Dr. Peters through the path I'd taken in the house. He agreed that the carpet stain could well be a bloodstain that had been cleaned up. The hole in the wall he didn't want to speculate on, but the diameter looked about right for a .22 caliber round. The small dried puddle on top of the water cooler was, to the best of his knowledge, blood.

Dr. Peters had to leave, as he had to autopsy a questioned death victim in Manchester. He said that he'd do ours as soon as the bodies were warmed sufficiently.

"X-rays first," he said. "And I'll be in touch with the lab team."

We waited in the house for the mobile lab, who arrived about half an hour after Dr. Peters left. They'd made remarkable time.

We showed the lab team the area we were most interested in, and then did an initial inspection of the rest of the house, as a preliminary, and to make sure we weren't overlooking anything that could be of primary importance. We didn't find anything useful.

What we did find was a normal home, with two possible exceptions. First, there were two PCs in the back bedroom. Both were on and running. Many farms were equipped with computers, so their mere presence wasn't unusual. The monitors, of course, were in the "rest mode," and I couldn't see what was on the screens. But, as I looked, the hard drive light on one of them flickered, and the faint buzz told me that the hard drive was being accessed for some reason. Running, all right. My first thought was of an elaborate security system. I didn't touch them, being a little reluctant to set activate an alarm. I also thought that an alarm system might explain one of them being on. But two? Maybe one as a backup? Legally, I couldn't even turn the screens on, as materials contained within the machines had the same constitutional protections as to privacy as anything else. I did make a mental note to ask Lamar why these were so much newer than our department machines. Curious.

The second possible exception was an extensive library, in the upper floor of the older portion of the house. Long shelves of computer books, weapons books, explosives manuals, an escape and evasion manual, and books on subjects such as the inner workings of the IRS, and countersurveillance practices. There were books describing conspiracies of several sorts, along with survivalist manuals, surviving Y2K, anti-federal government pamphlets, do-it-yourself legal volumes with emphasis on how to beat the IRS, the common law, and books on military history. Some of the latter volumes I had on my shelves at home. This little library was quite extensive, however, and tended toward the how-to end of the materials. On the table there were maps of North America, the United States, and Iowa, all shaded in a variety of colors in various areas, with no key. Some had arrows in red, some in blue, some both. Fascinating, like I said.

We had known for years that Cletus tended toward the vocal right wing, but this stuff was quite a bit more antigovernment than I'd expected.

The only possibility of additional evidence was the discovery of bedclothes in the dryer. They appeared freshly laundered. The reason that was considered possible evidence of "something" was that a woman on the lab team named Mary thought it unlikely that the wife in such a clean and tidy house would leave on an extended vacation without folding and putting away the laundry. She was probably right, but just try explaining that to the males on a jury.

The lab crew said right away that the dark areas I'd uncovered on the carpet did contain traces of blood. They also said that whoever had cleaned them up had done an exceptional job. Same for the area on the wall that looked to have been wiped clean.

A preliminary test confirmed Dr. Peters's judgment about the dried pool of blood on the top of the water heater.

This was a phase of the investigation that could easily lose the case. You not only had to locate and carefully examine all items of evidence, you had to preserve them in such a way that a defense team could conduct their own examinations. That took much, much time.

It looked like the lab team would be there for several hours. Lamar used the radio to order food brought to the farm. Great idea. About a minute later, Deputy Willis called from the end of the lane. The owner, Cletus Borglan, was here.

He was a about medium height and build, in his middle fifties. He was fit, from working as opposed to working out. He also had a loud voice, which he was using. Not particularly angry. Just loud.

"Damn, Lamar! What's goin' on here? Why the little army at my farm?" He was standing in the kitchen doorway, and was using a voice that would enable him to be heard in the machine shed.

"Been a problem," said Lamar.

"So I hear," said Cletus, loudly. "What are cops doin' on my property in the first place?"

"We're investigating a murder," said Lamar.

"What? How the hell can there be a murder here when there's *nobody home*?" He headed toward the archway, louder as he went. "What the hell are they doin' to my carpet?"

I was by the archway, and just stepped sideways into his path.

"Sorry," I said. "You can't go in there just yet. They're not . . ." I was going to say "done."

"Who the hell are you to tell me that I can't go in there?" Very loud, but he'd stopped.

"Calm down, Clete," said Lamar. "Like I said, we're here on a murder investigation."

Cletus spun around to face Lamar. "And I said, 'How the hell can there be a murder here if there's NOBODY HOME?'!"

Lamar stood his ground, and I stepped one step closer behind Cletus.

"Like I been trying to tell you," began Lamar, patiently, "one of my officers had a reason to come here, and look for somebody. He found who he was looking for, but not alive."

Cletus cut him off. "What happened? One of you guys get killed trespassing on a farm again?"

Lamar went white, and I suspect I did, too. Cletus was referring to an incident about five miles from his house, where Lamar had gotten shot and our civil Deputy Bud had been killed, attempting to serve a notice on a farmer and his wife. Our people had not been, of course, trespassing.

The outrageousness of the statement had Lamar temporarily speechless. Cletus, too, for he knew he had gone too far. Before he could try to make amends, though, Lamar spoke up.

"You stupid son of a bitch," said Lamar, quiet but not quite controlled. "Don't ever say anything like that again. Ever. You got that? Ever."

"I'm sorry, Lamar," said Cletus, still too loud, and not quite sincerely. "It was out of line. I didn't mean that."

Well, there it was, though. He'd thought it, and he'd said it, and that was that. Lamar looked at me and said, "You deal with him. I'm gonna step outside for a minute."

Thanks, boss. Thanks a lot.

"Why don't you have a seat at the kitchen table, Cletus," I said. "You quiet down, and I'll tell you some of what's going on."

He turned and looked at me, his face a bit redder than it had been when he first arrived. He said nothing, just walked over to the table, and sat. Then, "What's this country coming to when a man's ordered around in his own house?" He said it almost softly, like he was talking to himself. Almost, but not really. The softness made it deniable, though, if he were to be called on it.

"Just get a handle on it, Cletus," I said. "Things happen for a reason."

"It's my house. What'd you do if I just said to get off my property? Huh? It's MY property."

"Well, Cletus," I said, sitting across the table from him, "first I'd tell you that we have the right to investigate the crime without interference." I kept my voice soft and low, forcing him to listen.

"Bullshit." This was a little louder again. "What were you doing here in the first place?"

"And," I said, "if you persisted, I'd charge you with Interference with Official Acts."

"On my own property?" His voice was rising. "That's pure bullshit!"

Time to change tactics. "Look, Cletus," I said. "Suppose you invited some guys over for a poker game, you lost, got pissed off, and shot all of 'em. You actually think that the courts would allow you to say, 'It's my property, you can't come here?' I don't think so."

He didn't answer.

"So, if you want to calm down, I'll tell you as much as I can about what's going on."

Cletus looked me right in the eye. "Okay. Let's hear it." Very calm. Very matter-of-fact. It crossed my mind that Cletus had been raising hell for effect. Why? I had no idea. Sometimes people were just like that. Bluster, then calm.

Just as I was starting, Lamar came back in, fixed Cletus with a cold stare, and then moved over to the lab people. He didn't say anything, but Cletus was a little cowed for a few seconds.

I told Cletus Borglan just about everything I knew, with some important exceptions. I left out all reference to Fred. I just said we'd been informed that there'd been a burglary. I didn't describe how the victims had been shot. While I was telling him the details, he got up, went to the sink, and began making a pot of coffee. Being cool. He stood with his hips resting against the kitchen counter as he listened. When the coffee was done, he poured himself a cup, opened the refrigerator to get some milk, sat down, and took a long sip. He just looked at me, and smiled.

"My hired man is up here all the time. How come he didn't find no burglary? Care to explain that?"

"Don't know him, Cletus. Maybe that's something you should ask him about." I was unhappy about not being offered coffee. "You got an alarm system or anything?"

"Didn't think I'd need one. What with all you on the county payroll."

Because of Cletus and his attitude, the agent in charge of the lab crew decided that they better stay at the house until everything was done, rather than try to get past Cletus in the morning. The rest of us stayed right along with them.

That was all right. I was there when the bodies were removed, and saw a complete nonreaction from Cletus Borglan. In the dark, with the stark lights, the black hearses, the frost and snow, and all the officers and agents present, it was quite a scene. As I said to Lamar, it was too bad we didn't get a picture. It would have looked great on the Office Christmas Card next year.

I ended up back in the office, sitting alone at my desk about 0445, typing my preliminary report. It helps to do that. Organizes your thoughts. Sure. Well, in this case, there was damned little to organize. Fred let 'em off. They didn't come back. Who but Fred even knew they were there? Nobody.

Before I left the office, I left a note: ANYBODY WITH 43 ON FRED GROTHLER, A.K.A. GOOBER, LET ME KNOW WHAT YOU HAVE. 10-43 is cop talk for information.

I got home at 0547. It was amazingly cold. Minus forty-four degrees in still air. That's about thirty degrees colder than the temperature in your home freezer. The air was so still the smoke from the chimneys was just standing in straight lines. All the moisture had been frozen and precipitated out of the atmosphere, and the little frozen crystals were all over everything. I stuck my head in the door, and called out to my wife, softly, "Sue?" No answer. She was upstairs, sleeping. She was going to have to miss this.

I couldn't resist. I went to the sink, filled a large plastic cup with hot water, and rushed back outside. I heaved the contents of the glass up into the air . . . It dissipated in a puff, and was gone. Nothing came back down. I love to do that. I made four more trips, all with the same result. Just cold enough. It made my day. I was almost tempted to wake Sue . . . almost. She's pretty tolerant, but there are limits . . .

Six

Art and Lamar had decided to have a meeting of the investigative crew before the lab unit left for Des Moines. Swell. I hadn't even gotten to bed when they called. According to Lamar, both he and Art thought I'd better attend. Right. I'm sure Art did.

I'd just finished explaining to Sue that I'd been up all night, that we had a murder, and that she'd missed the experiment with the water in the air.

"Well, now you can get some sleep," she said, pulling her sweater over her head, and continuing to dress for school.

"Don't think so. That was the office, and they want me to be back in about an hour or so."

She stopped fastening her earrings, and turned to face me. "I don't want to sound mean, but you're getting too old to stay up twenty-four hours a day."

"Eh?" I cupped my ear.

"I said . . ." She stopped. "It's not funny."

As I came through the office door, I smelled fresh pastries. Great. I'm on a fairly strict low-fat diet. I stomped my feet to shake off the snow. I had on the same lace boots as yesterday, but was dressed in blue jeans, sweatshirt, and my own parka. Fortified with long johns, of course. It had warmed up, but was still minus fifteen or so. And, I admit it, I wanted to be in plain clothes just to prove to Art that I wasn't a "uniform." Ego. Always seems to be there when you don't need it.

Everybody was in the jail kitchen, seated around a long, industrial-sized folding table that had been in the kitchen since the 1950s. The initials of many prisoners were scratched into its top, along with a reasonably good checkerboard on one of the corners. Sort of a department heirloom. I grabbed a doughnut and some coffee, and sat down.

Lamar told us that the phones had been ringing like crazy since about midnight, with the media getting all worked up. So far, they hadn't put in a physical appearance, but he was pretty sure they'd be here by ten or so. Lamar hated media people, primarily because he was self-conscious. He also hated them because they seemed incapable of getting a story straight. He tended to leave terse, handwritten statements for the duty dispatcher to read to whoever called. He handed us all copies of his most recent effort.

THE BODIES OF TWO MALE SUBJECTS WERE DISCOVERED ON THE CLETUS BORGLAN FARM YESTERDAY. BOTH WERE FROZEN. THE CASE IS BEING TREATED AS A MURDER.

Great. I started to laugh, and drew a heavy stare from the boss.

"Jesus, Lamar," I finally got out. "You want to reword this?"

"What?" Gruffly, at best.

"Well, maybe you could put in something about the cause of death being undetermined at this time?" I grinned. "Otherwise, it sounds like they were killed by Jack Frost."

He looked at the note, and his eyes twinkled a little. "Write in the change," he said.

Lamar then announced that he'd talked to the two officers who had the responsibility to do the residence checks at the Borglan place. They had not had any tire tracks or foot tracks in the lane for the last eight to ten days.

The first case item of importance was Art's announcement that he had "ordered up" an Iowa National Guard helicopter for sometime today, hopefully to arrive before noon. He wanted to "scope out" the snowmobile tracks from the air. I just loved it when he used cop talk like that. He was the sort of guy who wouldn't say to his wife, "I always miss you, dear." Instead, he'd say, "I miss you, twenty-four-seven." But it was a good idea. I dearly wished we had resources like that in our department.

"I don't know what they have available," he said, "so I'm not sure how many of you will get to go up." Leaving absolutely no doubt that he would be in the chopper, regardless.

Over the years, I've flown a few times in Iowa Guard choppers, and knew we had a choice of two types: the OH-58, which held four; and the UH-1H, which held ten or more, and was called a Huey. I really hoped for a Huey.

Art said Dr. Peters was going to X-ray the two heads in Manchester in about an hour. The bodies were still thawing, or "defrosting," as he had put it. He said they were apparently able to remove the clothing by now, so the clothes had been seized, bagged, labeled, and would be relayed to the lab in Des Moines.

Next, the lab team had made several interesting confirmations at the house. The small hole in the wall appeared to be made by a .22 caliber bullet. They hadn't found any shell casing yet. But it was a fairly good bet that it had been deflected by one of the Colsons' heads, and was not traveling point first when it hit the plaster.

The marks in the carpet were originally bloodstains, somewhat smaller than the dark area indicated, and had been cleaned up. Placing the chairs over them had kept them damp longer than they would have been, and made them more noticeable to me. The stain under the throw rug was not blood. It appeared to have been grease, and was old. They could have taken up the entire sections of carpet, and bagged them. Cut them right out of the floor. They didn't, but had taken small inch-square samples in several places. Easier to replace for the owner. Not that Cletus had been appreciative.

The dried puddle on the top of the water heater had been confirmed as blood, too, and had dripped down through a crack in the floor above, near the top of the basement stair. There was a large bloodstain extending between the edge of the stairs and the wall. As one of them said, just like you'd spilled some liquid, and cleaned it up in a hurry. As you moved the rag, you'd push the liquid toward the wall . . .

They had found no rags, by the way. Bloody or otherwise.

Traces of bloodstains had been found in a kitchen drawer, and on a box of white trash bags contained therein. All blood samples were going to the lab. Comparisons to the blood of the victims would be made.

There were numerous fingerprints on the sliding doors, but they were old. (You can tell older ones if you use print powder, because they don't jump out the way really fresh ones do.) They'd fumed several items with cyanoacrylate, and had raised many prints. Most of them appeared female, and if the lab team had to bet, they'd say they belonged to Mrs. Borglan. They'd know when they got a set of prints from her for comparison. (Female prints are often finer, and smaller, than male.)

They'd fumed the chairs, and gotten some smudges. Nothing legible. Played hell with the chairs, though.

All trash receptacles had been checked, and nothing of evidentiary value was present. Same with clothes hampers. Attic in the old half was checked, and nothing was there. Crawl space above the ceiling of the new addition was checked. Nothing.

They were preparing scale diagrams of the scene, and would have them for us in a couple of days. They gave us a copy of the measurements taken, so we would be able to do our own rough sketches with accurate distances.

That was it. No murder weapon. No spent shell casings. No foot tracks, except the one on the back door that seemed to match the shoe on one of the bodies.

Oh. The marks that I had followed to the chair from the archway? The ones I thought were drag marks? They were fresh vacuum cleaner tracks.

"We're taking the vacuum cleaner and bag back to the lab with us." They did that, because sometimes the critical part of some evidence wouldn't make it all the way into the bag. They disassembled the cleaners completely, down to slitting and opening the hoses.

Well. You just never know.

Art spoke up. "It looks pretty much like that's all the physical evidence, then. Except the bag, and the bodies."

We agreed.

"Anything anybody needs before we let these people go back to Des Moines?"

Lamar spoke up. "When can we expect your photos?"

Four days, max, as it turned out.

But that reminded me. I excused myself, and hurried out to my car, and got the film I'd used yesterday, and hustled it back to our new secretary, Judy. "Could you get these developed, today or tomorrow, rush job?"

"Sure, I think, I'll check . . ."

"If you could take 'em down? I'm not going to have a chance for a while, and I don't want 'em to be delayed."

"What do you want, like, double prints?"

"Sure," I said. "One for us, one for the DCI people. Maybe a third for the official file, so we have something to work with. Just keep it cheap, or Lamar will have a fit." I hurried back into the kitchen, to catch the lab team.

I met the county attorney as I passed the dispatch center.

"I'm here to see what we can make of this." He sounded burdened, as usual. Being county attorney in our county, as in most of the state, was a part-time job. A large case could really hurt his private practice, which is where most of his income came from.

"Oh, it's a murder, all right," I said.

"Damn," he muttered, as we entered the kitchen.

"Our photos will be back in a couple of days, too," I announced. The lab people said, "Fine," but Art had a better idea.

"Why don't you give your film to the lab, they can develop it for you?"

I'd experienced that before. The state then kept the negatives. We always wanted to keep our own negatives. "That's okay," I said. "They've already gone."

"Where do you take them?" asked Art. "Dubuque?"

"No, right down town here, to the local drugstore. They'll be back in a couple of days."

After the lab team left, Lamar, the county attorney, Art, and I conferred. Actually, we argued perspectives, as they say. Art, who had a reputation for preferring the quick and dirty approach, insisted that Fred had done the deed.

"No doubt," he said. "Opportunity? You bet. I'm sure we can find a motive."

I disagreed. "Nope. Look at the scene. This is about the tidiest crime scene I've ever seen. Fred's not that careful. Not that patient."

"I'm not ruling out his having help, here," said Art. "An accomplice."

"Who," I asked, "Martha Stewart? Whoever cleaned up had lots of 'Helpful Household Hints' for the carpet."

"But, Carl," interjected the county's finest, "didn't you say that Fred had asked you if you'd charge him with murder if they were dead?"

"Yeah." Hard to argue that one.

"Speaking as an attorney," he said, grinning, "it certainly sounds to me like he had prior knowledge."

"I really don't think so," I said, leaning forward. "I think Fred was really worried that they might be dead, but I got the impression he thought they might have frozen to death. Not been shot. Don't forget, he was also worried that they were going to crap on him for missing his pickup assignment." I leaned back in my chair. "He just didn't want to be held responsible, that's all."

"Look," said Art. "Give me another suspect . . . anybody else. Then I might be able to cut Fred some slack. But, Carl," he said, leaning forward, "he was the only one who knew they'd fucking be at the Bergerman residence!"

"That's Borglan," I said. "The Borglan residence." He just

blinked. I shook my head. He'd just had to use "fucking," to show he was one of the guys.

"Yeah, I know," I said. "I hate the 'gut feeling' bullshit as much as you do, but I just don't think that Fred did 'em. It doesn't make any sense to do all the covering up, and then sit outside the farm and honk your horn. Whoever killed them cleaned up the evidence really well, and did it so that the hired man, or anybody else watching the place, wouldn't pick up on the crime. Right?"

"Possibly," said Art.

"Possibly" my ass. "So, why then sit on the road and draw attention to yourself, on the off chance that a cop might come along? I just don't think so."

"Well, with the bodies salted away in the shed, the only person who might stumble on them was the hired man, right?" Lamar was off on his own track.

We all agreed.

"Let's not rule him out," said Lamar. "He might have been at the place when the two guys showed up. He might have done it."

"That could be," said Art, "but what motive would he have, really? He could just watch them, and call the cops when they left."

"Maybe he knows Fred?" said Lamar. "Let's get this checked out, too."

"Sure," I said. "Will do."

"Murder makes the mind do strange things," interjected our prosecutor. He just does that sometimes. Tosses in whatever is in his head. He does it in court, too. Leaving an occasional flabbergasted judge in his wake.

"So, what's with the bodies in the machine shed?" asked Art. "Why there? Just for argument's sake."

"Not enough room in the refrigerator?" I just stuck that in. Well, I was tired, and I thought it was funny. Apparently, I was a little more tired than everybody else.

"The ground is frozen solid," said Lamar, quickly. "Can't dig anywhere, so you store the bodies. Just like they do at all the cemeteries this time of year. Either that or heat the ground. Mostly, though, just come back later, haul 'em away, and dig a hole someplace." Lamar looked around the table. "Nothin' in the machine shed the hired man would need."

That, of course, implied that the Borglans' itinerary was pretty well known to the suspect. I said as much. This led to a brief discussion as to how many people knew where the Borglans were. Many, as it turned out. But it brought the hired man right back into the limelight.

What I couldn't understand was why Fred would salt the bodies away, clean the house, and otherwise erase any sign of his presence, and then come to the cops. It just didn't make any sense. I said as much.

"It would have if he'd changed his mind," said Art. "Guilt working on him, especially after he contacts his aunt, to make his alibi, and sees how worried she really is."

"Hell," I said, "if he was feeling guilty, he'd just confess and get it over with."

"Look," said Lamar. "So far, I think Carl's on the right track, here. We have no evidence linking Fred to the scene, and no motive for him to kill them." He looked at Art. "I know we don't need to prove motive, but it sure as shit would help to have one." He looked at me. "For anybody."

"Do we have any idea yet," asked Art, "where they were selling the stolen guns? That might get us somebody who knows more about the three of 'em. More background."

Actually, no, we didn't. This was shaping up into a long investigation, any way you cut it.

Then the county's finest prosecutor came up with the most telling point against Fred, and one that I had been missing. "I get the impression that we're all assuming that Fred planned this out in advance. Maybe not. Maybe he was there, and they just got into an argument. Maybe it was spur of the moment. Or, just maybe, Carl, it went down like the Whiting case."

About ten years ago, a man named Whiting got into an argument with a drinking buddy at a remote river cabin. Killed him. In the presence of another drinking buddy. He'd convinced the survivor to help him dispose of the body and the evidence. The guy had done so, apparently frightened and glad to be alive. He also had no place to run. Or to call for help. Then Whiting killed the second man.

"Could be," I said, "but don't forget that Whiting was a really dominant sort of guy. Fred isn't. And Whiting was really a cold man. Fred isn't that, either."

"Oh, I don't know," said Art. "Standing there with a gun . . ."

"And," said Lamar, "we only have Fred's word that he dropped them off. He could have gone in with them just as easily."

"Well, anyway, you people hash this out," said the prosecutor, standing up. "I'm afraid I'm asking the Attorney General for an assist on this one, and I'm afraid I'm going to have to remove myself from the case, anyway."

"You're what?" asked Lamar.

"I do Borglan's taxes, there's a possible conflict here." He raised both hands to shoulder level, palm up. "I'm sorry. But I do think you should interview Fred."

"His attorney will never permit it," I said. "Even if he's innocent."

"Christ. It's not Priller, is it?"

"It's Priller," said Lamar.

Priller was a well-known obstructionist. A pompous, irritating, aggravating little twerp. But somehow he managed to be likable at the same time, because he never took it to a personal level.

Mike grinned and shook his head. "Well, gentlemen, I wish you all the best of luck."

This was a bit of a blow, as the county attorney would normally be available for the quick questions during an investigation, while the assigned prosecutor from the Attorney General's office would do the long-term prosecutor's stuff.

"Are you going to appoint a special prosecutor at the county level?" I asked.

He stopped for a second, on his way to the door. "Boy, Carl,"

he said. "I don't know that the county board of supervisors is going to approve that . . . it could be pretty expensive, and with a
state prosecutor assigned . . . But, I'll ask."

Expenses. It always came down to that.

It was only a few seconds after he left that our secretary stuck
her head in the door and motioned to me.

"Manchester PD called, and said to say that Dr. Peters was
on the way here, and that everybody should stay put."

"Really?" I relayed the information back to the table. It was
just a bit unusual. I hadn't expected Dr. Peters to come back up
today.

At 0945 we, as they say, reconvened. Being an opportunist, I
grabbed another doughnut.

Dr. Peters had brought a portable light-board device, to
backlight X-rays. We didn't have one. Who does, except hospi-
tals?

We watched, paying very close attention, as Dr. Peters described the film.

"Subject number one," he said. "This is . . . Royce Colson
. . . the fellow we looked at first at the scene. The one who was
on his back. Bullet wound in his right temple . . ."

The X-ray showed the hole, cracks in the skull, a little trail of
debris through the brain toward the left side, and a fragmenting
of bone on the left side.

"Through and through," said Dr. Peters. "Entered just behind the eye, into the sphenoid, right above the zygomatic arch.
Transverses the brain, and exits via the lower edge, just about
precisely at the squamous suture. Caused a stellate, circumferen-
tial fracture of the skull, as it did." He traced the points with his
hand as he talked. Good thing.

The bullet had gone in right behind the eye, kept pretty
level, and come out the other side a little farther aft, cracking the
skull completely around its circumference. The stellate or star-
shaped portion was a crack running up the side of the skull from
the entrance, and stopping near the top of the head.

"This victim may have been upright, and I suspect standing

erect, at the time the shot was fired." He looked at us. "I strongly suspect that the bullet which exited this man's head is the one discovered that made the hole in the wall of the Borglan residence." He paused. "The entrance wound is about two-tenths of an inch in diameter, so I think we're dealing with a .22 caliber bullet. Close examination of the wound, after washing the clotted blood away, reveals very intense tattooing around the entrance." He stepped back from the X-ray. "Photos will be available soon, I'm sure, but it was a nearly perfect circle, and I suspect we have a contact gunshot wound, here. I would also think it was made with the muzzle in contact because the projectile actually exited the skull . . . Lots of energy available here," said Dr. Peters.

The muzzle was in contact with the skull when the gun went off. This was usually an indication of a suicide, but hardly likely in this case.

"Self-inflicted?" asked Art. Thinking aloud again.

"I don't believe so," said Dr. Peters. "Let's have a look at the next one . . . this would be a Dirk Colson," he said, checking his notes. "Notice that both entrance wounds are from the top of the head, in the right rear portion of the skull." He pointed. "The second round entered just ahead of the first, also traveling downward. It caused these fractures here," he said, "that stop at the sagittal suture, and also stop at the hole made by the first wound."

"This second one travels in a path to here," he said. "Again in the basilar part, but on the left and more forward."

We could see that one, too. It appeared to be on its side.

"This is the one that caused the extrusion of the brain tissue out the first entrance hole."

I remembered that. Like frosting out of a cake decorator.

"Close examination of both these wounds indicated a contact or near contact gunshot, as well." He removed the last X-ray, and put one of each victim up on the board.

"Likely a double murder, then," said Art.

Dr. Peters said, "Oh, yes. And a bit more flavor, I think." He paused, pointing at the X-ray of Dirk Colson. "From the nature and path, I would strongly suspect that this second victim was in a lowered position, possibly seated or kneeling, possibly squatting, when the two wounds were inflicted." He cleared his throat. "With the shooter behind the victim."

"So," said Dr. Peters, "based on the angles of the bullet tracks, the second victim was shot by a gun almost directly above and behind him. Even with a .22 pistol, that would require that the victim be either on his knees or seated." He paused. "Well, absent a ladder." He shrugged. "However, given the fact that both victims would very likely fall just about right where they were shot, it would explain the bloodstains on the floor. With the lack of bloodstains on the chairs that were moved to cover the stained area of the carpet, I will say this: The major carpet stains likely were from each of the victims, that the stains occurred when they were lying on the floor, and that the blood came from their heads. With the stained areas nearly in the center of the room, there doesn't appear to be any item of furniture close enough to permit the second victim to have been shot while seated, or for the shooter to have stood upon while shooting."

"An execution, sort of?" I asked.

"I can narrow your parameters, Carl. I can tell you they weren't shot at a distance. I can tell you what the evidence tells me happened. An execution . . . is a possibility. A strong one. But a *possibility*. Not a proven fact."

"Execution," said Art, disdainfully, "in my book requires restraints, bindings, things like that. Could this, Doctor, have been done in the heat of anger, not in a cold-blooded style?"

"Yes."

Art shrugged. "Well, that still leaves us with Fred. He goes in with them, gets mad, and shoots both of 'em." He looked around the room. "Like they say, go for the simplest solution."

Keep it simple. Naturally. But I hate oversimplifications like that. In the first place, people are complex. In the second place, you can get too simple, and jump before all the facts are in. I said as much.

"Oh, sure, Carl," said Art. "I can keep an open mind. But I'll tell you the truth . . . it's gonna take a lot of evidence to convince me that it wasn't either Fred or the hired man." He shrugged. "I sure don't think it looks like it's anybody else."

Like I said, Art always liked the quick and dirty approach. I suspected he was right more often than not, but I was getting just a little weary of this approach. Simple is one thing, easy is another. If we went with Fred, the easy touch, we were going to cut off the rest of the possibilities. If I was right, and Fred hadn't done it, that would be a catastrophe.

"This still doesn't go down quite right with me," I said.

"It's probably just because you know Fred," said Art.

"Could be," I replied, "but I'll still reserve judgment."

What bothered me about all this was that I felt Fred would be more than willing to talk with us, and probably would be a great help, but Priller the lawyer would not give us any slack on the questioning. He'd want immunity or some such for the burglary charges and as Fred was still the primary suspect for the murders, giving away the burglary charges now would set him free. Then Priller would advise him not to tell us anything about the murder anyway.

That left us with the scene as our only source of evidence. The lab crew had all the materials from there. But we could still go out and look at the place again, especially the tracks left by the dead men on their way to the house. It does help, and you will sometimes get an insight if you look the entire scene over again, after you have developed a scenario. Well, that's what they tell you in the Academy.

Right.

We called Cletus Borglan, and he told us two things. One, it was going to have to be soon, as he was going to be leaving for Florida the day after tomorrow. Two, he wouldn't let us on his property without four hours' prior notice, and he and his attorney would have to be present.

We checked the forecast. A big upward bump in the jet stream was moving inexorably eastward. But ever so slowly. It was supposed to be warming steadily for the next five days.

Good. We wanted to see the tracks over the hill in the daylight. They were faint, we knew that. But we wanted to see if there was a way to tell how many people had gone over the fence and to the house. We'd better be sure about that before the snow started to melt again.

It took three hours to type the search warrant application, but Judge Winterman issued a warrant to search the property for the exterior tracks and patterns of tracks, from the roadway to wherever they would lead us. It was the first time I'd ever included a National Weather Service forecast in a search warrant application. I was kind of proud of that.

Art was in his slacks and sport coat. With wingtips. No overshoes that I'd seen, and just a dress coat. "You got anything warmer?"

"Don't worry about me."

"Well, I wasn't really worried. I just didn't want to have to examine another frozen body."

We contacted the Iowa Department of Natural Resources, and got a Fish and Game enforcement officer named Sam Younger to meet us at the office. Sam could track just about anything, and was sure a lot better at it than the rest of us.

As soon as we got the search warrant in our hands, we called Borglan, and got no answer. Tough. Out we went. Not so tough that we didn't leave orders for the dispatcher to call the Borglan residence every five minutes until she got an answer, though. Lamar, having once been shot by a farmer who didn't honor a court process, didn't want us taking any chances, either. Wisely, as he still needed a cane most of the time, Lamar also opted to stay at the office.

I drove us directly to Borglan's house. No vehicles. I called dispatch, and they said there had been no answer yet. I got out, and went to the door and knocked several times, calling out Cletus's name as well. Satisfied there was no one home, I slipped a copy of the search warrant into the sliding door. The legal requirements had been satisfied.

I thought it best if we started where the two brothers had,

so we linked up with DNR officer Sam Younger near the Bor-glan place, and I took everybody to where the tracks began. I ex-plained to Sam that we wanted to try to discover how many people had made the track. It was a good thing that I'd seen them the day before, because the snowplows had been by again, "dressing" the edges of the gravel road, and the deep ditch was now completely filled with road snow. Although we were just able to make out the disturbed area on the other side of the barbed-wire fence, where the tracks led over the hill, it didn't look too promising. Well, as they say, you gotta try. We waited for Art to pull a pair of black five-buckle overshoes over his wingtips. They had N C JAIL hand painted on the sides. Ah, yes. Don't worry about Art. He'd also apparently borrowed one of the quilted, knee-length coats the prisoners wear when they go out for exercise in the winter. Mustard-colored. He cut a fine figure.

"You look like a North Korean soldier," I said. He glared, but didn't say anything.

Crossing the ditch was especially difficult for those of us who were a bit heavier than the others. I was treated to the spectacle of Art virtually walking straight to the fence line, while I was knee-deep in snow.

"Hey, Houseman," he said, "how's the low-fat diet coming?"

I would have done something cute, like answer him, but I was too out of breath.

Sam, the Department of Natural Resources officer, re-sponded for me. "It's all the damned rice those North Koreans eat," he said.

We grouped at the fence, and Sam Younger scrutinized what he gamely referred to as the track. "You know," he said, "there re-ally isn't a hell of a lot left, is there?"

"It might help," I said, "if you see it in an angled light, like early evening."

"I'm sure," he said. He looked over at Art. "Is there any magic sort of thing you people do to lift tracks from under snow like this?"

"Nope."

"Well, then," said Sam, "all we can do is see if the tracks diverge into three separate sets as they go . . . How far is the farmhouse?"

"About three-quarters of a mile, just over the hill, here," I said.

Art propped his arm on the fence post, and took three or four photos of the very faint track leading up the hill. It was hard to see among the trees and large limestone outcroppings on the slope of the hill. He wanted photos before we crossed the fence and tracked the area up.

We crossed the barbed-wire fence, and followed the track. My over the hill comment had made it sound so simple. Actually, the hilltop was divided, and we had to go down a long reverse slope, and back up again before we reached the crest that allowed us to see the house. The track split into two distinct portions three times in that distance. Never into three, though.

Worse, on the way down to the house, it split into two discernible depressions, and they stayed that way for about a hundred yards, until we lost them in the multitude of tracks made yesterday and since. Just the way two men, walking together, would approach their target. Walking parallel, with about a fifteen-foot separation.

We stopped in Borglan's yard. There were now two cars there, and a pickup truck. Cletus Borglan opened the door just before I got there.

"What do you want?"

"We just wanted to let you know that we were done with the tracks," I said. I watched him eye Sam. Cletus was one of those who had no time for the DNR, especially their Fish and Game officers.

"Did you think they took a deer on the way?"

"No point in being sarcastic, Cletus," I said. "We were just trying to learn something from their route."

He looked at me with cold, unblinking eyes, and it was very much apparent that he didn't believe a word I was saying.

"Right," he said. "So, if they were burglars, how come there's nothing missing?"

"Well," I said, "I don't think . . ."

"We aren't allowed to discuss a current investigation," interrupted Art, quickly. "Everything must be held confidential while the investigation is active."

I had been about to say that they hadn't had a chance to take anything, but Art was right. Technically, anyway. It's just that the official confidentiality thing sounds so much like an attempt to conceal something. Besides, there was always some slack you could let out, but apparently, Art didn't want any going toward Borglan. I wasn't about to be so unprofessional as to argue the point in front of Cletus. Although, come to think of it, I wouldn't have been so unprofessional as to interrupt me, either.

" 'Investigation'?" asked Cletus, just as two men I recognized as being area farmers came to the door behind him. "Isn't that just another word for cover-up?"

"Cletus," I said, grinning, "I just wish I knew enough about what happened to know what should be covered up." I shook my head, and glanced at Art. "Anyway, just wanted to make sure you got that copy of the search warrant, and answer any questions you might have."

"Nothin' personal," said Cletus, "but I'd just as soon ask my attorney."

"I would, too," I said, turning to go. "That's what you pay 'em for." As I was turning, I could see through the sliding glass doors, and became aware that there were at least two other occupants of the house. As I walked away, I heard Cletus say, "That one's a deputy, and one is a damned game warden." I began to suspect that one of the unknowns might be his attorney. I didn't look back, because when there is a bit of tension in the air, looking back after you've done what you've come to do can get you into an argument. But I was certainly glad I'd dropped the search warrant copy off before we went for our walk.

The consensus among us was that we had achieved very little. This was expressed by Sam Younger as we walked back to the cars.

"Well, shit . . ."

We parted company with Sam, who had to go on a deer-poaching call. I was sorry there hadn't been anything more for him to get his teeth into.

Back in my car, Art and I did some serious thinking. I could remember very clearly that there had been no other car tracks when I drove into the Borglan yard the day before. With what I'd say was a high probability that there were two sets of tracks going from the roadway, over the hill, and to the farm; I just couldn't see how it was possible for Fred to have gotten there to do the deed.

"Simple," said Art. "One of the brothers was already there."

Well, I have to admit, I hadn't thought of that possibility. "Why?"

"Don't know, yet," he said. "But I'll figure it out."

"Well, one thing's for sure," I said. "*Somebody* was already there. Any way you cut it. It could have been Fred, too, for that matter. Could have been."

So. Two sets of tracks going in. Two dead bodies, both shot in the head. They hadn't killed each other, nor had they killed themselves. No obvious involved weapon at the scene. (There wasn't a .22 in the gun cabinet. All shotguns and larger caliber handguns.) No spent shell casings, which indicated to me a re-volver. The mess pretty much cleaned up. The bodies put in the shed, covered with a tarp, as if awaiting disposal at a later date.

"Who do you think was going to go back and dispose of the bodies?" I asked of no one in particular.

"Fred," said Art. Instantly. "Probably as soon as he got a buddy to help." He paused for a second. "Or, maybe, if he wasn't able to get a friend to help him out, that's why he just gave up and went to the cops?"

"Yeah?" I said. I just didn't think Fred had done it. I did have to admit, though, that I still didn't have another suspect.

"You still skeptical?" asked Art. "Well, that's good. Keeps us honest." Condescending. Immediately separating me from "them," the true professionals. I resent things like that, but there are simply times where you can't let it show.

I cleared my throat. "Which still leaves us with the snowmobile tracks," I said. "Time to talk with the hired man."

"I'd like to see 'em from the air first," said Art. "To see where they all go."

Well, sure. Who wouldn't? It was just that some of us weren't used to working with choppers available. We checked through dispatch for the status of his flying machine.

"They're supposed to be at the Maitland Airport in about ten," she said. "They report a 'window' of about an hour, and then they want to head back. There's a front moving in."

Reasonable, as they had probably come from Des Moines to Dubuque, refueled at the Dubuque Airport, and then headed up to Maitland International, as we called it. Reverse that to go home, and you're talking about three or more hours. Maitland International, also known as MAX, was a grass strip and one tin shed with a wind sock on the curved roof, and a large machine shed that was called a hangar. But it was ours.

We had just enough time to get to MAX, to meet them. I really hoped we'd get a Huey.

We hit the airport about fifteen minutes later, and there was an Army drab Huey sitting there. Yahoo! My lucky day.

We met the pilots and the crew chief, they opened the large sliding doors on the sides for us, and closed them as soon as we were secured in the canvas bench seats. We were held in by thin seat belts, and faced outward. Infantry assault helicopter, you know. Wanted to be able to jump out as soon as they hit the ground.

We were also each given a headset and mike, which we keyed by pressing a button that was clipped to our coats. I was on the right side and Art was on the left, with the crew chief in the middle. With a roar, we were airborne, and sliding over Maitland.

I gave directions to the pilot, and in about two minutes, we were able to make out the Borglan place. A minute later, we were over the Borglan house at 750 feet, and started following the snowmobile tracks to the southwest. They went over a small board bridge that crossed the stream, and then through a wooded area, along fencerows, and eventually came out at the hired man's residence. All of them.

We asked the pilot to go back, and tried to see if any tracks diverged. I made the mistake of asking them to orbit the little bridge area so we could get a photo. The crew chief slid the door open, so we could have "unobstructed vision, sir." Right. Cold, oh Lord was it cold, and my feet were hanging out over the edge of the fuselage, and we went into a bank with us on the down side, and there was nothing to hang on to, and I was so sorry I'd asked . . .

We got our shots, though. Art didn't seem to be bothered a bit by hanging on the edge of oblivion. I, of course, didn't let on. Having discovered the steel post toward the center of the cabin, I'd casually slipped my arm over the back of the seat, and grabbed on for dear life with my left hand. The crew chief blew my act when he said, "Don't worry, we haven't lost one yet."

He slid the door closed, again, and went back and forth between the two farms three times. We thought once that we had something, but it turned out to be a cow path.

They all went to and from the farms. No splitting off. Direct route. Then, once they got to the hired man's residence, they went all over hell. Whoever ran the snowmobiles apparently really enjoyed traveling about the countryside. There must have been fifty tracks radiating out from that other farm, some going through fields, some staying close to established paths. One particular set simply made circles in a forty-acre field. Somebody just playing around. Another several sets to and from a machine shed on what must originally have been a third farm. Big shed, with the empty foundations of a house and barn behind it. Storage for planting and harvesting equipment.

"Look," I said, brightly, on the intercom. "Crop circles."

There were also lots of black Angus cattle in the fields near the farm. Beef cattle. The hired man was likely using the snowmobiles to herd the beef cattle.

I suggested we fly the foot tracks that went from the farm, over the hill, and to the road; the ones we had just walked. We did, at about 1,000 feet. As we passed over the Borglan farm, I saw there were several people standing outside, looking up. I waved, but I don't think they saw me.

As we headed for the hill, our own tracks were glaringly obvious, but the track we had followed was pretty faint. We then flew the ridgeline, and there were no other tracks that we could see. We paralleled the roadway, and were unable to make out any points where somebody had crossed the fence line. We did a wide circle of the farm, and there were no tracks we could see coming in from anywhere. We did have one set of depressions that looked fresh. The pilot, at the request of Art, went into a low hover to give us a better look. Obligingly, the crew chief slid the door open, and in the freezing draft, we could see they were deer tracks. We came out of hover quickly, as the pilot wasn't supposed to descend lower than 1,000 feet, according to regulations.

Interestingly, I found it scarier to hover just above the tops of the trees than it was to orbit higher up. Better sense of height, I guess.

We flew back to MAX, thanked the crew, and were back in our car. Art and I compared notes. This is what we had, generally:

All the tracks out of the Borglan place go through the hired man's yard. This means

A. *He did the killing.*
B. *He has knowledge of who did the killing.*
C. *He has at least heard somebody go through his yard in a noisy snowmobile after they killed the brothers.*
D. *The killer is still at the farm.*

"I figure," said Art, "we can pretty well eliminate the 'D' above."

I figured we could, too. Although there were no foot tracks from the house going anywhere except to the machine shed. The only other track was the snowmobile track that was near the back door. If our killer didn't take the snowmobile, he would have to have been in the house when I was first there. I didn't believe it for a minute, but it gave me a funny feeling in the back of my neck, anyway.

My feelings must have shown on my face. "Got a case of the spooks, Houseman?"

"Oh, sort of . . ." I said. Then, "Nah, we searched that house thoroughly." But I remembered very well the feeling that I was being watched . . .

I just drove. Back in the days when I smoked, this would have been the time.

I picked up the mike, and called for dispatch to phone Borglan's hired man, and let him know we were coming.

Art read off the sheet he'd picked up at dispatch earlier that morning. According to his information, the hired man was a fellow named Harvey Grossman. His driver's license had said he was born in '62, five feet nine inches, 180 lbs., blue, and brown. I didn't know him, but Lamar had told me that he'd moved to our county back in '93 or '94.

I was getting a little worried. Art was pretty well established as thinking that Fred had done the dirty deed. I didn't agree, and thought that Fred was telling the truth. All well and good, and an indication of a balanced investigation. The part that worried me was that I thought it was very likely that we were just about to talk with the man who had murdered the two burglars. I mean, if Fred hadn't done it, and all the snowmobile tracks at the Borglan place led to the residence of one Harvey Grossman, who was left?

Just for the sake of arguing with myself, I assumed that Grossman had been at the residence for some reason, and had caught the burglars in the act. Perhaps there had been some sort of confrontation. Turned violent. *Bang. Bang.* And then, *bang.* Put 'em in the shed. Who else would even be looking in there until the Borglans came back? If, as he said, Cletus had been called back unexpectedly for business, then how could Grossman have known he'd be coming? Right. He couldn't. All the time in the world to dispose of the bodies, as far as he could have known. The forecast was for warming for the next week or longer. Just wait a few more days for enough of a thaw to get them into a shallow pit. Move the corpses later, if necessary.

"How certain are you," I asked, "that Grossman here isn't the killer?"

"Just about positive," said Art. "Why?"

"Well," I began, and ran my theory by him. Quickly, but with some feeling.

"It's a point." He waited in silence. "Okay, it's a good point. If Fred didn't do it, this Grossman dude is the most likely suspect. Sure. So . . . ?"

"Well," I began, again, "if he is a suspect, shouldn't we just come right out an advise him of his rights as soon as we see him? Let him know, and take it from there?"

"Jesus Christ, Houseman," said Art, "don't be so goddamned honest!"

"What?"

"No kidding," said Art, exasperated, and with uncharacteristic length. "Look. Keep the suspect business in the back of your head, but don't go getting carried away on me. Let the conversation flow. If he sends the right signals, then we hit him with Miranda and handcuffs all at once. Otherwise, lighten up."

"I know all that," I said, getting a little exasperated myself. "But, in court, if some attorney asks when I first thought this guy was a suspect, I'm gonna have to tell him it was before we talked with him for the first time."

"What did you do?" asked Art. "Watch the *entire* O.J. trial?" He sighed. "Don't worry about it. Fred's the shooter. Trust me."

Yeah. Right. As I drove, I reached back under my down vest, and unsnapped the restraining strap on my holster. I'd feel a lot better trusting Art if my gun was unsnapped when we walked to Grossman's door.

We pulled into the lane, and on the way to the residence, we drove through a nest of outbuildings. The house wasn't nearly the quality of the home place, but it was nice, and well-maintained, nonetheless. It and the outbuildings were white frame, and looked pretty sound. The door to the wooden machine shed was opened, and there were four snowmobiles parked inside. One thing that struck me about them was that none of them had the little orange flags, and none of them appeared to have registration numbers on the cowl. Cops with a patrol officer's background notice stuff like that. I was willing to bet Art hadn't picked up on that.

We got out of my car, and walked toward the kitchen door. I knocked. It was a courtesy not to go to the front door. Most farms reserved the front door for important occasions, and the back or kitchen door was used for routine entry. If we had been accepted at the front door, and none of us had removable outer footwear, we would have "tracked in" all sorts of snow and mud. Easier to clean a kitchen floor.

The inside porch door opened, and a man meeting Grossman's description came out.

"What can I do for you?"

"I'm Carl Houseman, deputy here in Nation County. The office called, and told you to expect us?"

"Somebody did. You got any identification?"

I fished out my badge, as did Art. He reached for my badge case, and I pulled my hand back a couple of inches. I grinned at him. "You just get to look, Mr. Grossman. You can't have it until you're hired." He didn't seem particularly amused.

"So," he said, having scrutinized three badges he probably had no way of telling were authentic or not, "what can I do for you?"

He wasn't even inviting us onto the porch. Not a good sign.

"We're here because you're the hired man at the Borglan farm, and they had a burglary." I moved closer to the door. "We'd like to know when the last time was that you checked the place, and things like that."

" 'Burglary,' " he said. "That's what you're calling it?"

"Well, it started out that way."

"I understand that a couple of cops got it?" he asked.

Christ, what was it with these people, anyway? Wishful thinking? "No, no. No cops. A couple of burglars got killed, though."

"By who?"

"Now, that's a good question. We thought maybe you could help us there."

Much to my surprise, he invited us in. "You might as well come on in, and we can get it over with."

Get what over with? I thought. I glanced at Art, and he seemed to be thinking the same thing. Damn. Could I be right?

Seven

Several cups of Linda Grossman's coffee later (I was really running on caffeine at this point), it certainly didn't appear that I was even close to being right. After we'd all gotten settled around the kitchen table, Harvey Grossman, wife Linda, and their nine-year-old daughter, Carrie, had pretty well explained things to us.

Carrie struck me as a pretty cool little kid. About four and a half feet tall and very thin, she had brown hair and brown eyes that were pretty intense. Especially when I showed Linda Grossman my badge. I showed it to Carrie next, including her in the business just like everybody else. Carrie examined it very closely, and nodded.

The Grossmans told an interesting story.

First of all, the entire household had been awakened about 2 A.M. on Sunday, by the sound of a snowmobile running through their yard at an apparently very high rate of speed.

"Just tore right through the yard," as little Carrie put it. "I hollered out, it scared me so much."

I could imagine it did. At 0200, with the temperatures hovering at minus forty or colder, no wind, over two miles from the nearest gravel road, which wouldn't have any traffic anyway, it would be just about as dead quiet as it could get. A high-speed snowmobile passing within fifty feet of the house would shatter that silence, and very likely wake the whole family.

Carrie had run to her folks' room, who had also both been awakened. Nobody could figure out who it was, since the Borglans weren't home. After settling Carrie down, and checking their baby, David, Linda Grossman had come downstairs and had a cup of cocoa, because she wasn't able to get back to sleep. She thought she'd heard another snowmobile, or possibly the same one, off in the distance, but wasn't sure.

All three Grossmans were certain that the snowmobile had departed heading southwest. Carrie had apparently heard it first, and said it sounded like it was coming from the Borglan place.

We asked, and Harvey told us that he'd been at the Borglans' on Thursday, and was scheduled to go there tomorrow. He hadn't been there since he heard the snowmobile. Some farm people are like that. He'd go up and see when it was time to do his job at the Borglans'. Otherwise, he had enough to do without taking an unnecessary excursion. Not what I would have done, but I was a cop and he was a farmer.

We asked the three of them for written statements, and they complied. Carrie was really cute, so very serious and studious, and showing off a bit for the company.

Mrs. Grossman, Linda, struck me as being somehow edgy. It took me a few minutes, but I finally recognized the behavior pattern. She seemed overalert, and kind of watchfully aggressive in a way that reminded me of an abused woman. Most people imagine women who are abused as shy, meek, and downcast all the time. Not so. Very often, they come on a bit too strong, in a way that will seem uncalled for, or out of character. The best defense is a good offense, and they are really trying hard to conceal the fact they're being abused. They become almost too gregarious. An overcompensation that will fool most people. Anyway, that's how she struck me. Abused, but not to the point of real hazard or flight. With my batting average being nearly zero at this point, though, I just filed it away. No point in embarrassing myself completely.

Anyway, she made a mean cup of coffee. I mentioned that.

"Thanks," she said. "I learned that when I worked at a hospital in Kansas City."

"You want me to put down the last time I was up at the other place?" interrupted Harvey.

"Uh, sure, yeah," I said. God, I was tired. I turned back to Mrs. Grossman to continue, but she was bent over her statement.

I almost got the impression that he didn't want her to talk to me. Not about her past, anyway. Abuse? Maybe. Or, maybe he just didn't want her talking about his past. Or, maybe he was just antisocial. God knows, it couldn't have been my charming ways.

I had an unsettled feeling that I thought had begun when Art and I had compared notes about an hour ago. I got more unsettled when I discovered I couldn't figure out why. The last time I'd felt this way, I'd left a burner turned on on our stove at home, before Sue and I took a short trip to Dubuque. I remembered it about ten miles out. That kind of persistent, almost ominous feeling. Coupled with my feeling that I was being watched up at the Borglan place . . . Lack of sleep? I thought that might have a lot to do with it. Especially since I felt no sense of fatigue at all, so I could assume I was still wired from the case. I refilled my coffee cup.

Then, as he finished up his statement, Harvey Grossman asked a question of his own.

"Just how were those burglars killed?"

Before Art could leap in with his standard disclaimer about how we just couldn't possibly discuss this, I said, "They were shot, Harvey."

"Oh."

Simply that. No further curiosity, no further questions. Didn't ask where, when, or why. Really didn't seem all that interested, either. It didn't tell me much, but it was the sort of thing I liked to hear and see. Most of the time, if you give a little, you get a little, and in the information business, that could become important at the oddest times. Harvey sort of owed me one.

We collected the statements, all three of them, and cautioned the Grossman family not to discuss anything that had been said with any outsiders. Standard procedure. They said they wouldn't. Also standard procedure. Except I believed Carrie.

As we were tearing off the pink copies of their statements and handing them back to them, I noticed that Harvey and Linda had both used military time as they wrote about the events of Sunday night. Things like: "We were upstairs by 2300," from Harvey, and "We went to bed about 2230," from Linda. Unusual. Carrie had said, "I was to bed at nine-thirty." I chuckled to myself. Two military times, and one Olde English.

Back in the car, the consensus was that Carrie had, single-handedly, eliminated her father as a suspect. She was absolutely believable. You can tell, especially with kids. Well, within their knowledge, of course. But there was no doubt that both her parents had been present when that snowmobile came blasting through the yard. And, if that was our killer, and it sure looked like it could be, she'd eliminated her whole family as suspects.

As we stopped at the end of the lane, before entering the roadway, Art said, "Looks like what we got left is Fred."

Sure did. Great news, except that I didn't think he'd done it.

We discussed things.

What we had was a fairly good circumstantial case against Fred. Sure. At this point, however, we had absolutely no physical evidence placing him in close proximity to the two victims when they were shot. None.

We had no evidence of animosity between Fred and his cousins. Fine. Interviews were required there, and we'd get on them. They'd be lengthy, though, and we decided to use whatever other officers we could.

We had to find out if Fred had access to a .22 caliber weapon. True, several .22s had been stolen in the course of the residential burglaries, but we didn't know where the weapons were. That had to be checked.

We had to try to see if it was a .22 rifle or handgun. That would be a good start, and we'd have to rely on the expert opinion of Dr. Peters for that. As soon as he could open the heads, he might be able to give us some idea.

.22 caliber ammunition comes in three flavors: short, long, and long rifle. Short being the least powerful, long rifle the most. Problem: the longer the barrel of the weapon, the higher the velocity of the bullet. So, a short fired from a rifle could hit with the same force as a long or long rifle from a handgun.

It gets worse. Pistols come in two basic types: revolvers and semiautos. Because of the fit of the pieces, a lot more gas escapes from the gap between the cylinder and barrel of the revolver than escapes from the sealed chamber of the semiauto. Yep. That means that a long rifle fired from a revolver might hit with the same force as a long from an auto. Even worse, with the small bullet and small forces we were dealing with here, the differences might not even be pronounced.

Then there would be the spent shell casings. Revolvers don't throw their empty shells out the way auto pistols do. Rifles have to eject the preceding cartridge case in some way, regardless. Art was assuming a revolver. I was waiting to see what the lab team found in the bag of the Borglans' vacuum cleaner. It would all be moot, however, if we didn't find the murder weapon. Only then would we be able to try to test to see if the bullets or shell casings came from that particular weapon.

I hated the .22 for another reason. The size of things made it very difficult to do comparisons, and they were all what they call "rim fire" cartridges. No pin striking the center of the cartridge, here. That would be too easy, because center-firing are all a bit off center, and that can be an ID point. No, with a .22, you have a small rectangular notch struck in the edge of the shell rim. Hence "rim fire." They aren't nearly as individually distinctive.

That's why it was always so very nice to find the murder weapon at the scene.

"I sure wish we had something puttin' our man there," I said.

"We're doing all right," said Art.

"I'd feel a lot better if we could place him at the scene. You know," I said, "even if Fred confesses, we can't convict unless we have some evidence puttin' him at the house when they were shot."

"You," said Art, "are just depressing the shit out of me."

I laughed. I couldn't help it.

It was pretty close to 1500 by the time we got back to the office. Waiting for us there were the press. About four separate units, three of them television. With them I recognized Nancy Mitchell, formerly of the *Des Moines Register*, and now with the *Cedar Rapids Gazette*. She was close to forty, fit, and a good sort. She had the unusual virtue in the media of being accurate. I had first met her when she'd helped us out with a right-wing case a couple of years back. The same one where Lamar got shot, and Bud got killed. She lost her partner, as well, shot through the chest while standing in the yard of the barricaded suspects' residence. He'd been about to go in to do an interview they'd requested. She and he had drawn straws for the interview. He'd won.

Nancy half waved when she saw me. I waved back. Unfortunately, the reporter for KRNQ thought we were waving at her, and hustled over to us along with her camera person.

"Can you tell us what's going on with the triple murder?" she asked, in her best "on" voice, pushing her epiglottis as hard as she could. "How many were officers?"

I don't function at my best with a light in my eyes, a mike in my face, and no sleep. The best I was able to manage was "Huh?"

Art, on the other hand, excelled. While I started to duck inside, he began to speak blather about "investigative confidentiality," "reasonable progress," and things like that. He was good. As I moved away, he was beginning a statement for another camera unit.

"Three?" I said, mostly to myself. "Where in the hell did they get three?"

I headed for my office in the rear of the building. I opened my door, and was startled to find Iowa Assistant Attorney General Mark Davies seated at my desk. He'd been recognized, and was avoiding the fourth estate by hiding in my office.

"Hi, numbnuts," he said, standing as we entered. "What took you so long?"

Every cop that ever worked with him liked Davies. He was intelligent, aggressive, energetic, and had a great conviction record. What more could you ask?

"I didn't see an ambulance," I said. "You must be chasing the media today, for a change."

"No, they're chasing me," he said. "Art with you some-where?"

"He's out there."

"Figures. I really think he wants to wear makeup someday. So," he said, "Nation County has another murder."

"Looks like," I said. "Double."

"Well, naturally. You guys don't do anything simple up here. I'm surprised there weren't little slimy space alien tracks around the scene."

"Obviously," I said, "you haven't seen the latest report . . ."

He chuckled, reaching past a little plate of pastry to a steam-ing cup of coffee. I made a mental note that our secretary was overimpressed by attorneys. "So, what we got here?"

"Depends on who you ask."

"Why don't we start with leads? You do have lots of leads?"

"Well," I said, thinking fast, "we have a possibility. Not much more right now."

He took a sip of coffee. "You mean to say that you've been out flying all over the county at *state* expense, and you only have a possibility?" He chuckled. "The director ain't gonna like that."

"What we have," I said, "is a fairly good circumstantial case. Unfortunately, it's against somebody I don't believe did it."

Davies sat back, and put his penny-loafered feet on my desk. "Hey, I do circumstantial. When I have to. Tell me more."

I did. Art came in about halfway through the briefing, and between the two of us, we gave Davies an accurate picture of the case to date. Just as we were through, Davies put his finger right on the thing that had been making me uneasy most of the day. I knew it as soon as he said it.

"You ever think," he said, chewing part of a doughnut, "that there might have been a snowmobile at the Borglan place the killer could have used to make his getaway? Borglan's got bucks. He could own a snowmobile or two."

Well, hell. Wouldn't have to drive in, just drive out. Placing Fred right back on the front burner.

"That way," he continued, "all you have to do is make a stolen snowmobile case, and leave the rest to me." He grinned. "Piece of cake."

If Cletus Borglan had been a bit friendlier, I would have called him right away, and simply asked. As it was, I went hustling out to dispatch, and asked Sally to run all snowmobiles registered to Clete. Zip. Nothing.

"Huh. That really sucks."

"Well, it surprises me all to hell," she said, "since he was the president of the Maitland Valley Snowmobile Club three or four years ago."

"He was?" I'm usually a bit snappier than that, but I was really beginning to feel tired.

"Same time my sister and her husband were in it," she said. "Why don't you check with the treasurer's office? They maintain their registration records for five years."

I explained to her that I didn't want to make a big deal of it by doing it myself. But that I, Nation County, and the State of Iowa would really appreciate it if she would just make one little phone call.

"I suppose the three of you're gonna give me a raise, too?"

"Sally, you've become so cynical the last few years. What would your mother think?"

She sighed. "I'll call you when *your* work's done," she said, picking up the phone.

I did the polite thing, and hung around. It only took her a few seconds. She wrote furiously, then said, "Beats me. They could." She hung the phone up, and smiled.

"Three sleds in Clete's name, one in his wife's. Last registered two years ago. Then stopped."

"He sold them?"

"No records of sale or transfer. He just stopped registering."

Well, that'd be in keeping with some of the books in his library. Several people protesting taxes and the like would stop registering their cars, getting driver's licenses, and things like that.

Sally was typing letters and numbers into her teletype.

"What are you running?"

"If I get the numbers, I can pull 'em out for several years back."

"Mildred," Sally referred to our county treasurer, "wanted to know if you guys thought the killers escaped on snowmobiles." She sat back smiling, as the printer began to whisper several sheets out.

You can't get away with a damned thing.

"Just a hunch," I said, ignoring the question, "but would you run all vehicles registered to Clete?"

"Shouldn't we include his wife, Inez, in this, too?"

I thought for a second. "Of course." You really shouldn't let dispatchers get ahead of you that way. Two or three hundred times, they begin to get ideas.

"Good," she said, radiating perky. She handed me the papers. "That's what you got there, along with the snowmobile stuff." She grinned. "Now run along and eat your doughnut."

Sally has always been efficient like that. Sometimes it's a game we play, and sometimes she really catches me about a step behind her. She's usually magnanimous enough to make it seem like a game.

On the way back to my office, I ran over the lists in my hands. Interesting. Four snowmobiles. Two four-wheelers. All six of them had once been registered, which meant that Cletus had, at one time, run them on public right of way. Two Chevy pickups, a Bronco, an Oldsmobile. The off-road stuff had ceased registration two years ago. The trucks and car, though, were current. The snowmobiles and the four-wheelers were registered to Freeman Liberty Enterprises, Inc. Only the oldest pickup was in Clete's name. The new pickup and the Bronco were also registered to Freeman Liberty Enterprises, Inc. The Olds belonged to his wife.

I shared that data with Art and Davies.

"How did you find out about this Freeman Liberty Enterprises, or whatever?"

"Same SSN on the corporate registration as is on Mrs. Borglan's driver's license," I said. "When Sally ran the DL numbers, everything with that SSN came back."

"Probably has his wife as treasurer of the corporation," said Davies, absently. "I'm not sure I like the name of this corporation, though. More right-wing shit?"

"Could be. There was some indication in the house, but not as strong as some we've seen." I was just being honest.

Davies thought for a second. "So, what does this tell us?"

"Well, he has right-wing leanings, maybe," I said. "And it tells me that it's possible that he gave his snowmobiles to his hired man." I just hate the "right-wing" label, because it's come to mean irrational in some circles. Sometimes it's right. Sometimes not. But to jump at that tends to skew your thinking.

Art looked at me, one eyebrow raised.

"There were snowmobiles in Grossman's machine shed. They didn't have registration stickers." I grinned. "Didn't have those little orange flags, either, in fact."

"Point for my man Houseman," said Davies.

"Since we have the VINs for the equipment, why not just go out to the hired man's place and check the numbers?"

A VIN is the vehicle identification number put on all motor vehicles by their manufacturers. In more than one place. They do that so a thief has a hard time selling them. Well, has a hard time selling them to somebody who cares, at any rate.

"Fine with me," I said.

"Good!" Davies stood up, and reached behind him for his coat. "Take me along. I'd like to meet him, and then we can swing by to meet Mr. Borglan and let me see the scene." He put an arm over his head, pulling on a coat sleeve. "If we're really lucky, maybe we can get to meet Mr. Borglan's attorney."

Art was reaching for his coat.

"Why don't you stay here?" said Davies. "Carl and I can just run out there. We wouldn't want old Clete to think he's too important. After all, he didn't die, two other guys did."

"What do you want me to do," asked Art, "while you're gone?"

Davies answered him as he stepped into the hallway. "Cop shit. Do lots and lots of cop shit."

We dodged what remained of the press by the simple expedient of going out a side door, and walking behind their cars to mine. It was far too cold for them to simply stand outside for hours. They were all sitting in their vehicles, which were pretty thoroughly steamed over, and never had a hint we were anywhere around.

On the way over to Borglan's, Davies explained that he would only be here today, had to go back to Des Moines, then a trial date in six days in Mahaska County. After that, a big forcible rape case in Bettendorf.

"No rush, though. It isn't like you guys are ready to charge that kid yet. It ought to take the lab another two or three days, at least, if there's any evidence there . . ."

"True," I said.

He went on, to reiterate the points he and Art had discussed when I was getting the snowmobile information. They'd covered the ground pretty well, because he ticked off the main points, rapid-fire, almost like he was reading them.

"And I understand that you don't believe the only logical suspect did it?"

"Havin' a hard time with it," I said.

"Houseman, I don't know what to do with you some of the time." He chuckled. "But you do know a lot about these people around here." He chuckled again. "From your uniform days."

"That would have been yesterday . . ." I looked over at him. "You got that from Art."

"Oh, yeah. He thinks relating to people is some sort of disease that comes from wearing uniforms. You having any problems working with your ex-chief deputy?"

"Yeah. But I can cope."

"What are you thinking about doing to settle the question about this suspect kid?"

"We got the cops in Oelwein talking to the family of the two dead guys. I figure I'll go talk to Fred's mom and sister tomorrow. Then Fred, if his asshole attorney will let me," I said, turning into Borglan's driveway.

"Check with me before you talk to this Fred?"

"I'll make sure Art talks to the aunt," he said.

It was getting a little dark, by this time, with the sun having disappeared behind Borglan's hill. Kind of pretty, with the sunlight across the little valley, and the shade in the yard. There were lights on in the living room, but I couldn't see anybody around. Three pickups in the yard, one of them brand-new, and one of them a twenty-year-old rolling wreck. Quite a contrast.

We knocked on the door, and after about fifteen seconds, during which I was sure we were being observed, Cletus answered the door.

"Mark Davies from the Iowa Attorney General's office. I'm here to look at the crime scene. I'm the prosecuting attorney in the murder case. I'll look around outside for a bit while you contact your attorney. Then I'll want to take a quick look around inside."

"I don't think so," said Cletus.

"We have this scale in the AG's office. Starts at Interference with Official Acts, goes to obstructing, ends up at coconspirator. A coconspirator, in this case, can get out in maybe fifty years. Talk with your attorney, while we check a couple of things out here." Very fast, but very pleasant. Said completely deadpan, and then ending with that infectious smile of his. Just like in court.

"I'll call him right now," said Cletus.

"Well, I hope to hell you will," said Davies. "It's cold out here."

While we waited, I showed Davies around. He was especially interested in the shed where I'd found the two bodies.

"No point in wading through the snow," he said. "Just reassure me that you could see a track leading to the shed from the house."

"Sure. No problem."

"You get photos of it?"

"It was pretty faint. I sure hope so."

"Me too." He looked over the garage. "Impressive. Not the 'poor' farmer, is he?"

"Hardly. Smart, and a hell of a worker. That, and a little luck, you can make it."

"Yeah." He cupped his hands, and blew into them, to warm his face. "Let's go bug Cletus. I'm getting cold."

This time, Cletus invited us in. "He says to cooperate with you."

"You got a good attorney," said Davies. "They are *so* rare these days. So," he said to me, "where did the dirty deed happen?"

I showed him. We spent all of five minutes examining the living room, the basement steps, and looking out the basement door. I was brief to the point of terse, not wanting to give anything away. Davies was even more controlled, just making little humming sounds once in a while. He took no notes.

There were at least two other people in the house. One was a sixty-year-old farmer I knew, but whose name I couldn't remember. I did know he was the owner of the ugly pickup in the yard, now that I saw him. The other man was about forty or so, and one of the people we'd seen here earlier today.

Cletus stayed right with us during the whole inspection. When we'd finished, Davies turned to him, abruptly.

"So, what do you think happened?"

"Huh?"

"You. What do you think about this?"

"I'm just wondering," said Cletus, "why the Iowa AG is involved in this."

"It's what you pay us to do," said Davies. "You have no ideas, huh?"

"Why would you want to know what I thought?"

Frankly, I was sort of asking myself the same question.

"Thought you could help us with what you thought they might be after." Davies paused. "And if you had any thoughts on who could have been here when they arrived."

"Beats me," said Cletus.

"You own any snowmobiles?" asked Davies.

"Nope. Not anymore, gave one to Harvey Grossman. Junked the rest."

"You just gave it to him? Just like that?"

"No use for the things anymore. He needs them to do chores."

We headed toward the door. "If you find anything unusual that we missed," I said, following routine, "let us know, would you?"

"You people sure do try," said Cletus. Once again, there was a sarcastic ring to his voice that bothered me. Like he was trying for innuendo, and missing his target. He was sure missing if I was his target, anyway.

We opened the door.

"My attorney said to cooperate, but not to say anything." Cletus shrugged. "I guess you'll have to earn your keep without me doin' your work for you." He paused a second, but couldn't resist. "But, like I said before, there was nobody home."

"You have any thoughts, check with your attorney, and then give us a call," said Davies.

"What about the black helicopter?"

I looked at the speaker, the forty-year-old I didn't recognize. "What?"

"We saw it," he said, with an air of accusation and defiance. "Who was flying it?"

"I don't know his name," I said, "but I was in it. I waved. Did you see me?"

Silence.

"Thanks again," said Davies, and we trudged across the yard to my car.

As soon as we got in the car, Davies started to laugh. " 'We saw it,' " he mimicked. He looked at me. "Houseman, you smart ass. You actually waved?"

"Yeah. They were outside, right under us, looking up. Just a reaction, I guess."

"How high were you?"

"Oh, thousand feet, more or less."

"An Army green Huey?"

I nodded.

"Black Helicopter. Great observers," he said. "Must have shaken the whole house. Hey, while we're out here, show me where they went over the fence." He sighed.

"Yeah. We better go to Grossman's and check the damned VINs on those snowmobiles."

On the way, I showed him the entry tracks. It was pretty dark by then, and I had my headlights on. I shined a flashlight out the window, showing him the path. All he did was make that little humming sound. With my window rolled down, I found myself thinking about how alert I was, again. Nothing like bitterly cold air to wake you up.

We went directly to Grossman's, and I cashed in my marker with a request to look at the VIN numbers on the snowmobiles. It took about five minutes, but I found them all, and wrote them down. I thanked him.

Davies gazed out the window on the way back. "You know, without anything linking him to the inside of that house, Fred could walk." He leaned back in his seat. "All we got him on is conspiracy to commit a burglary. That works. He said he took 'em there for the purpose of burgling. They sure were where he said they'd be. Packaged. Nicely packaged."

"What . . . you think he *delivered* them?"

He snorted. "No, probably not. But it's a possibility, isn't it? Somebody says, 'Hey, I wanna kill your cousins . . .' and Fred sets the boys up."

I thought about it for a second. "Too many possibilities, not enough leads," I said. "We could be chasing our tails forever . . ."

We drove about another mile.

"You get the feeling," I said, "that there's something missing?"

He snorted. "Like evidence?"

"Not so much evidence . . . more like *information*."

We got back to the Sheriff's Department fully intending to have supper with Art. Instead, we found a bit of a flap. Fred had bonded out on the burglary charges.

Eight

A rt was pissed off, and Lamar was simply frustrated. Fred's
bond had been set at $13,000.00, a so-called "sched-
uled" bond, that was used when a magistrate wasn't
immediately available to set one. Lawyer Priller found
one, though, and he convinced him to agree on a 10 percent
posting. Fred had left us for the princely sum of $1,300.00.

"Don't worry about it," said Davies. "I'm just glad you didn't
do something dumb, like charge him with murder."

As it turned out, that's exactly what Art had wanted to do, and
had been dissuaded by Lamar, who had maintained that there
was insufficient evidence to smack him with a murder charge.

"Let's put it this way," said Davies. "You lay a murder charge
on him, I've got forty-five days to make the entire case, unless he
waives his right to a speedy trial." He shook his head. "You know
about backlogs at the lab. No guarantee everything will be done
in forty-five days. I have other trials scheduled, in the next forty-
five days. You charge him now, he demands speedy trial, he walks,
free. Period."

He looked at Art. "What's the hurry? He ain't goin'
nowhere." He grinned. "I assume, at least, that you told him not
to leave town?"

"Absolutely." Art seemed a bit mollified.

I'd been checking the VINs I'd gotten from the snowmobiles

against the list Sally had given me. Two were from Cletus Borglan. I announced that.

"Is this, like, significant?" asked Art.

"Beats me," I said. "Just an error in memory, maybe." Cletus
had said that he gave Grossman one and junked the rest.

"I prefer to go to trial with a ninety-five percent chance of
winning," said Davies, ignoring the Art and Carl show. "The five
percent being the whim of the jury. I'll be happy with seventy-
five percent, and I've gone in with about a sixty percent chance,
but I really don't like to do that. Right now, this one would be
about fifty-fifty. Maybe less. With a circumstantial case, and a local jury, I don't think we could pull it off."

"What if the lab doesn't give us anything linking Fred to the
scene?" I asked. "Then what do we do?"

"If that happens," said Davies, "you do lots and lots of interviews, of lots and lots of people. And if we still come down with
Fred being the only possibility, then . . ." He paused. "Then we
go the grand jury route, get an indictment, and see if we can convince him to cop a plea."

"Nothing personal," said Art, "but that's not much of a plan."

"You are so right," said Davies. "And that's just the best possible scenario if the lab doesn't link him. The very best."

"So," I said, "where's that leave us?"

"The no-link bit, you mean?"

"Yep."

"That leaves us with very little," said Davies. "Or, to use a legal term, up Shit Creek without a paddle."

"Don't worry," said Art. "He did it, and the lab will find a
link."

Davies looked at him. "You must have taken a confidence-
building course recently."

"I just don't accept defeat," said Art, "when I know I'm
right."

I was glad for him. He was just full of admirable traits.

After much discussion, it was left at this: Absent any other
viable suspect, it appeared that Fred was the only person who

could have done the deed. Period. We took a short poll, and it was decided that we would diligently seek other suspects. And, in the meantime, we would do all we could to link Fred to the scene.

"We don't have much pressure today," said Davies. "Tomorrow, there'll be more. And each day we go without an arrest, the pressure increases. So long as you understand that."

"Just like always," I said.

The dispatch desk called, and said there were several members of the press in the outer office. Art and Davies took the job of talking to them. Lamar went out the unused back way. And I mean, unused. We never opened that door, and never shoveled the snow outside it. I last saw him slogging through two-foot snow drifts, going around behind the building. He really hates the press.

I was tired when I got home around 8:30. Sue had laid in a supply of frozen, microwaveable food. Murder rations, so to speak. Although I couldn't discuss details, I let her know that things were going slowly.

"How about Madison this weekend?" she asked.

Ooh. We'd been planning to do that since Christmas, and this weekend was the one per month I was scheduled off.

"Not sure. Let me see how it goes tomorrow . . ." Damn. Another delay would put us into March. Too long. It was going to be difficult, though, getting things arranged for a weekend off. If stuff happened fast, then we would be able to go in March. If it continued at this pace, we'd be going in August if we didn't go now.

"I know you're really into this case, but if we don't go now . . ."

"I know. Now or six months from now."

"I got lots of frozen vegetables today. Be sure to eat some." She smiled. "You need to be healthy, either way."

I put the frozen vegetables into my microwaved couscous, added a can of mushrooms, sliced a low-fat sausage, and topped the whole thing with fat-free grated cheese. Eleven minutes from opening the first package to a complete, satisfying, and sort of tasty meal.

"I don't know how you can eat that . . ."

"Oh," I said, "thanks. I forgot the Thai sauce . . ."

"God." She shook her head. "Your stomach won't last till spring. If you want to eat at a good restaurant in Madison, you better go soon."

That was about as close to a clincher as you could get. I popped the top of a can of Diet Cherry Coke, and silently drank a toast to Madison. Hitting directly on top of the Thai sauce, it produced an instant reaction, and I belched.

"You may have to go by yourself . . ."

I was just scraping off my plate, and opening the dishwasher, when the phone rang. It was Deputy John Willis, our newest officer. He was coming along nicely, and excelled at the snoopy kind of patrol work that would make him an excellent officer.

"Hate to bother you at home . . ."

"Sure you do." I picked up a notepad and pen. "Whatta ya got?"

"Well, you know, I got to thinking about Fred, and the Borglan place, and all that stuff. You remember last year, oh, maybe July, when we had that humongous fight in Dogpatch?"

Dogpatch was our name for Jasonville, a very tiny town in the west of the county, population about 100, and one very busy tavern. "Yeah," I said. "The one where we called everybody but the National Guard?"

We'd arrested over 50 people that night, which isn't bad for either a town of 100, or a department of 10. Most of the arrestees had been from out of town . . .

"We arrested Fred and his two cousins that night. Remember?"

I did now.

"Yep. I did the interviews of all three of 'em."

"Okay . . ." I said.

"I got the notes right here . . . Fred got into it with some grubby dudes from Dubuque, remember. And both his cousins jumped into to rescue him. And I got statements from the three of them. And all three say that they . . . just a sec . . . that they will 'give my life' for the other two. In each of the three statements, same thing."

"Exactly?" I asked. Strange.

"Exactly the same phrase."

"Damn . . ." I jotted the phrase down. "You remember how close together they were when they wrote the statements?"

"Well, they were in the same room . . ."

"Did they communicate with each other?"

"Well, yeah, they did . . ." He sounded disappointed.

"Great!"

"What?"

"That's at least as good, I think," I said. "Chummy, even talk it over and decide they will stick together through and through kind of stuff. Remember if they were sober?"

"I've got the PBT stuff here," he said. A PBT was a preliminary breath test, designed for use on the highway as a precursor to arresting for OWI and doing a real test on an Intoxilyzer. The PBT wasn't admissible in court, but was used a lot to give the officer a ballpark idea of the state of the subject. "All three of them were over point one oh, but not by too much."

"Fine."

"Fred's girlfriend bailed all three of 'em out, that night."

"Cool. You remember anything else they might of said?"

"No, sorry, I was kinda busy." He was apologetic, like he should have known that they were going to end up in a murder case or something. New officers are like that. Well, the good ones are, anyway.

"That's all right," I said. "No problem. This is good." I was having a bit of trouble getting the ballpoint pen to write, and grabbed a pencil. "What was the girlfriend's name?"

"Just a sec," he said, and I could hear paper being shuffled in the background. "Ah . . . Donna Sue Rahll."

"Get a DL on her, will you?"

"Will do."

"Thanks. This is good."

I normally hated to be called at home, but I loved it when it was something I could use. I didn't know Donna Sue Rahll, but the last name rang a very faint bell.

I joined Sue in the living room.

"Did I hear you say Rahll?" she asked.

"Yeah. Know anybody by that name?"

"Well, John Rahll is the man who runs the Maitland Economic Development Center."

"Oh, sure . . . tall man?"

"Yes."

"Any kids?" One of the many benefits to being married to a teacher.

"Oh, a girl who graduated a while ago. Becky, maybe," said Sue, absently, as she shuffled through some tests she'd brought home to grade.

"Or, how about Donna?"

"That's right, Donna."

So. Tomorrow's schedule was shaping up.

"You know where Donna might be, these days?"

She looked up. I usually didn't pursue her information so far. It was an agreement we had. You don't have to tell me about school stuff, I don't have to tell you about cop stuff.

"Last I knew, she was working at the Maitland Library. She had a year of school, dropped out. Came home. I think she might live with her parents."

"Okay. Thanks. That's plenty."

"So, now I get to ask a question?"

"Uh, maybe." I grinned.

"They said in school that you were flying in helicopters today, looking for another body. True?"

"Yes, I was in a helicopter today. It was really, really cool. But, no, we aren't looking for any more bodies."

"Thanks," she said, and went back to her papers.

Rumors can plague an investigation. Especially in a town like Maitland and a county like Nation. One of the seldom appreciated effects is that it retards the flow of information. Somebody has a truly important bit, but they hear through the grapevine that something else entirely is really important. They dismiss what they know, and begin to rely on what they hear. Consequently, they don't tell you their information, because it doesn't seem important. In our case, for example, the third body bit might convince someone that a snowmobile sighting they had on the night in question might not be significant. Because we weren't looking for snowmobile sightings, after all, we were looking for a third body. So that's where that triple homicide nonsense came from with the media.

"We were looking at snowmobile tracks," I said, hinting. "Not for a third body. If anybody asks . . ."

"Oh," said Sue, absently. "All right."

You do what you can. I went to bed. But before I did, I turned off the police scanner.

Nine

made an appointment with Donna Sue Rahll for 0915, at the Sheriff's Department. I went in out of uniform, to put her at her ease. That worked about half the time, and blue jeans were a lot warmer than uniform trousers.

Art was in Oelwein, interviewing the mother of the two victims, so I got to do the preliminary interview of Donna Sue all by myself. As it turned out, she was a bright, fairly attractive girl, who considered Freddie to be a phase of her life she'd just as soon forget. About the first sentence out of her was to the effect that she hadn't wished to associate with Fred for the last seven or eight months.

"So, I don't know why I'm here," she said. The second sentence.

I could tell that she was hoping for a short interview, because she'd left her blue parka on. Unzipped, though, to reveal the orange lining. There was hope.

"Any particular reason you broke up?"

She looked me right in the eye. "I don't see that that's any of your business."

"It isn't," I replied. "But it may be the state's business. There's a lot of interest in Fred right now."

She sighed. "This is all confidential?"

"Unless it has a direct bearing on facts material to the investigation. Then you may be questioned regarding things, in court."

"If I know something about the case, you mean."

"That's right," I said.

She stood, and said her goodbye line. "Well, since I don't know anything 'material,' about any kind of case, I'll leave, now."

"I think you might know more than you think," I said. "Why don't you sit back down for a minute."

She stopped, but didn't sit. At least the parka hadn't been zipped yet.

"I want to ask about Fred's two cousins, Dirk and Royce . . ."

She flicked out an insincere little smile. "The Colson brothers? The 'Weasels'?"

"Pardon?" I said.

"The 'Weasels.' That's what we call them."

"Why?" I asked, leaning back in my chair. I had her.

She sat back down. "Because they're greasy little shitheads who have no respect for anybody, and lie and steal and stick their noses in and think they're just great."

Well. It came out in a rush, and I suspect she felt a lot better for having said it. It sure helped me.

"Stick their noses in what?" I was already pretty sure about the "steal" part.

"Everybody's business." She exhaled hard, and started to shrug out of her coat. "They just cause a lot of trouble." She looked at me. "Why? What have they done now?"

It took me just a second. Then the little lightbulb came on in my head. We hadn't released the names of the victims yet. And if she'd severed relations with Fred, she might not have a way of knowing.

"You don't talk to Fred and his crowd much these days?"

"I have no time for them. If I saw one of them coming toward me, I'd cross the street."

"Ah." I gave her my most serious and concerned look. "Well, I'm sorry. Really. I assumed . . ."

"What?"

Had her good. "That you knew they were dead."

I figured I was ready for about any kind of reaction, but was surprised when she simply said, "That doesn't surprise me."

"It doesn't? Why not?"

"They 'party hearty,' and they drive too fast. We've all been telling 'em that. For years."

"Wasn't a car wreck," I said. I paused for effect, for all the good it did me. "They were murdered."

Her eyebrows shot up. "Murdered? Like, by somebody else?"

"That's what it looks like." By somebody else, indeed.

"Well," she said, "well, shit. Huh. Whadda ya know . . ." She paused. "That's something. Well, you guys know who did it?"

"It's beginning to look like it might be Fred."

"Oh, no. No, no, no way. Oh, no," and she started to chuckle. "No, not Fred. No."

In about ten minutes, she explained to me just what a foolish idea it was. Fred, in her experience, was absolutely determined to avoid conflict at any cost. He would take the path of least resistance every time. She'd known Fred since high school, and he'd always been that way. The only times she'd ever seen him angry, it was at himself.

"He'd do things like let the other kids keep their beer in his locker. Really. Just so he wouldn't have to argue with them. He'd fidget all day, worried that the principal would find out. But he'd never say no."

"Because the principal was one step removed, and the kids were right there?"

"Yeah," Donna Sue thought for a second. "Like that. You know he was busted for DWI back in high school?"

"Oh," I said, "yeah . . . I'm the one who got him."

"Well, you know the only reason he drove that night is that the kid who was the designated driver had gotten it for DWI before, couldn't afford to get busted again, and got drunk at the party anyway?"

"Didn't know that."

"Just like the beer in the locker. Knew he shouldn't do it, but just to avoid the hassle . . ." She shrugged. "Like I say, he's always been that way."

Judy came in with the coffee. It helped.

"What if," I said, "somebody asked him to do something he just couldn't bring himself to do? Could he get violent?"

"No way. If it got that bad, I swear to God, he'd just move to California or somewhere." She sipped her coffee. "He's just not aggressive at all."

"How about his two cousins? The 'Weasels'?"

"They're mostly just liars. Were, I guess." She shook her head. "They'd get him to do shit, you know? Like keep stuff for 'em that was hot."

"Were they violent?"

"Not really."

"I mean, like, if they got caught at a burglary . . . do you think they'd get violent then?"

"I don't think so," she said. "They'd just try to lie their way out of it. They could get pretty outrageous, sometimes."

"Oh?"

"Yeah. They used to laugh about one time, in Oelwein, when they were caught behind a store one night. They were thinkin' about sneaking in through the rest room window, and the owner came out with, like, the garbage. He started to jump in their shit in a big way. So they told him they were undercover cops. Convinced him, too." She giggled.

Bingo. Oh, Bingo indeed. "Really?"

"Oh, sure. They did that more than once, I think. It worked." She shook her head. "They could convince you the sun came out at night. Look you right in the eye and lie, lie, lie. Never blink."

When Art got back from Oelwein, I ran my interview with Donna Sue by him.

"And?" said Art, sort of impatiently.

"It explains a bunch of the stuff that's been bothering me," I said. "Why people kept assuming the two victims were cops, for one thing. Why it just didn't ring true. Why there had to be somebody involved we weren't aware of."

"Why's that? I must be missing something," said Art. "I didn't think she provided any other names?"

"Impersonating cops," I said. "If the wrong person was in that house, they might have killed them because they convinced whoever it was that they were cops."

"What you're doing is this: You have a theory that says Fred didn't do it. Okay? Yet all the real evidence points to the fact that he did. Then you feel that a story told by Fred's ex-girlfriend, about two dead men who can't contradict her, that you have no proof ever even happened . . . confirms your theory." Art shook his head. "This now requires the presence and the involvement of a third party, based on a supposition by you, based on a tale by another party." He shrugged. "Can't buy that, Carl."

I gritted my teeth. "But I think that's what happened."

"Based solely on your instinct," he said. Just a bit too sarcastically, for my taste.

"You have to start somewhere," I replied, evenly. "Your so-called instinct tells you where to dig. You dig, you get the evidence, you may solve the case. I don't guess a case. I never guess. You should know that by now."

"I didn't say 'guess'," he said.

"Do you realize the ramifications here? If I'm right, that would mean that Cletus had prior knowledge of the murders before he got to the house. He said something about the dead being cops." I paused, to let that sink in. "And that would mean, in turn, that he had contact with the killer or killers, who was the only person who would have heard them say they were cops. Of course, you would then have to characterize the killer as someone who would kill cops, as opposed to someone who would be relieved if they said they were fuzz."

"All based on a conversation that we can't prove ever occurred," said Art.

"You gotta admit, though, it does cover the territory," I said.

"So did the theory," said Art, "that had the sun revolving around the earth."

Well, he had me there.

"Tell you what," said Art, finally. "Make you a deal. You do this lead, your lead, and we'll do the straight-up case. If you score, fine. Okay?"

No way. If I'd do that, I'd take myself out of the mainstream investigation. Let him proceed, without me, the local yokel, getting in the way.

"Naw," I said, in my best aw shucks voice. "The officer with primary jurisdiction makes the deals." I said it very pleasantly. I couldn't afford to be offended. "I'll follow that lead, but not exclusively. I'll still work on the main case. But I'll go into my theory, at the same time."

He thought a second. Legally, it was my case all the way, and he was assisting. He knew that. But he also knew that without DCI, we were going to be left high and dry. He had to know that. God knows, I did.

"Damn it, Carl. The last thing we need is for the defense to get hold of something like this. As far as I can see, it's only going to be enough to confuse a jury. Which means that a killer walks."

The bit about a killer walking sort of pissed me off. I hate that sort of melodramatic crap.

"Look at it like this: If it occurred to me, it can occur to the defense," I said. "Even if my lead goes nowhere, we can at least be ready for the other side when they bring it up. Show 'em just why it doesn't work." I shrugged. "I don't mind the extra work." Top that.

"Okay. Fine. Fine with me." He held up his hands. "But don't come up with another theory. This is plenty."

A peace offering. Tentatively accepted. "Promise," I said.

"What did you find out in Oelwein?"

Not a lot, as it turned out. Nora, the mother of the two victims, was distraught, but had no idea who might have done it. A female cousin of the victims thought it might have been "some farmer." Oelwein PD had nothing on file, indicating that there was a feud or any other sort of problem that had anybody mad enough at the brothers to kill them. One of the more remarkable things, apparently, was the tacit acknowledgment by just about everybody that the brothers were, in fact, thieves.

"Fred's involvement in the burglaries or thefts never came up," said Art. "They may be grief-stricken, but they aren't stupid. Which means that we still have only his word that he drove for them." He stood. "I have to be getting back to Cedar Falls. We're going to be doing a polygraph on a suspect in a murder from Mason City. I have to be there."

Understood.

"When will you be back up?"

"Tomorrow, I hope. Why don't I just touch base with Davies, while I'm there?"

"Did you talk to Sergeant Thurman in Oelwein?" I asked, as Art was going out the door. He hadn't. I put in a call to him. Phil Thurman was an excellent officer, and had originally worked for our department before transferring to Oelwein PD. More money, better hours. His first cop job had been with us, I'd been sort of his training officer, and he'd been a real breath of fresh air. We'd hated to see him go.

"Sergeant Thurman."

"Phil, it's Houseman. How are ya?"

"Dad! Hey, understand you had a cool double murder up there! You got all the luck . . ."

"Sorry you left?"

"Just about! What can I do for you guys?"

I asked him about the dead Colson brothers. He certainly knew them. "Yeah, those two been a pain in the ass for five years or more."

I asked him about Fred. He knew him, too. "The quiet one. He was with those two a lot. Not a bad kid, you know? Just not too smart about who he hung with."

I asked him about the impersonation of an officer story. He hadn't exactly heard about that one. "Sounds just like 'em, though. Hell, it sounds just like half our store owners, for that matter." He did think that, since the store was open after dark, at least in the account I had, that he might be able to track it down. Most stores in Oelwein, as in Maitland, closed at five o'clock.

"Good enough," I said.

I told Lamar what Phil had said and asked Lamar if he'd like to have lunch at the buffet in the pavilion of the *General Beauregard*, moored at Frieberg. He declined, but I decided to drive up anyway. Hester Gorse was working the gaming boat up there, and I really wanted to discuss the case with her. I needed an unbiased opinion. I also needed a really good meal, out of the reach and notice of the local media. It was only twenty miles or so.

I called Hester at her office at the boat.

"Houseman, by God! You been busy?"

Just hearing her voice cheered me up. " 'Busy' ain't the word for it. Like to do lunch? I can bring you up to date, and see if I can get Art assigned to Minnesota."

"Yeah," she said, "I heard. Things okay other than that?"

"Things are interesting. Two corpses, no real suspects. How 'bout it?"

"Oh, you do know how to convince a girl. Sure. Love to." I could hear the grin in her voice.

The *General Beauregard* was moored in the Mississippi River, separated from its associated pavilion by a railroad track and a highway, both of which paralleled the river. The bluffs that formed the prehistoric banks of the river rose to over 100 feet, within a block or two of the boat. It was really a pretty setting. Even with the river frozen over, and the stark black trees outlined against the white snow.

The pavilion was a combination theater, office, and restaurant complex, containing everything to make the boat into a casino, as opposed to a simple floating slot machine. Iowa law forbade gambling on the land, so the boat was more or less a dedicated gambling platform. The pavilion provided the rest of a mini-Las Vegas aspect to the operation. Nice, in a way. Families could use the pavilion facilities without being near gaming, which some seemed to prefer.

Iowa also required that the Division of Criminal Investigation maintain a presence at each and every casino. The legislature neglected to provide any additional agents for that purpose, so General Crim. had to spread itself even thinner than usual to accommodate the mandate. They accomplished that by three-month assigned tours. No exceptions. This was Hester's turn in an eighteen-month rotation.

I hadn't seen her for several months, and hadn't actually worked a case with her for over a year. She was one of the best agents I'd ever worked with, and totally reliable. And very, very smart.

She was also a few years younger, and very fit. Something I tried never to bring into a conversation, and something she brought up every chance she got. She was waiting near the buffet entrance.

"Hi." She grinned broadly. "Looks like life agrees with you."

"Everything but work," I said. "It's a tough one this time. Great case, though. Fascinating."

We spent about half an hour in her office, and I ran through the basic details of the double murder. She was into it instantly.

"I don't think it was Fred, either," she said, "based on what you've given me. Does Art think it was him?"

"Yeah."

"You've got to understand, he thinks he's under pressure to produce a conclusion." She held up her hand, forestalling my protest. "I know, but it's true. You know him as well as anybody does. He's always wanted to be the best, and in his mind, the best is also the fastest to get the bad guy."

I finished up by telling her about everybody assuming that it was a pair of cops who'd been killed.

"That's what we call a clue, Houseman," she said, seriously.

We found a table in the main dining room, off in a corner. A couple of people spoke to me as we walked through the place, and a couple more eyed me closely. People I knew. I was with an attractive woman, not my wife. They were checking Hester out, and could be relied upon to keep an eye on us throughout lunch. I loved it.

I was in a fine mood. Hester noticed. "The case really tripped your trigger, didn't it?"

"Oh, yeah." I smiled. It really was good to see her. "I'll buy."

"Wow, Houseman. This must be the case dreams are made of. It's affected your mind."

We put our coats on the chair backs, and hit the buffet line.

I gave in to my conscience, and had the grilled chicken plate, with whipped potatoes, peas, carrots, and a roll. $4.50. Hester just picked up a taco salad. $2.98. Less than $10.00. I was encouraged. Easily affordable. Not that I'm cheap . . .

Just as the food arrived, so did our favorite reporter, Nancy Mitchell. She'd been through a particular kind of hell on our last murder case. She'd not only witnessed a murder, she'd also been threatened and generally put through the wringer. Helping us out, at out request. We owed Nancy, and we owed her big time.

"How're my favorite cops?"

"Have a seat," I said. "What the hell are you doing here?"

"Well, since you can't provide any information, it was time to work on a feature article about the boat. And have a great lunch, at the same time." She pulled out her chair.

"Lunch is on Carl," said Hester. "Great to see you again."

"I'd like you to meet Shamrock," said Nancy. "She's my photographer this week."

"She's welcome to join us, too," said Hester, standing and reaching out her hand to the pretty blonde with the cameras. "I'm Hester Gorse, DCI, and this is Carl Houseman, Nation County. He's buying lunch today."

I stood, as well, and shook Shamrock's hand. She was about twenty-two or -three, small, slight, and about as pretty a young woman as had graced Nation County in years. Really small, I noticed as I stood. More than a foot shorter than I was. Not more than ninety pounds, I'd guess. With camera. She looked like she was in junior high. Well, from my perspective, at any rate.

"Shamrock really your name?" Cops. We say things like that.

"Yours really Carl?" Big grin.

I was beginning to feel hemmed in. "I'm buying, cut me some slack." I grinned, and sat back down.

She laughed. I sure hoped that she didn't go the way of Nancy's last photographer. Shamrock could grow on you.

"So, Nancy," I said, "what brings you here?"

Nancy looked at Shamrock. "He just sounds that dumb. He's really not."

"You gotta take that on trust," said Hester.

"Should I leave?" I asked.

"Not till the bill comes," said Hester.

"The murders brought me to Maitland," said Nancy.

"I hope you packed," I said. "You're gonna be here awhile."

Nancy glanced around. "Lamar going to join you?"

"No," I said.

"Then I'll stay," she said, barely able to keep a straight face. "Wouldn't want to make him mad . . . We'll hit the line," she said, "and be back in a second."

Nancy came back with a taco salad. Shamrock appeared with a cheeseburger, cheese balls, and chocolate milk. Youth. Hers came to $4.50. Not too bad.

"So," said Nancy. "How you two comin' on this one?"

"Grinding it out," I said. Instantly on guard. Nancy was, after all, the press. "And it's not us two, either. Hester's just having lunch with me . . . Really," I said. "She's on boat rotation."

"Oh, sure," said Nancy. "Then you haven't told her of any of your great leaps of intuition this time?"

Hester laughed. "Now that you mention it . . ."

Thankfully, that got us off on what I would term "House-man's intuition," intuition in general, and ended up with women's natural intellectual superiority over men. It also got us to the end of the meal. Hester and I were engineering a graceful escape, when Nancy scored.

"So, before you two go running off, how come we were hearing that it was two cops that were killed in there?" She knew she

had us. I could tell, because she was still seated as we were standing. She knew we weren't going anywhere. The carrot had been
dangled.

We sat back down. "Where did you hear that?" I must have
looked interested or something. A crack in the poker face.

"Well, first from a neighbor down the road. Then from an
older man at the Borglan place."

Unfortunately, we all now ordered dessert. Another $9.00
plus tax. Pie all around.

"We heard some of that, too," said Hester, pressing her fork
through a slice of lemon meringue. "Do you know who these
men were?"

"I think one was a Grossman . . . hired man or something,"
said Nancy. "I'd have to look around for the second one's
name . . ." She carefully balanced large red cherries on the end of
her fork, with fragments of a beautifully crumbly sugared crust
clinging to the thick syrup.

"We don't know where that came from," I said, which was
pretty much true. Just who might have started it when they were
interrupted in a burglary. But they hadn't told anybody, that was
for sure. So I wasn't really lying.

"They were sure convinced," said Shamrock. She took a bite
of French Silk, topped with whipped cream and chocolate shav-
ings.

"Well, there weren't cops killed. So I don't know how that
got going," I said, again. I fiddled with my pumpkin pie, sans
whipped cream. My diet program.

"Maybe somebody thought they were cops?" asked Nancy.
"Good lead story, any way you cut it."

Ah. The stick.

"Wouldn't something more accurate be better?" asked
Hester.

Of course it would. But what could we do?

My thoughts were interrupted by the waitress. "Phone for
you, Carl."

I excused myself, and took the call at the phone in the

kitchen. It was Sally. The bodies were thawed and Dr. Peters was ready to do the autopsies. Would an officer be available at the Manchester Hospital in the next hour or so? Art was still busy, so it was going to have to be somebody from our department. Right. If I knew Art, he was ducking the autopsy, the same way he did when he was a deputy sheriff. He'd hated autopsies as long as I'd known him . . .

I walked back to the table. "Shamrock, I don't have my camera with me. Could we hire you to do some shots for us. In Manchester?"

Nancy knew an opening when she saw one. "Sure, she will," she said. "I'll come, too."

Hester shot me a glance, and mouthed "autopsy." I nodded. She grinned. We do think alike.

The deal was, the department got professional, first-class autopsy shots, for a reasonable price. Shamrock got to take two cameras in, taking whatever shots for herself that she thought she'd need. I'd provide death-related information, and they'd get to hear the comments of Dr. Peters. Just the latter, in itself, was one hell of a lot. I let on as if I was really sticking my neck out, but the truth was we had used professional photographers many times before. Although it was true that the *Maitland Examiner* newspaper was usually the provider. Nonetheless, it was a precedent, and I felt covered. There was a chance that Lamar would be pissed, but if the results justified this . . .

In exchange, Nancy and Shamrock would latch on to the folks who thought the victims had been cops, and find out what the hell was going on with them. Especially the older male subject at the Borglan place. For us. They'd tell us just the information that was in regard to the cop bit. No obligation to say anything else. Deal? You bet.

"So, how soon do we get to release this stuff?" Nancy got out her notebook, a pen, and poised.

"Not sure," I said, "but I can guarantee you get it before anybody else."

"Gotta have at least twenty-four hours on everybody, or no deal. 'Before anybody else' won't cut it."

"Okay. But there has to be at least one critical detail held back," I said. "Number of shots, for example. Or caliber."

"*Number* of shots?" said Nancy. "Oooh, I like it when you talk like that."

I turned to Shamrock. "You ever do an autopsy before? I don't want to have to get you a wastebasket . . ."

"All the time. Bread and butter since fourth grade."

"No distractions for the doc," I said. "I'm serious. If you start to quease out on us, just excuse yourself, and leave me the camera."

"Sure, boss," said Shamrock. "No problem."

As we left Hester, she gave me some of the best advice I'd ever had on a case.

"Houseman," she said, "the Art business is distracting you from the case. You try too hard to get along with him, you'll end up with a mess."

"Okay."

"I mean it. And keep in touch."

We headed off to Manchester, me going one way, Nancy and Shamrock another, to throw off any of their competition who might be looking at us. Since most of them didn't know me from a hole in the ground, I don't think they ever did catch on.

Dr. Peters had no problem with Shamrock the photographer, as long as he was not identifiable in the photos. Shamrock said there'd be no problem.

"She looked at the two bodies, covered by white plastic sheets. "I, uh, hope I do okay on this . . ."

"You'll do just fine," said Dr. Peters. "Just focus on the areas I tell you. We'll keep them to a minimum, just those that will grossly affect the investigation. Most likely," he said, pulling back the sheet on the first body, "just the heads . . ."

The bodies were both supine, naked, with the heads resting on shaped wood blocks. I'd seen the same kind of head rests in a TV program on Egyptian mummies, used in their embalming process. Commonality of form and function. They still looked damned uncomfortable. Both mouths were open, eyes open, a little mucus in the nostrils of the first one. Part of the thawing process.

External examination of the two victims revealed nothing out of the ordinary, with the exception of the three gunshot wounds. Each had a couple of routine tattoos, poorly drawn and poorly executed, on their upper arms. Their initials, apparently, with M.F.D. underneath.

"What's 'M.F.D.' stand for?" asked Nancy, in a hoarse-sounding voice.

"Mean Fucking Dude," said Shamrock. Her voice sounded a little weak.

"Oh."

"Got an eraser? I had it down as Mighty Fuckin' Dumb." I chuckled.

Actually, it went rather well, as autopsies go. I tended to get in quite close, and had to back away for Shamrock several times. She was having no problems at all, which was kind of too bad, as I had all sorts of "Shamrock" and "green" lines ready. Well, she was a bit pale, maybe. Mostly the smell, I think.

There were very clear "tattoos" on each of the three entrance wounds. Perfect circles made by the impact of unconsumed particles of gunpowder moving out of a gun barrel at several hundred feet per second. Because the particles are so small, they disperse and slow very quickly. Perfect circles such as these meant the end of the gun barrel was in contact with the skin when the shot was fired . . .

"Contact wounds," said Dr. Peters. "No doubt about it."

You just can't get closer than that.

He washed the head of Victim Number One, filling the drain gutters in the table with pale pink water, which ran down toward the body's feet, and into a clear tube which was plugged in to a large container. With the dried blood out of the way, the tattooing was even more pronounced. "Victim Number One, Royce Colson," he intoned into his recorder.

"We won't probe," said Dr. Peters. "We'll do sections. The X-rays have the gross angles for us . . ."

With that, he incised the skin in a half circle around the top of the skull, and proceeded to fold the scalp down over the victim's face. He picked up a small rotary saw, and began cutting around the circumference of the head, being very careful not to disturb the wounds. As he was beginning to cut, I peered in closer, and saw the entry wound. Small dark hole, with reddish and bluish discoloration around it. Big bruise, or, at least, it would have been. Fascinating to see one under the skin. The cracking of the skull was just barely visible. Not like a fissure or anything, just a hairline crack.

The smell of the hot bone under the saw, coupled with a fine mist rising from the work, lent sort of a surreal air to things. The whine of the saw was occasionally interrupted by a deeper tone as it encountered more pressure when Dr. Peters had to change position.

Nancy left the room. Wise move. I've never understood the derision some people heap on those who have sensibilities. I, for example, can look at blood and entrails all day without a twinge. Yet, if somebody vomits, I likely will, too. Which is the main reason I appreciated somebody having the courtesy to leave before they tossed up their lunch. But I also respected their judgment.

Dr. Peters removed the brain, and placed it on a small cutting board that rested on the victim's chest. "Let's see where this one ended up," he said, shining a light into the cranial cavity. "There! See, the dark spot right there . . ."

He was pointing to what looked at first like a small lump of clumpy bluish blood. If you looked really close, though, you could see it was a misshapen slug, in a glossy dollop of what appeared to be mucus. Cerebrospinal fluid, plus membrane.

"See," said Dr. Peters. "It was coming just about straight down the pipe, so to speak. Just missed the foramen magnum. Good thing, lot harder to find if it went down that road."

We stood back, while Dr. Peters used a probe to indicate the location of the slug for Shamrock, who took three photos with each camera. Dr. Peters then picked the bullet up, and used a very sharp probe to scratch an initial in the base of the round. He placed it in a bag, and initialed it, along with the date, time, place, and his name.

Dr. Peters moved over the victim's chest, to the brain which rested on the cutting board. With all the commentary he was muttering into his tape recorder, and with all the sight-seeing he was helping us with, I couldn't help noticing that he was very, very gentle with the cadaver. Almost like it was capable of being injured further. He reached over to a stainless-steel tray, and picked up a large knife. Looked to me every bit like a large piece of cutlery you'd find in a kitchen. Complete with a black plastic handle.

"Where'd you get the knives?" I was just making conversation, really. Mildly curious.

"Katie's Kitchen Korner," said Dr. Peters, as he judiciously sliced into the brain. "Set of four assorted sizes. Great for this sort of thing." He laid a large portion of the brain aside. "Not nearly as much as they'd ask for the same sort of equipment in a surgical supply store. And surgical supply stores rarely have sales." He probed the tissues with gloved fingers. "Don't need a scalpel for this . . . it's not like we have to worry about scars or healing . . ."

"Oh." I was imagining a TV commercial . . . And, wait, there's more . . .

"Wonderful set," he continued. "Great place to shop."

"Sure is," said Shamrock. "I got a ten-inch frying pan and a French whisk there last month."

"The whisks that were on special, near the checkout counter?" asked Dr. Peters.

"You bet," she said. "Great for meringue . . ."

That got her points.

"Ah, here we are," said Dr. Peters. "The bullet's track."

He pointed at the sectioned brain, and I was very hard put to see what he was talking about. "Where?"

"Here. Tissues swell back after the passage of a projectile like this one . . . but see the perforation in the membrane here . . . and the depression in this white tissue here?"

That I did. We studied the track for a few seconds. No real reason, but it was important evidence, even though we ourselves wouldn't be testifying about it. After a few moments, Dr. Peters began hunting for the second bullet. He looked at the X-rays. "Should be right about here . . ."

With the brain on the board, I had a difficult time maintaining my orientation between it and the holes in the skull. Not Dr. Peters.

"Here we go . . . fragment . . . and here . . ."

He pointed the track and fragments out to us. We 'studied' them, too. While we did, Dr. Peters was slicing some very fine tissues off the brain, and preparing them for the laboratory examination that would be done.

He opened the chest and abdomen, and we continued our tour. No remarkable evidence turned up. That was good. We sure as hell weren't expecting any. Dr. Peters did complain about the pain in his hands, though. Very, very cold inside the victims. You could see little sparkles of frost underneath as he removed the liver.

The second victim was much like the first, except for the additional wound and track. We found only what we'd expected, and pending laboratory examination, there had been absolutely no surprises. Good news. But the slugs were so mangled I still couldn't definitely identify them as .22s. Then again, I'm not a ballistics guy.

At the conclusion of the autopsies, I had a brief meeting with Dr. Peters, while Nancy and Shamrock sat in the waiting room.

I had a question I just had to ask. "Doc, would either of the victims be capable of any significant movement after the shots were fired?"

"I don't think so," he said. "Although Victim One might not have gone straight down."

"Royce Colson," I said. "The one with two wounds."

"Right. The first one went well forward, and might not have

laid him down immediately. Which may well have been the reason for the second. I would expect him to have been seated or kneeling. Didn't topple with the first shot. But both wounds came from just about the same angle, in just about the same spot. From the nature of them, not more than a second apart." He thought for a second. "The scene tells me that they weren't lying down when they were shot. The angles aren't right for that, given the clearance. And, if somebody's lying down, on a floor, for example, the shots would come in the front, back, or sides of the skull, not the top. And the one with the exit wound put the round into the wall. So, no, they were seated or kneeling, or standing. Not lying down."

"Why were you thinking they were lying down?"

"That's common in executions," said Dr. Peters. "Just as common as kneeling."

"You think that's for sure what we have here?"

"Now that I'm certain of the contact wounds, and the track . . . Yes. I should think so."

Ten

I t wasn't exactly a revelation, but there's always a certain sense of having sailed over a major hurdle, when the pathologist reaches a definite conclusion.

So, where did that leave us? Well, we were still in the creek, but with fewer holes in the boat.

"The lab results will be in a few days, I hope," said Dr. Peters. "There have been some problems lately . . ."

True enough. The state kept cutting the criminalistics laboratory budget, reducing the number of criminalists and analysts every year. There was such a backlog that they were currently unable to guarantee processing marijuana samples within forty-five days, for example. Doesn't sound like much of a problem, but since forty-five days is the limit for a speedy trial, it meant that a savvy defendant could get you in court before you had any confirmation of evidence. As in "acquittal."

We would have priority. But it still would be several days, at best, before the toxicology report came back.

"Any real problems with that?" I asked.

"Well," drawled Dr. Peters, "unless somebody got to them with an aerosol that caused instant paralysis . . . probably not."

"There's no sign of restraints," I said. "Is that going to give us a problem with the execution approach?"

"No," said Dr. Peters, "Not at all. The fact that there were no marks, I mean. Marks are caused by very tight restraints, by strong overpressure caused by someone resisting the restraints, or residue left by adhesives. And by length of time." He shrugged. "It's like wearing a belt with your trousers. It doesn't leave prominent marks when you take it off." He looked at me, and smiled. "Well, with some exceptions, of course."

"Thanks."

"Don't mention it." He leaned back against a stainless-steel sink. "Don't forget that many things can restrain. Fear. Surprise. Dominance. The totally unexpected."

He described a case where a man had shot three women in the lingerie section of a department store. The three had been several feet apart, when the man came in and shot the clerk. He turned, and shot the customer she'd been waiting on, and then walked over to another clerk and shot her. Only the first clerk had died. She'd been his ex-wife. The other two victims had both been rooted to the spot by disbelief.

"He was quick about it," he said. "If he'd hesitated a few seconds, either of the other two victims probably would have reacted. But he shot all three within two to three seconds."

"Pretty efficient," I said.

"Remarkably so. And he never said a word. Leant an aspect of unreality to the whole thing. The other two women said in interviews that they'd been so immobilized by disbelief that they didn't even become afraid until after they had been shot." He shook his head. "The third woman took several seconds just convincing herself that she'd actually been harmed."

"I can see that. Environment, too, don't you think? If it had happened in a parking lot, they probably would have been more on edge in the first place."

"Precisely so. Even more if it had been at night." He began to take off his lab apron.

"Then," I said, "let me try this . . . Okay, our two victims break and enter what appears to be a vacant home. They just gain access, when they're confronted. Let's say they claim to be cops, looking for a burglar. It's worked for them before, maybe even something they've planned to say."

"Yes . . ."

"So they're really prepared to talk their way out of the thing, and all of a sudden, somebody sticks a gun in their face and says, 'Kneel down and put your hands behind your head.' One of them says something bright, like 'What?' and gets shot for being reluctant. The other kneels, right?"

"I would," said Dr. Peters.

"And probably asks not to be shot."

"And . . ."

"And, while he's asking, the captor walks around behind him and pops two into his head."

"Could have been," said Dr. Peters. "Sounds to me like you have a theory you've been working on."

"Well . . . yeah. Sort of. Long way to go, though."

"I certainly couldn't rule that scenario out," said Dr. Peters.

"Sort of like 'Don't shoot, we're cops.' Then 'you're what?' 'Cops.' *Bang*. 'Don't shoot me!' *Bang, bang*." I thought about what I'd just said. "You know what, I'll bet nobody had to say, 'Get on your knees.' I'll bet he did that spontaneously."

In my mind, at least, another little piece drifted into place. "The second victim . . ." I said to myself. "Yeah . . ."

"Elapsed time . . . what . . . five seconds? Hi. *Boom*. Hello. *Boom, boom*. You go in . . ." I looked at the big wall clock with the sweep second hand. "Four seconds, maybe, if you have to wait for the first one to drop, and move to the second. All the way to ten minutes, once the second victim gets to his knees. Getting the first one dead, and the second one controlled is the key."

Back outside, where the air was fresh and cold, I met with Nancy and Shamrock.

"Well, that was fun." Nancy patted Shamrock on the shoulder. "I'm glad one of us is hardy enough for this."

"No problems," said Shamrock, who was busy ejecting the last roll of film from her "official" camera.

"Let's go sit in our car, and we can talk a couple of details," I suggested. "Where it's warmer."

Car meetings aren't the best way to do things, but cops have to use 'em all the time. It's cramped, the roar of the defroster muffles things, and the coffeepot is usually several miles away. But we managed. Shamrock transferred the required film to us, and we went over the ground rules.

"No number of shots," I said.

"Sure," said Nancy.

"Either specific or vague. None of the 'several shots were fired,' or anything like that. Just 'shot.' That's plenty. And no caliber. Nothing about a .22, or a .38 or anything like that."

"Okay, Carl. Not to worry."

"Now, how are you planning to go about getting us what we want?"

"Interview, like a follow-up. You know. Back to the ones who mentioned cops being killed. Like I'm following up a lead. Get talking. At least let them know I'm interested." Nancy turned to Shamrock. "She'll get some shots. One or two, with the interview subject."

"Don't take any chances," I cautioned. Unnecessarily.

"Yeah, right," said Nancy.

"We'll wait for you to call," I said.

"Don't let me dangle this time," said Nancy. She kind of grinned. Kind of. She'd done this sort of thing before.

"Wouldn't think of it," I said. I smiled.

Back in Maitland with only a few hours to go before my shift ended, I picked up a call from Jake at the crime lab. He was looking for Art, but good old Art was busy calling around for a parka on another phone. Dispatch gave Jake to me. Jake, himself, was in his middle fifties, and a really great guy. I'd known him for years, and agreed with the rest of the entire state that he was the best analyst the lab had.

We talked for a few moments about how the case was moving nowhere fast.

"Things," I said, trying to be profound, "aren't always what they seem."

"For sure," said Jake. "Like that cartridge case we found in our vacuum bag. I never would have guessed that in a million years."

There was a stunned silence on my end.

"Hey, Carl, you there?"

"Yeah. Did you say you found a casing from the Borglan crime scene?"

"Sure. Didn't Art tell you? I told him this morning."

Well, in his favor, Art had been a bit distracted by other things.

"No, he must have forgotten. Good news, though. Now, all we have to do," I said, "is match it to one of a million .22s in the world . . ."

"No problem," said Jake. "It isn't a .22."

"Pardon?"

"Not a .22, although you'd think it was. It's a 5.45 mm PSM cartridge. Very unlikely there'd be more than a handful of 'em in the U.S."

"What," I asked, "is a 5.45 mm PSM?" Out of the corner of my eye, I saw Lamar perk up.

"Same thing we asked," said Jake. "Turns out it's a Soviet handgun, issued to troops of various sorts. Mostly KGB, NVD, and State Security. Very rare. Collector's item, I'd say."

"About a forty grain bullet," he said. "Not much, about two and a half grams. But ballistically about the equivalent of a .22 long rifle. The gun looks a lot like a PPK. Barrel just over three inches."

"Automatic, then?"

"You bet, Carl."

"And you only recovered one casing?"

"I think somebody beat us to the clean-up," said Jake. "They just missed one."

"Any idea how you'd go about getting hold of one of those PSMs?"

"Not a guess, Carl. No help there at all." He thought for a second. "Maybe a gun show? Or a collector's magazine?"

Well. In a stroke, Jake had pretty well eliminated anybody

"average" in the area. I'd seen Cletus Borglan's gun cabinet, and nothing having any connection to a hand gun had been in there. Not necessarily a complete negative, but another difficulty.

He said to have Art call him. Sure thing.

I hung up the phone, and looked at Lamar. "You know anything about a PSM?"

"It's Russian," he said. "That's about it." He folded a piece of paper, and put it in his pocket. "Notes on the PSM and the cartridge," he said.

"I'm kind of anxious to hear what Art has to say about this," I said. But alas, Art had slipped out, no doubt on the case of finding a warmer winter jacket.

When I got home, Sue and I had a nice, late, no-pressure kind of supper. We cooked together, making spaghetti and fat-free meatballs, toasted garlic bread, a great fresh salad . . . It was nice. I would have had some wine, but opted for soda instead. Legally, we were always subject to being called out, and if somebody got in real trouble, I didn't want to let them down.

We ate in our dining room, as opposed to TV trays in front of the tube while watching the news. Nice. No conversation about work. For either of us. For about two minutes.

"How are things going with Art?" she finally asked.

"Fantastic!" Well, as close as you can come with spaghetti in your mouth.

She gave me a look of disbelief.

"Well," I admitted, "it might have something to do with his not being around today."

"Well, just don't let him distract you too much when he gets back," she said. "I know you'll do your best, but he's just not as important as your business."

We cleared the table, and I sat down in my recliner, started to watch the news, saw that the damned warm front was still off to the west, and slept for about an hour and a half. That was unusual, but welcome.

"Still tired from being up for about two days, like a teenager," said Sue. "But you're not . . ."

"I guess so." I stretched. "No, I'm sure not. The nap helped, though."

Consequently, when the phone rang at about 2115, I was almost ready to go. Full, not too tired, and a bit testy, but nearly ready. It was John Willis, the new guy. Like I've said, new but sharp. Respectful, as well. Not necessarily respectful of my enormous talent, maybe, but at least respectful of my age.

"Sir?"

"Hey, John. What's up?"

"Uh, could I pick you up . . . I've got somethin' to show you, I think . . ."

I went back to the living room, where Sue was reading. "Gotta go for a bit," I said.

"I thought so."

"Sorry . . . I'll try to get back as soon as I can."

"Something dangerous?"

"I hope not," I grinned. "I'm too full of spaghetti to chase anybody, or to run away, for that matter."

I went upstairs, and pulled on a uniform. I always kept my utility belt attached to my uniform pants. You do that with little fasteners, called "keepers," that loop over the garrison belt, and secure the utility belt in place. It was much easier with the newer nylon belts than it had been with the old leather ones. Anyway, as I stepped into my uniform pants, the utility belt with its pistol holster, magazine holders, walkie-talkie holder, chemical mace holder and can, and handcuff case was already attached. All you had to do was put on the right underwear for the season, put on and fasten the Velcro straps for your bulletproof vest, put on a shirt, pull on the pants, lace your boots, and fill the various holsters and holders as you were on the way out of the room. Since it was very cold, I had to take the time to put on long underwear. But I was still fully uniformed and equipped in under three minutes. I pulled on my dark green sweater and walked down the stairs.

"Just like a forest green Batman," said Sue, "heading out of the Bat Cave."

I locked the chamber of my S&W 4006 open, slipped a magazine into the butt, snapped the chamber closed with a loud clack, and dropped the hammer. Ready to go. You never knew.

"You better wear more than that down vest."

"I'll grab my parka from my car," I said. "I'm gong to be riding with John for a while."

"Be careful." She looked up. "If you're going to be late, give me a call. Don't call after eleven, though, because I have a faculty meeting at seven. With all the people out with the flu, I really have to be there."

"Okay." I leaned down and gave her a kiss. "Have a good day if I don't get back before eleven."

Eleven

As I walked out the back door, I saw that John's squad car was already at the end of the drive. The porch light caught the reflective five-inch, blue-bordered gold stripe on his white car. Not too good for hiding at night, but great at wrecks. I ducked into the garage, to my unmarked car, and pulled out my Canadian Army parka. The best way to not have to spend time standing outside was to take it. Its pockets were full of neat things, like a stocking cap, thermal gloves, individually wrapped granola bars . . . I also grabbed my black flashlight.

I opened John's back door, and threw in the parka. I stuffed myself into the front passenger seat. "Hi, John."

"Good eve'nin boss."

I reached down and picked up his mike. "Comm, Three's ten-eight for a while with Nine." You had to let them know where you were, and you had to be logged as working if you got hurt. Insurance companies can be a pain in the ass about that stuff.

"Ten-four, Three." In wrap around sound. John had wired the police radio to his stereo speakers.

"Cool," I said. "Sounds better than in real life." Actually, it sounded a lot more bass, and gave her a bedroom sounding voice. A bit out of character for Eunice, whose voice I recognized.

"You ought to hear Sally," he said, grinning. "Sounds the way you think she would in the morning. So to speak."

"Nice. I'll tell her you said that."

"Wish you wouldn't," he said, backing onto the street. "Things are scary enough . . ."

"So," I asked, as we straightened out and headed out of town. "What brings me out on a night like this?"

It turned out that John had been patrolling in the area fairly close to the Borglan place last night. He had found a level field entrance at the base of a wooded hill, and had backed in about three car lengths, to have coffee and a sandwich. All lights off, but with the engine running, he was eating his midnight meal when he thought he saw something move out of the corner of his eye. He unrolled his window a way, and listened.

"All of a sudden," he said, "there was this whine, and something came whipping by down the road. Going like hell, it went right off the roadway and down a little bank, and off into a field. Goin' like a streak of shit. But really quiet. I mean, really quiet. Spooky as shit."

"I'll bet." We were turning off the highway, and onto gravel heading toward the general area of the Borglan farm. "What was it?"

"That's the really spooky part. I couldn't tell. I really couldn't."

"Did you get a look at his taillights? Any tire marks in the snow?"

"Sorry. Sorry, he didn't have any lights at all. God, I can't believe I forgot to say that."

"That's okay," I chuckled. "No problem."

"It was really dark, and I didn't want to shine any lights in case I'd fuck something up, you know? So I just sort of sat there for a while, and waited, but nothing came back down the road. So I walked over and tried to see, but there weren't any tire tracks, so I thought I was seeing things." In a major rush.

"Slow down," I said. We were slipping along at about 60, and the road was about 100 percent ice and snow-covered. "You're driving as fast as you talk."

"Sorry. I suppose it wouldn't look good to have a wreck with a superior officer onboard."

"Not with a big, ugly older one, either. Now, then, you have no idea what it was? How big was it?"

"I just got a flicker of it as it went by. I couldn't really tell. Isn't that the shits?"

"Yeah. So . . . what are we doing now?"

"Well, I didn't want to fuck anything up, so I thought the two of us could go back down there now, and look out into the field and see what kind of tracks we had."

"Sure. You could have done it yourself, though." I wasn't really resentful, or anything. But I had been so comfortable . . .

"Here we are," he said, shutting off his headlights and sliding to a stop. He began backing into the little lane where he'd been the night before.

"Boy, it sure as hell is dark down here," I said. Only starlight, and it was partly cloudy. If the landscape hadn't been covered with snow, it would have been like a black hole. As it was, it would take several minutes for your eyes to even begin to adjust.

"Let's just sit here a minute," he said, "and then we can walk over and look." He pointed as he talked. "It came from that way, and went off the road over there."

From the left, going right. We were about fifty feet back from the road, pretty well covered by trees and large limestone blocks that had rolled off the hill years before. From what John told me, whatever it was would have rounded a curve, gone by our location, and dipped right off the road, over a small bank, and out into a field. According to John, the place where it had gone into the field was about seventy-five yards from our parking place.

"It pretty much had to be a snowmobile," I said. "Don't you think?" That explained my presence. The troops in the department knew we were looking at snowmobile tracks.

"That's kinda what I was thinking," said John.

"But, it was quiet?"

"Yeah, that's what got me, too. Never heard a quiet one in my life."

I opened my door. I felt dark adapted enough to walk across the roadway. "Let's go look. I'm getting really curious." I got out of the car, took one step, and was up to my knees in snow. Apparently, the little lane was elevated a bit. "I'm up to my ass in snow over here," I said, stomping my way back up to the surface of the lane. "Little ditch there."

"Shit, I'm sorry. There isn't one on this side."

"No kidding." Now my feet were cold, and going to get colder. The all-weather boots were great, but they sure weren't heated.

It's one of the peculiarities of the deep winter that the road is usually lighter than the surroundings. The paved roads are whitish with dried salt, and the gravels with packed snow. It makes it a lot easier to see the road in the dark. We squeaked in the snow as we walked across the road. Over to the bank. In darkness on the roadway, I became aware of the fact there was a bit of a moon, hidden from view behind the hill from our parking spot. The moonlight shadow of the hill reached out over the roadway. The field across the road was slowly lighting up, as a couple of clouds moved past the moon. It was like a postcard. We were standing on a roadway that curved very gently to our left, disappearing after about half a mile. It curved around a big flat field, maybe three quarters of a mile across. Like a quiet harbor in the Arctic.

We reached the bank, and I shone my flashlight on the area John indicated. Snowmobile track, all right. Fresh, with little crumbled bits and chunks of snow scattered on both sides. Straight out into the field.

I turned off my light. "Son of a bitch. Doesn't that track lead toward Borglan's and his hired man?"

"I think it does. Harvey Grossman, you mean?"

"Yeah."

I looked off in the direction of the track, letting my eyes readjust to the darkness. There was a discontinuity in the snow cover, about half a mile across the field. "You see that . . . that different sort of area . . . off that way, and just before the trees . . . ?"

He did eventually. "Yeah, that's that lonesome machine shed of Borglan's. You know, the one with no other buildings anywhere . . ."

Oh, yeah. The one where some of the tracks led from Grossman's place.

I walked back up the roadway, in the direction the snowmobile had come from.

"Was it this dark last night?" I asked.

"Darker, the moon was down by the time he came by."

"Hmm." We stopped at the point of the curve, about a hundred yards from our car. I looked at it. "You say he had no lights?"

"None."

I could make out the exhaust plume of our car because I knew to look for it, but not the car itself. Well, not clearly, at least. Too much stuff in the way, like brush, trees, and rocks. I began walking toward it. About sixty yards from it, the left front fender became visible. By fifty yards, you could begin to see the area of the driver's door. At forty or so, a shrub began to block the view of the left front fender again. A narrow range of visibility, but . . .

"It looks for all the world like he was coming around the corner, saw you, and ducked off the road." I looked back toward the curve. "The distances are right if he's goin' about forty-five or so."

"But he didn't have any lights . . ."

"Yeah, I know." So how did he see John? Night vision goggles, that's how. "I'll bet you look good in green light."

"What?"

"Night vision goggles. NVGs."

"Oh. Yeah, that'd do it."

"Sure would," I said. "Let's get back in the car before I freeze to death."

I stomped through the snow again, trying to hit my original tracks and not succeeding particularly well in the dark. But, back in the car, the heat felt good. I'd left my parka in the backseat, of course. Just too much of an encumbrance. Besides, the heat would warm up the granola bars enough that they wouldn't break my teeth . . .

We each cracked a window, subconsciously listening. To hear a railroad train over the loud hiss of the heater/defroster and the engine would have been quite a feat, but we did it anyway.

"Granola bar?"

"Yeah, thanks."

We munched in silence for almost a minute.

"So," said John. "What do you think?"

"I think we got something really spooky here," I replied. "I don't know why, but somebody with a silenced snowmobile and NVGs is touring the countryside. Near a murder scene. Where the killer probably left via snowmobile."

"I never heard of a snowmobile like that, with the goggles and all."

"I did once," I said, around a mouthful. "On TV. Finnish Army."

"Who?"

"The Army of Finland. They and the Swedes were on TV. They have special units that use that sort of stuff. Go a hundred and sixty miles per hour on lakes in the Arctic like that. Quiet, and run 'em at night."

"Yeah . . ." said John.

"No," I said, "I don't think we've been invaded. But military people use this kind of stuff. Or, at least, would if they needed to. Survivalists would probably know about it, then."

"Oh."

"Just have to figure out who and why," I said. "For starters."

I could just hear Art with that one. I'd be labeled the conspiracy theorist of the year.

"Don't tell anybody. I mean, anybody. Got that?" I was deadly serious.

"Yes, sir." So was John.

"I want you to keep working this area, but don't hang it out too far on this thing. All right?"

"Yes, sir."

"You did exactly right, last night, by not giving any indication that you saw it. He probably thinks he just blew past you and you weren't even aware of him. That's good. And . . ."

There was a rising whine, followed by a suddenly deepened tone, along with the crunch of snow and gravel, and a black object flew by on the roadway. And was gone. Just like that. He'd come from our right this time, and wouldn't have been able to see us at all.

We looked at each other.

"You see well enough to drive?"

"Without lights, you mean?"

"Yep," I said, making sure my seat belt was secure. I knew his answer.

"Oh, yeah," he said, pulling the gearshift lever down. And away we went.

Without any lights on, it was fairly easy to see the road. It wasn't possible, however, to see the speedometer, so I had no accurate idea of how fast we were going. Probably just as well. We were fishtailing a lot of the time, and I thought we were going to go into the ditch more than once. It might have just been my perspective, but I thought the ditches were getting deeper and steeper on my side as we went. Because of the curving road and the nearness of the hills, we were in and out of moonlight constantly. I really sweated those dark patches.

"You see him?" I asked.

"Nope."

"Let me know if you do . . ."

We rounded a curve and caught a little moonlight. Up, over a small hill, going about 50 on a straight stretch. Over the top and down, like a roller-coaster ride.

"Careful . . . there's a bridge here somewhere," I said. Just as we flew across it.

"Yep."

He accelerated.

"Watch it, the curves start again really soon . . . and be careful, he's gonna be kicking snow, might be hard to see . . ."

"I see him . . . I see him . . ."

So did I. We were just barely gaining on a darker spot about a hundred yards up the white snow-covered roadway. He was hazy or fuzzy or . . . of course. The rooster tail of snow I'd just reminded John about. He was picking up just enough from the roadway to make a snowy haze.

"Try not to lose him, but don't fuckin' kill us, either." I get all fatherly in tight circumstances.

"Okay."

I picked up the mike. "Comm, Three. Nine is in pursuit of an unknown vehicle, proceeding south on G4X. Vehicle traveling at a high rate of speed . . ."

"Ten-four, Three."

Whoever it was was apparently oblivious to our presence. He was pooping along at about 40 or so, and we were now gaining perceptibly. But 50 was a high rate of speed for us, considering the snow-packed and icy condition of the road.

If this guy really was using night vision equipment, my plan should work. Get in close, then hit him with all the light we had on the car. It should cause the night vision goggles to "bloom" on him, and he'd be unable to see for a few seconds. His first reaction should be to stop.

"In about a second," I said, "we hit every damned light we got. Top lights, high-beam headlights, spotlight, everything. Just get ready for a hard stop. When I say . . ."

"Okay . . ."

"Stay with the son of a bitch for another five seconds we got a chance here . . ." We were approaching a fairly sharp curve to the left. "Just before he gets to the curve . . ."

"Right . . ."

"NOW!"

We both worked switches, John taking the headlights and the

spotlight, and me getting the top red and white strobes, and hitting the siren on "yelp" for good measure.

The lights had a dazzling effect on us, as well.

"SLOW DOWN, JOHN!"

Too late. I watched the snowmobile careen off the right side of the road toward the trees, with us right behind him. We hit small stuff, not much bigger than brush, and came to a stop in a large snowbank. I lost the snowmobile completely, as it went over the snowbank we stopped in. We didn't stop fast enough to deploy the airbags, but I was sure as hell grateful for the seat belts.

I reached over and cut the siren. The snow we'd kicked into the air came thundering back down onto the hood. Then silence. The black night air was filled with tiny red and white flashing snow particles, slowly settling on the windshield.

"Well, fuck." I looked over at John. He was opening his door.

I tried to open mine, but couldn't manage more than a few inches in the deep snow that had been thrown alongside by our sliding impact. My outside view was considerably diminished by flashing strobes. "Want to kill the lights?" I pushed a little harder, and got about four more inches of opening.

"Sir . . ."

"What?" My door seemed to have hit an obstacle.

"Sir . . ." said John. I looked up, and in the flashing red lights I could see the outline of a figure in a dark snowmobile suit, helmet with NVGs tilted up, sprawled in the snow at the top of the snowbank. It wasn't moving.

"Great," I said, "we've fuckin' killed him . . ."

I pushed real hard, and the door opened another three or four inches. I squeezed out, into the knee-deep snow, and approached the supine figure as cautiously as I could. I could hear John crunching through the snow just above and to my left. He'd obviously gotten up on the bank.

"Careful, sir," he said.

"Yep." I could see both hands of the figure, gloved, with the left one out to the side, and the right one almost folded behind. I heard the peculiar steel on nylon sound as John drew his gun.

That meant that I was going to have to check the body. I really hoped he wasn't dead.

I took off my right glove, reached down, and worked the zipper at his throat, until I could get my first two fingers inside and feel for a carotid pulse. Strong. Good. I pulled my hand back, and pushed the night vision goggles up onto the top of his shiny black helmet, and carefully tested his visor. It slid up easily, and as it did so, I saw his eyes fly wide.

"Don't move," I said. "You've been in an accident . . ."

I took both his feet squarely in my chest. He lifted me a good foot off the ground, and propelled me backward about three. If it hadn't been for the bulletproof vest, he would have broken a couple of my ribs, at least. He'd moved so fast I hadn't even had time to react.

John, on the other hand, cracked off a round right past the guy's ear as he started to stand. He stopped so fast his momentum carried him forward on the bank, and he rolled head over heels down toward me. I rolled to one side, and got to my knees, drawing my own gun as John yelled, "Freeze, asshole!"

A great command, although not designed for "post-shot," and still better late than never. The man in the snowmobile suit froze, all right. He had both knees under him, one hand in contact with the ground, and he was grabbing at his zippered neck. Obviously trying to reach something inside the snowmobile suit.

His hand stopped when he saw my gun in front, and heard John ask a question behind him . . .

"Should I shoot now, sir? I got him . . ."

"Only if he moves," I said. I continued kneeling in front of the man, pointing my gun at his chest. "Both hands in the air. Slow, but do it."

He did. The visor of his helmet was still up, and I could just make out his eyes in the moonlight. As both hands cleared the top of his head, I rocked back, got my feet under me, and stood.

"Now lay down on your face, like you were going to make an angel in the snow. Hands way over your head . . . And turn your face away from me . . . That's right . . ."

He did as I told him, and I saw John put his gun away, and get out his handcuffs.

"Careful, John. Stay toward his hips, 'cause I'm gonna shoot him in the head if he moves. I don't want to get helmet fragments in you."

That was said for the benefit of the suspect, naturally. With his head turned away, he wouldn't have any idea where I was, and could only feel John put the handcuffs on. For a smart suspect, it would be a case of no data, no plan, no action.

The man never moved a muscle.

When John stood up, I told him to open the rear door of the car. He did, and then came back to us. I was taking no chances with this fellow, none at all. He was just too damned quick.

"Roll over, and get to your knees," I said. Not the easiest thing to do when you're handcuffed behind your back, but he accomplished it in one motion. I stepped behind him, removed my gloves, and patted him down. Large lump under the left arm. I knelt directly on the back of his lower legs and ankles, and reached around him and unzipped his suit. He was kind of squirmy, but never made a sound. With me on his legs like that, he had no chance for any leverage.

I reached in, and pulled out a .40 caliber Glock semiautomatic handgun. I dropped the magazine, jacked the chambered round out into the snow, and put the gun in my gun belt.

"Found a Glock," I said to John.

"Cool . . ."

"Got any more?" I asked, patting his sides. No answer, but no weapons, either. Not as far as I could tell.

"He's probably got a knife," I said to John, "but I can't find it with him kneeling down." Just a hunch.

I reached under his chin, and unstrapped his helmet, and pulled it off his head. Keeping it securely in my right hand, I leaned on his shoulders and pushed myself back to my feet.

"Walk on your knees to the car."

He spoke for the first time. "What?" He sounded exasperated and angry.

"It's either that or be dragged," I said, evenly. "We have rope in the trunk. It's not that far, and the snow's soft. You can do it."

He did, too. I stood on his right, and John stood about twenty-five feet away, at the open rear door of the squad car. He covered him every inch of the way.

When he got to the car, I said, "Just kneel right against the open door there, don't get in. You'll get enough warm air from the door."

No leverage in the snow. Besides, he was likely a lot warmer than we were. I sat his helmet on the roof of the car, and handed the Glock to John. "For the trunk, I think. And you'd better get us some backup," I said. "Good thing we called in the pursuit."

"I'm just glad you were along. God, I'd hate to explain this all by myself."

The flashing red strobe lights that were left were disorienting, to say the least. In the white environment, things seemed to leap toward and away from you with each pulse.

"Check your temp gauges, make sure the engine isn't overheating . . ." Snow up under the hood could block the radiator, loosen belts, throw belts, you name it. "If it's okay, keep it running." In this area of the county, the hilltops were a good hundred feet above the roadway, and pretty close, to boot. Radio communications with our 10 watt walkie-talkies would be chancy, at best. I wanted the 100 watt radio in the car available, if I could.

"Yes, Father . . ." came from the car. Oops. Let up, Carl. He's able to do all of that.

I got busy thinking. There was absolutely no doubt in my mind that the subject in custody was related to or involved with the two murders. None. I was as certain of that as I was of the fact that there was absolutely no real evidence to back me up.

Over my walkie-talkie, I could hear John's side of the conversation with the office. He mentioned that we needed assistance. That it wasn't an emergency, but that we had a suspect in custody. He promised to keep in touch until help arrived.

He joined me in watching our prisoner. Time to get some information.

"Who are you?"

Silence.

"You got a name?"

Nothing.

"Well, let me put it this way," I said. "Any ID you got is going to be mine as soon as we get that suit off you." In the ensuing silence, I recited his Miranda rights. No reaction. Nothing. "Right." The radio was blaring in the background. "I'll get the radio," I said. I trudged up to the front, and reached in for the mike.

"This is Three, go ahead."

"Three, One is ten-seventy-six. So is Seven. 388 is coming from Wheaton, ETA ten."

"Ten-four, Comm."

"Ten-fifty-one is also ten-seventy-six." That meant that a wrecker was also coming. Well, we needed one, no doubt about that. Unfortunately, that also meant a civilian at the scene, as well.

"Which fifty-one, Comm?"

"Eddie's Body Shop."

If it had to be anybody, I was glad it was Eddie. He was pretty good at keeping his mouth shut.

What we needed was a cover story. Something that most people could be told, something that would explain a chase of a snowmobile, and a subject in custody. We were going to need it in a hurry, too. I could see the faint flashing red lights way back down the valley. Probably Seven. Deputy Gary Oberbrech. Fairly new, and a good officer. He'd need to know some details, but I didn't think I wanted the whole world to know that I had my real suspect. Not just yet.

Two deer broke cover, about ten yards from me, and just about finished me off right then and there. "Holy shit," I said to myself, when I got my breath back. "That would a been cute,

Carl. Scared to death by a couple of nervous deer . . ." Ah, but yes. That was going to be it. Our cover story. "John!"

"Yeah . . ."

I walked back up on the road. "Listen up. Except for Lamar, everybody is told this is a poacher. Got that? We caught a poacher. Use 'poacher' every chance you get. Poacher."

" 'Poacher'? Okay, yeah, poacher . . . sure."

"Stick to that even if they torture you," I grinned. "Coffee, doughnuts, chocolate bars . . . the works. Don't give in. Except Lamar," I added. "Never lie to Lamar."

"Got it." He grinned back. "You know how close we came? I almost ran over the fucker, I swear. Another hundred yards of straight road . . ."

"Yeah. Close." I clapped him on the shoulder. "I'll bet you scared the crap out of him when you touched off that round, too." Bravado has its uses. Oh, yeah.

According to my watch, it was 2310 when we got our suspect to the jail, and field-stripped him down to his dark blue union suit. Three of us, Gary, John, and me. No chances. You gotta take the cuffs off to get 'em undressed. We did find a knife, a Gerber, underneath his bulletproof Kevlar vest, which was also dark blue. He hadn't said a word to that point.

"Pretty well equipped for a poacher," said Gary, dryly.

"Got a wallet here," said John, who was going through the snowmobile suit. He handed it to me. Junior officers will do that, I suspect because they think us older folk would like the privilege of opening the prize, or something. This time, I was glad that he had.

I opened the wallet, and found myself staring at a complete FBI identification set. Photo, document, everything.

I just looked at him for a long moment. He just looked back. Well.

I cleared my throat. "It says here you're Norman John Brandenburg," I said. "That right?"

"That's right."

"And that you're a special agent of the Federal Bureau of Investigation . . ."

Both Gary and John stopped their inventory of his gear.

"That's right."

"How do you want us to go about proving that?" I asked. I'd seen FBI identification many times, and this was about as authentic as you can get. Including subtleties like slight wear and scuffing.

"Just make a phone call," he said. "The office will confirm."

I thought for a second. "Field office?"

"Yes, but not a local one. I'll provide the number."

I'd asked, because I'd never known a local field office to be open for phone calls after 1700. Not that I was going to be satisfied with a phone call, anyway.

"How about I call an FBI agent I know, and we have him do it?" It wasn't really a question.

Special Agent Norman John Brandenburg didn't seem happy with that. "You shouldn't do that."

My first thought had been that it was a phony ID, and that we were getting a phony number. Now I was just about certain I was right.

"I think we'll do it my way," I said. "John, why don't you put the cuffs back on him, and sit him over by the booking desk. This won't take too long . . ."

I went out to dispatch, where Sally was monitoring the taping of our activities with our suspect. She'd arrived about 2245 for the start of the eleven-to-seven shift, and had made sure that the recording system was working well. Audio and visual.

"Well, holy shit," she said, in a conversational tone. "You think he really is?"

"Dunno," I said. "Got George's home number?"

She found it in a second, wrote it on a slip of paper, and handed it to me, all the time monitoring the activities in the booking room.

"Can they execute you for arresting a Fed?"

"No," I said. "But I'm not sure about embarrassing one . . ."

I dialed George from the "officer's" phone, at the end of the dispatch console, near the coffeepot and supplies. The pot was empty. We'd have to do something about that.

"Hello . . ." came the familiar voice of Special Agent George Pollard, known to us as George of the Bureau.

"George?"

"Yes . . . Houseman?" He sounded very surprised. He should have. I think this might have been the second time in five years that we'd called him at home.

"Yep. Got a second for a strange one?"

"Oh, no. Now what?" He knew the Nation County Sheriff's Department pretty well.

"Well, it appears that we may have arrested a federal agent . . ."

"What?!"

I chuckled. "Well, somebody who's claiming to be one, anyway."

"My God. For what?"

"That," I said, "is pretty much going to depend on whether or not he's a real FBI agent."

There was a small groan on the other end. "An FBI agent . . ." George cleared his throat. "I was assuming it was some other agency . . ."

"Nope. Fucking Big Indian, as they used to say."

"What are the charges?"

"Well, if he isn't one, then we start with impersonation, and go down the list to concealed weapons, eluding pursuit, and reckless driving. If he is, we just got reckless and eluding pursuit."

"My God," whispered George. "Do you have his car?"

"No," I said, unable to suppress a grin, "but I got his snowmobile."

Twelve

Who is it?" asked George, with an air of fatality. "I
probably know him . . ."

"A Norman John Brandenburg," I said. "According to his ID."

"You have his ID?"

"Sure do," I said. "Retrieved it when we stripped him. You
recognize the name?"

There was a profound silence. Then, "No. No, I don't. Look,
let me get right back to you, all right?"

"Yep. But make sure it's you. Tell whoever you talk to that we
deal with you only, because we're having a tough time trusting
this dude."

I caught a waving motion out of the corner of my eye. Sally,
waving me over to the bank of camera monitors.

"I will," said George.

I hung up the phone, and went over to the monitors.
"What?"

"Look at this," she said, her voice up an octave. Very unusual
for Sally. She pointed to screen three, which showed the rear of
the office and jail; and then to screen eight, which showed the
corner of the jail and the edge of the parking lot.

I looked, and didn't see anything. "What?"

"Right here!" she said, tapping the screen. "There, see, he
moved!"

By God. There appeared to be a figure moving around the back of the building, in the shadows thrown by the yard lights. It paused, then moved into contact with the building.

"What's he doing?"

"He's looking in the window," I said. "Call Twenty-five to the office, fast but quiet. Gary and I will try to get this dude."

I went flying back into the booking room. "Gary! Intruder out back, we can get to him through the kitchen door, come on!"

John started to move, and realized that somebody had to stay with the prisoner. He looked so frustrated it was almost funny.

Gary and I thundered back to the kitchen, through it, and onto the little service porch where we kept the washer and dryer. I picked up my walkie-talkie mike.

"Okay, where's he at now?"

"He just moved," said Sally, in a near whisper, "and he's just around the corner from the kitchen door. He might be trying to look in that back window by the old pantry . . ."

Our jail is over 100 years old, and has too damned many nooks and crannies.

Gary and I carefully opened the outside door, and slipped through. So quiet. The air was unbelievably cold, and I almost instantly started to shiver. I think it was the cold.

I just pointed to the wall to our left, and eased my way toward it. Our target ought to be just on the other side. Putting slowly increasing pressure on the thumb break of my holster, I silently unsnapped the restraining strap, and slipped my handgun free of the holster. I tried to get right against the wall, but drifted snow kept me about three feet away from the massive limestone blocks. We were at the edge of the shadow from the backyard light, but the bright moonlight illuminated us wherever we were in that little yard. We'd have to move very fast, around the corner, and try to get him before he heard us coming. It was going to be difficult.

Suddenly, there was a squeaking from the parking lot, as Twenty-five, the Maitland officer, drove up, responding to Sally's call. The parking lot was also on out left, placing the suspect between us and the Maitland officer. Now, I thought, if we can get around that corner fast enough, we can chase him right toward Twenty-five's car . . .

There was a brief flurry of footsteps, and the suspect came flying around the corner, fleeing from the line of sight of the Maitland officer.

"Freeze!" From both Gary and myself, same instant.

The suspect turned toward the sound, looked down the barrels of two handguns, tried to stop, skidded, slipped, waved his arms, and hit the ground on his back with a loud *thump*.

I love Iowa winters.

"Don't fuckin' move!" thundered Gary, as we approached the supine figure.

"Comm, Three, I think we got him," I said, into my mike.

"Way to go!" came from Sally. "It's on tape!"

"You okay?" I heard Gary asking. I looked down, and saw that the suspect was gasping like a landed fish.

"Fall knocked the wind out of him," I said. "He'll be fine."

Just then, Ira Tully, part-time Maitland PD officer, came huffing and puffing around the corner. "We get him?"

"Got him, Ira. Thanks for comin' up."

"No . . . puff . . . problem . . . puff . . . Carl."

Ira had just turned sixty, and worked one night a month. As reliable as the seasons, and a plumber in real life.

"Well," I said, "let's get on with it."

Between the three of us, we lifted the gasping suspect to his feet, and slowly and carefully frisked him.

"Don't puke on me, buddy," said Gary, consolingly.

Beneath his dark blue parka, we found another .40 cal. Glock. No knife. No bulletproof vest. I felt the Glock was plenty.

When we got him inside, we sat him down at the kitchen table. I didn't want him to be in contact with the other prisoner, who I assumed was an associate of his. He stopped gasping, and was merely breathing hard. He had a desperate air about him, not threatening, but sort of actively unhappy.

"So," I said, in a friendly tone, "who are you?"

No reply.

"Name?"

Silence, except for the heavy breathing.

I was getting a little tired of this approach. "Strip him," I said to Gary. "I'm getting sick of this shit tonight."

"James Hernandez," he said. He shook his head, and shrugged in a resigned way. "Special Agent James Hernandez, Federal Bureau of Investigation. My ID is in my back pocket."

"No shit? The real FBI?" said Gary.

I glanced at Gary. He'd missed the wallet. He shrugged.

We let Hernandez very slowly reach back, and produce his ID wallet. He opened it, and showed it to me. I reached out and took it, although he resisted for an instant. It looked real enough, just like the last one I'd seen a few minutes ago. I laid it on the table, while I wrote down the information. "It won't leave your sight," I said.

Sally stuck her head in the room. "Carl, George for you . . ." She had a huge grin.

"Right." I followed her back to dispatch.

"This is just so cool," she said, bubbling over. "I got the whole thing on tape, him falling, you guys pointing your guns at him, the whole thing . . ."

Dispatchers hardly ever get to see what happens as a result of their efforts. This was quite a treat. Not only for her.

"I'd like to see that sometime." Cops don't get to watch, very often, either. "We'll have to bootleg a couple of copies . . ."

I picked up the phone. "George?"

"Carl, I'm afraid that Norman John Brandenburg is a real agent." He sounded very worried.

"No kidding?"

"No kidding. I hate to complicate your life like this, but he really is one of us."

"George," I said, "you ain't heard the half of it. We just bagged a fellow named . . ." I looked at my note. "James Marteen Hernandez. Out trespassing behind the jail."

"Oh, no . . ."

"Yep. You guessed it. His ID says he's one of your special agents, too.

"Oh, no," he said, again. "You're right, that's who he is. He's assigned along with Brandenburg . . . I was supposed to contact him as soon as I could find him . . ."

"I know where you can reach him," I said, smiling.

"Look, Carl, I'll get back to you, but expect me there within an hour or so. I'll be coming up on this one. But keep it as quiet as you can."

"I'll try," I said, "but you really ought to talk with your agents about that."

"Yes. I'm sure somebody will do just that."

"Oh, George . . ."

"Yes?"

"Is there, like, a limit on agents? Or can we bag as many as we want?" I just couldn't help it.

As soon as the connection was broken, I turned to Sally.

"Where's Lamar?"

"Over with the wrecker, getting the snowmobile."

"Better tell him to get here just as soon as he can . . ." I grinned. "Nothing about FBI agents over the radio. George wants it kept quiet." I laughed.

"Can we do this?" she asked. "I mean, they're really FBI . . ."

"We can even savor it," I said. "They're going to be the butt of every Bureau joke for the next six months."

We moved Brandenburg to the kitchen with Hernandez, and got them some coffee. I explained where we were coming from.

"So, like, we have valid charges on both of you. I expect the charges to be dropped. So do you. But I can't release you without a bond being posted, until I hear further. Regulations, you know?"

They didn't say anything.

"Now, I don't know what the hell you were doing out there," I said, evenly, "but I don't like people screwing around in my county, no matter who they are. Care to explain this?"

They didn't answer. That was all right, I didn't expect them to.

"I don't know if you're aware of it, but we had a double murder in that area . . ." I stopped. Right there. The level of tension in the room went up an order of magnitude. "I don't believe it," I said, to nobody in particular.

"What?" asked Gary.

"Never mind just yet." I went to the door between dispatch and the kitchen. "Sally! How soon can Lamar get in here?"

Lamar got to the office about ten minutes later. I ran the whole thing by him, kind of fast.

"You think I should call Art?" Art was going home every night, some seventy-five miles or better. Saved the state a few dollars in motel accommodations. He was like that.

"No," said Lamar. "Not until we talk with George."

We drank coffee in near total silence, thinking, until George arrived. When Sally buzzed the electric lock on the door to let him in, neither Lamar nor I got up. George came through the door, looking frazzled, harried, and very worried.

He should have.

"Ho, boy," he said. "This is a fine mess, isn't it?"

"It just might be," said Lamar.

"What have you got on them?" George got out his little notebook. I explained the possible charges, and he wrote them down. "Right . . . right." He snapped the book shut. "I'll talk to them, and then to you, if that's all right?"

"Sure," said Lamar. "In private?"

"If possible," said George.

"You can use the booking room . . ." said Lamar. I grinned. Everything in the booking room was taped.

Not three minutes after we heard the muted, angry voice of George talking to his two fellow agents, George came back to our room. He looked thoroughly angry.

"They were told," he said, "that their supervisor is not happy."

"And who," I asked, "would that be?"

He sighed. "Carl, I'm not allowed to say." He looked at us beseechingly. "You understand?"

"Maybe," said Lamar. "We just have to know what they were doing when we found them."

"I'm not allowed to tell you that . . ."

"Well," said Lamar, "since they might be implicated in a murder or two, you might want to get permission to reconsider that."

George stood there, openmouthed.

"Let me tell you . . ." I said.

I did. All about the Colson brothers. The circumstances of their death. The fact that they'd been killed in the commission of a burglary, and that it was very possible that they had stumbled upon somebody in the house. Somebody who was very efficient. Somebody who might have killed them in order to cover their presence. I went a step further. I told him the secondhand information I had about their impersonating cops once, when they were caught.

"We're trying to confirm that," I said. "But if they did tend to do that, they could have identified themselves as cops to somebody who thought that was a great reason to do 'em." I waited a second. "So, it was either your guys, or somebody who thought they had been caught by your guys."

George looked stunned. I think mostly because I was even suggesting such a thing.

"I don't know if you have ever felt this way," I said to George, changing tack, "but I occasionally get the feeling I'm being watched. Ever have that?"

"Sure. You're supposed to pay attention to it."

"Yep." I paused. "When I was at the murder scene, I could have sworn I was being watched. Several times."

Nothing.

"When Special Agent Brandenburg of your Snowmobile Division ended up in the ditch," I said, "he was coming from the direction of the Borglan place, where the bodies were found. He was on a machine so silent it could hardly be heard. He was equipped with night vision equipment. He was running blacked out . . ."

Still nothing.

"So it was pretty obvious he was doing surveillance," I said. "Proximity would indicate the Borglan farm as at least a likely object. Why? Why would your people be watching our murder scene? Any ideas?"

"None," said George. "I don't know what their assignment is. Honest. I think that your assumption that they were watching your crime scene is reaching a bit, though . . . but to even think they may be *implicated* . . ."

"Then," I continued, "very shortly after we bring him here, his partner shows up. Not at the door. Not that openly, by a long shot." I studied George. He was embarrassed, but I believed him when he told me he didn't know their assignment. "No, we catch Agent Hernandez out behind the jail, like a common burglar."

"I can't explain . . ." said George.

"Somebody better, and it better be damned good," rumbled Lamar. "We'd all hate to have to bother one of our senators to find out for us . . ."

George blanched, and I think I did, too. That was a first-class threat.

"All I can do," he said, "is try to get the information for you. Let me try that . . ."

"Twenty-four hours," said Lamar. "Try hard, George."

"Oh, yes," said George. "Count on it. But, in the meantime, can I have my two agents in there?"

Lamar grinned. "Sure. We'll call a magistrate and recommend release on their own recognizance. But first, we do photos and prints. Standard procedure before release."

It was unsaid, but nonetheless a major threat. No deniability with photos and prints. Just on the off chance it might have occurred to somebody to try to deny this.

Thirteen

Lamar and I sat in his office. We could hear the Maitland town clock strike twice. The bell was exceptionally clear in the still, icy air. It was a very lonely sound.

"You got any confirmation at all that those dead kids claimed they were cops?"

"Workin' on it, boss."

"You really think the FBI people did the Colsons?" he asked.

"No."

"Me, neither. Too bad, though, in a way." He grinned. "I mean, we caught 'em. Just too bad they didn't do it."

I drew a deep breath, and let it out very slowly. "Yeah. Ain't gonna hurt to let 'em think we suspect 'em, though. We might find out what they were actually doing around there."

"They were pullin' surveillance on my buddy Cletus," said Lamar. "That's what they were doin'."

I held up my right hand, measuring less than an inch between my thumb and forefinger. "Cletus is this important . . ." I spread my hands at arm's length. More than six feet apart. "You gotta be at least this big before you get FBI surveillance. At least."

We were silent again for a few moments.

"So," said Lamar, slowly, "what the fuck were they doin' there?"

I shrugged. "Not a clue."

"But you *do* think they *were* there?"

"Oh, yeah. If not actually on the property, they were close enough to see . . . I'd stake my life on the fact that they were the ones watching me when I felt so spooked." I crumpled my decaf pop can. "The real question is whether or not they were lookin' in the place the night the brothers were killed."

"Witnesses . . ." muttered Lamar.

"*Professional* witnesses," I said. "If we're lucky, they got photos."

"Of what?"

"Won't know until they think they have to tell us what they had going. Your bit about the senator should get that machinery going real fast." I stood. "Gotta hand it to ya, boss. That senator bit was perfect."

"Thanks," he said, pleased. "Look, let's let Art do the details tomorrow. You come in a little late. Say nine or so."

"Okay." That gave me seven hours, give or take, from now. I let my feet slide off the edge of his desk, and stood up with a continuation of the motion. A low-intensity pain shot through my back muscles, catching me off guard. Must have been something I'd done in the last few hours. Probably when Agent Brandenburg had kicked me, and I'd gone flying backward. Great. I was going to be really stiff and sore tomorrow. "See you in the morning."

"This is getting to really bother me," said Lamar, as I headed for the door. "You think Cletus knows what's going on here?"

"Beats the shit out of me," I said. "How you gonna handle the patrol in that area? Two-man cars?"

"We ain't got enough people." He looked at me. "This ain't the only thing we got going."

"You don't want to use the reserve in this sort of thing, Lamar."

He sighed. "Yeah. But I don't want to send nobody down there alone, either."

Sue awoke as I slipped into bed. "What happened?" she mumbled. "You all right?"

"Fine," I said. "John went in the ditch. Took us a while to get his car out."

"Oh. Just so you're all right . . ." And she drifted back off to sleep. I wish I'd been able to do that. I lay there, wide awake, for a good hour, thinking about the events of the evening. I tried to turn on my side, once, and my back muscles advised me not to try that again. So I lay there, staring at the shadows on our ceiling. Thinking.

Nation County is about 750 square miles, about half of it hilly. A dozen small towns, and about 2,000 farms. Connected by 1,300 miles of roadway, 75 percent of it gravel. So, what were the odds of us meeting up with the FBI Snowmobile Detail so close to the Borglan place? Right. Not conclusive, but a very damned strong factor.

Not to mention the near certainty that the killer at the Borglan farm had fled via snowmobile, in the middle of the night; blasting right through the Grossmans' barnyard, and off to . . . Where? Unknown, but south, that was for sure. For how far? I smiled to myself. Until the snow ran out . . . But that was a very loud snowmobile, at least according to the hired man and his family. I grinned sleepily to myself. Not FBI issue.

But, then, there was the timing. The snowmobile, on the first night John had seen it, had been heading in the direction of Grossman's. North. When I'd seen it tonight, it was heading south. But when John and I had seen it, it was earlier than it had been when John had seen it the previous night. What did that mean? Nothing. The voice of my ninth-grade algebra teacher came to me: "If a train leaves Smallville, traveling west at sixty miles per hour, and another train leaves an hour later, traveling at . . ." Ugh. If there was a solution to my problem there, it'd have to wait . . . I was just too tired.

More work. And hopefully, a little more luck, before somebody else got killed. The bullet casing found by Jack and company, that weirdo Russian caliber, had to figure in somewhere, too.

I started to turn over. Whoa! My back hurt a lot more, and was going to be more than stiff in the morning. Great. I moved gingerly, and tried to stretch the muscles slightly. Bad idea.

I know I slept, though, because the telephone woke me up.

The phone couldn't have rung more than four times, or the answering machine would have kicked in. I fumbled with the receiver for a second. My voice didn't quite come out, so I cleared my throat, and tried again. "Yeah, Houseman here . . ."

"Hey, I get you up?"

Phil, from Oelwein PD. I looked at the clock. 0836. "Yeah, you did . . . or, you will have, when I'm awake."

"You old folks sure sleep a lot." He laughed heartily. "Hey, I just thought you'd want to know, I found the old fart that the Colson brothers told that they were undercover cops."

That perked me up. "No kidding?" I started to scoot up on my right elbow, and the pain in my back almost took my breath away.

"Yep. Last September or so, I believe. He was going out the back door, into the alley, to put some trash in the Dumpster, and hit one of 'em with the door."

"Really?" I had frozen halfway over onto my side. My back felt like somebody had taken out half the length of the muscles, and sewn them back together. "Tight" does not begin to describe it.

He laughed again. "Yeah, no shit, they were just getting ready to try to pry the door. He asked 'em what the hell they were doing, and one of 'em says, 'Be quiet, we gotta get in here, there's going to be some kids try to break in and we want to catch 'em.' Really!"

"Guts." The pain in my back was subsiding. Wonderful. If I stayed like this for four more days, I'd be fine.

"Oh, yeah. Told him they were undercover state officers."

"Didn't he ask for any ID?" I asked, gingerly moving into a more or less upright position by carefully swinging my legs off the bed, and letting their weight help lift me.

"Yeah, and you know what they said? The one with the little beard says, 'If you was undercover, would you carry one?' Just cool as hell."

I chuckled, myself. "Sharp," I said.

Phil laughed again, hugely enjoying himself. "It gets better! He wouldn't let 'em in, you know, so they got all pissed off, and left saying they would come back with their boss in a few minutes, and he'd better be there when they got back! You know what he did? The poor bastard apologized, and he fuckin' waited almost an hour for 'em to come back!"

"Must have been real, real convincing." I was sitting now, and the pain wasn't all that bad.

"Oh, yeah."

"Do you know if Goober was one of 'em?" I asked, hoping he wasn't.

"Who?"

"Fred, their cousin . . ."

"Oh! Him! No, not him. The two he described were the brothers. Just the two of 'em."

"Good." I just about had my thoughts collected. "You turn up anything more on Fred, while I got you on the line?"

"Just what I got from my old reports. Remember . . . oh, a couple of years ago, more 'n that, maybe? He was a juvie, and was breaking into taverns, and hitting the pinball machines?"

"Oh, yeah . . ." I'd heard something to that effect, but since it hadn't happened in Nation County, I never saw a report.

"All three of the boys that night," said Phil. "I remember Freddie was wearin' a fatigue jacket, and he made one hell of a racket when I chased him. Pockets full of quarters. We weighed the jacket. Thirty-four pounds of quarters." He had been chuckling to himself all through the recounting. "Every time I saw him after that, I'd ask if he had any change." He broke into laughter.

"I never saw a cop who enjoyed his job more than you do . . ."

Breathless with laughter, he managed to get out, "Yeah, ain't it a sin, though?"

"This is a good piece of work. Really. Can you write it up and send me a copy?"

"You bet. Oh, yeah, before I forget . . . when we busted the three of 'em with all the quarters, your boy Fred tried to take all the blame."

"Really . . ."

"Oh, yeah. Stuck together like dried cow shit. Really tight."

It was time I was up, anyway. And to good news, to boot. I went downstairs very gingerly, and enjoyed a great cup of coffee while leaning gently against the counter, looking for some old ibuprophen I'd acquired after a root canal. Found it. Twelve left, of 800 mg. Cool. I didn't think I could afford to miss work today. Of all days. So, prescribing for myself, I figured, "What the hell, take it with coffee."

Standing at the coffeepot, pouring my second cup, I looked at the outdoor thermometer. Twenty-six degrees. Same as the temperature inside a refrigerator. The warming trend had arrived. It was almost thirty degrees warmer than yesterday.

The phone rang again. I assumed it was going to be the sheriff's office. "Yeah!"

"Boy, you're nasty in the morning." Lamar, calling from the scene of the snowmobile incident from last night. He was with the lab crew.

"Sorry, thought it was the S.O."

I told him about Phil's call. Then he told me something.

"Did you ever look in Borglan's refrigerator that day?" He was deadly serious.

"I don't think so . . . but I think I might have seen a bit inside it when Clete was making his coffee . . . he got the coffee can out of the refrigerator."

"That's when I saw it, too. Notice anything unusual about the contents? Think, now. Think hard."

I did my best. "Nothing unusual . . . no more bodies . . . no, boss, I can't say that I did. Just a normal inside of a refrigerator. Why?"

"It was normal, all right," he said. "I remembered this last night . . . it was full of food."

"So . . . ?" I asked, even as it came to me.

"You don't leave your refrigerator stocked when you're planning to be gone for three months."

"Right. You're right. Son of a bitch, you're right!"

A minor problem, though. Cletus was now back in residence. Unless we had it documented during the crime scene examination, there was no way to prove it now.

"I already checked with the lab guys," he said. "They looked in there, just a cursory inspection. No documentation of contents, although Jake thinks he remembers seeing food."

Jake was a lab tech. He'd had no reason to inventory the refrigerator, and he'd sure as hell been busy with enough other stuff that night.

"Damn. But I can understand it. I should have thought of that . . ."

"Ain't you supposed to be workin' today?" Gruffly.

"Can't come to work if I'm standing here talkin' on the phone." Take that, boss. It did make me wonder when he slept, though.

I figured I'd go out of uniform, as much to remove the 15 lbs. of gun belt and gear as anything else. I might not be feeling much pain, but I sure didn't want to aggravate my back. As I got dressed, I went over things in my head. Not too bad, for a short day. Somebody had been staying at Borglan's. No doubt. Again, no conclusive proof, but we were on the right track. On the upside, we did have testimonial evidence that the Colson brothers had, in fact, impersonated undercover officers on a previous occasion. Thanks to Phil. I was in good spirits when I hit the office. I think it was mostly the ibuprophen.

Art's car was in the parking lot, along with a blue Ford sedan that had FBI written all over it. George, I was willing to bet.

I walked carefully up the steps, but the medicine was beginning to kick in, and I hardly felt a twinge. Cool. Now, if I could just stay awake . . .

Art knew George, as did most law enforcement personnel in our area of the state. I wasn't sure how well, but he certainly knew who he was. Both of them were sitting in the main office, and both of them appeared to be waiting for me.

"Hi," I said.

"You talk to Lamar this morning?" blurted Art.

"Yep."

"About the refrigerator?"

"Yep. I think he's right. I remember that, now, too, I think."
I was being oblique because I didn't know if Art had told George
anything, and since Art had raised "need to know" to an almost
mystical level in his own head, I didn't want to aggravate him unnecessarily.

"I don't think it proves a lot," he said. "No connection with
anything."

"Don't be so sure," I said. I looked at George. "Have you told
him . . ."

"No," said George.

I looked around to make sure we were alone, and then closed
the door. Dramatic, but fun. "We arrested an FBI agent near the
murder scene last night," I said.

"Oh, bullshit," said Art. "Get serious."

"It's true, they did," said George.

Art went blank-faced. He was one of those cops for whom all
status resided in the kind of badge you carried. Credential envy,
sort of.

"And," I said, savoring the moment, "after we got him to the
office, we busted another one who was sneaking around behind
the jail . . ."

"Correct," said George.

I thought Art was going to . . . well, swoon seemed pretty
close. His face got noticeably redder, and he said, "You gotta be
shittin' me."

We filled him in on the activities of the previous night. I did
most of the talking, and even George was aghast at the thought
that we had what I referred to as "the Hernandez bust" on video-
tape.

I did only fact. No conclusions. I wanted to see what everybody else would think. When I was done, George simply said, "I
keep telling these guys that you aren't a bunch of hicks. I keep
telling all of them . . ."

Art, who seemed to have recovered pretty quickly, just shook his head. "So, what does all this mean?" he asked George.

"Ask Carl," said George.

Art just looked at me.

"It means that our federal brothers-in-law have been watching the Borglan place, or at least that general area. Night and day. I'd guess for a while, at least. I'd suspect," I added, "that they know more about the murder of the Colsons than we do . . ." I paused. "But we're getting closer."

I told about my phone conversation with Phil. About the Colsons posing as undercover cops.

"That's nice," interjected Art, "but it's just a theory. That's all, and not a strong one. No evidence at the scene."

"No," I said. "The people who killed the Colsons suspected they were being watched. Long before those two poor bastards wandered in. They caught the Colsons red-handed, and the boys did what had worked before. They lied about being undercover cops." Nobody said anything.

"The problem was, they lied to some people who believed them. And who killed them because of it."

Art looked at George. "Well?"

George nodded. "Pretty close," he said.

Art and I both waited. George, who had taken a sip of coffee, looked up. ". . . what?"

"You can't just say that and stop," said Art. "Are you confirming, or just guessing, or what?"

George put his cup down. "Confirmation will come shortly. There's another agent en route who will provide more information. I was just, well, letting you know that you were on the right track."

"Do you know who the people in the house were?" I asked. "That much . . ."

George thought for a few moments. "No, I can't say. I can't give you that." He looked at each of us. "I'm really sorry, guys. I can't."

Fourteen

We'd just have to wait.

Our secretary, Judy, came in and handed me a package. Developed crime scene photos, those I'd had her take to be developed. As cheaply as possible, I remembered.

"Got a really great deal on these," she said, "three sets for the price of one."

"Hey, great! Thanks . . . they're quick for a change, too!"

I put the pack on my desk, and started to open the photos.

"My shots of the crime scene at the Borglan place," I said. "Let's see what we can find here . . ."

Art held out his hand for a set, and George scooted his chair closer to the desk.

I looked in the envelope, and just cracked up. Packed neatly inside were three sets of crime scene photos, all right. One set was a normal 4 x 6 inch series of color prints. Nice. The other two sets were about 2 x 3 inches . . . wallet size.

"You want . . . a . . . big set, or . . . a set you . . . can . . . carry with you?" I just roared.

"What?" asked Art. "What?"

"Here," I gasped out, handing him a set of the wallet-sized prints. "We got a hell of a deal, though . . ."

George looked over, and started to chuckle. "Oh, my God . . ."

There was absolutely no harm done, all we had to do was re-submit the negatives. But I kept seeing myself in court, holding up a photo wallet, and letting a hundred prints dangle in their linked transparent holders . . .

We went over the photos, one at a time. It was almost easier, in a way. I used the one set of larger prints, and each of the other two had a set of wallet size. They just picked out the ones they wanted to see . . .

Privately, I spent a lot of time on the group of photos I'd taken as I turned around and shot into the distance when I thought I was being watched. To see if there was anything there. Nothing I could pick up on. Outside the area that was fairly well lit, it had been so dark that the shutter had stayed open too long that there was virtually nothing but shake lines in shades of dark gray to black. Except one. South of the farm, there was a bumpy white streak.

I looked at it more closely.

"I see you ruined some shots, there," said Art. "Flash not go off?"

"Maybe . . ." I do some amateur astronomy, and one of the first things you do with your camera is just point it straight up, open the shutter, and let the stars make curved streaks in the time exposure. Like those "cars on the freeway" shots taken at night. That's what this was. Only it wasn't a straight, or even a curved line. It looked more like the path of a small firefly. One that was drunk.

"What's this look like to you?" I asked, pushing it toward Art and George.

"Flaw in the film," said Art, turning back to the other photos.

"Yard light," said George. "You have a lot of shake here, but I'd say it was a yard light off in the distance."

"Oh." I placed the print back in the stack, and continued looking at the others. Yard light. I hadn't noticed any yard light, but it sure looked like that's what it was. That meant there could be a farm yard with a view of the machine shed. I shuf-fled back through the pack of photos. Yep. Judging from the thickness of the streak, it was quite a way off. But that's what it looked like.

I noticed George kept looking at his watch. "When are the other agents coming up?" I asked.

"Well, hopefully before lunch. They did have a lot to do, though," he said. "They may only send one, anyway."

George and I sat in silence for a few moments. I looked out my window, and watched Delbert Jacobs unloading buckets full of sand for his driveway. He was one of the jail "neighbors," and a pretty decent fellow. He would dip the bucket over the rear of his pickup, which was apparently filled with sand, and carry the bucket to his sand pile, which was hidden from my view by a small pine tree. I watched him make two trips with the bucket, when it came to me. Back and forth went Delbert. And, as he stooped to pick up another load, it occurred to me that, if you were to film him, and freeze frame several shots, it would be very difficult to tell if he were moving the buckets of sand to his house, or from his house. A frozen point of time wouldn't necessarily yield much useful information at all. Just knowing his location at a precise moment wouldn't be enough. Movements. You had to watch his movements.

"Hey, George, how do we know Cletus was coming back from Florida the day I discovered the bodies?"

"Your office, wasn't it Lamar or Sally, were told it was Florida . . . Wasn't that it?"

"No, not that part. Not how we were told . . . How do we know he was really in Florida? I mean, we were told he'd be at the farm shortly, and he was. That he was coming from 'Florida,' and that was all. But, how do we know he was really *in Florida*? How do we know he wasn't back at his house several days before the killings? How do we know he wasn't the killer, especially when he's the first son of a bitch who says there are two dead 'cops'?"

"Damn."

"We've been assuming he was telling us the truth." I reached for the phone. "He could be a prime suspect. Well, duh . . ."

I picked up the phone and dialed the intercom. "Lamar, you get a second, you want to come back here . . ."

Our first move was to set the machinery in motion to check with the airlines to see if Clete had ever, actually, flown in the last few weeks. He could have used a private plane. He may never have gone to Florida at all. It was the first place to start.

George initiated a discreet inquiry into Freeman Liberty Enterprises, Inc., Cletus's corporation. It was probably an incorporation for tax advantage for his farming operation, but you never know. Regardless, it had to be registered with the Secretary of State of Iowa.

I checked with the county recorder's office, for any documents on file for FLE, as we began to call it. Same with the county assessor's office. He might own another farm, where he had access, that we knew nothing about.

I called Sally, and had her work on a list of members of the snowmobile club her sister, brother-in-law, and Cletus had belonged to. I wanted to talk to them about him ever running his sled with NVGs. Just a chance.

I love the feeling you get when you're working a lead. Much better than sitting on your butt waiting for the FBI to show up and tell you that everything they have is "need to know."

Just then, Art stuck his head in the door. "Just telling you, I gotta get back to Cedar Falls. Something's come up. I'll try to get back tomorrow."

I believe both George and I understood that Art was ducking out. I thought it likely that he had just told his office about our arresting two FBI agents, and that they had, wisely, told him to come in for a conference.

"I understand," said George. After all, Art and the DCI hadn't been involved with the two agents last night.

"I understand they found a cartridge case . . . the lab people?" I had to ask.

"Oh, yeah . . . Jake call? He has all the information. I don't know that it means much." Attaboy, Art. Screw up, so minimize it.

"We'll see what we can to with it," I said. "Have a good trip."

That's one thing about Art. You'll let him go, even if you have a bone you can pick with him. Just so long as he goes.

George and I continued in pursuit of Cletus Borglan, killer. Well, for about another five minutes, until Lamar got to my office.

"Boss, have we got something for you!"

"Fine, fine." He sat painfully in a chair. The gunshot trauma to his lower leg was bothering him again. He held up his hand, seeing that I was about to launch into something. "Just let me tell you this before I forget, and then you can talk to me all day . . ."

"Sure. Sure, no problem." I was feeling generous, having just solved the case.

"You remember my wife's sister, Arlene?" He waited for my nod. "Well, she lives in this little town in Florida, that is the same town where Cletus and Inez Borglan go in the winter." He pulled a small piece of paper from his breast pocket, and held it at nearly arm's length. "Same place where the Bensons, the Hazletts, the Rhombergs, and the Hefels have retired to . . ."

I knew all four couples. Two teaching families, one insurance man, and a retired farmer. Come on, Lamar, I thought. I'm gonna bust if I don't tell my news.

"Wife says they want to change the name of the little town to 'New Iowa' because of all the Iowans there." He smiled at the thought. "Anyway," he said, folding the paper and placing it back in his breast pocket, buttoning the pocket, and patting it down, "Arlene says that she was talking to Cletus and Inez down there, the night before Cletus left to come back up here, and they was pretty excited about something."

Uh-oh. "Down there the day before the killings?"

"Yeah. They were playing bridge, or something, over at Cletus and Inez's cabin. He got a phone call about eleven that night, that really shook him."

"In Florida?"

"Yeah, in Florida. You got somethin' in your ears?"

"Oh, no, I guess not. We were thinking that he might have come back before we thought he did. That's all." Damn. Damn, damn, damn.

"Oh," he said, absently. "Doesn't look like it."

"Sure doesn't," said George.

"Anyway," continued Lamar, "what Arlene says is that he got this phone call, and he just sort of went white. Real worried. Took the phone to the porch, but she heard him say, 'How could they find out?' maybe two-three times. She thinks," he said, confidentially, "that Cletus is up to some illegal financial stuff." He grinned. "Anyway, old Cletus kept lookin' at Inez, like there was something she should know. Finally, they went into the kitchen together to get the coffee and some crumbly stuff . . . what do they call that stuff?"

"I don't know . . ." I said. "Crackers?"

"No, that ain't it . . ."

"Oh, yeah, that crumbly cake stuff . . . yeah, I know . . ."

"Will you two," interjected George, "stop it!"

Lamar chuckled. "Anyway, Arlene heard him trying to whisper to Inez in the kitchen, and then heard her say, 'Oh, my God!' and then when they came out, it looked like she's seen a ghost."

I could just imagine Cletus whispering.

"Must have been pretty bad business news," I said. "The market crash, and we didn't hear?"

"Well, you know, that's the funny part," said Lamar. "I mean, you know Cletus. He ain't quiet about nothin' that bothers him. Hell, he ain't quiet about nothin' at all. But Arlene says that they never mentioned it the rest of the evening, and he left the next day. Arlene says that she talks to Inez the next day, and Inez ain't saying nothing about it."

"Hmm." I tried to be noncommittal.

" 'Hmm' is right," said Lamar. "I was thinking that it's too bad that there ain't some way to find out who called him."

"You got that right," I said. I was disappointed that Cletus was in Florida at the crucial time. Well, disappointed was a bit mild, frankly. The excitement was only a memory. Shit.

" 'Cause," said Lamar, "I got kinda curious, and I called Jack Reed."

Jack Reed was president of one of the local banks. Curious, indeed.

"I said, 'Jack, I got this attorney bugging me 'bout having to repossess some stuff from Cletus Borglan, due to some business failure . . .' " He smiled. "Jack says, 'No way.' Tells me that Cletus is in no way in any financial trouble. So I says, 'Anything happen that might have hit him on the stock market, or the futures market?' And Jack said 'No,' that everything was fine." He turned to George. "Jack's Cletus's banker."

"Oh."

That was one of the main differences between the new model FBI agent and the old model sheriff. The agent would spend eighteen hours getting information necessary to get an application together to ask the court for permission to dig into somebody's financial records. The sheriff would just go to the banker and ask.

"So, I figure that, since there ain't no financial information of a bad nature, there ain't no business problems up here that anybody'd get too excited about. So, I think, if it ain't financial, what is it?"

"Yeah."

"It's almost got to be a death in the family, like. But nobody in the family died."

"Yeah." I knew where he was going. I loved it.

"But, I got to thinkin' that maybe somebody 'in the family' was *involved* in a death. Or two . . ." Lamar grinned. "I think our man Cletus was told about the dead brothers a long time before we tried to fill him in."

"I think you're right," I said. Yea, boss.

"So I went one step further, and I got a tape here of the telephone conversation Sally had with Inez Borglan on the day the bodies was discovered. When she called to see if Cletus could come up, and he was already on his way?"

All calls made from dispatch are taped. Without exception.

He opened his other shirt pocket with a Velcro rip, and pulled out his minirecorder. He carefully turned the volume up, and placed it on my desk. George moved in a bit closer.

"I got it right at the part we want," he said. "You can hear the rest later." With that, he pressed "play."

There was some hiss in the tape, and voices coming over Sally's radio console were an irritation, but the conversation itself was clear enough.

SALLY: Inez, this is the Nation County Sheriff's Department. Could I speak with Cletus, please?

INEZ: Oh . . . oh . . . God . . .

SALLY: It's all right, Inez. Really. Could I just speak to Cletus?

INEZ: He's on his way. He left this morning, and he's on his way.

SALLY: He's coming here? Back to Nation County?

INEZ: I just knew it.

SALLY: Inez, how can I contact Cletus? Where's he flying in to? Cedar Rapids?

INEZ: He'll go right to the farm. You know.

SALLY: He's going to the farm?

INEZ: Harvey will get him to the farm.

SALLY: Harvey?

INEZ: Our hired man. Harvey will get Clete in Cedar Rapids. He's going right to the farm. I'm sorry. So sorry.

SALLY: That's all right, Inez. We can contact him. What time does Cletus get to Cedar Rapids?

INEZ: He left about two hours ago. I'm so sorry.

SALLY: Do you have a flight number?

Lamar stopped the tape. "That don't sound like much," he said. "But if you think about it, why the hell is she so sorry? What is it that she knew was going to happen?" He looked at us. "She sound really stressed to you?"

"Sure does," I said. And she had.

"Very," said George.

"Now nothin' against females, or anything," prefaced Lamar,

"but they do worry a lot, and it ain't that unlikely for a female to say she knew something was gonna happen beforehand, no matter what it is. Right?"

Lamar's idea of "politically correct" was to use old high school biology terms, like male and female.

"I thought that was just my mother," said George.

"When a male subject says he's 'so sorry,' he means he's sorry for himself, like when he gets caught. But," said Lamar, "when a female subject says she's 'so sorry,' she ain't sorry for herself, she's sorry for you. Or about something that happened to you."

"Okay," I said.

"I think," said Lamar, conclusively, "that somebody called Cletus and said, 'I just killed two guys at your house', and it was somebody that Inez knew was there, too." He hurried on. "And I think that whoever it was said that he'd shot a couple of cops. Like you say, Carl. But that's why Inez is so sorry. She's apologizing to the whole department for the cops being killed. Only she don't know she's doin' it."

He was right. Absolutely. No doubt in my mind. Again.

"Totality of the circumstance," said George. "Now, all we need is evidence . . ."

"I been thinking about that, too," said Lamar. "I think there's a chance that whoever called Cletus in Florida was calling from the murder scene. Cletus's house." He shifted in his chair, and winced. He'd put weight on that ankle. "So I was thinking that if somebody was to go to a judge, and just lay the whole thing out, and make a couple of really good points, maybe we could get a court order for Cletus's telephone records. Like, maybe a long-distance call made to him, from his place in Iowa to his place in Florida." He shifted back, more carefully. "So what do you two think?"

"Explain to the judge that this is a critical case . . ." murmured George, to himself as much as us.

What it boiled down to was this; a judge would take into consideration the bare evidence, but would listen to more persuasive arguments. First, we would get a bit of leeway, because it was such a serious crime. Then, it would be apparent that this evidence would go a long way to either get us on the track, or to eliminate Cletus completely. Most persuasively, though, I thought was the fact that the order to permit examination of the phone bill was not particularly intrusive. We wouldn't have to go on the Borglan property to get it, and we wouldn't disrupt the Borglan household in any way. As a plus, we could be pretty restrictive with dates, as well. We weren't going fishing, here. We could stipulate a three-day span, from Friday through Sunday. No more.

I thought we had a good chance. So did George. Lamar just sat there looking very pleased with himself.

As we were typing out the application, I thought about Cletus. He'd really had a busy day. He'd gone from innocent irritant, to suspected murderer, back to innocent, to accessory after the fact. By rights, he should have been breathing hard.

"So, what did you have to tell me?" asked Lamar

"Uh . . . nothing," I said.

Fifteen

The Febbies were still a no-show, so after we broke for lunch—a couple of fat-free hotdogs for me—we moved on with the Cletus lead.

Judge Oberfeld was polite, and you could tell he was obviously pleased about George of the Bureau being with us, but suggested we simply approach the county attorney and have a subpoena issued. We explained about the conflict of interest, and that there had yet to be a special prosecutor appointed, and that Davies was in court in Pottawattamie County and not available.

Mike, who was just coming on duty, took the resulting order, and headed to the phone company records office in Manchester.

George and I went back to my office. I got busy filling out my account of John's and my flying trip into the snowbank, in hot pursuit of a snowmobile. It ran to four pages, in which I took responsibility for authorizing the chase sans headlights. Not nearly as noble as it sounds, really, because department policy requires that the driver, regardless of authorization, operate the vehicle in a safe manner. Best I could do was share responsibility.

I had just finished the report, and signed it, when George said, "They're here."

I went to the window, and looked out over the parking lot. A dark blue Ford sedan was parked beside George's dark blue Ford sedan. Twins. I opened my mouth to make some sarcastic remark to him, when I recognized who was getting out of the second car.

"Oh, shit" was all I said. "Goddamn it, George. You could have told us in advance . . ."

Special Agent in Charge Volont, Federal Bureau of Investigation, stuck out his hand. "Deputy Houseman, how've you been?"

"Fine." We shook hands. "Yourself?"

"Except for the fact that some of the people assigned to me are idiots," he said, deadpan, "fine, thanks." He glanced around. "Sorry I'm late. Sheriff Ridgeway close?"

"Right here," said Lamar, emerging from his office. "You're lookin' healthy."

They shook hands, and Volont took notice of Lamar's limp. "Any improvement?" he asked, with a hint of warmth in his voice.

"Still bothers me some," said Lamar. "You want to talk in my office?"

As I followed Volont and Lamar into the doorway marked SHERIFF, I glanced at George. He looked a little apologetic. He should. Volont was the FBI equivalent of Machiavelli. We'd worked together before. Not exactly my kind of guy. If those two agents, Brandenburg and Hernandez, had been working for him, we were in deeper that I had thought. Much deeper. Volont was in charge of counterterrorist operations in a large chunk of the United States, and he'd worked with us once before. He was honest, fair, and very unlikely to share any useful intelligence with anybody in a rural Sheriff's Department.

I managed to keep any expression of joy off my face as we all sat down. The twinge in my back had nothing to do with it.

It's not often you get to watch a real expert at work. Volont was, among all the other things I thought he was, an expert in handling people.

He began by apologizing for any inconvenience his subordinate agents may have caused. He expressed concern about the snowmobile accident, and said that the Feds would gladly pay for any damage to our car. He further expressed concern for the behavior of Agent Brandenburg for kicking me, and for Agent Hernandez being so inept as to creep about the outside of the jail.

At that point, the con was in.

He then asked how we had come upon Brandenburg in the first place. Between Lamar and myself, we managed to tell the basic details of the encounter with the agents. We also gave a basic description of the two homicides, as background.

"I feel an apology is in order, for not touching base with your department, Sheriff, before we started the spot surveillance. I hope you understand, we have some problems with obtaining permission to divulge certain . . . aspects . . . of our work."

Smooth.

Lamar accepted that. No real choice. "But," he added, "I want to know why they were out there."

It was very interesting. Volont had just told us that he was sorry, but wasn't able to tell us the truth. Since nothing had been said to indicate that the "problems . . . divulging" had changed in any way, he had already warned us. Obliquely, but nonetheless, warned. So, now, he proceeded to tell us . . . well, not exactly the truth.

"We've had information," he said, "concerning a possible meeting in this area. Not specifically at the farm where the two killings took place. We were watching, to see who attended." He gave one of his familiar little tight-lipped smiles. "This is all concerning another matter, of course. One that has nothing to do with the area being observed." He shrugged, regretfully. "I'm sorry, but my agents tell me that you really can't see much of the Borglan place from their position." He paused. "So, we don't have any surveillance data we can share with you. I wish we did."

"Me too," said Lamar.

At this point, he'd really said he was sorry it had happened, he wasn't able to tell us the truth, he'd proceeded to tell us something other than the truth, and had just reassured us that it was all better. Very smooth. If I hadn't known him from before, he would have been a comfort. I was beginning to understand my feeling of being watched at Borglan's, though.

I glanced at George, wondering if he was buying this. I couldn't tell from his expression.

Lamar just said, "Maybe you should tell him some more, Carl."

I did. I told him that the Colson brothers had been known to impersonate undercover officers on previous, documented occasions.

"I see," he said. Noncommittal, but interested.

I told him that we had incontrovertible evidence that a person or persons unknown had called the Borglans at their Florida home on the night of the double murder. That, upon receiving that call, Cletus Borglan had left for Iowa the following morning. That he had appeared very concerned upon receipt of the call. That, upon arriving at his farm, he had indicated that he believed that two officers had been shot there, not two burglars.

I stopped.

Volont didn't bat an eye, but I swear I could almost hear relays popping in his head.

"Where," he asked, quietly, "did the call to the Borglans' Florida home originate?"

"Just a second," said Lamar. He picked up his phone. "Where's Mike? No shit? Bring it in, will you?" He looked at Volont. "Tell you in a few seconds," he said. He addressed me. "Mike got here a few minutes ago, and dropped off our letter . . ."

There was a knock on the door, and Judy stuck her head in, and held out an envelope. "Mike dropped this off a few minutes ago," she said. "I didn't want to bother you . . ."

Being closest to the door, I reached up and took the envelope from her. It was sealed, but it had the phone company logo on it. "That's okay, Mike should have said something . . ."

"Thanks, Judy," said Lamar. After the door had closed, he said, "Go ahead, Carl."

I carefully opened the envelope and removed the single sheet of paper. It was Cletus Borglan's telephone records, as requested by our court order. And there it was.

LONG DISTANCE
1. 1–11 ORLANDO FL 407-555-3344 1047 P.M. 8.5 DDD
NGT 2.87

One call. 10:47 P.M. Central time. Make it 11:47 Florida time. Eight and a half minutes. Direct Distance Dial. Nighttime rates applied. Two dollars and eighty-seven cents. That was it. One single call. But that was plenty.

"Just a sec," I said, reaching for the phone. Sally answered at dispatch. "Sally," I said, as evenly as I could, "what's the Florida number that the Borglans left for us . . . for contacting them if anything was wrong while they were on vacation?"

She sounded a bit stressed. "You need that right away?"

"Faster than that," I said. I could hear her muttering something to herself as I held my hand over the phone. "Just a second . . . I think we might have it . . ."

"Carl, that number is 407–555–3344. Orlando, Florida."

"Yee hah!" I startled her, but I just couldn't help myself. "I'll be damned."

"You guys must have lots of fun back there," said Sally. "Need anything else?"

"No, sorry about the yelling, just good news. Thanks!" I put down the phone.

"So?" said Lamar.

"So. So, the telephone company record here," and I held up the sheet of paper, "tells me that a call was placed from Borglan's residence here in Nation County . . . the murder scene . . . at about ten forty-seven our time . . . to a number in Orlando, Florida. The same number that the Borglans left with us on their residence check form. And," I added, "with the time difference, the call would have been received in Florida at about a quarter to midnight." I looked at Lamar. "Just when your source said it was." I was grinning all over myself.

"Well, bingo," said Lamar. "Just like we thought. Looks like our boy's been holdin' out on us. He's gotta know who it was that he talked to . . ."

" 'Source'?" asked Volont.

I looked at Lamar, and he nodded. "We have a source who was with Cletus Borglan when he received the call from Iowa," I said. Being as matter-of-fact as I could.

It was time to bring Cletus in. I said I wanted an arrest warrant.

"Let me contact Davies." For Volont's benefit, I added, "Iowa Attorney General's office. He's got this case." I spoke toward Lamar. "You can damned well bet Cletus Borglan knows where he is. And that phone bill should be enough to charge Cletus as an accessory in a double homicide. Let's just see how far his loyalty to these murderers extends."

"Even so," said Volont, "there will be arms, and people to use them, around him, too. Perhaps even the killers themselves. You'll may well need a TAC team, either way. It would be best to wait . . ."

I smiled. "Nope. I don't think so. I just have to have a warrant for his arrest . . ."

You have to know who you're dealing with. It always comes down to that. I got Davies on the phone, and did just exactly what he told me to do. I sat down, typed a complaint and affidavit against Cletus Borglan, affirming in part that he "received a confirmatory call regarding the double murder, from the murderer, at the murder scene, while at his residence in Florida. This is confirmed both by confidential testimonial evidence sworn to the court, and a telephone company record of that call, placed on the night of . . ." The "testimonial" part was Lamar's sister's account. He called her, and told her to write it out, get herself to the Orlando PD, swear to it, and have them Fax it to us. We teletyped them to the same effect, and referred to it as an FBI case. Volont made a telephone call to FBI, Orlando. Reluctantly, I think. But it was for them to assist in whatever way they could.

"You're going to have to move very, very fast, here," he said.

"Not just on this Borglan. But very fast on the suspects afterward, as well . . . They'll know just about as soon as Borglan's been arrested."

"We'll move fast," I said, "but we're going to have to find out just who the suspects are, and that's going to depend on Borglan."

The fax copy of Lamar's sister's statement was in our possession before I got my complaint and affidavit typed out. She was also remaining at Orlando PD until further notice, just in case the judge wanted to have telephone contact with her. The FBI, as it transpired, had given her a ride. Volont was a heavy dude, no doubt about it.

George went with me to the judge.

By 1626, I was slipping and crunching in my car down Cletus Borglan's lane. George was with me, more as encouragement than anything else. I had outlined my plan of attack, and Volont had dragged his heels. Lamar said I could pull it off.

Volont had said, "You're asking for big trouble."

Lamar had said, "Smaller than Waco." Not fair, really. But effective. I got to go.

I PARKED MY CAR at the edge of the little rise in Borglan's yard, where we'd descended to the shed to retrieve the bodies, a good hundred feet from Borglan's front door. I felt that ought to be enough. Ought to be.

I got out of the car. "Come on, George." There were two cars and two pickup trucks parked in Borglan's yard, all at the other end of the house, near the fancy garage.

The front door of the house opened, and I purposely opened the back door of my car, and reached for my camera bag. I kept an eye on the figures that emerged from the house through the back window. Sure as hell, Cletus detached himself, and came stomping over toward us, making loud noises. Two others followed, but hung back just a bit. Confrontation with cops wasn't something relatively normal people undertook lightly. Unless you were Cletus Borglan, and had yelled at cops for a long time.

I backed out of the car, and made a show of opening my camera bag. "You understand him yet, George?"

"I think it's something like 'What the hell are you doing?' or something like that."

"Cool." I rummaged in the camera bag. I was sort of worried about it, too, as it was my wife's camera. Sue had let me borrow it about ten years before. I just never got around to getting it back to her, and it had been acting up ever since the night of the Colson brothers discovery. I would have returned it to Sue if the department had bought me one, but people like Cletus had always objected to expenditures.

"Get off my property!" Cletus. Beautiful.

"What?" I hollered back, waiving, and watching him stomp closer. He was so determined he was causing a fine spray of whitish mud to splatter around his ankles as he came toward us. I looked back into my bag.

"GET THE HELL OFF MY PROPERTY! YOU BETTER HAVE A WARRANT!"

I looked up. Son of a bitch was fast. He was already at the back of my car.

"Hi, Cletus!" I grinned.

"EITHER SHOW ME A WARRANT, OR GET OFF MY PROPERTY!"

I checked the other two. They were a good fifty feet away, but coming on. Coming in for the fun, I thought.

By that time, Cletus had come around my car, and grabbed me by my shoulder. "YOU HEAR ME?"

I just stepped back, held out a copy of the arrest warrant, and handed it to him. As his eyes dropped to read it, I pulled my handgun out, and stuck it in his face.

"You're under arrest for murder," I said. "Get in the car."

"What?" He was too startled to even be particularly loud. He just stared at the gun barrel three inches from his nose.

George had stepped in behind him, and Cletus was hand-cuffed in two seconds flat.

"Watch your head," I said, as we stuffed him into the car, and shut the door.

"What the FUCK is going on here?" Cletus's support group was about twenty feet off the rear bumper.

I kept my gun in my hand, but pointed downward. "Cletus is under arrest for murder," I said. They both stepped forward. "Interference with this arrest permits me to use deadly force," I said, perfectly evenly. It was hard to say it that way. I was nearly laughing. "Think twice, gentlemen."

They were absolutely rooted to the spot. Stunned. These weren't hard-core professionals, obviously.

I got in the car, looked over at George, grinned, shut the door, and was backing up before the two men in the drive could even move. *Splash.* Not intended, but funny as hell.

As we hit the end of the drive, I let out a loud "YES!" and hit the gas.

"You can't do this," said Cletus. He didn't sound too convinced.

"You're under arrest for murder, Cletus," I said. "You might want to remember that you do have a right to remain silent . . ."

Cletus had made the big mistake. He was predictable. Altogether too predictable.

I looked over at George. "What'd I tell you?" He just grinned. I picked up the mike. "Comm, Three is ten-seventy-six, one ten-ninety-five."

In other words, we were en route, and we had one prisoner in custody.

"Ten-four, Three." She sounded relieved.

"Three, One?" That was Lamar.

"Meet you back at the office." He sounded pleased.

"Ten-four." Nonchalant. You had to be.

Sixteen

We got back to the office, and I was just getting my
proud little ducks in a row to begin booking Cletus into the jail, when Lamar approached me.

"Mike can start that," he said. He looked
very grim. "You come back here with us."

I thought it was sort of strange, but I went back with him into
his office. George and Volont were there. They didn't look too
happy, either.

"Sit down," said Lamar. "Special Agent Volont has something to tell you."

I didn't like the sound of that.

"First," said Volont, "you have to know two things. One, I'm
telling you this because events have, well, overtaken us here.
Two, the two brothers were killed by a single individual, acting
alone." He looked at me, evenly.

"Your surveillance team did witness the murders," I said.
Hell, that wasn't such bad news. Not at all.

"No." He sighed. "No, they managed to miss that, with the
same skill they demonstrated when you caught them."

He made a little pyramid with his extended fingers. "They
were killed by a man I've been tracking for years. You know him
as Gabriel."

"You're kidding me . . ." All I could think of to say.

"No."

Jesus. In the first place, it had just dawned on me that Gabriel, who was a professional in every sense, and was not only capable of killing without remorse, but who was also very able as well, could very easily have been at Borglan's residence as we were arresting Cletus.

"You might have said something a little sooner," I said. I looked over at George. "Or did you know?"

"No."

"That," I said, "violates just about every 'need to know' guideline in the book." It did, too. You were never supposed to expose an officer to danger in the name of confidentiality. Never.

"He isn't there," said Volont. Just a flat statement. "I'm just telling you this because you'll probably find it out from Cletus." He looked at me. "You do intend to interview him, don't you?"

"So where the hell is he?" I thought it was an appropriate question. "Gabriel, I mean. We'll need to find him as soon as we get a warrant for his arrest."

Volont held up his hand. "Just a moment. The Bureau has a source fairly close to our Mr. Nieuhauser," he said. "I receive the reports on a regular basis. Gabriel's movements and intentions are usually known to us in near real time." He sounded pleased. "We have to wait until Gabriel is at a location that we could discover by other means, before we can move on him. Otherwise, we reveal the informant, and place them at risk."

"That the purpose of your surveillance team, then?"

"One of them, yes. So we can reveal them at the proper time, with their data, and show that they were the ones who tracked Gabriel. Saving the life of the informant is a high priority." He made a tight little smile. "The irony is, now we can use you to confirm the presence of the team, now that you've . . . uhmmm . . . apprehended them, as it were."

I knew Volont just well enough to think that he would tell his superiors that he'd planned for the surveillance team to get busted by us. He was adept at that sort of thing.

"Our Mr. Nieuhauser, or Gabriel, has much unfinished business in this county. He'll undoubtedly be back, and we think fairly soon."

Volont said that he'd known Gabriel had been in Nation County since around Christmastime. He hadn't been precisely sure where, but he was now certain it had been the Borglan residence, at least part of the time.

No shit.

"I want that son of a bitch busted as soon as he sets foot in my county," said Lamar. "None of this pussy-footin' around like last time."

"Ah." Volont actually chuckled. "Understood. This time, we won't let him blow up Maitland."

"That's right." Lamar glared at Volont. "This time we just got two people killed . . . so far."

"So," said Volont, "please tell me more about the murders . . ."

I did. I even repeated some detail. Drive it home. When I got to the part about the Colson brothers very likely attempting to convince their killer that they were undercover cops, he nodded. "Really not the man to use that story on," he said.

I explained about the 5.45 mm PSM shell casing. He nodded again. No surprise to him. Well, now that I knew who the perp was, it wasn't a surprise to me, either. During the last incident with Gabriel, we'd found that he had been assigned to Europe a lot of the time he was in the Army.

I went throught the autopsy findings, and the best guess as to the manner of the death. He spoke.

"What he likely did was to shoot the first one as soon as the undercover cop story was brought up," he said, slowly. "The other one was probably on his knees, pleading his case by denying he was a cop. He was either shot because Gabriel had to conceal the death of the first, or because Gabriel was still convinced both were officers. From what you say, it seems he still thinks they were officers of some sort."

I continued with the part about Davies and I interviewing the hired man, our helicopter flight over the area, and ended with the snowmobile chase.

"So, to keep the ball bouncing," I said, "let me ask you a question."

"Go ahead."

"Just what is Gabriel's 'business' in Nation County?"

"Money," he said. "My sources tell me he needs financial support for his activities."

"He's here on a fund-raiser?" I asked.

"Of a sort. Not the fifty dollars for a plate of chicken type, though. He apparently intends to rob several banks in the area. Simultaneously."

Suddenly, it was one of those conversations where two threads spring up at once. While I said, "Several?" George said, "Simultaneously." And Lamar said, "Take him out now."

Lamar won for two reasons. He was proposing a course of action, and it just took him longer to get it out, so we all heard his last two words.

"You mean on the murder charges?" I said.

"You're goddamn right."

"Are they good enough?" asked George.

"You're goddamn right they are," said Lamar. "You know where he is, we go now!"

"Oh, I agree," said Volont. "We only have one problem."

We three just looked at him.

He looked at me. "Could I have some coffee, now?" Before I could answer, he continued. "The problem is, I'm not, well, precisely sure where he is. Are you?"

It all boiled down to the fact that, after the murders, Gabriel had split. Fast and clean, to parts unknown. Which was beginning to look like why the surveillance team stayed on location. To pick him up when he came back.

"This sounds a lot like 'The criminal always returns to the scene of the crime,' " I said. "Surely you have more than that to go on."

Volont smiled, shrugged, and simply said, "Of course." In that "If I tell you, I have to kill you" tone we all knew and loved.

We had to take him at his word. We sure as hell didn't know where Gabriel was.

"Another question . . . ?" I asked.

"Go ahead," said Volont.

"Just when were you intending to tell us about the bank robberies?"

"I would have given you twenty-four hours notice, naturally." He looked at Lamar. "You'd be right there."

For publicity. Not for any participation in the bust. That's not what he said, but it was what he meant.

"And now?" I asked.

"Now," he said, "you're in the loop. Right along with everybody else."

Sure.

As I headed back to the booking room, Lamar gave me the rest of the bad news. He'd decided to let DCI know we'd made an arrest in the Colson case. Well, that was all right, and I should have thought of it first. The unfortunate part was that Art was on his way back to Maitland. Just who I needed.

Booking Cletus had been a drawn-out process. His attorney had practically followed us in the office door. Well, actually, he'd followed us from Cletus's farm. He'd been one of the two people who had come out of the house with Cletus. He was a largish man, Ray Gunston out of Cedar Rapids. I'd heard of him. Well known, successful, and on TV a lot. Attorney to the rich and infamous, as we said.

Anyway, after forty-five minutes, Cletus was tucked away on a $250,000.00 bond. A tidy sum, but I wasn't at all certain he couldn't raise it in a hurry.

We'd also made the acquaintance of his other attorney. This guy named Horace Blitek had just walked in the office, and announced he was "at law, assisting in the representation" of Cletus Borglan.

"I wasn't aware that Mr. Borglan had any other . . ."

"I'm part of the defense team, Deputy. Mr. Borglan is a very important man. I received a call from his friends, and since I represent some of his corporate interests, he'll need me if he's compelled to raise a bond."

Sure. I notified Cletus, and he said that Blitek was, indeed, a member of the defense team. Gunston didn't seem too happy with the arrangement, though. I, for one, had never heard of Blitek. He hadn't given a card. I did notice, though, that his clothes looked a little worn, especially his shoes.

We'd notified Davies immediately, and he'd driven up when his court case had adjourned for the day. The first thing we did was brief him on Gabriel.

"Holy shit."

Well, he got that right. I'd just told him that Gabriel, whose real name was Jacob Henry Nieuhauser, was an ex-Army colonel, who had all sorts of Special Ops knowledge, and who was the man who had been so heavily involved in the case where Lamar had been shot, and one of our deputies killed. Not so damned long ago, either.

He laughed a little nervously. "You got extra security laid on for the building here?"

I explained how much good that had done us before. "Besides," I said, "it's not in the budget."

"We need a warrant for his arrest. Pronto."

Lamar took that one. He left for the judge's office. We were going to get a "confidential" arrest warrant, one that would be filed with the Clerk of Court herself, and sealed until it was executed. A nice thing to have, if we had to do anything unusual to effect the arrest.

DAVIES KNEW GUNSTON very well. Before we'd gotten to the kitchen, he'd said that the Cedar Rapids attorney was reasonable, but fast. "Tell you what," Davies had said. "He's gonna want to move this right along to a point. Only to a point. But he's assessing the case as he goes, trying to see if it works for him. Understand? He'll hustle your socks off, you let him, and he'll be persistent to the bitter end."

"Whether or not Borglan's guilty?" asked Lamar.

"No," said Davies. "Whether or not the case will generate enough billable hours to enable him to own Borglan's farms." He laughed. "For true. That'll be his first checkpoint. Shit, guilty, schmilty, he won't care. He gets paid either way."

I was surprised that Cletus was even talking to us, and said so.

Davies laughed. "Cheap discovery. He stops talking as soon as he knows what he wants to know. Well," and he chuckled, "whenever Gunston tells him to, anyway."

We didn't know a lot about Cletus, mainly because I didn't think the man had ever been arrested in his life. Not until now, anyway. Between Lamar's and my recollections, we were able to piece something together.

First of all, Cletus Borglan wasn't an extremist, not in the violent sense of the word. Neither was he a "Militia" man, or Nazi, or anything like that. Cletus was a fairly wealthy farmer, a truly successful farmer, who honestly didn't like the tax system. Well, who did? He also was very much pro-"family farm." Well, maybe it was more of an anticonglomerate farm stance, to tell the truth. Regardless, he really felt for the small farmer who was slowly going under. Cletus was a hard worker, who had inherited two farms, and bought another. Lucky there, and nobody knew it better than Cletus Borglan. He'd also been savvy enough not to get in over his head, when many others were mortgaging to the hilt to buy up more land, on the theory that the more they planted, the more they'd make. It had sounded good, but just didn't work.

His wife was a second-level administrator at an area education agency, had gone back to the University of Northern Iowa and obtained her MBA, and had set up their computerized farming operation. Between the two of them, they put in long hours, but with great success.

Having encountered him often over the years, I thought Cletus had a major flaw. Aside from predictability, that is. Cletus got

emotional about farming. Really. Whoever had invented the slo-
gan "We feed the world" hadn't done Cletus any favors. It was
too evocative of images of altruism. It should have been "We sell
food to the world."

Regardless, that was a trump card. Cletus was a crusader.

George, Art, Davies, and I were at the kitchen table, with
Cletus and his attorney Gunston on the other side. The whole
business was being conducted here because his attorney thought
it less likely that we had bugged the kitchen. Right.

We were closer to the coffee. We'd just got settled at the
long table when attorney Gunston stated that this was a "police-
dominated environment." Too many cops at the table, and we'd
intimidate his client. Right out of the late '60s, but still viable.
At the same time insisted that only "the deputy" do the interview, as I was the officer with superior jurisdiction. Sure. He was
trying to pick the less sophisticated officer, the one he thought
would do the worst job of interviewing his client. Me. Well,
maybe he'd get a surprise. Davies agreed, with the provision that
he too be present.

Art wasn't happy. George seemed a bit relieved. Volont
wasn't present, anyway, so it sure didn't bother him.

After a little flurry, we began again. I used the approach that
had always worked best for me, especially with an opposing attorney present. I presented facts, and asked no questions. Kept
either attorney from interrupting, and if Cletus wanted to say
anything, the ball was in his court.

"Cletus," I said, "I'm just gonna tell you what I got. I'm not
gonna ask any questions. I'd suggest you pipe down unless
they"—and I nodded toward his defense team—"tell you to say
something. That's what you pay them for."

I knew he'd never be able to do it, any more than I could
have in his place. But, having said it, I was on pretty firm
ground. I had also given my "sincere" shot to Gunston and
Blitek, hopefully taking just a tiny bit of the edge off the adver-
sary relationship.

"So, what happened was this . . ." And I started out with Fred dropping the cousins off. I went through every step, fairly quickly, but concisely and in a clipped near monotone. Well, I do have to admit getting a bit dramatic when I stood and showed how the two had been executed, with one pleading that they really weren't cops, in full view of his dead brother. But it did have the right effect.

"But the suspect shot 'em both, anyway," I said. "In your house. In your living room. Believing they were cops when he did it." I paused for effect. "In cold blood. With malice. First-degree murder."

I stopped. Silence. Cletus looked kind of sad, in fact. But not a word. Gunston was following very closely, but letting me run. He would. I represented great information, without his having to go through the discovery process. And I might make a mistake he could bring back to haunt me in court.

Blitek was another matter. "According to the common law, a free man is supreme in his castle. And any invited guest in his castle is the same person in right as the sovereign citizen."

Gibberish, but familiar gibberish. I now knew why Gunston hadn't been too happy with Blitek on the "team."

"Yes?" I shouldn't have asked.

"Based upon that, the so-called 'warrant of arrest' which you presented to Mr. Cletus G. Borglan, freeman, is refused for cause without dishonor and without recourse to him, and need not be complied with because it is irregular, unauthorized, incomplete, and is a void process."

"We'll make a note," said Davies. "I'll file it under 'bullshit.' Now, let's get on with this."

"Under protest," said Blitek.

"Sure," said Davies, cheerfully.

I started up again. "Now, when you got to the farm, you remember what you did first? No, don't answer that. I'll tell you, because I was there. You announced in front of five cops and three agents that a couple of cops had been killed." He started to speak, but I held up my hand. "Just a minute. Wait. Don't say anything. It's gonna get a lot better."

I reached into the file. "I have a statement from a witness that says you got a phone call in Florida, about the time the two brothers got murdered. Says you were all concerned, and that you left the next morning for Iowa. Because of the call."

Cletus just was going to burst if he didn't say something. "Bullshit!"

Well, it wasn't much of a defense. But I think it made him feel a little better. Gunston put a hand on his shoulder. "Let him go, Cletus. He's going too far out on a limb now."

Blitek just looked startled. I assumed it was because he so seldom dealt with evidence.

"You know, that's just what I thought." I put on my reading glasses, and looked down at the paper I held in my hand. I looked at it for a second, and then looked at Cletus. I looked over the top of my glasses, without raising my head. "I thought, 'There ain't no way to prove that, that's just hearsay.' " I stared over the top of those little glasses for all I was worth. Timing was everything.

"Until I got this," I said. "With this subpoena," I added. And I handed both documents to his real attorney, not to Cletus, not to Blitek. As Gunston looked at it, I said, "It's your phone bill, Cletus. A phone company record of the call being placed from your farm, to your place in Florida, just minutes after the Colson brothers were killed. In black and white."

Cletus was very pale. Gunston didn't look all that good, either. Silently, he passed the bill to his client. I thought Blitek was going to trip as he got up and stood behind Cletus, peering over his shoulder.

You could have heard a pin drop, as they say. I don't know how I ever did an interview, before I got those glasses.

"You want to stop, or do you want me to give it all to you now?" I asked. Quietly. All for effect. They'd have gotten the phone bill on discovery, anyway.

Cletus looked up. "Go ahead," he said, in as close to a whis-

per as he could probably get. I looked at Gunston. He nodded.
Nothing to lose, there. Besides, I think he was really curious.
Blitek I ignored.

"We've been following Gabriel for years," I said. Call it a
white lie. "We" as in "We the People . . ."

That was when Cletus surprised me. He turned to the side,
and threw up on the floor.

Seventeen

Thursday, January 15, 1998,
1848

Nothing like heaving on the floor to bring a party up short. We made Cletus clean up his own mess. Jail rules. Got him a damp cloth for his forehead. He was all quivery for a few minutes.

"Tell me the truth, now," said Davies to Gunston. "You trained him to do that, right?"

Gunston wasn't particularly amused, and told us that the interview was over. We'd abused his client for the last time. We were Nazis. Truth was, he was running up his tab.

Cletus had other ideas. "Just stay with me, here, will ya, Ray? I gotta explain here. I gotta."

"Be careful," said Blitek. "Think about what you say. I can't caution you strongly enough . . . be careful."

An attorney who got $25.00 an hour probably would have said it wasn't worth it. Ray Gunston, who was closer to $2,500.00 an hour, let the clock run.

Cletus did the only thing he could, as far as trying to exculpate himself. He told us that he'd been snookered in, was afraid of Gabriel, and didn't know how to get out of the matter. He also explained something that had been making me wonder ever since we did the crime scene.

"He wanted to use the computers in the house while we were gone," he said. "He calls it 'distributed computation,' or something."

" 'Distributed computing,' " I said. "Sure. Put a bunch of little computers on big problem. Use their time, then put it together at the end."

"Yeah. Tied in with a bunch of other equipment. All over the country."

"For what?" I was curious.

"You'll see," he said. Right. I got the solid impression that he didn't know, either. I stopped with that line right there. Distributed computing was all we'd need to know to get some smarter cops on it. But I really wanted to get hold of those computers.

Cletus said that he just thought that Gabriel would use the house while they were gone. Then be out of there before they got back. No problems. No troubles. No complications except a bit of an electric bill.

Mostly true, I thought. Easy to make up, hard to disprove. He was only telling us what was supposedly in his own mind. No way to prove it either way. Then he interjected something into the rather standard tale of woe that led me to believe him.

"I thought they had to be cops, too. Feds. I thought he was right. I thought you were all lying to cover up the Feds."

Let me tell you just how glad I was that Volont wasn't in the room.

"Gabe's well known, and wanted around here," I said. "He's been involved in other killings, you know."

"He's a hero around here," said Cletus.

"You wouldn't think so if you'd been there, Cletus," I said.

Davies had let me converse with Cletus for long enough. "So, Cletus," he said, "where is he?"

Cletus just looked at him with a firmly closed mouth.

"Ray, here, will tell you that what I'm about to say is the truth. Your only chance is to cooperate. Saying you're sorry ain't gonna cut it. Neither is 'I was afraid of this man' when you so clearly cooperated with him."

"You offering a deal?" asked Gunston.

"I'm offering a chance," said Davies.

"My client will never cross the BAR," said Blitek.

"Pardon me," said Davies, "but what is that supposed to mean?"

"Common law applies on the lands, lakes, and the rivers. The law of the sea only applies on seawater. Salt and fresh water cannot be mixed, because God did not make salt water potable. This is the basic contradiction between the law of the land and the law of the sea. Cletus G. Borglan is a citizen under maritime law, and the laws of the land are not his. Where salt and fresh water meet is the BAR, and we will not cross it." Blitek paused for breath.

"What's your position on piss?" asked Davies.

Blitek opened his mouth, but Gunston put a hand on his shoulder. "Not now." Simple, nearly sotto voice, but it shut Blitek up as if you'd closed switch. Interesting. Obviously didn't have much time for the man, but was in complete control of him.

I'd also noticed that, all during the time Cletus had been talking about Gabriel, Gunston hadn't batted an eye. I made a note. I really didn't want to forget that.

Gunston asked to talk with Cletus in private, so we took them to a little jail conference room, with a tough plastic window, and shut the door. I didn't lock it, although I was authorized to do so. I didn't feel they'd pose much of an escape risk. Blitek stood outside, looking forlorn.

I showed my note to Davies. "Yeah," he said. "I know." He then gave me an elbow in the ribs. "Good job," he said, just like W. C. Fields. "Made him regurgitate."

"Hey," I said, "I didn't know . . ."

"Ah, you're a mean one, Houseman."

"Yeah, right." I took a sip of coffee. "Don't you suppose it could have been the reaction from anybody in Cletus's position, though? I mean, here he was, totally committed to an ideal. And a cool leader. He must have totally believed in the man." I took another sip.

"From what you people tell me about this Gabriel character, yeah, he would have." Davies grinned.

Gunston stuck his head out. "We're ready to go back to the kitchen, now."

We got there, and I was all prepared to get some good information. We did seem to have Cletus where we wanted him. Didn't work that way, though.

"My client," said Gunston, "is in danger of his life. I demand that he be moved, and that every security precaution be taken to ensure his safety."

"We'll do what we can," I said. Gunston was just blowing smoke, as far as I was concerned.

"To protect him from a known killer? Deputy, I'd suggest you move my client to the Linn County jail."

I laughed. I couldn't help it. "Last time we had somebody involved with Gabriel at Linn County," I said, "somebody else associated with Gabriel fired at them with a LAWS rocket and took out a chunk of wall."

I'm sure Gunston remembered the incident, but I'd be willing to bet a million dollars that he'd never heard that it had anything to do with Gabriel.

Apparently, Davies hadn't, either. "No shit? Was that this dude?"

"Ah, I guess I let the cat out of the bag on that one." I looked squarely at Gunston. "The point is, neither you, nor I, nor your client is safe if Gabriel wants to take us out. Anywhere. I'm deadly serious, Mr. Gunston." I gestured around the room. "But I think we're marginally safer here than we would be on the road."

Gunston didn't seem particularly worried. "Even if he stays here, we feel he's talked enough this evening."

Like Davies said later, Gunston had learned enough to begin to build a long, expensive case. I suspect my statements regarding Gabriel made it all that much easier. I didn't really care about that part. I suspected Cletus had told the truth, as far as it went.

"If your client were to let us know where Gabriel is," I said, "I'm confident that he could be taken into custody fairly quickly. Eliminate the whole problem."

"You don't know where he is?" asked Cletus.

"No, I don't." Then, afraid I'd given too much to him, I added, "Well, not exactly."

Cletus turned to Gunston. "I think it'd help if I told them what I know about that," he said. "It can't possibly get me in more trouble if they go get him." Before Gunston or Blitek could get a word in, he said, "He scouts banks at night. He's gonna hit some banks, and he's making detailed plans of them. For his troops. Calls it Operation Just Cash."

Cletus had been told that Gabriel intended to hit five banks in the area, three of them in Nation County. First, Maitland, First Iowa. Grand Vista, Federated Bank and Trust. Terrill, People's National. One in Dubuque County, and one across the Mississippi in Conception County, Wisconsin. Five. Sounded impressive at first. Until you figured the five would probably net him $10,000.00 in cash. It was apparent to me that Cletus had been sold a little bill of goods. Normal, I thought. Gabriel wouldn't want any details about a real plan in the hands of the likes of Cletus Borglan.

Too bad for Cletus. He'd opened the bag, but we already had the cat. No bargaining points there. But after he spoke, both his legal advisers just raised hell.

Cletus went back to his cell. He said he really didn't want to bond out. In his shoes, I wouldn't, either.

In any case, it was way past my bedtime. I said as much to Lamar.

"Yeah, get some rest," he said. "This is your weekend off, isn't it?"

Oops. I'd forgotten about that. Our schedule went something like this: seven days on, two off; seven on, two off; three on, two off; two on, three off. Yeah, I know. Took some deputies months to get used to that. But the "three off" was a Friday, Saturday, and a Sunday. The only Friday, Saturday, or Sunday we got in a month. Tomorrow was my day off. Sue wanted to go to Madison and a part of me did too. But I knew the other part wouldn't let me.

"Uh, yeah. I guess it is."

"Don't you think you better take the rest of it off, then?"

"Not now . . ."

"Okay," said Lamar. No reason for him to argue that. I'd just go on building up comp time for eternity.

"Maybe I could get next weekend?"

"If you can get somebody to switch," he said. "We're still shorthanded."

When I got home, I explained the situation to Sue. It was one of those times when she got really mad, but was totally reasonable.

"I expected that," she said. "I always expect that."

"Look, I'm really sorry. We can try for next weekend . . ."

"There's leftovers in the refrigerator," she said. "Scalloped potatoes and ham. I'm going to bed."

As she started up the stairs, I had two choices. One, I could say something apologetic, and she'd start to lose it, and we'd have a fight. Two, I could stay downstairs, and she'd lay awake for an hour, getting madder and madder.

I hate to say it, but I let her go up the stairs. I just didn't have the energy to argue.

I put the scalloped potatoes in the microwave, and heated them up. I took a plateful into the dining room, and ate in silence. I hated that schedule. I hated the size of the department that made you find your own replacement for an unscheduled day off.

The potatoes sat in my stomach like concrete. Most of the ham chunks were still cold. I didn't care enough to take them back to the microwave.

I took my plate out, scraped it off, and decided to go upstairs to bed. I'd just have to say something to Sue, the frustration was building to a point where I wouldn't be able to sleep, anyway.

I got into the bedroom, and Sue was asleep.

I remember counting, lying there, staring at the thin strip of street light coming through the curtain. I remember making a mental note to myself that I had reached 22,500.

Eighteen

Friday, January 16, 1998,
0802

I woke up, showered, shaved, and went downstairs for coffee. There was a note on the pot from Sue. She and a neighbor gal had gone to Cedar Rapids to shop. She had already taken the day off from school and chose to make the most of it without me. She planned on being back after supper.

There being no point in sitting around the house, I checked the Weather Channel on TV. There was a great worm of a jet stream, moving up and down over the Midwest. Huge cold masses were sliding down from Canada into the dips in the stream. We, however, were just getting the benefit of a sort of peak. Warm Gulf air was just moving into the area. The forecaster said we should enjoy it. Shortly, the arctic air would be back as the hump of the jet stream moved east. It was warming up, and forecast to be above twenty degrees most of the day. A "January thaw," as they call it, was in the making. If it got over thirty-two degrees, it would really start to mess up the gravel roads, with standing water, and softened surfaces giving under the wheels of traffic, and making ruts. Then it would freeze hard, again, and those ruts would be like steel trenches. In the meantime, the water on top of a frozen roadbed made for some really greasy driving. They say wet ice on wet ice is the slipperiest surface known . . . much slipperier than Teflon.

I got to the office at 0842. Three plus hours early, since I was now going on to a noon-to-eight shift.

I found myself wandering about the jail kitchen, waiting for the fresh coffee to brew, when Sally came in at shift change. She came out to the kitchen to store her supper in the refrigerator, and stopped to chat for a few seconds.

"Hiding from work?" she asked.

"Kind of. Just waiting for a phone call . . ."

She opened the refrigerator door, and put her lunch bag inside. "You making fresh coffee?"

"Yep. Want some? Be glad to pour you a cup."

"Sure. You must want something special," she said, pulling a folding chair up to the long, institutional table.

I interrupted the pot, poured her a cup of coffee, and took it to the table. "Here. Well, yeah, I sort of do."

"Like, what?"

"Well, I'd like to know what impression you got from Inez Borglan, when you talked to her the other day."

"None," said Sally, and took a sip of the coffee. "Strong," she winced, and put the cup down. "To tell you the truth, I was busier that a cat burying shit. I didn't have any 'impressions' of anybody, that day."

"Oh." I went back to the pot, and poured myself three-quarters of a cup, and let the brewing continue.

"That hardly seems worth a cup," she said. "Anything else you need?"

I sat down opposite her. "What can you get me regarding Inez? Or Cletus, for that matter." I took a sip of my own coffee. "Just right. Anyway, I need anything you can dig up. Any criminal history at all, even misdemeanors. Any contacts out of the area, and why."

"It'd help if I had someplace to start. Misdemeanor stuff isn't likely to be in the CCH or NCIC." She was referring to the Computerized Criminal History and the National Crime Information Center. They were very useful as places to start a background check.

"Try the town in Florida where they have their cabin," I suggested.

"Okay . . ."

"Anything you can find. Anything."

"Do what I can . . . but I'll tell you right now, this coffee isn't all that good."

There was a knock on the open kitchen door. We looked up, and there stood Shamrock, all big eyes and smiles.

"Mr. Houseman? They said I'd find you back here . . ." She looked around the room, and her eyes settled on Sally. "Hello, ma'am," she said. "I'm a photographer. Just call me Shamrock."

Oops. Sally stood, drawing herself up to her full five feet. "Ma'am" was referred to as "the M word" around the department. Especially if delivered by a younger woman. "Glad to meet you. I'm a dispatcher. Sally will do. Coffee?"

"Oh, sure. You bet," said Shamrock, coming through the door. She grabbed a chair and pulled it around to the end of the table, then sat.

Sally glared, turned, got a cup from the cupboard, poured the coffee, and set it down in front of the pretty photographer. "Can I get you anything else?" It was a very pointed remark, I thought. I would have said no. I would have said, "No, thank you," in fact.

"Some sugar, maybe?"

I'd seen Sally use chemical Mace on a gal once. The slightly flushed face below her red hair looked very familiar. "Sure. Anything else while I'm at it?"

"No, that's fine," said Shamrock, brightly. Actually, she and Sally were very similar in appearance, except for the hair color. Even with Sally being a good ten years older. Something I made a mental note to never bring up.

Sally came over with a box of sugar cubes. It's really hard for someone of ninety pounds to stomp effectively, so she overcompensated and almost glided across the floor. Tense, kind of, but more like a coiled spring than a stiff board. No. No, more like a stalking cat.

"We went back and we talked to the old dude at the farm and he told us some stuff and I think it's pretty good," said Shamrock. About ready to burst. She was really getting into this.

There was another knock at the door, and Nancy stuck her head in. "Hi?"

Sally sort of knew Nancy. "Hi! Come on in!"

Nancy glanced at Shamrock. "I don't suppose that's decaf," she said.

"Nope, full strength," I said.

"Just what she needs, more zip," said Nancy, pulling up a chair. "Sugar, too, I see?"

Sally was already getting a cup for Nancy. "Should I have gotten her parents' permission?"

"Mine," said Nancy, "at least."

"I just can't wait to tell what we found out yesterday," said Shamrock. She gestured toward Sally. "Is she cleared for this stuff?"

I really didn't think Sally's back could have gotten stiffer. She started to turn, and I told Shamrock, "She's gotten clearance on federal cases. She's currently cleared for the most sensitive cases in our department."

"Cases," added Sally, sweetly, "that you'll probably never even hear about."

"Oh, good!" said Shamrock. Genuinely glad. Innuendo-proof, I saw.

"So, what you get for us?"

Shamrock looked at Nancy.

"Oh, go ahead, kid," said Nancy. "I'll just translate as we go."

Shamrock began talking in an excited rush. "So, okay, we went back to the farm . . . and the old guy I said had told me that there were two dead cops was there. He's called . . ." And she looked at Nancy.

"Hubert Frederick Brainerd," said Nancy, slowly. Sally and I wrote it down. Nancy had known enough to get a middle name. "And he's from near Waterloo." She smiled. "And don't forget to tell them he's about fifty."

"Yeah, like she says," said Shamrock. "So I walk up to him, and I go, 'We heard other people say there really were two cops that got it on Tuesday,' and I go, 'so we want to talk to you again.' " She looked at Nancy, who threw her an encouraging smile. "So he goes, 'I told you so, didn't I, sweetie,' " said Shamrock, in her deepest voice, and tittered just a bit. "He gives me this look, and then says, 'You might want to look into the ATF records on this,' and I go, 'No kidding, the ATF?' "

"That's a direct quote. 'You might want to look into the ATF records,' " said Nancy. "We don't have a clue on that one. Just what he said."

"How in the hell . . ." I couldn't believe he'd said that. Or that he thought a reporter would be able to go to the ATF and check their records, for that matter.

"Don't know," she replied. "Just what he said. Go on, Shamrock."

"He says that the ATF has been hanging around for a long time, ever since that other cop got killed up in the park, and then that undercover cop got killed. He means Nancy's previous photographer, we think. And that the cops have been trying to get even, and that they fly over all the time, and that they send vans all over with listening devices." Her eyes were wide. "Really. 'Helicopters, jets, and reconnaissance satellites' is what he said."

"Oh, boy." It was all I could say. I guess I'd been secretly afraid of this, ever since I'd seen the survivalist and antigovernment books at Borglan's house. The same old problem: How do you prove that something isn't there? Tough. But when people get excited about it, it gets a lot tougher.

"He told me all about taxes, and how you really didn't have to pay them. How it was a conspiracy to take everybody's money and give it to the rich and the Jews, and the Chinese, and things like that." She glanced up at me. "Anyway . . . he said that the media was being fed lots of lies by the government, and that we should check out our sources better. I think that's about it."

"He took quite a liking to Shamrock," said Nancy, dryly. "Almost like I wasn't there at all." She addressed her photographer. "Tell Mr. Houseman about the little buildings . . ."

"Oh, yeah. He also said that there was a secret government listening station right near there, with a satellite communications antenna, and that it was where the ATF went to send their reports to Washington. He showed it to us, it's just over the bridge, it's gray and a little building. Only it says 'U.S. Geological Survey' on it. Has an antenna, though."

She was right about the USGS station. They had set several in place over the last few years, and improved flood control considerably. Of course, if you're paranoid enough, you can concoct just about anything.

"Well, I didn't know what to say, because I know he's full of shit on that one, and then he goes, 'I got it right from the mouth of the horse.'"

"That's 'horse's mouth' dear," said Nancy, with a wicked little grin.

"Right. Anyhow, he goes, 'We know it was cops.' And I go how does he know that, and he goes, 'Because the owner of the house knows. He don't lie.' Just like that, he said it!" Shamrock took a big gulp of coffee, and shrugged her shoulders. "Well, that's what he said."

"That *is* what he said." Nancy got up, went to the sink, and poured a little cold water in her coffee cup.

"I'm sure." I pushed my chair back. "Well, you've done really well, here."

"Just wait," said Nancy. She sat back down, cup in hand. "Tell him." She glanced at Sally and me. "You're not going to believe this."

Shamrock just sparkled. "I asked him if I could take his picture. He goes, 'Sure, how about over here,' and he stands in front of the mailbox. So I go, 'How about you pointing at something for me?' and I take the first shots. And he goes, 'How about this?' and he walks over to his car, and points at the bumper sticker that says something like 'Remember April 17' or something, so I get some more shots of that."

"April 19," both Nancy and I said, at the same time.

"Oh? Well, okay . . ." said Shamrock.

"Couple of bad things happened on April 19," I said. "A lot of Branch Davidians died in Waco, Texas, on that date, and a couple of years later, the Murrah Federal Office Building was blown up in Oklahoma City. Lot of people died there, too."

"Oh, sure," said Shamrock. "I know about those. Sure."

"The sticker say anything else?" I asked.

"Not that I remember," said Nancy. "But you'll get a photo of it." She gestured with her hand held out, like a traffic cop telling me to stop. "Just a second. Don't go anywhere. It gets still better."

"Three of his buds came out of the house," said Shamrock. "Two men and a woman. I got them on film, behind him, and I don't think they know I did. Good shots, I think."

"They politely asked us who we were," said Nancy, "and then politely asked us to leave."

"The one with the gun looked scary," announced Shamrock, "but I think I got a shot of it, too."

"What kind of gun?"

"Assault rifle," said Nancy. "You people up around here seem to have lots of them."

Well. "I can't believe you got that," I said. "Good job. More than a fair trade for an autopsy." I looked at Shamrock. "I wish I knew how to get information like that."

"You start," said Nancy, dryly, "with walking around with your coat unzipped, a jersey shirt, no bra, batting your eyes, and saying, 'Oh, golly gee' as often as you can." She reached out and put her hand on Shamrock's shoulder. "Faked him right out of his bib overalls. She's like the daughter I never had."

Shamrock laughed. "Yeah, right." She was blushing.

"Well, maybe the bratty little sister, then." Nancy patted Shamrock. "Whatever, you'll do until some young stud with a camera shows up."

"Shamrock, why don't you come with me to the local newspaper office? They can develop prints there. You can use their facilities."

"How do you know that?"

"Trust me," I said.

I had the damp prints in my hand by 1040. There they were,

big as life. I recognized Linda Grossman right off, and I recognized one of the men with her as having been behind Cletus Borglan in the doorway when Davies and I were out at the house on Wednesday. Chunky, about forty or so. He was the one with the weapon. Looked an awful lot like an SKS or AK-47. I could just see the middle part of the barrel clearly. Way toward the rear, and partially hidden by Harvey Grossman, was a white male, looked about fifty, taller than Harvey, so I'd guess about six feet. Didn't recognize him, but since I'd never actually seen Gabriel, it didn't mean much. Nancy thought she had, and I was prepared to take her word for it. I didn't see any weapons other than the one SKS.

It was the only photo showing the unknown male. The rest were of a portly fellow who just had to be Mr. Brainerd.

I was standing damn near on top of Shamrock, peering intently at the photos. "They aren't looking at you, are they?"

"No. I don't think they knew we were there right away."

"Really?"

"Nope. Good old Hubert had walked us down the lane for a ways. They couldn't see us from the house. When they came up the lane, on foot, I don't think they were aware we were where we were." She stopped. "That wasn't very clear, was it?"

"I got the gist," I said. I was looking at the next photo. "This must be Hubert."

"Yep."

"Looks friendly enough."

"Oh, he's friendly, all right. Downright gushy."

I laughed. "Wiles are one thing, but you gotta learn to use them in increments. You don't want Hubert asking you to marry him."

"Good photos, aren't they?" she asked.

"They're great! Really good."

"Thank you." She smiled very sincerely.

I got back to the office just before lunch, and almost literally bumped into Art in the entrance.

He greeted me with "You know when I forgot to tell you about the lab finding a shell casing?"

"Yeah?" I said.

"Well, anyway, they did, as you know. A strange one, but my sources . . ." The way he said "sources" implied that his were much better than mine. I'll never know just how he does that. ". . . tell me that good old Fred would go to a gun show occasionally. Opportunity, again."

I smiled. With my telephone evidence, I felt I could be magnanimous. "Still have to link him with a gun of that sort, though." I held up the copy of Borglan's phone bill. "I think this might change the, uh, direction of your investigation?"

Art looked at it for a few moments, and at first seemed gratifyingly startled. Then he lowered the phone bill, and gave me the best example I'd ever heard of bending the evidence to fit the theory.

"Insurance scam." That was all he said, but he did it with such conviction I wondered if I'd missed some printing at the bottom of the bill.

"What?" I truly didn't understand.

"Insurance scam," he repeated, patiently. "They called Borglan to tell him they were inside. He must have commissioned them to break in while he was gone, and was going to split the insurance take with them."

I was speechless. So was George, who'd been in the rest room, and had stepped back into my office just as I'd showed the phone bill to Art.

"I'm thinking that, when Fred heard just how much the take was going to be," continued Art, "he decided to kill the brothers and keep it all for himself."

Ignoring, of course, the likelihood that Fred wasn't in the house. That there wasn't enough "take" in the whole house to make that worthwhile, anyway.

Any thoughts of clueing Art in evaporated. So, that left me right where I was, with the additional burden of keeping Art busy, but also keeping him ineffective. The last thing I wanted was for him to pop up at the wrong time, and blow the whole case. Accomplishing that could be a career in itself. Getting rid of him temporarily, though, turned out to be pretty easy.

Lamar stuck his head in the door and asked where we wanted to eat.

"Let's go up to the boat," I said, "and have lunch with Hester." My unstated plan worked, as Art excused himself by saying that he wanted to talk with Fred's attorney about an interview with Fred. Fat chance. But a distraction for him. All well and good.

We went in my car, and on the way, I handed the photos that Shamrock had taken over to Lamar and George.

"Check out the dude in the rear. I never saw the man, but I'm told that might be Gabriel."

Lamar just shrugged. He'd never actually seen Gabriel, either.

George had seen at least a photo. He was pretty quiet as he looked at the photo. Then he put it down and leaned up into the front seat between Lamar and myself. "I believe it's him," he said. "When was this taken?"

I told him, and he got on his cell phone. We could hear him talking softly in the backseat, but couldn't quite make out what he was saying. I knew it had to be Volont, though. Just by the tone of George's voice.

As we drove down the bluff side road into town, you could see the *General Beauregard* tied up at her own dock, all white and glittery in the sun. The *Beau*, as they called her locally, was a Mississippi River boat, a false side-wheeler, with the tall, almost delicate smokestacks that Mark Twain would have seen every day on the river. She was a false side-wheeler because she was really driven by a screw at the stern, with two bow thrusters for maneuvering. The big paddle wheels were for show. The main deck was about three feet off the water, with the top of the stacks clearing at about seventy-five feet. She was especially pretty from a distance. As you got closer, the red neon tubing on the side-wheels got a little much. She'd been glitzed up for the gaming trade.

She was moored alongside her own pier, which also supported a large restaurant and entertainment pavilion, with offices on the third and fourth floors.

We three walked down the dock, and I was, as usual, amazed at the number of people on and around the boat. She was about two hundred and fifty feet long, and three decks were full of gaming machines, tables, and bars. They told me that she could carry nine hundred gamblers, and I had no reason to doubt them. Thing was, it was always crawling with patrons. Not nine hundred every time, of course, but she averaged about four hundred and fifty, twenty-four hours a day, seven days a week.

She featured three decks of gambling, from about five hundred slot machines to blackjack tables, poker, dice . . . well, just about everything, I guess. Glittery, glitzy interior, complete with chandeliers, a gift shop, and a day-care center for children of gamblers, all surrounded by double-pane glass, attended by about ten crewmen and fifty dealers and assorted casino personnel. They said that if she ever sank, the hardest rescuing would be prying the hands of the sixty-five-year-old ladies from the handles of the slot machines.

The best thing about her was that she provided about three hundred jobs for our area. Not too bad. She was, in fact, the largest single employer in Nation County.

We entered the pavilion, and went directly to third floor. Iowa DCI maintained an office for the gaming officers up there. One "real" DCI agent, and two "gamers" per shift. Most of what they did was check the electronic gaming machines, and make sure they paid off at the right odds. We could hear Hester as we got close to their office.

". . . and the reports on the applicants for dealer will be on this desk no later than ten A.M. Understood?"

DCI had to do background checks on every boat employee. Including deckhands.

Lamar knocked on the door. It opened rather rapidly, revealing Hester and two young gamers. "Hi," he said. "Is this where we can apply for a job . . . ?"

Hester was glad to see us, and surprised we had George in tow. She also was ready to eat, and took us down to the pavilion buffet. God. About a hundred yards of great food, all hot and steaming, from ham to potatoes to soup, to scrambled eggs and sausage, to glazed chicken . . . I was in heaven. I only took the low-fat offerings, of course.

"I see," said George, "you found the low-fat fried shrimp."

"But I took rice. If I take the rice . . ."

"Oh, look, Carl. Fat-free chocolate éclairs . . ." Hester even pointed them out.

Lamar suggested the four-inch-thick Iowa chop. "Low-fat gravy, isn't it?"

Dine smart. That's me.

I had a Diet Coke. To prove I was serious.

As we sat down, I gestured about me with my fork. "Must be nice . . . I mean, so this is where they send you when they're mad at you . . . I mean, when Lamar gets mad at me, I end up standing out in the rain, up to my ankles in hog manure."

We showed her the photos. She looked at George, quizzically. "You've seen him?"

"No. But I've seen photographs. This looks like the same man, but . . . but . . . yes, I think it's him."

"So," asked Hester, "what are you guys going to do about it?"

"I've been told to wait," said George. "At least until we can fix his location in real time."

"How are you going to do that?" I really wanted to know.

"Beats me."

Lamar took a deep breath. "I know better than to go rushing in there . . . maybe better than any of you. But I don't want this son of a bitch walking away again." He glared at us. "Not again." He spoke to George. "You got any guarantee that he won't just walk away?"

George pursed his lips. "No, Lamar. He won't walk away this time."

I wished I knew how he could be so certain about that. Judging from the look on her face, so did Hester.

Nineteen

When we got back to the office, I'd fully expected to see Volont. Lamar picked up his messages.

"Our friend Volont is out tailing Linda Grossman," he said. "Thinks she'll lead him to our boy."

"You're kidding . . . he really doesn't know where Gabriel is, does he?"

"Doesn't look like it. I hope he's really good at following somebody in the open country . . ."

We'd found that the urban folks were pretty funny when it came to tailing people in rural areas. They were used to congested traffic. Out here, when you and your quarry were the only two vehicles on the road, it was a bit tougher to remain inconspicuous. When you were in our hilly country, to boot, you had to be within 200 yards of your subject or you lost sight of them. With myriad intersections, farm lanes, and field entrances, if you lost 'em for more than a few seconds, you could lose them completely. The best way was to have a good estimate of their destination, and get to a spot where you could see some of the roadway from a distance. Spot-check. Actually, following was out of the question, unless you knew for certain where they were headed. If you knew that, there was no real point in following them at all. Just go where they were headed, and wait.

"You want to guess what else?" asked Lamar.

"What else?"

"He's got Art with him."

"You've got to be kidding me . . . he's briefed Art?"

"Yep. I guess he feels that with Art with DCI now, he don't need us to help him get around the county."

"Great. Just fuckin' great. Art ain't ready for this." I just shook my head. "Christ." Saying "Christ" brought the image of Art following Volont to the gates of hell. "Volont just got a disciple," I said. "Matthew, Mark, Luke, and Art."

Lamar chuckled. "That's funny."

"You think he's really gonna hit five banks at the same time?" I looked at the map of the county on the wall behind him. "Doesn't make sense to me."

It really didn't. With the wormy roads, the small banks, the smaller take . . . it was folly to try that. With a "team" he'd put together from locals, it was worse than that. Three of the banks had large vaults with time locks. Unless you were pretty good at cracking safes, you'd have to hit the bank during business hours if you wanted to get anything to speak of. Even then . . . $10,000.00 wasn't much, for the effort, the risk, even the equipment.

"Cletus escaped yet?"

"What?" I'd caught him thinking about something else.

"Cletus ain't busy, is he?" I laughed.

He wasn't, but his attorney had spent the night at the local motel, and had already convinced the judge that Cletus needed a bond reduction hearing. Lamar was to have Cletus in court in about fifteen minutes.

"I'd sure like to talk to Cletus about those little 'training sessions' Gabriel's been giving." I looked out the window. I couldn't talk to Cletus, naturally, without his attorney being present. No real problem. It gave me time for a long coffee break.

I grabbed a cup, and stood at the window overlooking the parking lot and the town below. The sky was bright blue, and it looked almost like spring. It was still below freezing, but relief was on the way. In a few days, we'd be back in the deep freeze.

All the warm interlude would have accomplished was to make the gravel roads a little harder to drive, with the mud tracks becoming hard as iron when they refroze. But it was nice, anyway.

Lamar and Cletus came down the hall from the cell block, Cletus in his orange coverall and handcuffed in front. Lamar was limping a little more than usual. Changes in the weather really did affect his leg.

I went out to my car, unlocked it, and started the engine. We'd transport Cletus in my car, and I wanted it warmed up. I left the engine running, and came back in to grab my vest. I met Lamar and Cletus at the door. "I'll be right with you," I said, walking into the secretaries' office to get my vest off the hangers.

I got it, and as I turned, I saw them descending the wooden steps toward the parking lot. Lamar in the middle of the steps, Cletus on the right, near the rail. That way, handcuffed as he was, Cletus was supported on both sides if he started to slip. Suddenly, Lamar froze, and Cletus turned to his left, and just about knocked Lamar over as he stumbled into him. Then I saw one of the wooden posts supporting the porch roof just split in half. No noise. Just splintered and split. It was like slow motion.

Lamar hollered, "Carl!" and tried to grab Cletus and haul him back up the stairs. Cletus, with his balance already thrown off, wasn't able to use his hands well enough to grab the railing, lost his footing, and started to tumble down the steps. Lamar reached down for him, and the porch floor behind him erupted in splinters.

Bullets. Those were bullets. I tried to get my coffee cup on the counter as I hurried by, missed, and drenched the carpet. Judy yelped, totally unaware of what was happening outside.

I flew out the front door, just in time to see Lamar and Cletus falling in a heap at the foot of the steps. I started toward them and the pillar next to me made a *thump*-cracking sound, like it had been struck with a large hammer, and splinters smacked into my left cheek and shoulder. I ducked, and saw the sidewalk ahead of Lamar start to puff in several places as rounds struck it. I jumped down the steps, slipped, wrenched my damn back again, and almost fell on Lamar. I grabbed Cletus just as Lamar got back on his feet.

"Behind the cars," he gasped, and we started dragging Cletus through the wet slush toward the line of parked cars out in the lot. I thought Cletus had been hit, and fleetingly wondered if he'd die on us.

Just as we got to the first car, there was a thunking sound, as if you'd hit it with a golf ball. Several golf balls. Dust flew from under the fenders, and one of the tires went flat with a *bang*.

We kept dragging Cletus, to the second car, and then the third. We heaved him up to the front of the fourth, and collapsed behind him.

I grabbed my walkie-talkie. "Comm, ten-thirty-three, ten-thirty-three, shots fired, parking lot!"

One of the newer dispatchers was on duty, I think her name was Grace. "Ten-nine?" 10–9 means for you to repeat your traffic.

"This is Three, this is ten-thirty-three, somebody is shooting at us in the parking lot!" I gasped for breath. "Get assistance!"

The golf balls started up again, working toward us. *Plunk, plunk, bang, plunk*. A tire.

"Where is that fucker?"

"Can't tell . . ." I couldn't, either. Nor was I about to stick my head up and look. I could hear the dispatcher say something on the order of "Three . . . thirty-three . . . uh . . . courthouse . . . I think . . ."

Of course. We couldn't hear the gunshots, and neither could she. She was assuming that we were at the courthouse. That's where she knew Lamar had been headed.

I brought my walkie-talkie back up. "We're here at the jail. Shots fired. Get an ambulance!"

"You hit?" Lamar sounded terribly concerned.

"No. You?"

"No. Who the fuck is the ambulance for?"

"Him," I said, indicating the orange heap that was Cletus.

"Shit," said Lamar, "he ain't hurt, he's just scared."

We didn't hear any more plunking sounds. The shooting had stopped. The question was: Had the shooter given up?

I cold hear dispatch again, this time Sally's voice. My confidence increased. Cautiously, I raised my head over the fender of the closest car. Nothing. I ducked. Nothing.

"See anything?"

"Nope." I was acutely conscious of the icy water and mud soaking into my shirt and pants. "Let me look again." This time, I drew my gun.

Up, peek, down. Like playing a child's game. I put my left hand on the fender and splayed my fingers out as far as I could. Reference points. I popped my head up, and looked over the top of my thumb, concentrating for about a second only on that sector. Down. Up, with the index finger as my reference. Down.

"Anything?"

"I can't see shit," I said, "but I don't know where to look."

Cletus started to make retching sounds.

"Not again . . ." said Lamar.

I bobbed my head up, referring to my little finger. Nothing. Down again. Cletus was still making the noise. "You suppose it could be the jail food?"

"They say," said Cletus, spitting, "I got a nervous stomach."

"No shit?"

I could hear a siren start up downtown. Couldn't be the ambulance yet. Cop car.

I saw a dark blue Ford slowly pull into the lot. Well, originally dark blue. This one was spattered with light tan mud, white road salt, and grungy as hell. Volont. Car might as well have had FBI plates. Although it was so covered with mud you wouldn't have been able to read them. They monitored a completely different set of frequencies, and obviously were unaware of our problem.

"Looks like the Spook's back," I said. As the Ford turned into the parking slots, I saw it had a large dent in the right rear quarter. "Dinged up, too."

We watched Volont and Art get out of the car, and look at the dent. Both were in suits, with the same light tan mud speckled halfway to the knees.

I got into a crouch, gun still in my right hand. "Get down!"

They both looked at me, startled. Volont comprehended first. Me. The gun. The holes in the nice cars. He nearly vaulted the car closest to him, drawing his gun at the same time.

"Come on!" he yelled at Art.

Art stood still for a split second, just long enough for another golf ball sound to make him turn his head. I dropped, just as Art dove between two cars.

Volont duckwalked toward us. "Where is he?"

"Can't tell . . . I don't know where to look . . . rifle, I think . . ." Giving a hint that the shooter could be a long way off.

"Prisoner hit?"

"No," said Lamar. "Keep down."

Art crawled out on our end of the cars. "Who's doing the shooting?"

"Somebody who's a piss-poor shot," said Lamar.

The sirens were a lot louder. I stuck my head up, and saw two brown state patrol cars nearly at the lot. I holstered my gun, grabbed my walkie-talkie, and switched to the mutual aid frequency.

"This is Three, we're down behind the cars. Shooter is in the direction of downtown, has a rifle. There are five of us here . . . keep low . . ."

They slid to a halt, and both exited their vehicles, getting down behind the fenders, handguns drawn. Just like in the movies.

We waited. It seemed like an hour, but it was closer to a minute. Finally, Lamar spoke up.

"I want to get him back inside," he said. "He'll be a lot safer there."

"Fine." Great. We have to drag Cletus, in his high-conspicuity orange suit, to boot. With a lousy sniper, who can't hit the broad side of a cow's ass, aiming at Cletus, and more likely to hit me by mistake. But I didn't say it, because Lamar was thinking the same thing. "Might as well," I said. "I can't dance . . ."

"I ain't goin' with you, by God! They might shoot me by mistake!" Cletus spit again.

"You damn fool," said Lamar. "It's you they're after, not us!"

Cletus began retching again. Apparently, it hadn't occurred to him.

"Can't we wait until he's done? I don't want to haul somebody who'd heaving all over me."

"Yeah," sighed Lamar.

We waited. I looked at the hole in the outside of the fender next to my head. I bent down, and looked back into the fender well until I saw daylight. Toward town, and in the top of the hood. Downward. Hard to do, since we were just about the highest point in town. Except for the grain elevator, about a half mile away. I peeked up over the fender. Sure. There was that huge concrete elevator, standing off in the middle distance, bigger than life. To hit us from there, the path would be downward.

"I think he's on the grain elevator," I said. Nobody contradicted me. I glanced around, and as far as I could tell, none of us had anything but a pistol. We couldn't even shoot back.

Volont got over beside us, and we told him our little plan.

"The sooner the better," he said. "I'll help."

The three of us grabbed Cletus, Lamar and Volont by an elbow, and me by his securing belt.

"On three . . . one, two . . ."

I was reminded of that movie, about Butch Cassidy and the Sundance Kid. Where they counted before running into the guns of that South American army . . .

". . . three!"

It should be an Olympic event. We hit the porch at full tilt, the three officers panting and straining, Cletus moving his feet very rapidly, but completely ineffectively. Judy, who was watching from behind her file cabinets, saw us coming, and opened the door just in the nick of time. We all let go of Cletus at about the same time, he tripped, and skidded across the linoleum floor for about ten feet.

We took a moment to congratulate ourselves. Then I realized we'd abandoned Art and the two troopers out in the lot.

It dawned on me that I hadn't been aware any shots fired during our portage of Cletus.

"You think he's gone?" Lamar was puffing, and wincing. His leg was probably hurting him quite a bit. He'd moved awfully well, though.

"I don't know, Lamar. But I wouldn't . . . just stand around out there . . . for a while." I was still breathing hard, too. And my back hurt like hell. But we'd gotten the first order of business done. Cletus was safe.

The next problem was how to get to our cars and get down to that grain elevator. There was just no place else the shooter could be.

I took a quick peek out the safety glass panel in the steel outer door. Then a longer one. Nothing. I was wondering how I was going to tell if he really had quit and left, when there was a sudden puff of packed snow and concrete dust in the middle of the parking lot. It was kind of hard to see, and I wasn't absolutely certain what it was. Two more puffs, each closer and about a half second apart, struck the parking lot. Then a solid plunking sound as something hit the wooden support for our porch roof.

I ducked. Late, but better than never.

"I know what his problem is," I said.

"He's still there, then?" Volont was sitting on the floor, with his back to the pop machine, which was against the outside wall. Smart. I should be so smart.

"Yeah. He's there, all right. His problem is, he can't see where his shots are going . . . unless he hits something that throws up debris or something . . ."

"So he can't correct his aim," said Volont.

"Yeah."

"Probably alone, then," he said, matter-of-factly. "That's why snipers should always have a spotter."

I filed that away. Like I would ever need it.

Lamar was on the phone to the people who ran the elevator, telling them they had a sniper on the roof, some 100 feet over their heads. It took him a minute to convince them. They couldn't hear the shots.

I was on my walkie-talkie, getting the Maitland squad car down to the elevator, to make sure there was nobody getting away. If the suspect hadn't gone up the interior elevator shaft, and then to the roof, he'd had to climb a long ladder.

"Want to try for a car?" asked Volont.

"Not just yet . . ."

I got on my walkie-talkie to the Maitland car again. "Hey, Twenty-five, you see anything down there?"

"I can't see nothin' here . . ." came the stressed voice. "But somebody just made a hole in my roof! I'm out of the car."

Still there, all right. But now, having taken the time to shift his aim to the much closer Maitland squad car, I thought he'd have a tougher time readjusting and zeroing in on us.

"You know," I said to Volont, "he really can't hit shit. You want to try for my car?"

"You mean the local can't hit shit, or the sniper can't hit shit?"

I grinned. "Neither one."

"Well, let's go," he said. "Just get your car keys in your hand before you go through the door."

"Okay . . . it's unlocked, and the engine is already running. Just get in and stay low . . ."

Volont and I went flying out the door, and down the steps three or four at a time. I nearly lost my balance, on the last four, and ended up scraping my hand on the sidewalk. I almost fell again, as I stopped suddenly at my car door. Running bent over, my back started to act up, and I hollered, "Shit!" as the pain flew up and over my right hip as I jumped into the car.

"You hit?"

"No, no . . ." As soon as Volont has his legs in the car, I put it in reverse and stepped on the gas. We shot backward so fast I was afraid I'd sprung the open passenger door. I slammed on the brakes, and spun the wheel to the left, sliding us around on the drive. Into drive, and we shot out of the parking lot, bottoming out at the end of the driveway. Volont got his door shut, I hit the flashing lights and siren, and we were off.

"Not bad," said Volont. "Not bad . . ."

"We're out of his line of sight," I said, turning left at the bottom of the long hill toward the courthouse, "until we come around that next corner."

"So we won't do that, will we?" said Volont.

I grinned. "No, we won't." I cut the siren, and we came to a smooth stop at the point of the curve leading to the elevator. "Let's go between those houses," I said, "and we should have a good view of the side of the elevator with the ladder."

I got my AR-15 out of the trunk, inserted one thirty-round magazine, and put a second one in my back pocket. I contacted dispatch on my walkie-talkie, and told them where we were.

"Uh, Comm., let's see if we can get some more people around this thing, the . . . uh . . . elevator. Stay low, but we need to see all four sides . . ."

"Ten-four, Three."

"And you might want to page the fire chief. We need people to be warned to stay off the street. And call the school, and tell them to keep everybody in, even after school, if they have to. Explain it to 'em." The school was about as far from the elevator as the Sheriff's Department.

"Ten-four."

"How's Twenty-five?" I asked her.

"I'm just swell . . ." came a squeaky reply. "But he's shot my car four or five times now. I'm behind the co-op garage over near the river."

"Stay there, Twenty-five," I said. "We can always fix the car."

I put on my green stocking cap. This was going to take a while. Volont had already gone between two of the houses. I moved in behind him.

As I reached the area where the backyards began, I could see his hand go up. "Careful," he said. "I can see him." He had his handgun out, but it was down by his side.

I looked up, way up. There, at the top of the elevator, to the left side, was a bump that might have been a head, with a long stick out in front. Rifle. The base of the elevator was about 150 feet from us. With him up in the air, say 90 to 100 feet . . . Geometry class, years ago, had addressed this very issue. Pythagoras. I remembered the name. I remembered it was a theorem. A squared plus B squared equals C squared. And I realized I'd have to do a square root in my head to be sure. Right. I started to adjust the sights on my rifle.

"How far away would you say he is?" I asked Volont, casually.

"Oh, about a hundred and fifty to a hundred and seventy-five feet."

"Thanks." I backed my sights all the way down to the 100 yard combat setting. At this distance, a bullet from my rifle, even going uphill, would only drop about a quarter of an inch below my aim point. If that.

Volont glanced back over his shoulder. "Can you hit him from here?"

"Yep." I looked up as a loud *crack* sounded above us. He seemed to be still shooting toward the jail. "If I can see enough of him, and there isn't much wind."

Just as I said that, the sniper stood, and changed position. He disappeared from our view. All I had been able to catch was that he was wearing a mustard-colored hooded coat, with tan gloves. And that his rifle had a scope. A split second, and he was gone.

"Moot," said Volont. "You happen to have a bullhorn in your trunk?"

"Nope. Fire Department has one, though." I handed him my walkie-talkie mike.

While we waited for an intrepid volunteer fireman to go to the station, get the bullhorn, and bring it to us, we sketched out a plan of attack.

"I'll talk to him, and see if I can get him to give it up," said

Volont. "If he starts shooting at anything but the jail or police vehicles, we take him out." He looked at me. "If that's all right. I really don't have much jurisdiction here. Your call."

"Sounds good," I said. "Problem one . . . we're in about the only location that can engage him. If you shoot from the other sides, the missed rounds are going to fall in town."

He looked at the target area. "Right."

"So if he does something really stupid, it better be on this side of the building."

"If not," said Volont, "we go up and get him."

"What's this 'we' shit? I don't do heights."

"How long," he asked, "will it take to get a TAC team in here?"

"About two hours," I said. "Maybe a bit longer. They're state troopers, and they have to come from all over."

"Helicopter?"

"I doubt it."

He sighed, audibly. "You people do need resources, don't you?"

I almost held out my hand.

The volunteer fireman got to us. There seemed to be some problem with the bullhorn, and he'd brought extra batteries. It was one of those items that was hardly ever used.

While Volont checked out the bullhorn, I looked very closely at that concrete grain elevator. The only way up, from the outside, was via that caged ladder. I remembered the first time, as a kid, I had thought about climbing it. I couldn't reach the ladder. I double-checked, and saw that the bottom rung was about seven or eight feet off the ground. Still, apparently. There was an aluminum stepladder, erected but on its side, under the cage. Obviously how our man had gotten up. Kicked it over, probably on purpose. That told me that he'd at least thought about somebody trying to climb up after him. All he'd have to do is lean over the edge, and shoot down into the circular cage. Anybody climbing up was not only going to get hit, they were going to get hit by plunging fire, along their longitudinal axis. In other words, the bullet wouldn't go through your shoulder and out. It would go in between, for example, your neck and your collarbone, and come out somewhere near the bottom of your pelvis.

Ugly concept.

There were three landings, each about twenty to twenty-five feet up the ladder. Open platforms, they had rails about four feet high. From the last platform on, anybody on that ladder was a dead man. At night, maybe, you could get as high as two platforms up, without getting shot. But by the third . . .

I saw the sniper pop up, and crack off a round down toward the right side of the building. Toward Twenty-five, the Maitland officer. Or, likely, his car. I pressed the "talk" button on my walkie-talkie mike.

"You okay, Twenty-five?" I asked.

"You bettcha . . ." came the reply. "But I think my car's dead."

"He's just keeping your head down," I said.

"He sure as hell is," he said.

"YOU ON THE GRAIN ELEVATOR! THIS IS AGENT VOLONT OF THE FBI!" came booming and crackling right behind me. Scared me nearly to death. He'd apparently gotten the thing fixed.

There was no response.

He tried again, this time adding that the suspect should surrender.

I was looking up at the top of the elevator, my rifle at my shoulder and aimed where I'd last seen the shooter, when he came popping back up at the other end of the tower. As I brought my rifle to bear, he cracked off two rounds and disappeared.

"Son of a bitch!" hollered Volont.

"Sorry," I said, "but I almost had him that time . . ."

I turned, half expecting him to yell again. Close. There was a neat, round hole in the rim of his bullhorn, and he was scrambling back behind some concrete steps leading into the side of one of the houses.

He put the bullhorn back to his face, and I turned toward the elevator. This time, I had my rifle pointed at where our sniper had popped up moments ago.

"YOU MIGHT AS WELL GIVE UP. YOU'RE SUR-ROUNDED, AND CANNOT ESCAPE."

Succinct, you gotta admit.

Nothing. I was all set to light him up, and nothing.

I lowered my rifle, and joined Volont behind the steps. Quickly.

"Now what?"

"You looking for suggestions?" he asked.

"Yah."

"Wait him out."

"Okay," I said. "It's gonna get awfully cold up there tonight. He could well freeze to death."

"You got a problem with that?"

"Not in the least."

We were both looking up when the sniper's head bobbed up. Arms extended into the air. No sign of his rifle.

"Shit," I muttered, "I think I could hit him now . . ."

Volont gave me a withering look, and picked up his bullhorn. "ARE YOU SURRENDERING?"

Faintly, we could hear a voice, but we couldn't make out the words.

"WE CAN'T UNDERSTAND WHAT YOU'RE SAY-ING!"

". . . I kill him?" wafted down from the top of the elevator.

"DID YOU KILL HIM? IS THAT THE QUESTION?"

". . . yes . . ." came back. Along with something else we lost.

"I DON'T KNOW WHO YOU MEAN. YOU DIDN'T, I REPEAT, DID NOT KILL ANYONE!"

That should have been good news to a man who was about to surrender. If you're under fifty, the difference between twenty years and life can be a long time.

With that, the sniper simply stood up, and began climbing over the top rail. Apparently, it wasn't good news to him.

"Shit," I said. "He's gonna jump . . ."

He extended both arms in a cruciform, like he was going to do a swan dive or something.

"DON'T DO IT . . ."

He teetered there for a second. Composing himself for the jump. He just needed to screw his courage up a little bit more.

Then, unexpectedly, he slipped. His feet just went out from under him, his butt smacked into the rail, his arms flailed, and, instinctively, he caught himself.

Our suicidal sniper was now hanging by his hands about 100 feet over our heads. Instinct having taken over when he slipped, it looked like he had lost his resolve. He looked to be hanging on for, as they say, dear life.

Two volunteer firemen thundered past me, followed by an ambulance EMT and Volont. They rushed the fallen stepladder into position, and began climbing frantically toward the top of the elevator.

The fire chief came up beside me. "We ain't got a ladder that will make it more than seventy-five feet," he said, simply. "They better hurry."

"Yeah."

"Funny, isn't it, I mean the way they want to jump, and then they don't?"

"Sure is," I said. "I wonder why he just didn't shoot himself."

It took, oh, probably a minute, for them to get to the top. It seemed like an hour to me, and I was just an observer. They had to go over the rail, and then about twenty feet to my left, before they could get to him. I could hear them hollering to him to hang on.

It was very close. Too close for me.

The two firemen each grabbed at him over the edge, and then the EMT reached way down, and caught the back of his coat in her hands. I could just see the top of Volont's head, and supposed he was pulling on her waist. They all seemed to freeze that way for an instant, and they all sort of heaved together, and the dangling sniper slid back up, over the rail, and they all disappeared from view.

"Know who he is?" asked the fire chief.

"Not yet," I breathed. "But we will . . ."

By the time they got back down, there was a little crowd of us waiting for them at the bottom of the ladder. Lamar and I, Art, the two troopers from the parking lot, several firemen, and a couple of EMTs.

Volont suggested the troopers handcuff the sniper. As they did so, I got my first clear look at him. I was flabbergasted.

Our trembling, nearly collapsing sniper was none other than Horace Blitek, the screwy member of the Borglan defense team.

You could have, as they say, knocked me over with a feather.

We hauled him up to the hospital in an ambulance, to be checked out.

We were met by my old friend Dr. Henry Zimmer at the entrance to the emergency room of our thirty-bed hospital. As soon as Henry had heard there was a sniper, he had prudently called in two extra nurses, a couple of lab and X-ray techs, and his junior partner, Dr. Paul Kline. Consequently, as soon as Horace Blitek was out of the ambulance on his stretcher, he was nearly mobbed by attention.

"So, this is the guy everybody's making such a fuss about?" said Henry.

"Yep. In the flesh," I said. "He did try to jump, Henry. You might want to know that."

"Depressed," asked Henry, "or just in a hurry?" He chuckled, and started in to the ER, where Horace Blitek could just barely be seen through the little bevy of nurses and ambulance personnel. "We'll see if we can't cheer him up . . ."

While they attended to Blitek, I got a chance to talk to Volont and Art.

"All he had was an SKS. The pauses were to reload. Just had loose ammo in boxes. No clips." Volont shook his head. "He had to reload by hand after every few rounds."

The SKS doesn't have a detachable magazine, but it was a favorite of some survivalist types, for some reason. Semiauto rifle, 7.62 mm. Chinese manufacture of an old Soviet design. They cost about $75.00, which may have gone a long way toward their popularity.

"So, why didn't he shoot himself?" I asked.

Volont grinned. "Out of ammunition. Not even proficient enough to save one for himself."

"So," said Art, "now we just have to find out why he was so pissed off."

Henry pronounced Blitek fit a few minutes later. "Just some bruises on his forearms, and on his butt. Otherwise, he's just a picture of physical health."

"Thanks, Henry. We just needed to be sure."

"You might want to have a psychiatrist check him out, though. He's really upset. Told me that he's let Gabriel down, and that Gabriel is going to 'get' him." He clapped me on the shoulder. "You do get some strange ones for us, Houseman. But a personal feud with an archangel . . ."

"Yeah . . ."

Volont and I conferred. Based on what Henry had just said, we really needed to talk with Blitek. Even in his possibly mentally disturbed state.

"We won't be able to use anything we get against him . . ."

Volont shrugged. "Then we don't use it against *him* . . . but we use it to get Gabriel."

We took Blitek to the office, and began making the arrangements for an emergency committal to a mental health institute, for evaluation. He had, after all, attempted suicide. But we'd have at least two hours before the arrival of the mental health referee, who would examine him.

While we had been at the hospital with Blitek, two state troopers, Art and George, had been to the top of the elevator. Lots of shell casings. 7.62 mm. The rifle. Some brown cardboard ammo boxes. Nothing else, though. Courtesy Maitland PD, chains and padlocks had been installed on the caged, exterior access ladder, in three layers, where a cop in a car could see them. A potential sniper could still climb to the top, but it was hoped that he'd at least be more obvious. The area was pronounced secure.

Pronouncement be damned, I noticed that almost everybody was suddenly using the back door to the office.

Twenty

Friday, January 16, 1998,
1717

We sat Blitek in a chair in the reception area, while we tried to find a room without bystanders where we could interview him.

"Cletus and his attorney are in the interview room," said Lamar. He indicated Blitek, sitting bedraggled in the corner. "Shit," he said, "he looks like somethin' the cat dragged in."

He did. At the hospital, they had pretty well undressed him, looking at what turned out to be minor injuries, and prodding and probing to make certain there was no internal damage. Typically for those under emotional duress, and on the downside of a suicide high to boot, he had then replaced his clothing in a rather haphazard manner, not tucking in his long john top, or buttoning his plaid shirt. His fly was unzipped. His boots were untied, with the laces dragging on the floor. He was sitting in a small wooden chair, with his head in his hands, and his elbows on his knees; his disheveled gray and brown hair sticking straight out between his fingers. The only bright element in the picture was the touch of silver provided by the handcuffs.

We decided the best place for him was the kitchen. Available coffee, rest room, and no phones. We kicked everybody else out, including the troopers and Maitland officers who were regaling a small crowd of late arrivers with lurid descriptions of the monster sniper. They looked a bit silly we as brought Blitek in and shooed them out.

We sat him down, and I went out a different door on my way to get note tablets and pens for the interview. As I did, I had to excuse my passage though the interview room containing Cletus Borglan and Attorney Gunston.

Cletus looked kind of bad, and Gunston was being all protective. "Did you manage to get whoever it was? Is this area secure now?"

"Oh, yeah," I said. Just passing through. I was on my way back with the tablets before it occurred to me, I excused my way through the interview room again, and hit the kitchen with a plan.

"I think," I said, "we'd be better off doing this interview in your office, Lamar." Way back on the other side of the building.

As he started to protest, I motioned him over by the sink. "I just came through the interview room," I said, in a low voice. "Cletus and his attorney are in there, and they don't know who the shooter was."

I could almost see the cartoon lightbulb come on over Lamar's head. To arrive at his office, we would have to transit the interview room occupied by Cletus and company.

"Let's take him back to my office," said Lamar, in a loud, clear voice.

We paraded past Cletus and Gunston. Lamar, Volont, Blitek, and me. Slowly, of course, so that Blitek wouldn't trip on his shoelaces. Blitek's head was down, and in his state, I don't think he even noticed who we were passing by. None of us said a word. Except for Lamar, who simply said, "Excuse us, please," as he led the way through.

I glanced at Cletus, who had the now familiar pre-heave glaze in his eyes.

It was much more crowded in Lamar's office, but it had been worth the trip.

Blitek, in a mumbling sort of way, told us some interesting

things. Gabriel had, in fact, told him to "take out" Cletus. Blitek had been assigned what he called a "cosniper," a fellow named Rollings. He never showed. Blitek was just sufficiently frightened of Gabriel that he undertook the "mission" alone. He thought that might have been a mistake. In retrospect, sort of.

"Well," said Lamar, kindly, "you gotta do what you gotta do."

Blitek had told Gabriel, as it turned out, everything that had been said by Cletus at the interviews. Including the fact that we knew about the phone call from the Cletus Borglan residence to the Cletus Borglan residence, so to speak.

Shit.

He also told us that Gabriel was still planning some sort of major operation for Sunday? Something to do with cash, and banks, but probably not what Cletus had described.

"You mean, 'had been planning,' don't you?" I was fairly certain by then that we had just lost Gabriel again.

It was the only time that a spark of life showed in Blitek's eyes that day. He had almost a religious fervor about him. "Gabriel says that there's no way you Zionist puppets can interfere. You can't stop him. It's a military operation, and you don't have a chance." He kind of giggled, like a kid. "There's going to be no betrayal this time!"

We decided the best way to find out was to talk to Cletus. By now, both Davies and Attorney Gunston were at the jail. Gunston said we could talk to Cletus, but that he was making arrangements for a doctor to attend his client and perhaps give him a sedative.

"No sedative," said Davies. "We wouldn't want you to say that we'd talked to him under the influence of drugs, would we."

I stood on the front porch of the jail with Volont, Davies, Art, and George. It was the best place for a fast private meeting. Nobody else seemed to want to hang around in view of the grain elevator.

"So, how do we proceed?" George kept glancing at the elevator in the distance. "Well, he's seen Blitek. He's got to be aware that everything he's said has already been given to Gabriel."

Volont looked around. "I'd say he's just about ripe, if we can protect him."

"We can't," said Art. He'd been a deputy in Nation County long enough to know what our resources were. Now that he was a state officer, he knew what they had available. He was right.

"We can," said Volont.

He was right. They probably could. For me, it was just a question of whether or not we could convince Cletus of that. I had absolutely no problem with giving him up, in exchange for getting Gabriel. We'd intended that all along.

"I'm not authorized to make deals," said Art.

"I am," said Davies.

"Not without the permission of the local prosecutor," said Art. Knowing full well that, as yet, there really wasn't one.

"We'll talk about that one again, after you've passed the Bar." Davies kept his voice light, but there was no mistaking the fact that Art was being shut down. He turned, and looked at me. "I think you and I should do the interview, since you've established something of a rapport with Mr. Borglan."

"Yeah," I chuckled. "I make him puke."

"And that a representative of the FBI should also be present, to make the 'protection' offer." He smiled, brightly. "A gesture of good faith . . ."

Volont, Davies, and I were in the "interrogation kitchen," as Davies referred to it, and Lamar was bringing Cletus out of his cell. Attorney Gunston was waiting to talk to Cletus before we did, in the secure room.

"Now, let me see," said Davies. "Paper . . . pencil . . . briefcase . . . vomit bag . . ."

"Give me a break," I said. "It was probably something he ate."

Volont said, "We don't ask directly about Sunday?"

Davies and I agreed. "How about the banks? How direct for details?" I wanted to have the interview parameters really clear on this one.

"Whatever you need on that," Volont said. "Don't forget that

Attorney Gunston was at the Borglan farm before he knew Cletus was being charged. I don't like the possible connection here to the rest of that group."

"Right," said Davies. "We should have Cletus pretty nervous, right now. Let's try to keep the edge on him as long as we can." Leaned back in my chair. "What about Florida, and the call? More detail?"

"I do that one," said Davies. "Remember," he cautioned, "we have him on a solid aiding and abetting of a double murder. We don't want to forget that."

"By the way," said Volont, "you do know his real name is Jacob Henry Nieuhauser?"

"Nieuhauser?" asked Davies.

"Gabriel . . . his full name is Jacob Henry Nieuhauser."

Davies wrote it down.

Cletus and Gunston entered the kitchen, guided by Lamar, who backed out, locking the door behind him. Our defendant and his attorney sat down at the long, old table. As far from the three of us as they could get.

We got off to a really good start, what with Blitek having been Exhibit A and all. Until Gunston said, "You have no direct evidence that Mr. Blitek was shooting at my client, here. He could well have been attempting to facilitate my client's escape, instead."

Weak. Stupid, really. Last try.

"He just told us his assignment was to kill Cletus, here." Davies grinned across the kitchen table. "That would be your client. Make no mistake." He looked at his yellow tablet. "If your client can tell us some things about Jacob Henry Nieuhauser," he said, slowly, "we may have an offer we can put on the table."

"We'll entertain an offer," said Gunston. "Even though my client has done nothing wrong. But, if as you say, he was the target this morning, then you must guarantee him protection."

"We may make an offer, depending on what your client is willing to share with us," said Volont. "As for protection, we think he's safe in this building for now. If we move him at some date, you must understand that you will only be informed after the fact."

Gunston, still aggressively defending, looked at Volont. "And just who might you be?"

I love it when this happens. Especially with somebody like Volont, who can place a 600 lb. badge on the table.

"Special Agent in Charge Volont, Federal Bureau of Investigation, Counterintelligence Unit." I don't know, it just sounded so good. Gunston looked startled. Cletus looked like somebody had reached into his chest and grabbed his heart.

Gunston, who deserved much credit, managed to say, "I didn't know the FBI had jurisdiction in this kind of case."

"It's not the murder that particularly concerns him," said Davies, also obviously pleased to have Volont at the table. "It's what you might call collateral matters. Very large collateral matters."

Cletus didn't vomit. I was relieved. His face began to redden, though, as he looked at each of us in turn. His gaze kept moving back to Volont, and he finally said, "What do you want from me?"

"We should confer . . ." was about all Gunston got out.

"No!" Cletus was scared silly, and getting pissed off that his attorney seemed to be dragging his feet at his salvation. "Just promise me protection. That son of a bitch is a professional killer!"

We quickly completed what Davies later said was the "fastest, strangest" deal and information exchange he'd ever done.

Mercifully, it was also vomit-free.

Cletus was given federal protection, and his charge of two counts of Conspiracy to Commit Murder was reduced to Obstruction of Justice, to which he would enter a plea of guilty. Quite a deal, indeed. Until you consider that, if tried in Nation County, he probably would have gotten at least as good a result.

In exchange, he gave us Gabriel on a platter. Well, as far as I was concerned.

Jacob Henry Nieuhauser, whom he had known for several years, had come to him for a place to stay while he scouted "five handy little banks" that he intended to take off. These banks apparently had been part of his original plan back in June of 1996, when events in our county had conspired to thwart him.

What banks? Cletus didn't know. But the number five had been mentioned.

He'd let Nieuhauser, a.k.a. Gabriel, use his home, while Cletus and his wife were wintering in Florida. Low-profile, no problem. He'd received the phone call, all right. From Gabriel, who had told him that he'd become aware that he was under surveillance by some cops for about a week or so, and had been preparing to "take measures to throw them off the trail" when the cops had broken into the house. He was certain they were cops, because they'd told him they were.

I thought that was pretty sad.

Cletus said that Gabriel had killed one, then tried to question the other. The second brother tried denying that they were cops, even though they'd originally said that they were. Since the young man was adamant about it, after a few minutes of questioning, he'd killed him, too. It had been "necessary." His cover was being blown.

Of course there had been no information. Neither of the poor damned Colson brothers could possibly know shit about what Gabriel wanted. Talk about terror. Especially for the second one to go. I tried to make that very clear to Cletus, but he was so worried about himself I don't think it took.

The computers were engaged in what was called "distributed computing," a network of over 100 machines each working on a small portion of a project. But he didn't know of what kind. Where was Gabriel now? He didn't know, but he was sure that he was around. The banks were scheduled to go down soon, and he knew that Gabriel wasn't going to be put off this time around. The cause needed money.

We made Cletus disappear this way: We called for an ambulance to come to the Sheriff's Department. When they arrived, we told them that we needed a special favor. Volont and I accompanied Cletus and his attorney in the ambulance to the hospital. Volont had called for a chopper. It arrived, and we made all the right fuss to have Cletus look as if he were on his way to a major trauma center. Put him onboard in a stretcher and everything. Four FBI agents were in the chopper. Volont insisted that Gunston accompany him. Insisted by way of placing him in protective custody. No kidding. I never thought they could really do that.

As Volont said, it kept both of them out of the way for a good seventy-two hours.

He told me that the Huey took them to Waterloo, where they would be held at a National Guard facility.

We divided the rest of the evening between trying to figure out how to prevent the bank robberies.

I enjoyed eating dinner in Lamar's office. Cheeseburgers delivered by Maitland PD and Judy. Being the only person in the room on a low-fat diet, they tasted fantastic to me. Somehow, I'd become convinced that, if I ate that stuff under these circumstances, it just didn't count. You know. Like when the waiter delivers the wrong thing to your table, and you get stuck with lots of gravy . . . I think I burned off most of the fat calories with frustration, anyway. We had real problems.

Let me just say that the bank jobs fall into two possible categories. First, there are robberies, which by definition would have to occur while there were people in the bank. Second, burglaries, which would occur when the banks were not occupied. The second was the least dangerous for all concerned, but the first was a hell of a lot more likely to get you into the safe. It would very likely be open during business hours. Open meant daylight. Closed meant night.

My point, and the one that stuck the whole operation together from our end, was just what Volont had always preached. Gabriel wasn't a "criminal" type, he was a soldier. There was a very big difference in approach.

I said as much.

"What?" asked Art, in rare humor. "Are we talking air strikes here, or what?" He was happier than hell to have the double murder solved. Knowing him, I figured he was only giving us half his attention, with the other half trying to figure out how he could claim credit for the entire case.

I think the most difficult thing to do as a cop is to predict what robbery or burglary target will be hit, how the suspect will do it, and when. I've worked on Task Forces where some of the best cops around were trying, and just couldn't get it to add up.

I shared one with the group. I told about the time that eleven counties and the state were trying to bust a group that was breaking into implement dealers at night, stealing tools, chain saws, snow blowers, lawn mowers . . . anything that could fit in the back of a pickup or a van. By the time the Task Force got involved, these boys had done almost thirty jobs.

We had drawn in the locations of each hit on an area map. Tried to find a center of gravity for the dots. One of the cops had an MBA, and did an analysis of the center of distribution that would have earned a promotion in the real world. We tried to determine which direction they would go by date of occurrence. We tried to determine how they would possibly scout a potential target. We did sort of a market analysis on items that were best stolen in particular seasons. We tried to find where they lived by correlating locations of burglaries. We skewed the maps by driving time instead of distance from possible origins. Then . . .

We got information from a snitch as to who they were. We followed them, and on the third night, busted them in a dealership. So much for pure "intelligence." Oh, yes. The kicker.

"We asked them how they determined what target to hit," I said. "Turns out that they'd buy a case of beer, put it in the van with the five of them, and start to drive aimlessly around. When the beer ran out, they'd just go to whatever implement dealer was closest, and bust in. No plan. Really skewed our maps on a couple of occasions when the driver had got lost, once in the fog." I chuckled. "We never thought to correlate the radius with driving conditions on a particular night."

"The point being?" asked Art, who had also been on that Task Force.

"Well," I said, "those were criminals we were dealing with. Nobody knows criminals better than a bunch of senior cops. And we couldn't predict what they were going to do next." I looked at him. "And here we are, trying to second-guess a professional soldier. Like, what are the odds?"

He glared.

"Unless we have a professional soldier in our midst," I said, "this is going to be very interesting." I was hoping that Volont would call in somebody from the U.S. Army, as an adviser. I hoped that one for a long time.

As usual, the real problem was that we didn't have enough information. Things like "five banks simultaneously" are worthless. We needed to know just who was working with him. How competent they were. How many associated did he have? Hell, just which "five banks" would be nice! And the really big question: Why hit five mediocre banks and get little, when you could go to a metro area, hit one for the same effort, and get a lot? I secretly suspected that our lack of officers had something to do with it. George put it pretty well when he said, "Carl, nothing personal, but with two to three of you on a shift, a bank robber could be fifty miles away before you could block very many roads."

"Frankly," said Volont, "they could be a long way before you could block this parking lot."

Art resented that, bless him. His face got kind of reddish, and he got a familiar, sour look on his face. I noticed that he didn't have a rejoinder.

Anyway, don't misunderstand. I love doing the map thing, drawing radii, plotting routes, assigning units, all that good stuff. Wonderful board game. Delightful. But in this case, with the information we had, it was pointless. It was like doing a map exercise on a blank piece of paper.

Volont had resources at his disposal that, given a day or two, could accomplish virtually anything. Really. Somebody would come up with a miniscenario, mark a map, and Volont would start saying things like "We could put a team here and here . . . a surveillance team here and here . . ." Wow. Really. Resources like that just trip my trigger. He talked about "helicopter landing zones," with the solid assurance of a man who utilized them all the time. But it was futile, having the resources and nowhere to use them. Like standing in front of a game machine that took only nickels, with a ten-pound bag that contained only quarters clutched in your little hand.

We stuck with it, though. We had nothing else to go on, or so I thought.

The intercom buzzed, and I answered. Judy, with a phone call for Volont. He took it out in the reception area. He was back in less than a minute.

"If you gentlemen will excuse me for a short while, I have some other business to attend to."

We did.

Just like so many other times, that little interruption broke the train of the meeting, and everybody just about simultaneously decided to take a break.

I took George aside out in the kitchen, when I went out to make a pot of coffee and he tagged along for the exercise. "What did you interview Nancy and Shamrock for?"

"Mostly to find out what they knew, and to tell them they couldn't use anything they had learned about a particular individual."

"George, damn it, it's our murder. We can deal with the press if we want to." The coffeepot had stopped gurgling, and was in the hiss-and-steam phase, which meant the water reservoir had emptied. The flavor was best then, before all the water had dripped through. I turned the pot off, and pulled the basket.

He shrugged. "We mostly wanted to shut down anything about Gabriel. They seemed to understand. Including the film."

" 'The film'?" I stood there with the pot in one hand, and a cup in the other, and nearly poured the contents on the floor.

"Shamrock's film. I asked her to let us keep the strip of negatives that contained the photos of Gabriel. Two frames."

I chuckled. "You mentioned Gabriel?"

"Volont specifically told me to. As Nieuhauser, of course. Not Gabriel. But this Nancy is pretty sharp. She picked up on it right away."

"Yeah." I poured my coffee, and put the pot down. "So, you don't think you pissed them off totally, then?"

"Oh, no. They were very nice." He poured his own, adding fat-free milk and sugar substitute.

"How is that shit?" I asked.

"Awful. Milk and sugar are good, though."

"Thanks." I took a sip. "Doesn't Volont realize that he just drew Nancy's attention to Gabe?"

"I'm sure he does," said George. "I'm just not clear as to why."

He sipped his coffee, looking a bit worried. "Can I trust you with something?"

"You bettcha."

He closed the door. "This is supersecret, and you never heard it. I'm deadly serious about this."

He sure appeared to be. "Fine. I'm good for it," I said.

"Okay . . . here you go. Don't ask how I know this, either, by the way. I can't tell you." George took a deep breath. "Okay. First, Gabriel is supposed to be leading Volont to some 'big man' in the antigovernment movements. Really big man. Gabe was Volont's snitch. At some point in the past. For sure. Volont squeezed him a few years ago, over some arms sales or something. But Volont's lost control of him. As if you hadn't figured that part out."

I just nodded. I figured this was not the time to demonstrate ignorance.

"Volont's pissed. 'Cause now old Gabe is simply getting ready to make a hit to fill his own pockets, and run away to somewhere. Not for the 'movement.' That's all phony as hell, now." George looked around, just checking, I guess. "None of this 'five banks' thing is for anything other than Gabe. All his associates don't know this, but he's just using them for his own purposes."

"And Volont knows all this?" I asked.

"And a hell of a lot more," said George. "He's got people on the inside, I'm certain."

"I'll be damned." I thought for a few seconds, wondering who that could be. "And he's probably known this for a while now, hasn't he?"

"You could say that," said George.

"I know what that Spook stuff's like, George. Are you sure Volont is right about him not doing this for the 'movement,' or anything like that? Could he have misled Volont?"

George grinned. "Wheels within wheels. Just know what I've been told," he said.

"Sounds true," I said. "You know what they say about 'doing it for the movement.' Just means you don't have to pay the help."

Fascinating. Unfortunately, it didn't change a thing as far as murder and bank burglary were concerned. Ideology aside, we still had the same problems going on.

"Thanks, George," I said. "A lot." He'd taken a large risk to tell me that. I just wished it had been something I could have used to stop the "five banks" stuff, or to have prevented the deaths of the Colson brothers. But I did file it away, and very carefully, too.

Twenty-one

Saturday, January 17, 1998,
0714

'd made it out of bed at 0702. Nearly a record. After a quick shower, I'd pulled on sweatpants and a shirt, and made a pot of fresh coffee. The Weather Channel gave me a new shot of my blue and pink worm, coiling through North America. The upward bump was edging closer and closer. Ah, warmth was on the way. Soon.

Sue didn't flinch when I got up. Still mad about Madison, I guess. I promised myself that I'd make it up to her somehow, but then thoughts of the "five banks" took over. I decided to go see Hester again and get her thoughts before hitting the office. I called George and he agreed to come with me. He must be as addicted to the buffet as I am.

The three of us sat looking out at the red-neon-framed *Beau*, glittering in the clear morning and reflecting on the small patch of liquid water that surrounded her. The Mississippi, except where the slight heat from the *Beau*'s pumps and disturbed water flow kept it from freezing, was covered with a thick coat of ice. Hester told us that she'd seen cars carrying ice fishermen on it as late as yesterday. It was warming a bit, though. I would hesitate to drive on the stuff myself, now.

"So," said Hester, wistfully, "things looking up?"

We brought her up to date on the interviews, and the "five banks" business.

"Five?"

"Yeah, five. Why five? We don't have the foggiest."

"Does Gabe have access to a good safe man?" asked Hester.

"Not that we're aware of," said George. "But with his training in explosives, he probably could do it very well himself."

"Daylight," said Hester. "I'll bet on daylight. He can't be in five places at once, and explosives require a high level of competence."

"That's true." We'd spent the better part of the afternoon on it, and Hester had just zipped in with an excellent point we'd overlooked. Another reason I liked her so much.

"How much cash you got floating on the old *Beau* out there?"

"Oh, maybe thirty to fifty thousand at any given time. They use some tokens, coins, and cash, but it's hauled to the banks very regularly . . ." She grinned. "You thinking piracy?"

"Well, I was . . ."

"They keep the cash on hand to a minimum, just for that reason." She suddenly got very serious. "They might have a lot more than that in the local bank," she said. "Especially on a weekend . . ."

" 'Bank'?" It was George's turn to look concerned. "We considered this one, but felt that the cash flow would be small. You know. The workers here wouldn't get that much cash on a payday . . ."

"They take it off the boat," said Hester. "It's gotta go somewhere. I think I heard they distribute it between several banks, but I'm not really up on this operation yet. Want me to check?"

"I'll check," said George.

"So," said Hester, "Super Agent Volont have the principals wired on this one?"

"Everybody but Gabe," I said, grinning. "He says he's lost him, and I think that's true."

"Even if it wasn't," said George, "I think he'd be a lot better off trying to take him out in the world, than he would be trying to arrest him wherever he's holed up." He shrugged. "I think we can be pretty sure that Gabe will find us."

I couldn't have agreed more. Gabriel would be able to not

only hold off a small army, but I wasn't so sure he wouldn't take the offensive and break out. With lots of unnecessary bodies in his wake. The man was really good at that sort of thing, and I believed he had access to more dangerous tools than even the FBI did.

"So where's Volont?" asked Hester. "I would have thought he'd be with you two."

"Last we saw of him," I said, "I think he was off to meet one of his famous sources." I took a sip of coffee. "I wonder who they are, anyway?"

"Wouldn't it be funny," said Hester, "if he was calling a psychic?"

That made my day.

As we left, she said, "Hey, look on the bright side. At least you know who did the brothers in the shed. The big case is all over but the shouting."

"Yeah, and Art'll take care of that."

When I got back to the office, I met with Mike Connors. Since he'd been with the department for over fifteen years, he was pretty much in charge of the night shift. He was also renowned for being able to keep his mouth shut.

I checked with him on the general stuff happening with the night shift. Who or what was moving. Anything suspicious. Mike just shook his head.

"You might want to keep an eye on all the banks in the county . . ."

He raised an eyebrow, but said nothing. He'd been one of those tunnel rats in Vietnam. It took a whole hell of a lot to get a rise out of him. Whether it was a case of the chicken or the egg being first, I couldn't tell you.

"We might have a problem there," I said. "There might be somebody scouting some of 'em. You seen anything unusual . . . ?"

"Sure."

"But don't tell the other people on the shift," I said. "Just you and me for now."

"Got it."

"Hey, by the way, do you know either Harvey or Linda Grossman?"

He smiled. "Linda. You should remember her, too."

"Me?" I grinned. "Sure I do, I just met her a couple of days ago."

"No, no. She was a Perrin. Married a fellow named Voshell before she got hitched to this Grossman guy. You remember now?"

Not at all.

"You remember Nola Stritch?"

Did I. She had been heavily involved with the whole Gabriel business back in '96.

"Linda's her sister."

" 'Sister'? I didn't know she had a sister . . ." I was dumbfounded.

"Yep. Well, half sister. Nola's maiden name was Jaekel. Divorce in the family. Little sister's maiden name was Perrin. Linda Perrin. Remember her? Charlie Perrin's kid. We got her twelve, thirteen years ago for beer."

It never occurred to me to question a beer ticket from a dozen years ago. He had that kind of memory.

"I'll be damned," I said. "Be really aware around the banks. You remember the Gabriel dude who did all the shit at the courthouse?"

"Oh, yeah . . ."

"He's back, and he's the one we think is going for the banks."

He got very serious, very quickly. "No shit?"

"No shit. Without any names, bring the night folks up to one hundred percent, okay? I think something's gonna happen between now and Sunday."

"Yep. Who else knows about this?"

"Me, and Lamar. Sally, at least part of it. Two DCI. FBI, of course. Gabriel," I added, grinning.

"Right."

"And Mike? One more thing. I think it's about one hundred

percent that Gabriel offed the Colson brothers. You can figure he's in a mood."

George came in with a look in his eye.

"Let's take a drive up to the Frieberg bank."

I drove. Less conspicuous that any U.S. government Ford. Even if George had drawn one of the better ones. Forest green as opposed to navy blue.

"This could be a good day," I said.

"Let me guess. You're thinking, 'Thirty minutes of Frieberg. Minimum of thirty minutes at the bank. Time for lunch. The pavilion of the *General Beauregard*. Buffet.' " He looked up from studying the photographs of the field. "Right?"

It's embarrassing to be that obvious. I said as much.

"We all have our needs," he said.

The news we got at the bank took the fun right out of the day. In response to the ruse that we were engaged in a routine survey of all banks, the branch manager had been very reluctant to talk with us, even though he knew me on sight. George hit him with the Credential from God, and we got the straight dope right away.

It seemed that this little branch bank was often holding more than five million dollars in cash. Cash.

"Why didn't you tell us?"

"Well, it was all so hush-hush, you know. The casino people told them that nobody was supposed to know." Consequently, nobody did.

We asked where it was. All in the new vault. He checked his computer screen. "Well, right now, we're way down. Only one-point-three million."

Swell. And when did they expect the ante to rise?

"We do our greatest business beginning Thursday with the last deposit of the day. By end of business on Friday, we normally have about three-point-five million, and by start of business on Sunday, after the weekend drops, probably a little over five million."

Holy shit. And, it turned out, they had somebody in the bank on odd hours. One employee, to supervise the cash deposit and exchange. The casino was open, after all, twenty-four hours a day. And it appeared that there was no deposit slot in the area that could handle that volume of cash, without forcing the boat courier to spend an unconscionable amount of time standing around with the trunk of the car open.

"I wouldn't worry too much," he said. "We expect nearly half a million to be in coinage. Maybe more. Nobody would ever take that much weight in coins."

"Uh, just how much would that be?" I asked. "Would it weigh, you know?"

"Well," he said, "a thousand dollars in quarters weighs about fifty pounds. That would make ten thousand dollars weigh in at five hundred pounds, a hundred thousand dollars at five thousand pounds . . . so half a million dollars in quarters would run in the neighborhood of, oh, say twenty-five thousand pounds."

George and I looked at each other. I chuckled. "Nobody without a dump truck."

It was noon before we connected up with Hester in her office. I went right to the phone, while George gave her the bad news.

"Hey, Sally, can I talk to Lamar?" I waited, watching Hester react. I'd never seen her jaw drop before. "Lamar? Uh, I think we found the bank that's gonna get the most attention."

The term "flurry of activity" doesn't even begin to approach what was happening in the next thirty minutes. We were wanted at meetings with both Lamar and Volont, and even Art was trying to contact us. I dug my heels in, and finally convinced everybody that we'd attract a lot less attention at the DCI boat office than we would back at the Sheriff's Department.

Hester caught on immediately. "You're shameless. You know that, don't you?"

"It's the only buffet in the whole damned county," I said. "You've just become desensitized because you get to eat here every day."

"You do, too," she said.

Yeah. Anyway, as we waited for the conference to congregate, I asked Hester if she had some quarters. She fished six from her purse. I asked George, and he came up with four. I added them to the seven I had in my pocket, and stacked them on Hester's desk.

"You got a ruler?"

"Houseman," she said, fishing around in her desk drawer, "what are you doing?"

She handed me a ruler. I stacked the quarters, and removed two.

"There's fifteen quarters to an inch," I said.

"Well, I always wanted to know that. Thanks, Houseman. Can I have my ruler back now?"

"Sure. You got a calculator?"

This time, she didn't say anything. Just pushed it over to me.

"Did you know that a million dollars in quarters would weigh about fifty thousand pounds?" I asked.

"No."

"That'd be four million quarters. At fifteen to the inch, that would be a stack just about four-point-two miles high."

There was a pause. "Can I have my quarters back, now?"

"Oh, sure." I handed them to her, and gave George his. "The banker said they'd likely have at least half a million dollars in change at the bank, over there. Since they use quarters on the boat, I figured that'd be a hell of a lot of quarters." I smiled. "Four-point-two miles, stacked."

She just stared at me.

"Twenty-five thousand pounds," I said.

Hester sort of giggled. "Is there a point to this?"

"Yeah," I grinned. "That's a lot of fuckin' quarters."

It was a great lunch. And, with any luck, the conference would last until suppertime. We did need to be there, though. You could see the bank from Hester's window. You could also see about three easy routes to and from, and all sorts of places for the good guys to hide. Not to mention the bad.

After lunch, I took Volont aside for a second.

"Did you know that Linda Grossman was Nola Stritch's half sister?"

He waited a beat. "Really?" No expression.

"Really. Just found it out. Want me to check further?"

"Sure. But not a high priority. Not now."

Just then Art and George came up, and the four of us rode the elevator to third. I made a mental note to tell George about Linda and Nola. Just in case Volont "forgot."

Back in Hester's office, we got down to it in earnest. One of the first rules is you never, repeat never, take the bad guys while they're in the bank. One of the other first rules is that you never, never prevent them from leaving. And in our case, you wanted to positively encourage them to think they had a clean getaway ahead of them. This leaves you with two basic choices.

First, you take them on the way to the bank, in which case you have a potential problem with proving that they actually intended to hit the bank. You also have a bit of trouble when you don't know just how they intend to do the job in the first place, and just who is involved, and what they might be using for transportation. So, that was out.

Second, take them shortly after they've left the bank. Wait long enough to not jeopardize the bank staff, but move soon enough to catch them before they could disperse. That was the only sensible plan. If they actually went to the bank, of course. There are no certainties.

"What if they get the cash courier instead?" Art, sitting on the edge of one of the boaties' desks, was the first to put that card on the table. I think we'd all been dreading dealing with that.

"He needs mucho cash," said Volont. "Why go for part, when you can get it all?"

"How big a part?" Hester has a way.

"What?"

"How big a part can they get if they take out the courier? How much do they transfer, and when?"

Hester, George, and I found ourselves walking onto the boat, headed for the security office, and asking ourselves a question. How do you tell the chief of security about what we thought was going to go down, and then get him to be nonchalant? Well, you just don't. Do the basics, but leave out the hot information. Besides, the three of us were bound to get his interest up.

Harmon James was the head of security on the *General Beauregard*. Nice guy, about thirty-five, fit, bright. Probably made three times as much as I did. He already knew Hester. He met George and me. As we sat, he pressed an intercom button and said, "Agnes, could we have some coffee and mints, please?" I heard a voice on the other end. There hadn't been any secretary in evidence.

"So, what can the *General Beauregard* do for you?"

If it had been a month or two before the bank job was going to go down, we'd have had a little more leeway. As it was, I was the designated liar.

"We're going to have a disaster drill, and we need something that will involve federal, state, and local law enforcement. You're all we could think of." I shall likely rot in hell.

We talked a bit. Agnes brought the coffee. She was as close to a showgirl as you could get. Short black skirt. Net stockings. Heels. Classy white blouse. Not your typical government employee. The mints were chocolate-covered.

"How do you get a job like this?" I was flattering him. I was also very curious.

He'd been a deputy sheriff in Nevada. No kidding.

"Yep," he said, "this is where we go when we die . . ."

After that, I began to think we could trust him.

At any rate, we did find out the information we needed. They never transferred more than a quarter of a million at a time.

"That's what dictates the scheduling. And that's the beauty of it," he said. "There's no way somebody can get onto our schedule, because there isn't one. Different employee takes it each time, different vehicle, different route. No way to even know how much we've got onboard. Works."

"Cool." I thought it was.

"We were going to use an armored car service," he said, "but there isn't one available, except the one that services the banks. They can't fit us on anything like the schedule we'd need, and they aren't about to buy a new truck just for us. We really don't want to keep much more than five hundred thousand on the boat, anyway. And even that is divided up by a cash cage on each of three gaming decks, and a counting area under the waterline. A hit on one of them, and all of them are notified and close down. Piece of cake." He had a glimmer in his eye. He knew. Or, rather, he suspected. Either way, I had the feeling that things were going to tighten up on the boat for the next while.

"And," he said, "we transfer coins once a week. Lots and lots of quarters." He grinned broadly. "They accumulate around our slot machines the same way they do on your dresser at home."

As we left, I purloined another chocolate-covered mint.

They sure seemed to have it covered on the boat. Security at the bank, though . . . a different question all together. As with most banks, they relied on structures, not people. Structures, and lots of alarm functions that were going to alert law enforcement.

The guessing game was going on when we got back to Hester's office.

"Why Sunday?" Art was saying. "Why not Friday or Saturday?"

"More money." Point to Lamar.

"If Gabriel is still around after all this excitement," added Hester.

"He's here," said Volont. "Don't worry about that."

"Well, now, just a minute," said Lamar. "Let's clear this up right now. Do you actually know he's here, or are you just guessing?"

Volont, I'm sure, wasn't accustomed to being talked to in quite that manner. He handled himself well, I thought.

"He's here, Sheriff. What we do is use several things. Elimination is one of them. We have informants in three or four places he is most likely to be if he isn't here. He's not at those places. We use deduction based on knowledge gained over a long period of time. He's invested heavily in this operation, with the heaviest investment being the two Colson brothers that he killed. He doesn't like to do that. He's got plans. Accomplices. He needs the cash. He'd not the type to let a subordinate run the main operation. He's here. All the indications are, he's here." He looked at Lamar.

"So," said my boss, "you boil it down, and skim off the fat, you're still guessing. I'm not saying it's not a good guess. But it is a guess."

"That's right. But it's a truly good guess, and it's right." Volont flicked out one of those tight little grins of his. "Let's see what to do with the bank."

"Good guess" my ass. Volont was lying through is teeth, and if I hadn't had that conversation with George, I'd have bought it hook, line, and sinker. He was good. As it was, I was now certain that he knew exactly where Gabriel was. And he really was close.

In the end, we decided to go really light on the other four banks. Whichever ones they might be. The main forces, so to speak, were to be concentrated on Frieberg. The "daylight, bank open" plan was to set up around the bank, at enough distance to ensure they would be well clear of the place before we hit them. Roadblock vehicles, surveillance teams, chase cars. All concealed. Manned mostly by FBI and DCI SWAT team members.

Our "nighttime, bank closed" plan was very similar, but brought the ring in a bit closer. Both plans included a helicopter on standby at Maitland Airport. We felt we had to use Maitland, because the only other airport with gas and any sort of facility was just across the Mississippi from Frieberg, in Jollietteville, Wisconsin. A Huey sitting there, so close to the Freiberg bank, would possibly be spotted by the bad guys. Tip time. We did send a delegation across the river, to meet with their people, and let them know they might have a bank robbery on Sunday, too. Just being neighborly.

For our cohorts in Conception County, this was a definite "need to know" situation. They were just across the Mississippi bridge, a trip of 1.6 miles without a turnoff. The actual width of the Mississippi there was about a mile, but the approaches on both ends of the bridge extend the trip. The Iowa and Wisconsin spans met on a small island in the middle. I really mean small. No structures, just a lump of dry ground about halfway across. Once on the bridge, a bank robber either had to cross, stop, or come back. No exits. Besides, if we actually got into a pursuit, crossing the bridge was as good a route as any for flight. The 1.6 miles would go by in a minute, literally, in a high-speed pursuit. Without forewarning, it was very possible that Wisconsin wouldn't be able to get the bridge blocked in time.

Covered on that one.

Lamar was still skeptical of the entire plan. "Don't forget, we want him for murder. Two counts, at least. Maybe more if we re-open an old case. What's wrong with, we see him, we grab him?" He addressed Volont directly. "Is it good if we let him commit a bank job, too?"

"No, it isn't. Not at all. But," said Volont, "it is important that we be sure we have him. If we go to take down a suspect in a car, based on a glimpse of somebody, we might get the wrong man. We might tip off the right man. We can be sure," he said, emphatically, "that he'll be with the bank team. I have good information on that. Very good."

"Wait a minute," said Lamar. "You keep pullin' this information out of your hat every time you need it, and we're supposed to buy it." He looked around the room. "Doesn't it seem that way to you all?"

Before any of us could answer, Volont spoke rapidly. "My rules keep me from telling you certain things until you demonstrate a 'need to know.' When you ask the question, I can sometimes give an answer under those rules."

Lamar sighed, and stood up. "I gotta get back to the office." And he walked out. Just like that.

Well. There was a pretty thick silence after he left. I broke it with "Looks like you better be right on this one." I could say that. I'd been shot the last time Volont had made a mistake. In the vest, admittedly. What the hell, it's the thought that counts.

"Confidence," he said, blandly, "is high."

I thought what Hester had said about a psychic. I caught her eye and grinned at her, but she was too worried to catch it.

We made tentative assignments, and the call went out to begin gathering reinforcements. I headed back to Maitland. Tomorrow was Sunday. Sunday was Bank Day. Time was getting short.

Twenty-two

Volont stuck his head in the door. "TAC team commander will meet with you out here in a few minutes. He just landed." He was gone as quickly as he'd appeared.

George had hardly had time to "pop to". "We gotta plan, I guess."

"Yeah." I rummaged through the box, looking for another doughnut with little sprinkles on it. "I think this is as close as Volont ever gets to orgasm."

George started to laugh, caught it, but still had a dribble of coffee on his chin. "Don't say those things!"

"Oh, yeah, before I forget . . . Remember Nola Stritch?"

He sure did.

"Well, Cletus Borglan's hired man and his family? The Grossmans?" He nodded. "Turns out that she's Nola's sister. Half sister, anyway. Neat, no?"

"Well," he said, "I'm glad Volont finally told you."

"He didn't tell me, George. We found out on our own."

"Oh, then you must be the one who told Volont," he said, lamely.

"Well, I thought so . . . You know, George, I've been thinking about all this. You guys are really throwing a lot of resources at this. I mean, really. Surveillance for God knows how long. TAC team. It's a lot like last time. Only more, you know?"

George smiled. "Just consider it part of the Peace Dividend."

I thought that was a strange thing for George to say.

"I've been led to believe that this was sort of a vengeance thing between Gabriel and Volont," I said, slowly. I looked at my empty coffee cup. "I've been buying into a cover story, haven't I?"

Silence.

"Not blaming you, George. You bought it at first, too. But something's different, and I think it's that you know a lot more than you're being allowed to say. Now."

He smiled, ruefully. "I couldn't tell you even if I did. Could I?"

I spoke very quietly. "The whole damned Bureau has just been relentless with this Gabriel dude. Obviously for several years, going back to before I ever knew about him. And still. Still at war with him." I pushed my cup away, and my chair back. "It's no vendetta, where he screwed Volont, and Volont is just screwing back. Is it?"

Before he could answer, I grinned and said, "Don't tell me, you'd only have to kill yourself." I was sort of kidding. He surprised me, though. He gave me an answer.

"No. It's much more than that. Volont really doesn't give a damn about Gabriel, at all. He just knows him fairly well." He shrugged. "If it helps, I only found that out a few months ago, myself."

We were interrupted by Sally, who knocked on the door frame and announced we had a guest.

The FBI TAC team leader was top-notch. Higher, in fact. Excellent individual, very precise, and completely without pretense.

"This could get to be a real zoo," he said. "We really don't have a lot of good data, do we?" Smart, too.

He knew damned well that I hadn't called him in. I couldn't. Neither could George. That being the case, he didn't have to worry about hurting our feelings.

"Not a lot." I handed him a cup of coffee, and our file on the banks, the schedules for deposits, and the plans of each building. "I do think the Freiberg bank is the main hit, though."

He looked at the possible banks sheet. "I agree." He looked up, sharply. "You guys just found out about the cash on hand yesterday?"

We told him how that had happened. He grinned. "Always the last to know."

We went over again the list of other possible banks. We hit upon a compromise. FBI TAC would take on the Frieberg bank, while the Iowa State Patrol TAC team would put two men on each of six little banks, in plain clothes. A tactical reserve of eight FBI TAC officers would be at the Maitland Airport with a helicopter, ready to respond to whichever area seemed to need them.

I just love resources.

As a gesture to goodwill between departments, our county officers would be assigned as roving patrol near each of the banks. Iowa State Patrol units would be assigned to each area as well, with the majority being around Frieberg.

Each local police department in a town with a "targeted bank" would be notified, and would have an officer on duty, but not obviously around the bank.

I held my hands up off the table, palms toward the TAC man. "That might be a problem . . ."

"Oh?"

"Uh, well, you see, of the six 'possibles,' only two are in towns with police departments."

The TAC man seemed somewhat taken aback. "Just how big are these towns, anyway?"

I pointed to them on the map, and told him the population of each town as I did so. "Three hundred, two fifty, four fifty, two hundred, eighteen hundred, and twenty-six hundred." The last two were Maitland, the county seat; and Frieberg. "Maitland and Frieberg have local departments."

"Gonna be difficult for the surveillance teams not to stand out," he said.

"Let me tell you," said George. "Rush hour consists of three or four cars . . ."

The TAC commander gave me a quizzical look. "In such small places . . . how much money do you think they'll get?"

"Twenty-nine ninety-five," I said. "Hey, don't ask. Reliable informant says, 'five banks.' Volont says, 'five banks.' All in the same area. We figure that'd be here."

"Same area . . . same time?"

"Yep. That's what they said."

"Well, then, that's what we prep for." He grinned. "Good exercise. We can get inconspicuous here, we can hide just about anyplace."

"If you can hide in these little towns," said George, "you can hide on a gym floor." He looked kind of sheepish all of a sudden. "Nothing personal, Carl."

"You never can tell about these little places," said the TAC commander. "They'll surprise you."

As our plans developed, it became painfully apparent that "Sunday" was a period twenty-four hours long. We had no idea when on Sunday they were going to hit. If they hit at all, of course. Consequently, it was decided that we'd be up and running for the full twenty-four hours. Lovely. I thought I'd probably go home for supper, get a nap in, and be back out around ten or so. It looked to be a long time before we got much sleep.

It was almost time for dinner when the intrepid Nancy called.

"Not on the phone. How about dinner? Just you, me, and Shamrock. It's pretty good stuff."

Where do you meet for lunch in a small town with two restaurants that were bound to be filled with either cops or press? Not the office. I couldn't afford to have them see any of the prep people who were beginning to arrive. Too cold for a picnic. Which left one place. "Can you pick me up a fish sandwich? Bring it to my house . . . You know where I live, don't you?"

She did. I called Sue, and told her that I had to have company for dinner. She thought that was nice, and suggested I get home a few minutes ahead of our company, and tidy up my breakfast dishes. She was going out with a friend, anyway. I told her that I'd have to go back out about ten. She wasn't too enthused about that, and reminded me about the dishes again.

"Can you please get home before your company comes? I left some homework on the dining room table . . . if you could move it to my desk . . . and there's some really good rice in the freezer, if you need it."

"Thanks. Do we have any potato chips or anything?"

"Some in the cupboard on the right. Use the good green dishes. Not the good china, but the good but not everyday things." She thought for a second. "And the good glasses. Those other ones are just too old."

"Okay."

"Don't eat too much. See you, Batman."

By the time Nancy and Shamrock hit the house, I had cleared the table, set it, put a couple of condiments out, started a pot of coffee, and had remembered paper napkins. I was rather proud of myself.

"Jeez," said Nancy. "You expecting company?"

We unwrapped the sandwiches, poured caffeine-free diet pop all around, and sat down to eat. I took a couple of bites, and then asked the question.

"So, what you got this time?"

Nancy took a drink of pop, and put her glass down. "You know anything about a bank robbery going to go down in Nation County on Sunday?"

I thought I carried it off rather well. "Sure. You too, eh?"

"You serious?" she asked. "You do know about that?"

"Sure." I took a drink of my pop. "Can I ask you a question?"

"Shoot."

"Just how in the hell do you find this shit out?"

She grinned happily. So did Shamrock. Nancy pointed at the blue-eyed little elf with the camera. "My girl Friday, here. You gotta give it to her, Carl. She's good."

According to the two of them, they were in one of the local

THE BIG THAW 261

bars on Wednesday night. Relaxing. One of the local denizens hit on Shamrock. Gently, to be sure. But a hit, nonetheless. Being bored, she played him for a while, with Nancy right at the table.

I asked who. Didn't know his name, beyond Terry. They described him as about twenty-five through thirty, nearly six feet, and with "nice buns."

"That'll look good on a police report." It had to be Terry Waterman. The only guy I could think of in the county with a strong ass.

"Be creative," said Nancy. "Anyway . . ."

Terry found out that Shamrock was with the media. Trying to impress her, he said something on the order of "I just might have a scoop for you . . ."

"And I go, 'Oh, right,' like that," said Shamrock. "And he goes, 'No really, there's something big going down on Sunday.' And I go, 'Oh, sure.' "

She must have said it sweetly, because, as the evening wore on, he got more specific. Apparently, with both details and proposals. After the second time she refused to go home with him, he really turned on the charm.

"So he goes, 'You want to cover a bank job, sweet lady?' and I go, 'Maybe.' So he goes—" and she lowered her voice about two octaves—" 'This is gonna be a record breaker. Five hits at the same time. Five. All close.' "

Five. There was the magic number again. And all close.

"No shit?" I took another slug of pop. "What else?"

Nothing. She'd still refused to sleep with him. So he got angry, called her a "media tease," and left.

Shamrock was laughing so hard she almost fell off the chair. "Mmmedia teeeasse!"

I was glad to see the local boys were still as adroit as ever. I laughed, too, but it wasn't easy. Five. Five.

When the gaiety subsided a bit, I pressed. "You sure it was five?"

"It was," said Nancy. "Five hits, and all close together. That's what he said."

I excused myself, and went to the phone. Fascinating. I called the office, and got George and Sally looking for information on Waterman.

When I returned to the table, I popped the question. "So, what would you like in return? I suspect this little dinner isn't going to cover it."

As it happened, Nancy had a plan. All I had to do was tell her where the hits were going down, and they'd just "happen" to be in the area. Might even get a shot or two of the thing in progress. Scoop of the century. Hint, hint.

Or, as Shamrock put it, "That could make my whole career. Honest." The eyes had it, so to speak.

"Look, you two. I only have fair information on one location. I'll give you what I have, but you gotta promise to stay back where you won't get into trouble." I shrugged. "If it actually goes down. I'm not going to promise anything more than a fifty percent chance at this point."

Of course they would. Went without saying. Nancy I could really believe, as she'd been in the crap before, and wanted no more. I felt I could rely on her to keep Shamrock from getting carried away.

I took a deep breath, and let it out very slowly. "Right. Okay, look, sometime on Sunday, we think there may, and I emphasize may, be a hit on the bank at Freiberg."

"No shit! This Sunday?" Nancy was genuinely excited. It dawned on me that they hadn't had any idea of the reality of the bank hits until I'd confirmed it. They'd been guessing. Maybe "hoping" would be a better word. But they obviously hadn't expected anything so soon.

"Yeah," I said, "tomorrow. Don't make me sorry I told you . . ."

"No, no. But that's the little bank just up the street from the *Beauregard*, isn't it?"

"Yep."

"Fantastic," said Nancy. "You can see it from the boat. We'll be able to do a phony shoot from the boat, and pick up the bank really good . . ."

"How far to the bank?" said Shamrock.

"Eight hundred feet? Right, Carl?"

"About."

"Great! I've got a five hundred millimeter Schmitt-Cass in the car . . ." Shamrock, I thought, was going to be happy with this arrangement. Good. I didn't want either of them getting in close.

"What time?" asked Nancy.

"For the hit? Don't know. Sunday is all I have."

"You trying to tell me that you guys are going to set up on it, full force, for twenty-four hours?"

"Yeah."

"Good Lord, Carl," she said. "You really like these marathon things, or you just have bad intel?"

"I'm just in this for the food. You decide." I smiled. "Look, if you two get any more, let me know. But for Christ's sake, don't breathe a word of this to anybody else."

"You mean, like, the competition? Get real." Shamrock had that eager look about her. "They can buy my frames, man. Big bucks. Big, big bucks."

"Take a deep breath, dear," said Nancy.

Shamrock stuck out her hand. "Thank you, Carl. I mean it."

I shook her hand, a little surprised. "Hey, it's nothing definite. Just a chance, here."

"Oh, no," she said. "That dude Terry really wanted it, last night. He didn't lie."

"We'll talk about evaluation as we get ready," said Nancy. "Lust makes guys stupid, but it doesn't make 'em tell the truth." She laughed. "He was just stupid enough to let it slip."

Because we were to be on duty for twenty-four hours straight, I tried to catnap after Nancy and Shamrock left. Right. Like I could just go to sleep. I did try. Sat there, watching TV. Dozed once, I think. Not for more than forty-five minutes.

I kept the Weather Channel on and saw that my favorite blue and pink segmented worm of a jet stream was making progress. Tomorrow would be much warmer. A real, sudden "January thaw," in all its glory.

That was Iowa, for you. In eighteen hours, the temperature could change fifty degrees or better. Much better, in this case. It looked like we'd hit thirty degrees by 3 A.M., and go up from there.

God bless warm fronts. If we were going to have to be outside for any period of time, warm was so much better . . .

When I got back to the office a little after 2200, they gave me everything I'd requested on Terry Waterman. I would have liked to haul him in, but good sense prevailed. After Sunday, either way, Terry would pay us a visit. Beforehand would just tip people off. With his inadvertent contribution, however, the estimates on Sunday actually happening went nicely past the fifty-fifty level.

The main control point was designated as Hester's DCI office at the *General Beauregard* pavilion, in Freiberg. It was just about on top of the main target bank, it was well equipped with communications devices, it had its own teletype and fax, and it was warm and comfortable with many creature comforts. I came drifting in about 2230, having picked up Sally at Volont's request. He wanted a top-notch dispatcher with us. Hard to argue.

When we arrived, we established Sally with the radios, and a good land line to the Nation County Sheriff's Department, and to the Conception County Sheriff's Department across the river. Both were to be contacted on special phone numbers which were not to be used for routine calls until further notification.

She had the base station portion of the FBI scrambled radios, and a small base set with local police, fire, and ambulance frequencies. She was all set.

I picked up the scrambled walkie-talkie I'd been given. FBI issue. Looked a bit older than I'd expected. Almost as old as my new one for the Sheriff's Department. "What's the range on these?"

"Couple of miles, line of sight," said George, clipping his inside his jacket.

"Totally secure?"

"Absolutely. Programmed to a different code every time, downloaded before each operation. No duplicates. You can even say 'fuck' on these and the FCC won't ever know." He grinned broadly.

I was sorely tempted, but decided not to push my luck. I've always hated being first.

I don't know if you've ever noticed this, but in a law enforcement crisis situation, there are cops at two general locations. One is for management, and it always has the same general features: warm, dry, and a place to take a leak. The other is for the non-management folks at the pointy end, and tends to be cold, wet, and a mile from relief. It's just the way of things, I guess. There's an added dimension with long-term situations. Management always manages to find chairs and couches. The pointy end gets to stand in the rain, or lie in the snow. As we were setting things up in Hester's office, I thought about that.

"You know, guys, I sure feel sorry for those poor bastards gonna be out in the weather . . ."

Anyway, we all moved into the area of the *Beauregard* in ones and twos, over a period of a couple of hours. Easy to do, since the gambling operation produced the only consistent, large crowd in the county. By midnight, we'd been set for nearly an hour.

Everybody checked in on the scrambled radio, and we sat down to wait for Gabriel's Operation Just Cash to begin.

In a leap of originality, the call sign for the Command Post was "CP." Well, you want everybody to be clear, and we hadn't had time to do any better. At the CP were gathered Volont, George, Hester, Art, Sally, and me.

We had designated the five likely banks "Alpha, Bravo, Charlie, Delta, and Echo." Keep it simple, like they say. The observation points were numbered for each site. Very easy, as Freiberg was designated "Alpha," and was the only one with more than one observation point.

Alpha 1 was located on the roof of a two-story commercial building across the street from the Freiberg bank. There were two FBI TAC people there. The advantage of this location was that it provided a clear shot down the alley behind the bank. They had been instructed to vacate their location at first light, and to return after sundown. They could be seen from the bridge approach in the daylight, and we didn't want them compromised. They would remain in the building, and if something went down, they could be back on the roof in less than a minute.

Alpha 2 was in a vacant second-floor apartment, in the rear of a building diagonally across the alley from the bank. There were four TAC officers there. They had the best view through the drive-up teller's glass booth, and were able to see about a third of the interior of the bank, with a partial view of the bottom of the vault door. They could also cover part of the alley. If something started, two of them would exit the building, and take up positions behind a four-foot concrete wall that divided the alley from the rear lawn of the building, and enabled them to engage the general area of the bank from ground level.

Alpha 3 was in the residence of a Freiberg police officer. The two TAC officers assigned that location were in a bedroom on the second floor. It was about half a block from the bank, and in an elevated position about ten feet up the bluff that paralleled the river. Access was via a steep stair. Their view was of the front of the bank, and they were only able to see a small part of the interior due to their height. If necessary, they could reposition themselves, but it would take time, and they would be out of sight of the bank for a period of time before they could reach the secondary position along a retaining wall. That was a bad location, anyway, as they were exposed on their left.

Alpha Mobile was an older van, parked at the edge of the lot belonging to the convenience store across the street and to the west of the bank. Again, two TAC officers were there. Plainclothes, they were considered critical for daylight operations, as they could see much of the interior of the bank, and both exits. They looked to have a very long day. Movement was to be at their discretion, but was presumed to be done only to block access to the bridge ramp.

Alpha Chase consisted of two unmarked cars inside the Freiberg Fire Department. They were in a vehicle bay vacated by a pumper that we had persuaded the fire chief to park outside. We hid them because we felt that Gabriel was likely to pick up on them before they were aware of his presence. Four TAC officers were assigned here.

Last, but not least, was Alpha Foot. One male and one female TAC officer, plainclothes, were available to stroll by any location we wanted, to double-check and get a ground view of any situation. They were currently upstairs in the Freiberg Public Library, which was a full block removed from the bank, and where they'd be able to enter and leave without being observed by anyone in or around the bank.

We all had diagrams on a Xeroxed sheet. The bank was in the middle. Alpha 1 was to the right of the bank, close to the edge. Alpha 2 was below the bank, but close. Alpha 3 was in the upper left corner. Alpha Mobile was about halfway up the page, on the left edge. The boat was on the lower right corner, Hester's office was opposite that, and the chase cars were way over on the lower left corner. The river was indicated on the extreme right edge. The two north-south streets that formed Freiberg proper were parallel lines about three inches apart. The east-west streets were indicated by three parallel lines evenly spaced down the page.

The tension was high for about the first hour. Nobody said much, and everybody was grabbing a look out the windows of the darkened office every few minutes.

By 0230, we were making trips to the adjacent office, and grabbing coffee. By 0345, some of us were staying in the coffee room for as much as half an hour at a stretch.

At 0351, we all watched a train go by on the tracks between the *Beauregard* and the pavilion. A slow train.

I was in Hester's office about 0400, and saw Nancy and Shamrock walking across the parking lot, and heading toward the *General Beauregard*. Not a bad vantage point. I silently wished them luck with the photos. It had occurred to me that a good set through a telephoto lens could do us wondrous good in court.

About 0412, our radios crackled to life.

"CP, Alpha Two has suspicious movement."

"Alpha Two?" It was as though Sally had been waiting for just that call. "CP, we've got a brown Toyota four-door with Illinois plates, who's just started his third pass by the bank in five minutes."

"Alpha Two, Alpha One, is he eastbound? All we have is headlights."

"Ten-four, eastbound."

Silence. The tension was back.

"Uhh, Alpha Mobil hasn't seen any Toyotas."

"And Alpha Two has the suspect vehicle back on the street facing west . . . and they seem to be stopping to speak with a female subject walking east . . . on the north side of the street . . ." There was a silence of maybe ten seconds. "And she's in the car, and I think she should go for about twenty-five bucks . . ."

"A hooker?" I couldn't believe it. "Right here in River City?" I started to laugh.

"We've had rumors a couple of them are trying to work around the boat," said Hester.

"Well, I think you can mark those 'confirmed,' " said Art.

A flurry of activity like that, and now everybody was pumped with nothing to do. You don't want to leave the area, in case you miss something. So you just hang in there and fidget. And think.

I tried watching TV. My favorite, the Weather Channel, showed the blue and pink worm arching almost above us. Fantastic. Warmth, and on schedule.

By 0540, we were no longer pumped. Hester called down to the buffet, and ordered a bunch of rolls and orange juice.

By 0630, it was getting light, and Alpha 1 was stood down for a thirty-minute break.

I think we'd all reached that scratchy stage, when the sun comes up and you haven't slept, and you've had so much coffee that nothing would feel better than to brush your teeth and take a long, hot shower. And then pull the shades, and get into bed.

"Hey," said George, brightly, "only seventeen and a half hours of Sunday left."

With the sun coming up, the boat looked gorgeous. The sky had some high cirrus clouds, and was all pinks and grays. Out on the Mississippi, steam was coming up in the ice-free area around the *Beauregard*, and also out in the open main channel.

"I hate sunrise," said Hester.

There were large vertical pillars of steam coming off the ice. They were fun to watch, and lent a spooky air to the whole thing.

By 0700, the sun was theoretically rising. I say theoretically because those neat tendrils of steam were turning into a thick fog. Over everything. Visibility was dropping.

"Would you look at this shit?" said Art. "We're not gonna be able to see a damned thing." He turned from the window. "Well, they'll call it off, now. You can't see well enough to make a get-away in this crap."

I should have realized this could happen. The land and the river were very cold, and damp. The warm, moist air coming up from the Gulf was causing the problem. The jet stream. The problem was that there was almost no wind. Maybe 5 to 7 mph. Just enough to keep the warmer, wet air moving over the river and the land. Not enough to blow the fog away. Visibility was down to 500 feet.

Volont shook his head. "No, they'll do it. They have to."

At first, I thought he meant that "had to" because we were all ready for them. But the more I thought about it, the more it began to sound like Gabriel and company were not about to stop for anything.

"He must really need the money," I said.

"He does."

At 0828, the radio rasped again. "Alpha Two has a female subject approaching the bank."

It turned out to be the odd-hour teller. The first clue was

when she produced a set of keys and unlocked the door. I was glad they could see her. In the fog, we couldn't even see the bank anymore.

"She's alone?" asked Volont. It appeared so. That wasn't part of the plan, as she was to have been joined by a young FBI agent who was going to pose as an apprentice teller.

Volont got busy on his radio. He looked up. "My man seems to have gotten lost in the fog," he said. "He thinks he made a wrong turn . . ."

No plan, as they say, ever goes as written. Volont got on the secure radio, and had one of the team members on street level get out of his gear, lose his FBI jacket, and hustle to the bank as a customer. He'd just have to stay there until the "apprentice teller" got himself unlost.

No problem, really. Just like the first scratch or dent in a new car. You simply hope it's a small one.

By 0910, I was tired, hungry, and bored out of my mind. I had thought that, if any time was best, it would be just before the bank opened, but after the tellers had arrived.

At 0912, Alpha Foot called on the radio, and advised they'd "go for a walk." That meant a general reconnaissance about the area of the bank, on foot, that would probably take thirty minutes. Volont called, and said the lost "teller" was now assigned to a team, and left the other agent in the bank.

At 0914, Sally, George, and I went down to the buffet, and played like we were just tourists. Scrambled eggs (special no-fat variety), and bacon, with pancakes and butter and syrup, and orange juice and coffee and toast. Like I said, I was hungry.

We ate in silence for a few moments. Looking out the windows, at the *Beauregard* in the fog. You could still see her fairly well, but we were only about 200 feet from her at that point. Visibility was down to about 300 feet, here at ground level. The garish lights were creating a pinkish haze around her, in the dim light of day. It seemed to be getting thicker.

"Well, only fourteen hours to go," said George, with false optimism.

I raised my hand to attract the waitress who was roving with the coffee. "Piece of cake," I said to George.

By 0940 we were back in Hester's office. I looked out her office window, and could barely make out the *Beauregard*. "Hell, we can't see shit from here." I looked at my watch. "I think I'll take a walk over toward the bank. Anybody else want to come?"

No takers. I double-checked my walkie-talkie, put on my green windbreaker, was just starting out the door when everything started to go to hell.

"All units, Alpha Mobile has ten-thirty-three traffic. Alpha Mobile has three armed suspects getting out of a tan Chevy van in the bank parking lot!"

Twenty-three

The presence of the armed suspects was confirmed almost instantly by Alpha 2, who added, "And Alpha Two has the van moving toward the bank, right behind the suspects . . . I think . . . I can barely see it . . ."

The fog now began to play more of a part in the proceedings.

"Alpha Three can't see anybody . . ."

"Alpha Four no viz at all."

"Tell everybody to hold position," said Volont, straining with the rest of us to look out the window.

Sally's voice crackled over the radio. "All units hold," she said, as if she did it every day. At the same time she picked up the telephone and looked at Volont. "Time to wake up Conception County?" It was a good question. If the suspects headed off over the bridge, we'd have maybe seventy-five seconds before they were in Wisconsin. He nodded. She began to dial.

This was a very critical time. We didn't want them to know we knew they were in the bank, or that we were anywhere around. This was a time to build the robbers' confidence, and lure them into the open. Well, that's what the book said.

"Hello, Betty," said Sally, into the phone. "We're up, but not running."

Then, for a time, nothing seemed to happen.

"I can't believe this shit," said Art. "They just walked in. From nowhere. Didn't check it out or anything."

"It's the fog," said Hester. "Nobody could see 'em coming for more than a block . . . they could have been around for a while."

We were all in a state of amazement. I don't think anyone in the room had ever seen a bank robbery actually go down before.

"Remember," said Volont, "we let 'em come out."

"Sally," said Hester, "why don't you check on the other banks? See what they have."

I thought that was a good idea. Apparently, Hester hadn't been as mesmerized as I had been.

Sally got on the phone to our own Sheriff's Department. No activity with any of the other banks. The silent alarm for the Frieberg bank had gone off, so our department and Lamar had known just about as soon as we had.

So far, so good. I thought my heart was going to bang right through my rib cage.

"How long they been in there?" George was nervous.

I guessed. "Two-three minutes. Seems like a long time, doesn't it?" I wanted desperately to get down to my car, and head over toward that bank. Worst thing I could have done. It was very likely that, somewhere, there was an accomplice looking for just that sort of thing. An accomplice with some means of communicating with the three inside the bank. Even though my car was unmarked, it did have a cop feel about it. Extra antennas, for one thing. Cheap, with almost no trim, for another. I would really stand out if I were to stop where I could see the bank. And unless I was guided by an angel, there was no way I could time it right and get there just after they left. Nope. But maybe on foot . . .

"I think I'll just walk over that way," I said. "Any takers?"

Volont had to be up at the Command Post. Banks were federal responsibility, and he owned the resources. Art didn't even respond. George shook his head with a rueful grin. He'd go if Volont thought of it, basically. Which pretty much left Hester. It was her office, though.

"Sure," she said, grabbing her trench coat and turning to Art. "Don't worry," she said, "I trust you not to snoop."

Three minutes later, we were on the paving, and walking

briskly toward the bank. "I think we can see even less down here," I said, with a chuckle.

"Ah, but it's good to get out."

I glanced at her. "Why don't women ever wear hats in this kind of weather?"

She looked at my head. "Gee, I dunno, Houseman. Maybe 'cause we don't look as good in a baseball cap?"

I was wearing my blue U.S.S. CARL VINSON ball cap, with the yellow printing.

"You suppose?"

"I'm sure of it."

I stepped into the street, and nearly fell. Great. Ice. The warm air that produced the fog apparently lost the fight on the surfaces. The damp air was being used by the frozen ground to make a fine glaze of ice.

"Careful, Houseman. I don't want to have to carry you back . . ."

As we moved into the alley behind Alpha 2, Hester came up on her secure radio and informed them we were around, and might be strolling in the vicinity of the bank. They acknowledged.

The bank, in the thickening fog, appeared absolutely unremarkable. If you didn't already know, there was no way to tell what was happening inside. Even on a clear day, I suspected . . .

"Professional, real professional." I should learn, someday, not to overestimate the qualities of criminals. "Sure glad I'm not the agent in the bank."

There was a *thump*, more felt than heard. I looked at Hester.

"Beats me," she said, swiveling at the hips to look around.

Then the bank alarm went off. The audible. A heart-stopping steel bell and striker that I was sure could be heard for a mile or more.

That was a bit unexpected. We'd anticipated the silent alarm to go when they went into the vault. It should have, and it had. There was a safety on the vault, even though it was unlocked and half open during dropoff hours. You'd have to watch that vault for a long time before you caught on to the fact that the tellers tapped a button under their counters before they turned and walked to the vault. We got the silent alarm in the Sheriff's Department.

But now we had that damned audible.

The radios came to life. "Alpha Two had a . . . uh . . . loud report, from the bank. Just prior to the alarm."

"All units hold," said Sally, "until further." That had to be at Volont's direction.

"Gunshot?" wondered Hester.

"Sheriff's Department advises that it's the fire alarm in the Frieberg bank . . ." came Sally's voice, over the secure radio.

Fire?

"Alpha Two second team is at ground level, and they say they can't see smoke . . ." came over the secure radio.

"Three's very close to the bank," I said, "and I have no smoke . . ."

" 'Smoke'?" Hester grumbled. "In this fog, you couldn't see smoke if your nose was on fire."

Moments later, the team in the deputy's house announced that they'd come down the steps to street level, and were in their secondary position. "Alpha Three is at the little wall. We have no smoke, but there's something . . . uh . . . going on in the bank . . . stand by, One."

They were on the opposite side of the bank, with a much better view to the inside.

Radio traffic really started to pick up. "Alpha Foot is between Alpha Mobile and Two, going toward the bank, and we need instructions . . ."

"Alpha One is back on the roof . . . But we can't see much in the weather."

"Yeah, guys, Alpha Three sees some sort of activity on the inside of the drive-up window . . ."

"Alpha Two has the same. It looks like they're putting in insulation around the window."

I looked. Sure as hell. A man in a ski mask was holding what appeared to be multicolored clothesline around the edges of the teller's window, while another man was taping over it, all around the window frame of the thick, bulletproof glass. They were moving quickly, but clearly not attempting to hide their actions.

Hester and I stood by a parked car, which was between us and the bank. Less conspicuous, like we owned it. Watching, through the thickening fog, as the men at the drive-up window completed their task.

"What the hell are they doing?"

"Beats me," she said. "Sticking something around the inside of the window."

"Uh, Alpha Two thinks it might be det cord," crackled over my radio. "Inside the drive-up window."

The fire siren on top of the city hall began to sound. That could be activated in one of two ways; either by pager from the Sheriff's Department, or manually by somebody either at the fire station or the city hall.

Sally was on the radio in an instant. "Automated fire department pager and siren activation," she announced. "The firemen's personal pagers were activated first. The alarm's at the Frieberg Community Savings Bank."

So. While we had been standing there, volunteer firemen all over Frieberg were being automatically paged to go to the bank. But there were no indications of a fire.

Almost in slow motion, we could see three or four rotating blue dash lights, as individual volunteer firemen began driving to the fire station. I reached for my mike. "Three to Alpha Chase . . . when the firemen get there, tell them we have a robbery in progress, and have them stand by! Do not let them respond to the bank until further notice."

I can think fast on occasion.

"Right, right," said Volont, over the radio. "Good move. Right."

"Three," crackled Sally's voice, "the Sheriff's Department advises that the alarm was not, repeat not, activated in the auto mode. It's a manual activation." Information right off the screen at the Sheriff's Department. It could tell how the alarm was activated. The dispatcher up there had probably just noticed the mode, in all the activity. Strange. A real fire would have activated the auto alarm. Somebody at the bank had set it off manually.

As proud as I was of my warning to the firemen, sometimes even your best isn't enough. I watched in silence as three firemen went directly to the bank instead of the fire station. I could tell because of the little, flashing blue volunteer fireman lights on the dashes of their cars as they pulled into the lot. They obviously intended to make sure people were out and planned to don their equipment when the apparatus got to the scene. Standard procedure in rural areas, where some of the volunteers might drive right by the threatened location on their way to the fire station. I saw them head toward the bank. They started in, and I saw the last one put his hands in the air.

"Uh, Alpha Two believes we now have three firemen as hostages."

"Alpha Three confirms."

"Ditto Alpha Mobile."

Damn. Or, as Hester said, "Shit."

"Come on, come on," murmured Hester. "They can still get away. *There is still time to get away.* You don't need hostages, damn it."

"Maybe not," I said. "But they sure have 'em." I radioed Sally. "See if we can get a good guess as to how many people were in the bank when they went in."

Alpha 2 responded with "We believe five, plus the odd-hour teller, plus three firemen."

Nine people.

"Well," I said, disgusted, "that ought to be plenty."

As I spoke, a second vehicle approached the bank from out of the fog, pulled into the lot, made a turn, and backed toward the bulletproof teller's cage. A white panel truck with a potato chip logo on the side, it stopped about fifty feet away, and Hester and I watched in fascination while there was a puff of white and a loud *crack* and the drive-up window flew out of its mountings and slammed into the paving. I could see the shock wave hit her hair, making it fly back. Fascinating.

"It was," said Hester, even as we ducked down behind the car. "It *was* det cord he was putting up . . ."

"Alpha Two here . . . did you see that? They've blown the window."

Even as he spoke, the truck backed up toward the brand-new opening, and bumped into the wall.

"Well, I guess those windows are designed to resist pressure from the outside, not the inside," Hester mused. "Pretty slick."

"How long you think it takes to load a couple of million dollars?" I asked, cautiously raising my head to look over the hood of the car. "Ten minutes?"

"I'd estimate fifteen to twenty," said Hester, glancing at her watch. "And if they bother with the change, maybe as much as an hour."

A radio crackled again. "Three, it's Twenty-nine," said Sally, on the secure frequency. 29 was the local car, Frieberg PD. "He's going nuts, people keep running up to him and asking him what the hell he's doing just sitting there when there's an emergency at the bank."

Taxpayers are sensitive about that sort of thing. It was my call, being the highest-ranking local officer within range.

"This is sort of going to shit," I said, to Hester. "Comm, tell him to go to the bridge ramp and stand by there . . . nobody can even see him over there. Not in this fog." I turned to Hester. "Uh, does anybody you know have a Plan B?"

Just then, somebody tapped me on the shoulder, and I nearly jumped out of my skin. I turned, and there was one of the TAC team officers.

"No disrespect," he said, "but would you two mind moving? You're fouling our line of fire."

That was about as nice a way as he could have done it. In person, and not over the radio where everybody would have heard.

"You bet."

"Hell, Houseman," said Hester. "We're just in the way, here. Let's get back up to the CP."

We arrived back at the Command Post in time for a major event. Just after we quickly briefed George and Volont on what we'd seen, the phone rang, and Sally picked it up. After a couple of seconds, I became aware that there was no conversation. I looked over at her, and her face was as white as I've ever seen one.

"Yes. Sure, yes . . . just a second . . ." she managed to get out. "Mr. Volont," she said, "it's for you."

"Take a message," he barked, still looking out the window, vainly trying to see the bank.

I could see her listen intently, and then look about her frantically. She covered the receiver. "Hester! Do you have a speaker phone button here? Where is it? Hurry!" With that, she got the attention of everybody in the room. Hester didn't bother to tell her, just reached over and flicked a small button of the side of the phone base.

"It's on," said Sally.

"Mr. Volont?" asked a heavy, sarcastic voice. "You there for me today?"

"Who is that?" asked Art.

"This is Gabriel," said the voice. "Where's Special Agent in Charge Volont?"

Twenty-four

T his is Volont."

The speaker phone wasn't quite the quality it could have been, but I suspected it hadn't cost the state that much, either.

Gabriel chuckled. "I'm so very glad it's you. We have some business to conduct."

"Not until you surrender the hostages," said Volont.

"No, no. You never understood *planning*, my boy. No, the way it is is this . . . my people will drive away from the bank when they signal they've finished their business. They will drive away unmolested. Period."

"Not that easy," said Volont. "As long as they have hostages in there, they don't leave."

"Call the bank," said Gabriel. "Ask to speak to the teller. We had a man pull the fire alarm, to set it off. We wanted some firemen present when we set off the charges to open the drive-thru window. Just in case of fire." He chuckled. "We care about the citizens."

"Won't work," said Volont. "We've got the bank sewed up tight. Nobody leaves."

"Want to do an exchange?" asked Gabriel, lightly. "A lot for a few? Maybe some of your people? I'll give you a great exchange rate. Two of your agents on the street for the one in the bank."

"I think not," said Volont.

"You 'think not,' do you? My, my. I'll have to get back to you in a minute." The line went dead.

Volont reached over and took the microphone from Sally's desk. "All units, be extremely cautious. There may be other suspects in the area, and we have information that leads us to believe they know we have an agent in the bank."

"How'd they ID him?" asked George. "Did they watch him go in?"

Volont shook his head. "He wasn't the one I'd picked, remember? My pick got lost in the fucking fog." He sounded disgusted. "The replacement is Unger. Built like a fullback. Moves like a cat. Looks nothing like a clerk or teller. They probably just took one look and neutralized him."

Sure. The agent in the bank would have been under very strict orders not to endanger anybody, so if they picked him out right away . . . I would hate to be in the shoes of the "lost" agent when Volont got hold of him.

He resumed his conversation on the radio. "Each post . . . check your six, very carefully," he said. Warning the agents to make sure there was nobody trying to maneuver into position behind them.

As he put the mike down, a klaxon began to sound in the distance. We all looked toward the bank. No apparent activity there.

"What is that damned thing?" asked Hester.

The phone rang, and Sally answered. We were all expecting Gabriel, I think. She listened for a second, and leapt to her feet, looking out the window toward the *General Beauregard*. We followed her gaze. Through the thickening fog, we could make out what seemed to be thick green smoke coming from the after section of the boat. Green.

"What burns green?" asked George.

"The horn sounding off is the fire alarm on the boat," said Sally. "This is our office, and they've got a fire alarm on the boat."

There was a small marine band radio on top of a filing cabinet in a corner of Hester's office. It came to life.

"*General Beauregard* to the DCI office in the Port of Frieberg," came a calm, clear voice. "This is Captain Hanson, calling the DCI office at the Port of Frieberg."

Hester picked up the mike. "*Beauregard*, this is Agent Gorse. Go ahead."

"Ma'am," said Captain Hanson, "there's a man here with a mask on and a gun to my head, who says I'm to call you and give you a situation report on my vessel."

Hester was more self-possessed that I was at that point. She actually answered in a normal tone of voice. "Go ahead with your report."

"Well, ma'am, first of all we don't have any fire. I repeat, there is no fire. We have some intruders who pulled the alarm and say they just set off a smoke candle. Then my engineer tells me that we have an engineering casualty in that somebody has set off a little bit of explosive that has disabled our engines. We don't have a fire. We still have generating capability, but we can't move the boat under her own power."

"Right," said Hester.

"Then," said the captain, "the head of security tells me that the cash cages on the oh-one, oh-two, and oh-three decks and the counting room on the second deck have just been forcibly entered by armed men. They are going to remove all the money from the ship." He paused.

"Yes . . ." said Hester.

"And I'm to tell you that we don't have any casualties yet."

Silence.

"Captain?"

Nothing. Hester picked up her binoculars, and looked toward the *Beauregard*. "I can't see for shit . . ." She paused. "The green smoke is letting up . . . I think . . ."

The marine band radio came back to life. "DCI?"

"Go ahead, Captain," said Hester.

"This man says that they are to be allowed off the boat unhindered, or they will sink her." You could faintly hear some other voice in the background. "And he also says that they are going to break our radios here, and that they've confiscated all the walkie-talkies from security. I guess this is the last trans . . ."

It apparently was.

"Fuck," said Art. He did have a way with words.

"We don't negotiate yet," said Volont. "We don't know enough."

"This isn't yours," said Hester. "There are about six hundred people on that boat. This is us and the sheriff only. We have jurisdiction here."

I would have been just as happy if she had left me and my department out of it. "We'd appreciate your help, though," I said.

Hester glared at me. I shrugged. She and I had no assets on the ground in this one. Ours were all at the other banks . . . A lightbulb might as well have come on over my head.

I held up my right hand, and counted on my fingers, out loud. "One, the Frieberg bank. Two, the cash cage on the oh-three deck. Three, the cash cage on the oh-two deck. Four, the cash cage on the oh-one deck. Five, the counting room on the second deck." I grinned. "That's our 'five banks.' And they're close together, just like everybody said."

In the silence, I told Sally to contact the Sheriff's Department, and have all the troops watching the other areas head for Frieberg. "Ten-thirty-three all the way, please."

Nobody argued.

"You want the chopper up here, too?" asked Sally.

"Yeah, if it can fly in this stuff. Might as well have her close. The airport across the river will be just fine, if the fog permits. Otherwise, anywhere close they can land."

"The fog's just along the river," interjected Sally. The higher areas are clear. They don't have any fog at all in Maitland . . ."

"Excellent." I looked at Volont, who was calmly staring out the window, toward the vague shape of the *Beauregard*. "Trying to do it to us again, isn't he?"

He didn't answer.

Art, bless him, was doing his usual muttering to himself, and came up with a good point. "So, how is this supposed to work?"

he asked, rhetorically. "I mean, he gets his people out of the bank
. . . okay . . . then he gets off the boat with those people . . . they
leave, and we get them, right?" He looked around. "I mean,
what's the advantage here? How's he gonna sink the boat after he
leaves? Why would he sink it after he left?" He kept tapping his
foot on the side of a metal desk, unconsciously. "I don't get this
. . . all we gotta do is watch him leave, and hustle the people off
the boat . . ."

Good point. One I somehow was sure Gabriel hadn't overlooked.

"Let's get boat security up here," said Hester. She spoke to
Art. "Get our bosses informed, and get supervisors and hostage
negotiators on the way. Get a second TAC team, too."

"Maybe," said George, "we should call the bank like Gabriel
suggested we do?"

George always comes through in a pinch. Volont just nodded
at him. George waved his hand at Sally. "What's the number of
the bank?"

Sally, who was on the phone to our office, getting everybody
heading our way, simply reached over and threw the phone book
at him. In itself it was no big thing, inasmuch as the phone book
for all of Nation County is less than an inch thick. But it was the
thought that counted, and it helped to break the tension. Especially since George was caught off guard, and missed the book.

Our secure radio came back to life. "CP from Alpha Two?
Two things, up there. One is that, ah, we have *another* truck backing toward the bank. And there seems to be a problem on that
gambling boat . . ." Alpha 2 was about 100 yards closer to the
boat than we were. They apparently could see her, anyway.

"Yeah, and Alpha Mobile has the new truck, too. Straight
truck, double axle, with a lift gate."

Maybe they were going to take the change as well. Regardless, it sure looked like they weren't worried about time.

"I've got the teller on the line," shouted George. Since nobody else was talking at the time, it sounded sort of strange. "She
says," he said, in a more normal tone, "That everybody is just

fine, and that they are going to set off another explosion." He held his hand up for silence. Nobody was talking. "Uh-oh, I've got a fireman coming to the phone now . . ."

"Calm down," said Volont.

George looked surprised. He hadn't realized he was shouting. "I see . . . I see . . . yes, that's very considerate, isn't it? Yes . . ."

He looked up. "The firemen say that they've been allowed to watch, and that the bad guys are going to take out a section of wall with explosives, so they can load straight into the truck on that side. That they will seek shelter in the vault, and that the firemen are supposed to be ready in case of fire." He was back on the phone. "Right, all right. Yes, we will . . ."

The secure radio came back up. "Alpha Three can see inside the new truck . . . and it looks like they have one of those . . . oh . . . portable forklifts . . . a dolly forklift? It's near the back of the truck, and they seem to have like fifty-five gallon drums in the back . . ."

"Jesus," said Art. "They gonna blow up the whole bank?"

Volont turned on him. "Of course not. The drums are likely empty and will be used to contain cash. So the forklift can move them quickly." He spoke to Sally. "Tell the units to expect a section of wall to go with a minimal explosion. That we've been forewarned."

"CP to all units," she broadcast, "we have been informed that the suspects intend to blow a hole in the bank wall. They say not to worry about anybody inside."

Well, that was to the point.

"Tell Alpha Chase to have the fire department roll toward the bank," said Volont, "and have a pumper go near the boat. Tell 'em not to cross the river road, but to stand by right close."

Sally did as she was told. Cool, calm. It was absolutely necessary for her to be that way. Any sign, even the slightest, of panic on the control net, and things could go to hell in a basket. As if they hadn't already.

"You were right about him needing money," I said to Volont.

"Looks like they're going for the coins, as well." I paused, waiting for a response. None came. "You're going to have to tell me just why he's in such goddamned desperate need of cash," I said. "This is ridiculous."

"Greed" was all he said.

" 'Greed' my ass," I replied. "He's risking or threatening hundreds of people here. That's not just greed. That's a hell of a lot more than just greed."

"We've got activity at the boat," said Hester, using her binoculars. "A stretch van is backing up to the riverbank."

We peered into the fog, and could just make out the van as it crossed the railroad track and stopped about ten feet from the river's edge. There was no real riverbank there, but large chunks or rock had been used as riprap, with the paving running right to the water's edge. The hull of the *General Beauregard* was about six feet from the paving. Some vague figures appeared—they must have gotten out of the van on the side away from us—pulled two sections of what looked like some sort of ramp from the rear, huddled over them, and then bridged the gap between the shore and the bow weather deck of the *Beau*. In the swirl of the fog, I thought I could make out a shadowy figure crouching near the van, with what looked like a shotgun.

There was a lull in observable activity.

"I can't tell for sure, but I think I count a minimum of nine suspects that I actually saw get out of the van . . ." said Hester, in a monotone of concentration. "Plus at least three or four already on the boat, one per deck, probably more. Say . . . about"—and her voice began to pick up inflections again—"fifteen? Total, with a guess at the number in the van . . ."

"At least," said George.

"And we're . . . what, until reinforcements arrive?" We all looked at the roster. Counting the two local cops, we were nineteen.

"Well, shit, we've got 'em outnumbered," I said.

"Easily," said Volont.

"What about the other boat agents?" asked George. "How many are working now?"

"One," said Hester. "Let me check where he is . . . shit . . . he should have headed toward the boat when the fire alarm went . . ."

Harmon James, chief of security for the *General Beauregard*, came flying into the office, face red, and eyes wide.

"Jesus Christ, they've stolen the boat!" He held up his little pocket walkie-talkie. "I don't know who these people are, but they're talking to me on my own radio!"

The mystery voice was saying, ". . . like I said, your security people are all tied up right now . . ." and uttered a short laugh.

He stopped waving his walkie-talkie and looked at the group of us. "Well, why aren't you all doing something!"

At that point there was a rolling, basso profundo *boom* that rattled the windows. We all looked at the boat, and there was nothing. But over at the bank . . . there was a large area of fog that was slowly turning reddish brown. "Wow! Uh, Alpha One has an explosion at the bank."

It took me a second. "That's gotta be brick dust . . ."

Sally was up on the normal fire frequency, talking to the Frieberg fire chief. "Negative, we have contact with the people in the bank and they will be fine. There are bank robbers in the bank, and there are . . . are . . . pirates on the boat. Just get close and stand by."

George and I both said, " 'Pirates'?" at the same time.

"Well, what would *you* call them? Boat robbers?" She was embarrassed, but not about to back down. She had a point.

"They're hauling stuff off the boat," said Art.

Sure as hell. The van had turned on its fog lights to light the way of two figures pushing a two-wheeled garden cart across the plank.

"Tell me what you have onboard for security," said Volont to James, the security chief.

"Six security officers. Two female, on this shift. One of the officers is a trained emergency medical technician. Not armed. By law." He looked disgusted. "Why, you want us to retake the boat?" He stared at Volont. "Who are you, anyway?"

I held up our little diagram. "We have FBI snipers at four locations. The bad guys have hostages in the bank, and they have hostages on your boat. About five in the bank. How many hostages can we figure on the boat? Five hundred?"

"Closer to six hundred right now, maybe six hundred and fifty." He looked at the diagram, and went up in my estimation about three notches. "You knew about this yesterday, didn't you?"

"Not about the boat. Just the bank."

"That's almost worse," he said.

"Sally, get an ETA for the reinforcements, would you?" Hester pulled her service weapon, and checked the chamber. A Glock 9 mm. "I think we should act as soon as possible."

The phone rang. Sally put it on speaker. It was Gabriel.

"So," he said, "now you know how it's going to go. We won't hurt anyone unless it's absolutely necessary. We will proceed according to our plan, and you can just watch." I could tell he was grinning.

Before Volont could answer him, I just said, "Well, okey-dokey."

There was a brief pause. "Who was that?"

"Houseman," I said. "Hello again."

"Ah, my favorite deputy! Haven't seen you since you snooped around Borglan's. I'm honored."

"Thanks." The fuzziness in my photos must have been Gabriel hightailing it out of there. Confirmation of my paranoia . . .

"I fear this won't look good on your record, Deputy." He had to be still grinning. "What brings you here?"

"I'm here to arrest you for murder."

"Ah. A sad business. But business can be risky, sometimes. Let me speak with Super Agent Volont."

"I'm here," said Volont.

"I know you're there, you sad bastard. I just hope you can remember what I'm going to tell you. Are you listening?"

Silence.

"I know you are. So. We will leave the boat, first. Well, most of us. One or two of us will stay behind. For a while. Long enough to ensure you don't do something silly when the rest leave the bank." He paused. "Are you getting this?"

Volont wasn't going to give him the satisfaction of an answer. "I am," I said.

"Well, I don't give a fuck about you. You're just a deputy in Nowhere County. Agent Volont's the one who's important here. Aren't you?"

Believe it or not, Volont sort of brightened up at that. "I've taken down all you've said."

"Then pay even closer attention to this. We are in constant communication between each other. If my men from the bank, or from the boat, are followed, the boat goes down. With all the passengers."

"Got it," said Volont.

"Good day," said Gabriel, and the conversation was over.

"And who the fuck was that?" asked James, of boat security.

We kind of told him.

Our radios came to life again.

"CP, Alpha Foot's over by the boat, now. We're in a good position for the van."

"CP, Alpha One has a clear shot at the pilothouse, if you need it. We and the top of the boat are in lighter fog . . ."

They sounded very professional. Well, they should have. They were. And that got me thinking about professional versus amateur. Us versus them, as it were. We were pros. Even us deputies from "Nowhere County." I have to admit, that pissed me off. Besides, there were about a half dozen deputies from "Nowhere County" on the way. Along with several state troopers and a state TAC team. And a federal TAC unit in a Huey. Resources. A bunch of 'em.

"Hey?" I interrupted at least two conversations. "Listen up. We're pros, right?"

"We don't need a pep talk," snapped Art.

"Just think about it for a second. Who are these people Gabriel is using for his troops? Think about it."

"So?" Art was having none of this.

"He's got one guy in the bank who knows explosives, right?"

"At least one," said George.

"I'd bet one," I said. "Maybe two on the boat, but for sure one. That's three sharp dudes out of fifteen. Who are the rest of them? Amateurs he's picked up. Nobodies, not when it comes to this stuff."

"They seem to be doing pretty well so far," said George.

"But they haven't encountered any resistance. All the real troops we have are being held on a tight leash. Gabriel counts on that. He knows nobody wants a hostage hurt, so he's betting one hundred percent that he gets a cakewalk, courtesy of us. Right?"

"But, Carl," said Hester, "he's right. We can't risk a hostage. Especially with Gabriel on the boat. He *will* do the deed, and we know that."

"Think this way. He's got, what, three guns, two or three drivers at the bank, right? That's six of them, with five question-ables, against four to six really professional, really capable FBI TAC team members." I looked around. "So, we got 'em out-classed at the bank. Just tell our people there to take out the driv-ers of the trucks as they leave. We already know he isn't going to leave any of his people behind at the bank. Right? No point."

"But the boat is full of people . . ."

"Right. But look. We hit the trucks as they leave. Nobody at the boat can see the people at the bank. Not in this fog. So, what do we have there? We shoot, and anybody left alive in the truck either has to sit in the driver's seat and get himself shot, jump off the unit, or hunker down in the damned thing and hide. Piece of cake. We can scarf them up."

"Pointless," said Volont. "That just leaves six hundred or more people on the boat."

"But, unless Gabriel stays behind on the boat himself, if his peons hear that we just took off six of their finest, what are they going to do? Sink the boat? For what purpose? It's tied up at the fuckin' pier, for God's sake. All the passengers have to do is walk off!"

"We always figure seventeen feet under the bottom," said James. "That would swamp the oh-one deck, so all the passengers and crew would have to go to the second and upper deck. That could take some time."

"But not enough for her to turn over, is there?"

"No, I don't think so . . . look, let me get one of the captains here. He lives just up the street. Five minutes, and he can answer all your questions." He picked up one of the phones.

"Anyway," I said, "he can't sink her instantly. To do that, he's have to open up the whole bottom. *Boom.* Probably blow the boat right out of the water if he did that, and he'd kill and injure lots of people. Including the members of his own team. Even himself."

"We can't count on that." But Volont was coming around.

"I think we can," said George. "He's not bluffing. But he'll sink her slowly, because he has to. I mean, fifteen minutes, even . . . right? Getaway time . . ."

"That's what I think," I said. "And with them tied up at the pier for the winter months, all they have to do is walk off. What I'm saying is that I think it's a risk we might be able to take. With the shock effect of taking out the trucks as they leave the bank."

"Well, we better hurry," said Hester, "whatever we do. I do know that those little bastards are about as busy as they can get, moving that money into the trucks. We aren't going to have much more time, and we need the fog on our side for a while. I don't know how long that stuff will last."

Sally informed us that the chopper with the TAC team would be above Frieberg in two minutes. They reported zero visibility really near us, but could land on the bridge deck, which was above the fog ceiling.

Volont had been getting hold of himself gradually, since Gabriel's first call. He began to speak with his old decisiveness.

"Have them set down on the bridge." He indicated the playground that had been built for the kids who came with the gamblers. Summer only. "A two-man sniper team to the bridge ramp where they can command the best exit from the bank. Four to the boat. Have Alpha Chase pick 'em up. Leave the rest with the chopper." He smiled. "Wouldn't want anybody to steal our Huey."

"I think they might be done at the boat," said Hester. "We're gonna need a decision pretty soon . . ."

I really thought that Volont was ready to take out the trucks. I really did. And he might have, if Gabriel hadn't had another little surprise for us.

Twenty-five

They're pullin' their ramp away from the boat," said Hester. "I counted seven suspects coming off with the last load. They're all getting in the van."

Suddenly, there was a loud, double-cracking sound. It was accompanied by what looked to be a momentary ripple in the fog all around the *General Beauregard*. Weird sight.

"Jesus!" said Art. "They're sinking it!"

"No . . . no . . . no, they're not! Not yet, anyway." Hester pointed, but I couldn't make out what she was looking at. Not at first. But, then, as I watched, I could see the bow of the *Beauregard* slowly pull away from the pier, as the boat herself slipped slightly sternward, with the current. They had blown off the bollards and cleats from both ends of the boat. The thick cables attaching her to the pier, with no grip on the boat, slowly slid off her open weather decks and dropped into the icy waters of the Mississippi.

"Where can she go?" I asked.

James watched, horrified. "There's sort of an ice-free area around the hull . . . warm water from bilge pumps, stuff like that. She can go a ways out into the water, but she'll hit the ice in a little ways, and stop, I think . . ."

As he spoke, the stern of the *General Beauregard* disappeared into the fog, while she came around by the bow. She stopped, her bow about 100 feet from the riverbank, and about 90 feet from the pier. Out of reach. No engines to propel her.

Art said something that, in other circumstances, would have had me rolling on the floor. "That rotten bastard really does think of everything."

"It's time to do something," said Volont. "We can't let him call all the shots . . ." He moved Sally aside, and picked up her mike. "Alpha Mobile, get down to the intersection and block off the street before the bank. Alpha Chase, do the same on the cross street and keep that stretch van where it is." He fumbled for a second. "How the hell do I talk to the fire trucks on this thing?"

Sally pressed one of the frequency keys.

"Fire units, bring a truck into the exit from the bank parking lot and stay there. Use any auxiliary light you have to shine on the building. Bring a truck to the boat landing, to the dock, and park there and try to keep the public away. Shine your floodlights toward the boat." He looked at Sally again. "Now the police cars?"

She pushed another button.

"We need some units to block the bridge approach, some to surround the bank." He took a deep breath. "We need three or four squad cars to block the road north and south of Frieberg. And Twenty-nine, Twenty-nine, you go to the bank and provide support for the fire truck."

That was good. That was very good. The north-south road through town was bordered by bluffs for two or three miles each way. No side roads. No turnoff except to a vacant summer dock area to the south. No way to go around a roadblock.

And 29 now had something useful to do.

Actually, it looked like it was just a matter of whether or not the cop cars could get here before the bank trucks were ready to pull out with all the money.

I watched Volont give Sally back her microphone. "Try for some ETAs for us, see when the cavalry is going to get here," I said. "And make sure Conception County has the other end of the bridge blocked."

Her answer told me she was still in top form. "Get me some coffee, would ya?"

I did.

What was happening now was that Gabriel's little army was actually being shown the opposition for the first time. We should begin to find out what they were made of real soon. I was betting on jelly, at least for the majority.

The growl of an engine, and the sound of the chopper blades as the Huey settled down on the bridge deck was a nice effect. We couldn't see them, of course. Neither could Gabriel and his people. But the noise was unmistakable.

None of us could see anything moving or changing at the bank, but at the boat, the headlights of the stretch van moved slowly up from the dock. Apparently, they saw the fire truck and the two TAC team agents from Alpha Chase blocking the road and the agents taking cover with their M-16s. The stretch van simply stopped. They didn't appear to have taken this development into consideration. Just what we intended, and just as I thought. Amateurs. Finally, I thought, things are beginning to move in a direction we've chosen.

Volont spoke into his secure radio. "This is Volont. If the van advances, you are authorized to use deadly force to prevent its leaving."

The van promptly backed up.

"What the hell . . ." was Hester's first reaction.

"I'll be a son of a bitch," said George.

Art comprehended last. "They can hear us!"

Not only hear, but understand. They'd cracked the scrambled code of the secure radios.

"Well, now we know what they really needed all the computers for," I said. Another fucking surprise. Did his own download from the code banks. Slick. "Where did the FBI get those secure radios?"

"GSA, I suppose," said George. "Where the government shops . . ."

"From the Army," said Volont. "Via the NSA development people. Damn."

Gabriel, as an Army Special Operations soldier, quite likely was familiar with those radios before the FBI even purchased them. Even I knew that much.

"We'd better let the troops know," said George.

"Wait a second. If he doesn't know we know . . ." Volont was up to his old tricks.

"No." George glared at him. "No games. He's smart, and he knows. We have to tell our own people."

Volont came up with the ultimate leader's cop-out. "Then you tell them."

George knew it. Hell, George was an MBA. George had had all the "corporate think and manipulate" classes you could name.

He reached in his jacket and pulled out his walkie. "CP to all units. The security on this frequency has been compromised. Repeat, this is no longer a secure frequency." He replaced his walkie-talkie, and looked out the window toward the boat. "There."

"Well," I said, "there goes my chance to say 'fuck' on a radio."

The phone rang. Sally put is on the speaker phone as soon as she realized it was Gabriel.

"Didn't think you'd have the balls, Agent Volont. I planned for the eventuality, but I really didn't think you had them."

"Life," gritted Volont, "is full of surprises."

I didn't think that was a particularly good choice of words, all things considered.

"Oh, it is," agreed Gabriel. "Indeed. Now, I'd recommend getting your people out of the way of my people, or we're going to be producing victims." He paused, and then chuckled. "By the boatload, as it were."

Volont's face was several shades lighter than normal, but he stood his ground. "Completely counterproductive. Victims mean bad publicity. Victims mean no money for you. Victims, and your goals are done. Gone. Because with victims, we take out your whole team, and the horses they rode in on."

Yeah. Me too.

"I think I'll tell the crew to hand out the life jackets. You have five minutes," and the line went dead.

". . . 'tell the crew to hand out the jackets,' " said Hester. "He *is* on the boat."

Nice.

Volont spoke to James of boat security. "All right. Get all your rescue units up and running. All lifeboats, all rescue craft. We're going to need them in a very short time."

James stared, and then barked out a laugh. "All available 'rescue' equipment is on that boat, out there. Two thousand PFDs and one sixteen-person inflatable boat."

"What?! What's a PFD?"

"Personal flotation device. A little half-assed life jacket that looks like a piece of gym mat with straps. As for 'units', it's fucking winter, mister. The three rescue launches are in storage, with the oil drained out of the motors. They can't run on ice, anyway. That's all we have."

"My God," said Volont.

"It's just a damn riverboat," said James. "In a river that's thirty feet deep. We meet all the Coast Guard requirements, and we don't put out from shore in the winter. What do you expect?"

"We can round up about half dozen ice boats," said Sally. "Maybe ten people each . . . but it'll take time . . ."

"Get on it! Jesus H. Christ, life jackets and a rubber boat!" Volont turned to George. "Get over to that Huey and see what sort of good they can do us in a rescue."

"You might as well let me give you all the bad news at once," said James. He did. If a passenger used a life jacket, in the water out there today, they would live about fifteen minutes. That was, if the current didn't carry them under the ice. If they were to be recovered after ten minutes, since the average gambler was about fifty-eight years old, they would likely still die of exposure. The nearest hospital was in Conception County, across the bridge.

They had two ambulances. Frieberg had two ambulances. Our entire county could muster another six. By calling in everything available, and declaring an extreme emergency, we still wouldn't be able to get more than a dozen ambulances to Frieberg in the first hour.

With twelve ambulances, at eight to ten minutes per trip, into an ER that held six, into six hundred and fifty passengers in the water, meant that more than six hundred of them would be dead in fifteen minutes. But that was assuming they went into the water.

"How deep is it out there?" I wanted to know.

"Winter depth we've never really looked at . . ." said James. "It's low. Probably lower. That's for sure."

I picked up a phone book. "Anybody mind if I call the lock and dam? To get the depth?" Nobody did. I got the lock master, and he had the data in about a second. They could only give me the main channel data, and the general river stage at Frieberg. They said it was fourteen feet.

I motioned James over. "How much does the boat draw? Like, how deep does she sit in the water?"

He thought for a second. "I'd have to check to make sure, but I think it's seven or eight feet."

I grinned. "Really . . . Look at this." I showed him the figure fourteen, underlined. "That's the current river stage data from the lock and dam, with the measurement taken by the robot sensors under the bridge, here. So it's the depth of the water about five hundred feet from the *Beauregard*." I thanked the master.

I went over to Volont, who was on the phone to the Coast Guard station in St. Louis. He was quite exasperated, from the tone. He hung the phone up, and almost ran into me as he turned. "What?"

"I might have the first surprise for our side, I think. Look at this."

"Wait . . . what?"

"That's right," I said. "If the sensors are accurate, if she sinks, she goes down six or seven feet. And stops on the bottom."

"What's going on?" asked George.

"If Gabriel blows the bottom out of the boat, the people on the lowest casino deck are just going to get their feet wet." I handed him the paper.

The phone rang again, and I expected it to be Gabriel. Nope. It was Lamar, for me.

"What the fuck is going on down there?"

I told him, being sure to get in the good news about the water depth.

"I thought you told me this was going to be a simple goddamned bank robbery at five goddamned banks?"

I explained the part about the five locations. How it all fit the information we had. Just in a different way. "Neater 'n shit, Lamar, you think about it . . ."

" 'Neat'?"

"Well, yeah." I explained just what we had in as positive a light as I could. Not easy. I also said that we appeared to have Gabriel pretty well bottled up, and with a TAC team and a Huey, it was virtually impossible for him to escape. And this time, we even had his photograph.

He decided to come down.

"Before you do, Lamar, be sure to get a couple of people on Nola's sister's place. Linda Grossman's. If we would miss him, for some reason, that's where he might go."

" 'Miss him'?! 'Miss him'?! If that son of a bitch disappears this time, all of you better disappear right along with him!"

I thought that was a little unfair. But the message certainly was clear.

Volont was apparently encouraged by the river depth. He was on the no longer secure radio. "Alpha Chase, you clear to take out some tires on the stretch van?"

"Roger that."

"Stand by . . ." He turned to me. "Come on, Houseman. Let's go down by the tracks."

We hurried out of the pavilion, down into the deepest fog I'd ever experienced. We headed due east, and stopped just behind the big fire truck. In the intense light from its big halogen flood lights, we had a pretty good view of the stretch van. Just sitting there, filled with very still shadows. Several of them.

Volont picked up his radio, and gave the order to shoot out the tires on the van. "Do it."

I'd never seen that before. It was a bit of a disappointment, really. There was no discernible firing, either visually or audibly. Just a popping sound. The front and rear tires on the right side of the stretch van just went flat. Instantly. I think I might have seen a little bit of dust or something, or maybe just rapidly condensing air as it blew out of the tires. Very unremarkable. But now the little group in the van was totally screwed. Their vehicle was immobile. The only other refuge had been the boat, which was now across about a hundred feet of icy water. The concrete area they were parked on offered no cover whatsoever, for at least twenty yards in any direction.

The first three cop cars came around the bluff from the south, and stopped about fifty yards from the van. Now, I figured, we'd see just how disciplined the boys in the van were. If they fired even one round, they were all as good as dead. It would be like shooting fish in a barrel.

"Let's let 'em stew until we have a lot of people here," said Volont, "and then get 'em out of the van."

I looked around. We were pretty much alone, with the nearest fireman behind the truck. It was now or never.

"Look," I said. "This is all out of proportion. Way the hell out. What's really happening, here?"

I waited a very long ten seconds. Very quiet, except for the muter roar of the fire truck engine.

"Let's go back over here," said Volont, pointing to the edge of the bluff about a hundred feet behind the fire truck. "Where we don't have to shout."

We stood close to the bluff, and he told me what Gabriel was really doing. Well, that's what he said. I don't doubt him.

"I've been on Gabriel several years," he said. "You know that."

Yeah, I did.

Was I aware of the term "weapons of mass destruction"?

"You mean, like, nuclear, chemical . . . biological things?"

He did. Apparently, this had all started for Volont when the Soviet Union began to dissolve. "You know what the acronyms ADM, MADM, or SADM stand for?"

No, I didn't.

"That's atomic demolition munitions, medium atomic demolition munitions, and small atomic demolition munitions. Know what they are?"

" 'Atomic' rings a bell," I said, sarcastically.

"Right. Well, in the U.S. Army, those are small nuclear devices used like land mines. They were developed to block tunnels and things, blow up harbor facilities, to stop the Soviets when they invaded Western Europe. Engineering tools."

He made them sound like bulldozers.

"The Soviets had the same sort of thing." He flashed a tight smile. "For when Western Europe invaded them, no doubt."

"That figures . . ."

"So, first of all, Gabe resigns his commission, and makes noises like he's going to start his own little state out west. Fill it with his followers, and declare independence from the U.S.A." He looked up. "Of course, secession meets with disapproval at the federal level." He smiled again.

"He's going to war?" I asked, incredulous. "He's nuts."

"Not exactly. Our people on the inside say he puts it this way . . . The only countries that gain respect from the U.S. government are nuclear powers. Therefore he wants some nuclear weapons. As a deterrent. To ensure his independence."

"Jesus H. Christ."

"The devices came on the market after the Soviets went belly up. That's when I got involved. Back in '95, he made inquiries, and was told that it would cost ten million bucks." He shrugged. "Cheap, but they're only about five kilotons or so of yield. The higher yields, twenty-plus kilotons or megaton range devices, they go for a hundred million."

"Nuclear suitcase bombs," I said. "My God."

"Well, not 'suitcase.' These weigh over one thousand pounds in the packing crates. We would classify them as ADMs, actually."

"He could deliver them in a pickup truck," I said.

"Oh, yeah. They're also designed to work underwater. Lots of possibilities. And much easier to use than missile warheads, for example. No fusing options like impact, proximity, delay . . ."

"God."

"But that's why he needs the money. He's a bit short. That's why he's going to try to take even the coins. Time is running out, and he's afraid somebody else is going to buy the devices."

"Oh. Well, sure." A nuclear layaway plan had never occurred to me.

"He was trying for the banks last time. Just didn't get it done. But he has the plan, he has the volunteers, he has the infrastructure, right here. So he comes back." He shrugged again. "Nothing personal, but Nation County is easy pickings."

"Yeah."

"It's a warrior, with a war, Houseman. He doesn't want to kill the people on the boat. Really. Would be bad for 'international relations,' once his little private country is set up." He paused, and then, "But he will kill them, all of them, if he has to. For the survival of the state, so to speak."

"But he doesn't have them now? The nuclear weapons?"

"No."

The sense of relief was enormous. "I mean, I thought there was a special unit that worked that sort of thing . . ."

"There is. They kick in when nuclear weapons are actually in play. Right now, they're just monitoring things very closely. Right now, it's our baby." He stopped. "Until he should get some. Anything you'd like to ask?"

"Any idea what his targets are?" I had a vision of our courthouse under a small mushroom cloud.

"I don't think he has any. We're not here to prevent nuclear terrorism, really," he said. He smiled. "We're just trying to prevent the great state of Gabriel from becoming the world's smallest nuclear power."

I took a deep breath. "So, why are you telling me this?"

"Just so you'll know, if we end up with six hundred frozen bodies in the Mississippi, that they died for a good cause." He looked around. "Let's go back to the office. Don't tell anybody." He grinned. "Not that they'd believe you."

"Carl," said Sally, "call the office, ten-thirty-three."

After my chat with Volont, a local "emergency" just seemed to lose its punch.

I called the office. The duty dispatcher said, "I have a female subject on the phone, calling from the gaming boat, and she wants a number for you right away. Says her name is Nancy . . ."

"Give it to her," I said, and hung up. "Hey, guys?" They looked my way. "I think we have a contact on the boat."

I explained quickly about Nancy and Shamrock. The little deal we'd made. The fact that I'd seen them board the boat early on.

The phone rang. "Command," said Sally. "Yes, he is. Would this be Nancy?"

She handed me the phone.

"Houseman, you bastard," said an angry whisper, "if you knew about this, you turkey, I'll get you for this. You did. Didn't you?"

"No, none of us did," I said. "We were as surprised as anybody . . ."

"Not fuckin' quite," she whispered.

"Uh, well, yeah. Yeah. Are you two all right?"

"Just great. Get us out of here." There was a bit of commotion. "There. We're in the ladies' john on the middle deck," she said.

"Anybody hurt?"

"Not that we saw. What the hell's going on? Why did we leave the pier? Who are these people?"

I did my very best to explain, and gave her a fast summary, leaving out as much of the negative as I could, just to keep from worrying her unnecessarily about things that were already past. I was concerned for the two of them, but I was also really happy to have a voice on the boat.

"So, what are they doing now?" I mean, since she was there, she might as well be useful.

"They aren't in here, Houseman." Dryly. Sarcastically. But she was calming down.

"Nancy, it might help us get you out of that mess if you can tell us what's going on . . ."

"Houseman, you got us in this mess. You get us out." At least her voice sounded almost normal, now.

"Try to find out how many of the bad guys are still on the boat. And where they are."

"What, are you nuts?" Reasonable question. She paused. "Well . . ."

"You gotta admit, it's a great story," I said, trying to cheer her up.

"I'm not interested in a posthumous Pulitzer," she whispered. "I gotta go . . ." and broke the connection.

"Is anybody hurt?" asked Hester. "Are they going to be able to help?"

"No casualties as far as they know. And, sure, I think they're going to be able to help a lot."

Volont decided to crank up the pressure.

"Alpha One and Alpha Two, can you take out some tires on the suspect vehicles at the bank?"

"Alpha One. No problem with the one on my left . . ." came crackling through the radio.

"Alpha Two can do the one on the river side, but we can't do the potato chip truck in the middle."

"Uh . . . just a sec . . . and Alpha One might be able to do the right front on the chip truck." The spotter paused. "Yeah, he can, he can do that one."

"Take your shots," said Volont.

We, of course, couldn't see a thing of the truck tires. Or the trucks. Or even the bank, by now.

"Alpha One has put two grooves in the big truck tire, the one with the lift gate, but just can't get a good shot. Will change aspect, and try again. The other trucks are disabled."

"Roger," said Volont. "Well, so much for the coins. That ought to move things right along."

With her stern against the ice, and her bow pointing into the slow current, the *Beauregard* had slowly pointed her bow to the left, toward our side of the shore. We were now able to barely make out about the first seventy-five feet of her bow, just about ten windows back along the deck. It looked strange, the front end just jutting out of the fog.

I heard Hester say, "Come on in . . ." and a large man of about forty-five entered the room. "This is Captain Olinger, an off-duty captain of the boat," said Hester.

"Glad to meet you," said Volont. "I can see some activity on the front end of the boat, Captain. Can you tell what they're doing?"

Captain Olinger looked carefully through Hester's binoculars for a moment. "Well, it looks like some amateurs are preparing the rescue boat for launch," he said. "One of them is trying to release the boarding ladder . . . Not much of a sailor, is he?"

"Captain," said Volont, "these people have threatened to sink the boat. Can they do it?"

The captain looked down at Volont. "Beats me. What do they have to work with?"

Volont cleared his throat, embarrassed and irritated. Nobody likes to ask a dumb question. "Maybe I should ask what it would take to sink it?"

"And you are?"

James intervened. "He's FBI," he said.

"Oh. Well, she's got five watertight compartments. If the doors are properly closed . . . you'd have to breach the hull on either side of each of two of the transverse bulkheads to sink her. Flood two of the compartments." He looked back out the window toward the *Beauregard*. "I'd say that'd sink her, all right."

Twenty-six

I got busy about then with another phone call from Nancy and
Shamrock. They had been on a quick scouting expedition,
and had made careful observations.

"There are about five or six onboard, and they're doing
something up front with a raft, or something, and they're pissed
off and worried about something to do with that van on shore."

Not bad. "What are they worried about the van for?"

"I don't know. But they don't seem to know why it's still
there, like it shouldn't be . . ." Nancy's voice, though rapid, was
pretty calm.

"They got that right," I said, with just a hint of pride.
"Where are they?"

"Up front. One or two above us, but the others are out on
deck, as far as I can tell. Are they going to leave us?"

"I don't know. They might." I was really encouraged. If they
were talking so that Nancy could overhear, and if they were worried about the van not moving, they weren't the best of troops.
That meant that we might be able to handle them like ordinary
criminals, not like pros.

She slowed her voice way down. "Are they going to sink us?"

"They can't."

"Oh, right, Houseman. Just like *Titanic*."

"No, really. You're in fourteen feet of water. That means the
bottom of the boat is only seven or eight feet above the river bot-

tom. Worst you can do is get your feet wet. Best thing for you two to do is to go up one deck."

"I'm gonna get a drink," said Nancy.

"Yeah, right . . ."

"No shit, Houseman. The bars are still open. Hell, these idiot terrorists are letting people do their thing. There are still a bunch of people playing the slots."

"You're kidding?"

"No. For real. The only thing different is that there aren't any boat security people or any dealers around." She said goodbye, and broke the connection. To go get a drink, presumably.

I shared the information with the group.

Hester thought it was a good idea. "I mean, it keeps the people calm. It lets the gamblers go back to their thing. Keeps everybody happy. Why not?"

"Especially now," said Volont. "With about half your people sitting in that van. You don't really want to do crowd control. Keep everybody happy, like there wasn't any problem at all. Pretty smart."

"Call the bank," said Volont. "See how things are in there."

Sally did, on speaker phone. You could her the phone ringing, and then a man's voice.

"What the fuck is taking so long?"

"This is a police dispatcher . . ."

Click.

Well.

It was time to discuss things. We did. Not at length, naturally, but we got a bunch of thoughts together, and found that we were in substantial agreement on most points.

Stopping the van was an excellent idea, and had taken control from Gabriel. It hadn't put us in control, not yet. But there was at least more of an even playing field.

The boat, while it could be hurt, wasn't going to be sinking in the traditional sense. Passengers might be jeopardized in the long term, but not immediately. The captain explained that he thought the worst danger was that, since the engines would become inoperative if submerged, and that since the upper decks were mostly windows, it was going to get pretty damned cold on-board it they did anything drastic.

Not an urgent thing, at least not in the current environment.

We had apparently put a lot of pressure on the bad guys at the bank. Good. We also got confirmation that they couldn't see anything but the boat's stacks from the bank, in the best of times. Therefore, they were probably unable to see the stopped van at the boat dock. Uncertainty. Good.

We didn't want the gunmen to panic. All we wanted to do at this point was severely undermine their confidence, and it looked like we were making good progress there. All we just had to do was hold our ground, wait for the negotiator, and make preparations to get the passengers off the boat as soon as we could. Hester had an excellent suggestion.

"Get a couple of ambulances in—close, but not in the hazard zone. But obvious. Let 'em wonder who they're for . . ."

The group in the stretch van ought to really appreciate that. We had Sally call the ambulances to the scene.

We also started to marshal school buses across the river, in parking lots of the Conception County Sheriff's Department. If we had to off-load a bunch of passengers, we'd want a way to get them to the nearest shelter. In this case, the school gym.

Based on Nancy's report, and the reaction on the phone at the bank, it appeared that cracks were starting to appear in the opposition's confidence.

The loose talk around the passengers was a very good sign, and the voice on the bank phone sounded stressed as all get-out. And we hadn't heard from Gabriel for a while. Busy with the troops?

"Like I said, they don't have a lot of really good people in this," I said. "Just a couple. Discipline is going to be a problem."

"Lack of training," said Volont. "But not a failure of leadership. Gabriel is a very strong leader. Don't underestimate that."

"But with untrained people, he's going to have to be right

there. The ones that are separated from him, they're the ones who are going to start coming apart." Hester kept looking at the boat. "Makes me wonder, though. They're getting sort of nervous on the boat. They are really nervous at the bank. You suppose he's in the stretch van stranded on the ramp?"

Interesting thought. If he was in the van, it was the best thing that could happen to us. If we could take that van, and let the boat and the bank be fully aware of it . . . Decapitate the whole operation. How far could the rest of them be from surrender, if we took the stretch van and Gabriel really was in it?

"Alpha Lead," called Volont on the radio, "report up here ASAP." He was calling the TAC team commander. Volont beamed at Hester. "I like that idea."

By the time the TAC team commander arrived, we had something of a plan. The little group in the stranded stretch van was really dangling out there. No place to hide. No place to run. In a clear fire zone, especially with the boat now away from the dock. There was absolutely nothing to prevent us from taking them apart, if necessary. All we had to do was come up with a plan to convince them that we were about to do it if they resisted in any way, and then simply arrest them. Piece of cake.

The team commander agreed that they could be taken out without a problem. Arresting he wasn't so sure about.

It became a matter of approach. If, as we hoped, Gabriel was in the van, we'd have to be careful not to make any mistakes at all. One false step, and he'd grab any possible advantage.

The team commander, who was aware of Gabriel's background and the likely anti-Fed mentality of his group, suggested that we have either a local or a county officer go with him to approach the stretch van.

No names, but I looked around the office. I was the only one who fit that bill.

We came up with our plan. "You sure you're comfortable with this?" What could I say? No? Of course I wasn't comfortable about it. I didn't want to do it. One of those lovely little moments, when you agree with everything that was going to be done, but had a little reservation about who was going to get stuck with it.

"Just remember, we aren't going over there to arrest anybody. Just to give them something to think about."

"Like shooting the pale deputy?"

He laughed. "You'll be fine."

I hoped he was right.

The view of the stretch van from street level was a bit different. We were much closer, for one thing, and the fog wasn't much of a factor. You could see at least one head inside. The driver. The rest were fairly well obscured by shadow. I mean, it looked kind of lumpy in there, but you couldn't make out individuals. It was hard to believe there were seven of them in there.

The stretch van was down by the bow, as they say, with both front tires flattened, and the right rear as well. Although I knew it wasn't intentional, leaving that one tire up was a good thing. The occupants had to be just a little more uncomfortable, with a list like that. If we'd been able to shoot out all four tires, they'd have been on an even keel. Kind of reminded me of the old-fashioned interrogation chairs, with the front legs an inch shorter than the rear. The sensation of being about to slide out of the chair apparently made the interviewee most uncomfortable.

The engine was running, presumably for the heater. Even with the flat tires, I had to remind myself that they could move if they needed to. Just not too far or too fast.

We stopped just across the street from the stretch van, near the front of the fire truck. As planned, we climbed up into the cab, and scrutinized the radio and siren boxes, until we were sure we could turn on the truck's PA system. I was always a little nervous with an unfamiliar siren box. You had to turn the rotary switch to "PA" and then activate the siren switch. With this one, and we'd been warned, you also had to switch the mike box over from "radio" to "PA," or you'd just set off the siren. We were extracareful, because we didn't want to startle the occupants of the stretch van into something regrettable. Like shooting us, for instance.

Click. Click. So far, so good. Key the mike. Well, you can't win them all. We both had our heads down, and pulling the mike to my mouth only got it about three inches from the radio. Feedback. The resulting squeal sounded like fingernails on a blackboard, magnified about a thousand times. It only lasted about half a second, but it scared the hell out of me. I released the "talk" button, and slid back across the passenger's seat, so that my feet were on the paving, and just my elbows were in the truck.

"Wanna try that again?"

"Shit," I said. "Yeah. Should have thought of that." I cleared my throat, and stood on the running board with the mike in my hand. I keyed it again, and there was just a hiss from the speaker on the roof of the truck. So far, so good.

Following that squeal wasn't easy, so I figured I'd better keep it simple and straightforward.

"Two of us are coming over to talk to you. Don't shoot. Understand?" There was no reaction. I put the mike down. "That okay?"

"Don't do much public address work, do you?" said Adams, with a grin. "It'll do. Let's go."

We both stood in full view of the stretch van, took off our coats, and turned slowly. No obvious guns. We'd decided earlier that losing the coats would have to be enough. Cold made your voice shake, and that wasn't what we wanted, so we weren't about to take off our shirts. Just let them know that, if we were armed, they could probably get off the first hundred rounds while we fumbled for our guns.

Butterflies wouldn't do my feelings justice, as we walked across that street. I can't remember being so tense in my life. Not only were we in a perfect position to be gunned down in our tracks, but I was going to have to act self-possessed. And I was now very cold. It was awfully damp, and the breeze was picking up as it came upriver from the south.

We approached on the passenger side. We got about five feet from the window, and were staring eye to eye with a man in a ski mask. Armed with what looked like a Mack 10 submachine gun.

There was a face at each of the two side windows, also with a ski mask on. I couldn't see any guns, but I had no doubt they were there.

We just stood there. "Roll your window down," I said, rather loudly. Nothing. "Your window," I said, a bit louder. "Roll it down." The eyes in the ski mask didn't even blink.

I realized that, with the engine running, and the defroster on, it might be a bit hard to hear. But, honest, I was beginning to wonder if we might be all wrong, and dealing with some foreign nationals who didn't speak English.

"Roll down your window," said Adams. Also quite loudly. No reaction. The eyes just stared. No reaction, although they had to be able to see our lips moving, at least. We stood there for another thirty seconds. No reaction. Neither Adams nor I wanted to take our eyes off the occupants of the van, and neither of us should get any closer. The last thing we wanted was for them to grab one of us as a hostage. But this was turning into the stupidest moment of my career. I took two steps forward, and stayed well ahead of the door handle, so that if he did open it, the door would be between me and him. That way, if they tried to grab me, I could turn and run. I'm slow, but catching me in the middle of the street would have been really dumb on their part. It would take three of them to drag me back. Size does count, sometimes.

Thus emboldened, I continued the eye contact with the passenger, and motioned downward with my hand. "The window. Open the window." Loud enough to be heard. Clear enough to be understood, or so I thought. Still nothing. It was like he was drunk. Stupidly drunk. Or stupid with fear. Ah.

I pulled my right hand back, made a fist, and struck the hood just in front of the windshield. Hurt like hell. At the same time, I yelled at the top of my lungs, "OPEN THE FUCKING WINDOW!"

He energetically cranked the window down, at the same time yelling back, "BE CAREFUL OF THE FUCKIN' HOOD!"

Ah, communication.

"Hi," I said, in a more normal tone. "My name's Houseman, and I'm a deputy sheriff in this county. I think it's time you surrendered."

Even under that mask, I got the feeling this "warrior" was about nineteen or twenty. "We ain't gonna surrender. We . . . we . . . demand safe, uh, safe passage." It was just like he was reading it. "We don't acknowledge your laws. We don't have to obey the laws of this state. We're freemen, we're twenty-one, and you have, uh, no rule over us."

Oh, God. Gabriel, you asshole, I thought. Using these people for this, and the kids, to boot.

"Look, son . . ."

"I'm not your son! You have no force over me!"

"No, you're younger than any kid I'll ever have," I said. "The point is this. There are about twenty armed officers around you. If we open fire, you will be shredded like hamburger. You understand that?"

"We aren't in your jurisdiction."

"You are *completely* within my jurisdiction. Period. No question."

A voice came out of the rear, somewhat older. Well, at least a little deeper. "You ain't got thirty cops in this whole county! Liar! He's lying, Timmy."

"Adams, you want to show them some ID?"

Very slowly, Adams's hand came into my field of view. I could see the black nylon ID case opened up, and it was apparent that the passenger could see the ID.

"Tell them what you're doing here, what you do," I said.

"I'm the commander of the FBI Tactical Response Team that has you surrounded. The team that took out your tires in one second. From rooftops, from between the buildings, from behind the cars." He said it very slowly and clearly.

Silence from the stretch van.

"We want you to think about this," I said. "We'll come back

later and talk. If you want to talk to us, come out with your hands in the air where we can see them, and stand in the middle of the street. We'll meet you halfway. Got that?"

The kid nodded.

"Okay. We're going to go now. I trust you. I hope you trust me."

"We won't be far," said Adams.

I thought there was a small movement in the rear of the van, and froze. Nothing.

"Don't even think about it," I said. Bravado city. I fervently hoped it was just somebody adjusting his position for some innocuous little reason.

We backed away, well into the street, where we turned and walked quickly back behind the fire truck.

As soon as we rounded the corner, I grabbed for my coat. "Fuck!" I was just so glad to be back.

"Yeah!" said Adams. "You know, you're lucky you weren't shot when you hit that hood."

"Shit, I didn't know what else to do. I've never seen anybody freeze up like that."

"Fear. Pure, stark fear. I've seen it, but it took me a second to catch on to it this time."

"That fuckin' Gabriel ought to be shot for recruiting that kid."

"You got that right."

We walked the hundred feet past the pavilion, and took the elevator to Hester's office. We dutifully made our report.

"Just a kid, huh?" Volont was pacing. "All kids?"

"I don't think so," I said. I looked at Adam.

"I don't think so, either. I think he might have been coached by somebody."

"I'll tell you one thing, though." I spoke with conviction. "Gabriel ain't in the van."

"I completely agree," said Adams. "No sign of leadership. No sign of aggression. No sign of confidence. He's not in there."

I could tell by the look in Volont's eye that, if Adams hadn't agreed, he wouldn't have believed me. I just hate that. I was there. I'm as bright as anybody. But I'm not FBI.

"I can't believe," said George, "the way you hit that hood. Definitely not in the manual."

"Hey, I didn't volunteer for this one. Believe me."

Twenty-seven

f Adams and I were right, we had Gabriel either on the boat
or in the bank. Fifty-fifty chance, I suppose, but I'd been pic-
turing him on the boat all this time. I tried to remember, and
thought it was something he'd said . . .

"Anybody . . . didn't Gabriel say something that led us to believe he was on the boat rather than in the bank?"

"He said he'd 'tell the crew to hand out the jackets' when he
implied that they would sink the boat," said Hester. "At least,
that's the way I took it."

"Me too," said George.

Apparently, everybody agreed. "Maybe we could call the boat
and ask to speak with him?" Why not?

"We tried the boat while you were talking to the van people,"
said Hester.

"The land lines disconnected when she was cut adrift. They'd
do that," said James.

Hmm. "Well, then, let's call the bank again. Ask to speak to
him."

"Let me," said Art. "I'm good at that. Anybody got any name
I could use to get 'em to talk to me?"

"How about Roger Bushnell?" Sally blushed as everybody
stared at her. "Should work."

"How so?" asked George.

"The first uniformed cop that drove up to the stretch van ran the plate. It's just what they do. Comes back to a Roger Bush-nell"—she looked at her notes—"of Eden, Wisconsin. Plate expired three years ago. No other vehicles registered to him. Should be, if he registered cars anymore. I'll bet he doesn't because he doesn't believe in the vehicle laws." It all came out in a burst.

"Where," asked Volont, "did you find her, and why were you so lucky?"

Excellent question.

Art dialed the bank. He was on the speaker phone. It rang twice, and the gruff voice answered with "Hello."

"Hey," said Art, in a slightly deeper voice, flatter in tone than normal. "It's Roger. You hear from Gabriel yet?"

"No. Roger who?"

"Bushnell." He pronounced in without inflection or emphasis on a particular syllable. I would have said, "Bush NELL." He was apparently right.

"Okay, Roger. What's the password? You better give me the password."

He had him there. Art, though, really was good at this. Rather than make some lame excuse, or sound like a cop caught in the act, he just said, very loudly, and slightly away from the mouthpiece, "Look out! Cops!" and pressed the disconnect. He grinned, also pleased with his performance.

We were impressed. He'd not blown his cover, and left them worried and concerned, most likely. Good deal. And the icing on the cake was that we now could place Gabriel on the boat.

Unfortunately, knowing and arresting were two different things. I mean, it was surely a simple problem. Basically, all we had to do was figure how to get to a boat 100 feet from a dock. Well, maybe just a bit more complex. We had to figure how to do it with a stretch van filled with armed men between us and the boat. With people on the boat who would certainly, in the spirit of Sally's "pirates," repel boarders. Not to mention possibly sink it, or blow it up.

"Just what kind of fuel does she burn, Mr. James?" asked Volont.

"Diesel. No real fire hazard."

"Gabe tends to like explosives," I said. "If memory serves."

"Not under his own butt." Volont seemed sure. I wondered.

"If he starts her sinking," said Captain Olinger, "I'd suggest running cable, hook them to a couple of large wreckers, and pull her to shore."

We explained the method he'd used to blow off the cleats.

"No problem. There are structural members that would be accessible, and would bear the load. Do you want me to start rounding up the materials?"

We did. He got right on it.

Moments later, the phone rang. It was Gabriel. It was for me, at least at first.

"Deputy, did you enjoy your little chat with my people?" Confirmed he wasn't in the van, I thought. Well, given the fact that he would lie whenever necessary, maybe a 90 percent chance.

"The one is just a kid," I said. "Way too young for this shit."

"You're never too young, Deputy. Go to Fort Bragg and check IDs sometime."

"This one's been brainwashed."

"Welcome to the real world. But I digress. I want you to know I've talked with them, and I've given instructions to shoot on sight if anybody even tries to approach their position again."

"Don't you think 'predicament' would be a better choice than 'position'? These guys make Custer look safe," I said.

"Modern weapons . . . no. Never mind. But I wouldn't try them. They have a long reach." He sounded kind of mysterious. Rocket launcher? We knew he'd stolen a bunch a few years back. Good God, if they were to just step out of the van and fire a couple of LAWS rockets at the *General Beauregard* . . .

"Let me speak with Volont."

"I'm here."

"Stop playing with my people," he said. "In a short while, we'll be leaving. Stay out of the way," and he terminated the conversation.

"I think," said George, "we're definitely getting to him . . ."

About a minute later, the phone rang. Nancy, for me.

"Houseman," she whispered, "how are you coming with getting us off here? These people are starting to act kind of squirrelly."

"The bad guys or the passengers?"

"Don't be silly," she said. I thought it had been a pretty reasonable question.

"We're getting there," I said, trying to be a comfort.

"No progress, huh? You're gonna have to do better than that. One of the passengers is a little tipsy, and went over to one of the ski masks and asked him for a light. The ski mask knocked him down with his gun, and threatened to kill him."

"No shit?" We must be getting to the ones on the boat, too. I couldn't figure that out. They were the ones who cast off, apparently stranding themselves in the river. With explosive charges that had obviously been placed by them. Planned. With Gabriel there for leadership. So, what was screwing up their program? Something to do with the stretch van?

"No shit. This isn't a good situation here, Houseman. Not at all."

"Who's in charge? Can you tell?"

"It's supposed," she said, testily, "to be you."

"No, but in charge of the bad guys. Where's the leader? Where on the boat, I mean."

"I don't have the faintest. I didn't even know they had one."

Hester signaled me. "The suspects in the your little van seem to want to talk . . ."

"Gotta go. Hey, talk to Hester, will you?" I handed Hester the phone, and headed for the elevator.

When Adams and I got to the van, the young male I'd talked to was standing in the middle of the street, with his coat still on and his hands in his pockets. He was making everybody very nervous.

Adams and I approached him, and stopped when we got to the curb on our side of the street. "Put your hands where we can see them, would you, Timmy?" I shouted. "We'll keep ours out in plain view, too."

That seemed to work. He took his hands out of his pockets, and kept standing there. We approached.

"What do you want to tell us?" Adams was a lot better trained than I.

"We been talking. We don't think you can do this, but we . . . we know we have rights under your laws. Right?"

"Sure. Same as anybody else. Isn't that right, Deputy?"

"Absolutely."

He nodded. "Okay, then. Then we want to surrender under the Geneva convention."

He sounded so damned sincere, and so scared . . .

"Just tell me your name, and I'll accept your surrender," said Adams. "I'm authorized to do so."

"Oh, good . . . Timothy Frederick Olson."

"Maybe you better tell your friends that we can accept your surrender. But only if you lay down your arms."

"Oh, oh, sure. Oh. Be right back, okay?"

"Okay."

"This is Alpha Lead," said Adams. "It looks like they might come out. If they do, get a team here to secure them."

Neither of us looked at the other. We didn't want to take our eyes off the van. "Are we going to be this lucky?"

"Well," he said, "if the kid is any indication, we sure are."

"I agree. And why else send him? Just to blow away two older cops?"

"Speak for yourself."

About ten seconds later, they began to emerge from the van. Seven men, still with their ski masks on, but without any visible weapons. They were all dressed in olive green trousers, boots, and patterned rust brown, gray, black, and green rain smocks. They sure hadn't all been dressed like that when I'd seen them on the dock. They must have put them on while they were waiting. Solidarity?

As they walked toward us, Adams barked, "Hands on your heads, gentlemen, and please roll the ski masks off your faces."

They did. I didn't recognize any of them. As the kid I'd talked to went by, I stopped him for a second.

"Why did you all put on the same clothes?"

"If you catch us out of uniform, you can have us executed as spies," he said, very matter-of-fact. "It's in the Geneva convention."

I shook my head. "Go on with the others."

"Did I hear him right?"

"Afraid so."

"Boy. Twenty-two years in the FBI, and I never heard that one before."

But, now, regardless of anything else, our most direct path to the boat was cleared. The odds were getting better all the time.

Twenty-eight

We reassessed, as they say. It was decided to begin to bring rescue equipment toward the boat, since the threat in the stretch van had been neutralized, and we could begin to bring people in a bit closer. We called the main office, and asked for Captain Olinger to come back up to the DCI office. We needed to plan.

Sometimes it's hard to see any real progress in a given situation. I mean, here things were, with better access to a boat we still couldn't get to, which was still occupied by several hundred gamers as hostage, held by a few armed individuals who were not about to let us get much closer than we were. A small increment, at best. But, I thought, progress, nonetheless.

Until I talked with George.

"You know, what we've done is eliminate the only suspects we could hold hostage . . ." He looked at me, startled at his own thoughts. "If Gabriel ordered them to surrender, he just saved their lives, eliminated the threat that they could be killed or injured, and has kept the ante the same."

"Smoothed out the lines," said Adams. He shivered in the cold, damp air. "Looks like we just rescued some of his people for him."

Art had come up while we were talking. "Well, that means we got some people to charge if things go to hell on us."

Always practical.

Captain Olinger came in. "You have a plan? I understand you have a plan . . ."

Lamar arrived a few moments later. I'd never been so glad to see him in my life, because I knew what was coming, and I honestly didn't want the decision on my shoulders. We had another little impromptu get-together. The upshot was that, to pressure Gabe and to force his surrender, we had to take the bank. Volont really pressed Lamar, because it was Lamar's decision. His primary jurisdiction.

"He's a soldier, Sheriff. He is. He won't kill just to be doing it. I know that. You know that. Once we take the bank, the whole reason for his whole operation is over. Done."

Lamar looked at him for a moment, and then just walked off a few feet, stomping his good boot in the slush. "Carl, Hester, come here, will ya?"

We stood with him, nobody saying a word. Finally, he asked our opinion. "So, what do you think?"

"My best guess," I said, "is this: He hasn't hurt anybody on the boat or in the bank. We have no indication that he's going to do bad things on the boat. Unless we do, I say wait him out."

"I agree," said Hester. "When he has to try to feed several hundred people out there on the water, he's done. Forty-eight hours or less, and he just drops into our laps."

"So, you don't think we should try the bank, then?"

We both said, "No."

"Unless he does something to the boat?"

Right.

"Even then, it depends on what he does. As sheriff, it's my call." Lamar was quiet for a few more seconds, and then he turned back to the FBI agent in charge. "Let it wait. Plan it, set it up, and then wait. It ain't time, yet."

I thought it was a fine decision.

We just got back into Hester's office at the pavilion, when the phone rang. Sally made her now familiar "It's Gabriel" signal, and put him on speaker phone.

"Let me speak to Volont."

"This is Sheriff Ridgeway. I think you'd better talk to me, first."

"The sheriff himself. Well, this is an honor. What kept you?"

"Business," said Lamar. "Why don't you just knock off the shit, and give up. You know we ain't gonna let your people out of the bank. You know you're gonna have to give up the boat. Why prolong things?"

"I hate to disappoint you," said the heavy voice, "but I have other plans."

"We all got plans, son," said Lamar. "Doesn't mean a lot."

Gabriel actually chuckled. "You've got balls, for a gimpy old fucker," he said. "I think you'd give me a lot tougher time than Special Agent Volont." The humor left his voice like he'd turned off a switch. "My plans tend to mean quite a bit," he said. "Please direct your attention to the boat." He broke the connection.

We looked. We couldn't see anything farther back than the bow. Nothing.

Suddenly, there was a cloud of yellowish brown billowing up from inside the fog, and a distant *thump* that you could feel in your feet.

"Shit!" Lamar turned to Volont. "Get 'em to move on the bank," he said.

Captain Olinger, the off-duty boat captain, rushed to the window.

"What? Who the hell is he?" asked Lamar. They hadn't had time to be introduced, I explained as Olinger began to describe things.

"Watch her," said the captain. "If she settles by the stern, that might be good. It looked like the smoke was from the port side, maybe aft of the paddle wheels . . . she should settle by the stern . . . yeah, see . . ."

It did look as if she was getting a little lower in the water, and I could have sworn I could see more of the surface of the decks than I could a few minutes ago.

There was a spreading stain on the water, emerging from the fog from the direction of the after portion of the *Beauregard*.

"Is that fuel coming out?" Lamar always worried about fires.

"I don't think so . . . no," said Captain Olinger. "What it looks like is sewage."

"Sewage?" I was surprised.

"Yeah . . . there's a ninety-four hundred gallon sewage tank, just above the propeller shafts, straddling two big void spaces . . . and it looks to me like she's open to the river around void five and the engine room."

"Is it sinking?" asked Lamar.

"Not yet," said Captain Olinger. "Just a minute . . ."

There was a sudden jet of water coming through the fog, from the side, about the middle of the boat. Low.

"Pumps," said Olinger. "Automatic."

"Will that work?" asked Hester.

"It helps. If that's it," said Captain Olinger, "then she won't sink." He pointed to the security diagram on Hester's bulletin board. "She's got six transverse watertight bulkheads," he said, "and it looks to me like the holing occurred about here . . ." He drew an X near the stern. "Worst case would be on both sides of the bulkhead that separates the engine room and void five." He smiled. "If that's it, then she's stable right now."

"How stable," asked Hester, "is stable?"

"Really stable. She can stay like that forever and not go down another inch."

The phone rang, and Sally put it on speaker. It was Gabriel.

"Impressed?"

Nobody answered.

"Oh, come now. Surely you appreciate the talent, here?" He sounded amused. "I'm assuming that you have somebody accessible who can tell you about the boat?"

He anticipated just about everything, I guess. Well, you would have, if you'd planned this long enough.

"This is Captain Olinger."

"Ah, Captain. As you've probably determined, I've flooded the engine room and the last compartment aft. If you haven't, you know it now."

"I had."

"Good for you." The humor was back in Gabriel's voice. "The next charge is set to open what you call void four, with the next charge after that at the generator room."

"There's a ten thousand gallon fuel tank in void four!"

"Stay calm, Captain. The charges just let in the water. They're not set to even affect the fuel tank."

"How can you be sure?" Volont stuck his two cents worth in.

"Ah, Super Asshole in Control Volont! You of all people should know I can do that."

None of us in the office spoke.

"Let my people out of the bank when they signal you to do so, allow them to proceed where they wish, and I won't set off charges two and three. Ask the good captain. Charge two will put her on the edge, and charge three will sink her. It's your call."

The phone went dead.

"Well," Art said, "it's good to know that she's only sitting a couple of feet off the bottom."

"Who told you that?" asked Captain Olinger.

"The lock and dam," I said.

"They use an average depth of the river in an area," said the Captain. "Before we ever berthed the *Beau*, we had to dredge a channel for her, to avoid bottom debris and to keep her props from eroding the bank. Out two hundred feet, and four hundred feet north and south."

We looked at him.

"Right now, she's sitting in forty-five feet of water. That'd be enough to submerge her to the pilothouse."

"Can we tow it to shore?" George was right on top, as usual.

"Take a lot," said Olinger. "She's got no propulsion, and she's carrying another . . . Oh, say, fifteen tons of water now. Not a job for your average winch." He pointed in the general direction of the *Beauregard*. "Find enough power, attach a good cable to that big tow ring just below the weather deck at the bow . . ."

We decided that the first step would be to get several hundred feet of cable rounded up, connected, and think of a way to get it to the boat in a hurry. What to attach it to on the bank, to pull such a load, was the largest problem. It was also a problem we had to solve before we went for the bad guys inside the Frieberg bank.

George wondered about a wrecker. No way. Couldn't overcome the inertia, according to Captain Olinger.

Lamar solved that one. "Sally, get hold of the railroad. See when they can have a couple of those big diesel engines on the track by the boat landing . . ." He turned to the captain. "That be enough?"

"Oh, it sure would," he said, grinning. "Plenty. Hell, you could water-ski behind her with that kind of pull."

"Now we just got to figure a way to get cable attached to the boat without getting somebody shot." I looked at the dock area. "Can we get an iceboat up here?"

Our local iceboats were 16-foot aluminum flatbottoms, with caged aircraft engines, much like a swamp boat. Ice, water . . . made no real difference to the iceboats. I'd ridden in one for the first time at a drowning last winter. They just slowed a bit, hit the ice at a slant, and rode right up on it. Same thing going from the ice back to the water.

"We can probably get an iceboat here in fifteen minutes," said Captain Olinger.

"Let's do it," said Lamar. "I want everything in place when we decide to go . . ."

"It's time for the bank," said Volont.

Lamar looked first at Volont, then at Adams. "How long's it gonna take?"

"Ten minutes from 'Go,' " answered Adams. No hesitation.

"How are you going to do it?" I thought that was covered under "need to know."

Adams told us to look out the window toward the bank, one at a time, as he talked. He never looked, himself.

"The only operable truck they have is the one with the lift gate on the rear. Hydraulic. We can't get a good shot line on the tires. This turns out," he said, "to be a good thing."

He explained that there were a couple of blind spots in the bank. The bigger of the trucks had been the one the robbers had backed to the hole they'd blown in the wall. The hole wasn't quite large enough to accommodate the rear of the truck, so they'd had to leave a gap of about four feet between the end of the truck and the bank wall, to accommodate the powered lifting gate. His officers had been watching the robbers move the 55 gallon drums of money between the truck and the bank. They said that there was a good chance they could get in by approaching in the blind spot, creeping the wall, and just walking in through the hole in the wall when the power gate was in the down position.

They'd also had good views through some of the windows and were aware of the position of most of the hostages. Most.

In addition to the entry team, there would be four more TAC team members moving along the other blind spot, who would rush the door after the others got inside.

"Have the robbers locked the doors?" asked Lamar.

"The big glass doors? Doesn't make any difference," said Adams. "Not really."

Lamar stood looking out toward the boat. "What are your odds at the bank?"

"Good," said Adams. "Not perfect, but good. Given this situation, it's not likely to get any better."

"And the hostages?"

"Good, too."

"But not perfect," said Lamar. "Never is, is it?"

"No, it never is," said Adams.

Lamar kept looking out at the boat. "Damned if you do, damned if you don't," he said, mostly to himself. "Lose six hostages in the bank, or over six hundred on the water . . ."

"We have to go now," said Volont, "or the window of opportunity closes."

"Are you sure?" Lamar turned. "If they get to leave the bank, do you think he'll sink the boat?"

"He will, to cover his escape," said Volont.

"And if we take them out of the bank . . . ?"

"Then there's no point to continue the whole business," said Volont. "The soldier surrenders to save lives. Much better press that way."

"I hope you're right," said Lamar. He turned to face Adams. "Take 'em out of the bank."

We left the office to Lamar, Art, and Sally. The rest of us hustled down toward the bank. Adams left first, and just disappeared into the fog. It was that thick. You could only see about fifty feet before things started becoming indistinct.

I could see the tops of the heads of the five TAC agents who were to go through the hole, as they moved along the bank wall. Then they all ducked down, and I lost them to the fog, the trucks, and the low wall. We waited. And waited. Nothing happened. We waited. I suppose it was all of twenty seconds, to tell the truth, but it felt like a year.

Suddenly, the three TAC agents in the second group popped around the corner of the bank and rushed the main door, disappearing inside in the blink of an eye.

Nothing.

Then, the so-called secure radio crackled to life. "TAC One needs an ambulance at the bank, NOW!"

Sally ordered the ambulance in, and about half a dozen uniformed officers from both our department and the State Patrol moved in with it, running alongside . . .

Nothing, again.

Then, "Okay, TAC One has lots of healthy hostages, two dead suspects, one wounded. No casualties among the good guys."

"All right!"

"Yes!"

"Way to go!"

"Could *somebody*," crackled Sally's voice, "come back up here? He's been on the phone again, and Lamar wants you up here when he calls back . . ."

We got back to Hester's office, and had to wait for almost a minute for Gabriel to call. Lamar looked worried and pleased at the same time. No dead or injured hostages. But we still had to coax Gabriel off the boat.

The phone rang. Gabriel.

"What have you done at the bank? You stupid sons of bitches, what have you done?"

He knew. He was, after all, listening to our radio traffic. I also noticed that his cell phone sounded weak. His batteries were wearing down, I thought. More pressure.

"You might as well give up," said Lamar.

The connection went dead.

This time, water didn't just boil up by the *General Beauregard*. This time, there was a fountain of water more than fifty feet in the air, as the next charge went off. It came shooting up out of the fog, followed a moment later by a thunderclap that rattled our windows.

Captain Olinger had assessed the damage to the *Beauregard* almost before the water plume subsided.

"Void four," he said. "She'll be down a good foot to two feet at the stern with that one . . . I sure as hell hope the fuel tank wasn't ruptured . . ."

People burst out onto the forward weather decks of the *Beau*, climbing the exterior steps to the next deck. As she settled, I could see the water creep above the bottom of the glazed panes toward the rear of the boat. That would put the cash-counting rooms, rest rooms, and coin room into the water. The blackjack tables and the lower bank of game machines would be getting damp, as well. And that water was damned cold.

"If security is being restrained," asked George, "who's moving the people around like that? The bad guys?"

"The dealers and the waitresses," said Hester. "And the deckhands. They're trained for that."

As she spoke, we could see the black slacks and white ruffled blouses of the employees going to the big lockers, and begin handing out the personal flotation devices. They seemed calm.

The passengers, though, were starting to move toward the edge of the decks, and you could almost see them thinking of jumping in. So far, the icy water and the small PFD they'd been issued seemed to be dissuading them from leaving, but it was a funny thing. I was certain that as soon as the first one jumped, we'd get lots more. Anybody in that water for more than ten minutes was as good as gone, especially given they were mostly in their fifties.

The *General Beauregard* stabilized again, with the portion of the deck we could see angling down at about a 15 degree angle, and the last half of the main deck had to be awash. Steam was wafting out of the gangway doors, where the warm air inside met the cold water.

Just seeing her like that gave me butterflies. I fully expected something to give way, and for her to slide stern first beneath the water.

The phone rang again, and we all expected Gabriel. I know that Sally did, because she put it on "speaker" automatically.

It was Nancy, her voice sort of quivery, and no longer bothering to whisper.

"Houseman, this fucking thing is sinking!"

"No, no, it's not. Not yet." I am sometimes honest to a fault.

" 'Not yet'? 'NOT YET'!"

"No, we have a captain here, and he says it's not. Here. Just a second . . . This is a lady we know, and she's on the boat," I said to Captain Olinger, gesturing for him to help.

"That's right, ma'am," he said, loudly. "It's not going to sink after that explosion. Please tell the rest of the passengers that . . ."

"Get us OFF this thing!"

"We're working on it," I said. "We gotta clear this line . . ."

"Nancy, isn't it?" said Volont. "Could you look around and get a number on the terrorists for us?"

"What? What? Not on your stupid little life," she said, and hung up.

"Wait a minute," I said, after Nancy had terminated the

conversation. "Wait . . . What's happening here? I mean, Gabriel doesn't kill for no reason, right?"

"No reason in his own mind," said Volont.

"Right. So, the stretch van has been eliminated . . . and now the bank is back in our possession. So, what the hell is he doing still trying to sink the boat?"

I didn't get an answer.

"Is there any indication that he's suicidal?" I asked. "I mean, if he's not, now that the other aspects of the operation are done for, there's no point in continuing to play with the boat. He won't sink it. He'd be sinking himself."

"I wish I could count on that," said Lamar.

"We gotta keep up the rescue effort . . . sure we do," I said. "Just to be safe." I pointed to the crippled gambling boat. "What we really gotta do is understand that this might be a distraction."

"For what?" asked George.

"For him getting away," I said. "Get some surveillance on the other side of the boat. The river side. Gabe's going to try to make his getaway while we try to save the passengers. He's got to have a plan to get himself off that damned thing . . ."

We set up an observers point in an iceboat, about 300 feet east of the *Beau*. They said they could see everything, and there was no movement that looked like the bad guys were trying to get off the thing. We also closed off the Mississippi River bridge. We closed the thing off completely, and had officers and agents observing the riverside of the boat, watching the bluffs above the fog line, and making sure nobody had gotten off and was climbing to safety.

"Crap, do you think he's going to wait for dark to make his move?" Good old Art.

Shamrock called with Nancy's phone. Interesting news. "Nancy has been, like, upstairs, and she says to tell you that the robbers have changed their clothes. Like, they are blending in, you know? Like you can't tell them from the rest of us."

"Okay . . ."

"And that she thinks there might have been, maybe, six or seven, like at first? And that nobody has been hurt yet, so far as she knows."

"All right . . ."

"And," said Shamrock, "I got some great shots of them, Houseman, great, like at the truck, and pushing people around out here."

"Good for you."

"If we sink, I'm going to throw my film out onto the ice. I taped the cans shut, and I taped them to this stupid little life jacket, and I'll throw it out if we sink. Don't forget to look for it . . ."

The big railroad diesel yard engines arrived a few moments later. The attendant fire departments had rounded up sufficient cable. Now, it was time for volunteers to get the cable out to the boat. Although it always surprised me, there was no shortage of volunteers. It was quickly determined that a DNR officer who was off duty and was on scene with the Volunteer Fire Department would drive an iceboat out to the *Beau*. He was accompanied by a state trooper with arms like tree trunks, who would handle the cable and attach it to the *Beauregard* when the time came.

Both men were given two Kevlar vests, the outer one with plates, to protect them as well as possible from any shots fired at them during their mission. They also wore large orange life jackets. We almost had to lift them into the boat.

Volont issued the order to have half the FBI TAC team sharpshooters become visible to those on the boat, and to let them see the rifles with the scopes before they settled into a shooting position on the roof and the dockside. The four of them were each accompanied by a spotter, with a fairly large scope mounted on a tripod. About half a dozen state troopers and four of our deputies were also made prominent, with rifles. The message to the suspects on the boat was pretty clear. Try to take a shot, and see what happens to you. It was the best we could do.

"All shooters have a green light," said Adams over the once-secure radios. "Anybody on the boat with a gun, take him out. Spotters, if a shot is fired, give the location to everybody on the radio, not just to your shooter."

We watched as the iceboat's prop revved up, and it slid off the ramp and began to move toward the *Beauregard*. The original plan had been to carry the cable to the *Beau*, attach one end, and then move back to shore, and attach the other end to the big yard engines. That was changed, when it was pointed out that if they were shot after attaching the cable to the gambling boat, we'd lose them, the cable, and any other chance of towing the *General Beauregard* to shore. It was also determined that we could begin to tow immediately when the cable was attached to the boat, if it was attached to the yard engines beforehand.

Consequently, with the cable already attached to the yard engines, the iceboat crabbed slowly toward the stricken *Beauregard*, trailing cable over the side. It seemed to take forever, with the DNR officer exposed by sitting in front of the huge propeller cage, and the trooper on his knees in the open bow, cable in hand.

"All shooters, if anybody tries to detach the cable after it's in place, take them out." Adams was talking his sharpshooters through the scenario.

The iceboat moved steadily on, with the trooper in the bow occasionally looking over his shoulder to see that the cable paid out properly. I could feel my pulse in my neck.

When the iceboat was about ten feet away from the tow ring on the *Beau*'s bow, the secure radio crackled to life.

"Alpha Two Spotter has a masked subject with a long gun. He's, uh, on the main deck, and he's behind the glass, just right of center."

I couldn't see him, as there were lots of reflections in the glass.

"And Alpha Two Spotter has the same subject moving to the shore side of the boat, and, and . . . He's coming out onto the deck . . ."

I saw the glazed door open, and a man step out onto the deck with what looked like an AK-47 in one hand. He was in a green coverall and was wearing a dark ski mask. He started toward the bow of the *Beau*, about twenty feet from him. He brought his other hand to the rifle, and began to bring it to his shoulder.

"Shoot," said Adams. Very calm, very matter-of-fact.

I didn't hear a thing, but the man with the rifle just suddenly fell off the deck into the icy water, as if he'd been backhanded by a giant.

The iceboat edged closer to the bow of the *Beauregard*. All of a sudden we could see a myriad of small splashes erupt in the water around the small craft, and a twinkling from the boat. Automatic rifle fire, and a large bit of it.

"Let's suppress the fire, people," intoned Adams. "Get all of 'em. There's at least one shooter on the river side of the deck . . . Suppress that asshole . . ."

An occasional star appeared in the glazed area of the *Beauregard*, but I couldn't see anything else happening. The sharpshooters were having a hell of a time getting a clean shot at any shooters on the boat, because the passengers were bunched up all over the place. The firing at the iceboat did seem to slacken off, though, and it kept edging closer and closer to the bow. When it got within about ten yards, it should be concealed from the shooters by the bow of the riverboat. A safe zone, although temporary. It slid up to the bow, and we all let out a little cheer.

"Let's not get happy, people," said Adams into his radio. "They gotta get out of there, too. Find the shooters. Take your best shots, but be careful." He said to me, as an aside, "We gotta make a decision as to whether or not to accept collateral damage. We hold a shot to save a passenger, we could lose several hundred in return . . ."

He seemed awfully calm, for all that to be going on in his head. My respect for him went up another notch.

We watched as the trooper clambered back to the front of his boat, grabbed the towing ring of the *Beauregard* with one hand,

and the cable with the other. Surely, and with what appeared an easy motion, he drew them together, and began to fasten the cable to the ring.

"He makes it look easy," said George.

He did, too. Slicker than hell.

We all began to make noises of relief, when there was another explosion on the *Beau*, throwing up a gout of water, oil, and mud.

"There she goes!" hollered Olinger. "Damn it, they've sunk her for sure now!"

True enough, the *General Beauregard* began to settle noticeably, and by the stern.

"Get those fuckin' yard engines moving!" hollered Lamar. "Now, Now!"

As the *Beau* started for the bottom stern-first, the yard diesels began to slowly take up the slack on the cable. Too fast, and they'd tear the towing rig right off the bow. Too slow, now, and they'd lose some 650 people to the icy water.

"Fast as they can," muttered Lamar.

The DNR iceboat accelerated rapidly, and came flying onto the concrete ramp at about 30 mph, lofting and skidding up the concrete slab for about 100 feet, before coming to rest behind a tin shed. The sense of relief was enormous, if fleeting.

As the *Beauregard* took on more and more water, her weight increased. As she settled deeper and deeper, the drag on the hull also increased. I was beginning to wonder if the yard engines were gong to be able to pull her in at all. So was Captain Olinger.

"It's gonna be goddamned close," he said.

As we watched, she began to glide toward us, but it was pretty obvious that she was going to be down a good amount before she got anywhere near the shore.

The hatchway doors along the lower deck began to open up, and passengers began to stream out toward the upper decks.

Suddenly, there was a belch of smoke from the two yard engines, and they began to move rapidly up the railroad tracks, being very careful not to gain speed too quickly. A few moments later, and the *Beau* had developed a noticeable movement. She was coming in.

She was also going down. The main deck was nearly awash for its full length, and the increasing angle at the stern had caused water to lap onto the rear portion of the second deck. It was going to be awfully close.

"If she strikes the bottom with her stern," said Captain Olinger, as much to himself as anyone, "I don't think the yard engines will be able to overcome the drag . . ." He looked at Lamar and said, "If that happens, we'll lose her."

The gunfire from the *Beauregard* seemed to have stopped completely, and many firemen were converging toward the area where it looked like she'd beach, if she were lucky.

"Do we have any fire trucks with really long extension ladders?" asked Adams. "She's pretty close now . . ."

"Nope," I answered. The tallest occupied structure in Nation County was three stories tall. Hook and ladder trucks weren't available.

Suddenly, the *Beauregard* seemed to lurch, and swayed over to her left, before righting herself. I could see some ten or fifteen passengers lose their footing, and slip and slide into the water.

"Fuck!" Lamar yelled at Sally to get the rescue crews into the water with whatever boats they had available.

"Struck the bottom," said Olinger, "but she bounced a bit."

The bow of the *Beauregard* was about 25 feet from the ramp, and the emergency personnel were beginning to prepare plank, netting, and a short section of floating dock that they'd detached from a long, beached dock about 50 yards from the water. The *Beau* was also way down at the stern, with water beginning to lap around the glazing at the rear of the third deck.

Suddenly, both the *General Beauregard* and the yard engines stopped, with the tension causing the bow cable to sing.

"Back the engines down!" hollered Lamar, into his walkie-talkie. "She's stuck . . . stop . . ."

Before he could finish, the cable snapped clear of the bow ring on the *Beau*, whipping and snaking through the air, flashing toward the yard engines. It struck one of the fire trucks near the ramp, rocking it, and throwing an extension ladder into the air.

Then, stillness.

The *General Beauregard* was stopped about ten feet from the end of the concrete boat ramp. We'd won.

Twenty-nine

Let's go," said Hester, as she and Art grabbed a stack of papers.

"What are those?" I asked, heading for the door right behind them.

"Xerox photos of Gabriel, to hand out to the troops. We don't want Gabe to slip by us, they gotta know what he looks like," said Hester.

I figured Volont wouldn't be too pleased. What the hell.

We ran all the way from the pavilion to the dock area.

Fire, rescue, and boat security personnel were busy preparing the portable ramps to carry the passengers to the dockside, and most of our officers were getting ready for a fight in case the suspects were crazy enough to resist. I was still very worried about that. Smart money would just surrender. But, then, smart money wouldn't necessarily have tried to rob the damned boat in the first place.

As the passengers were being very professionally handled by the boat staff and the rescue people, cops were everywhere, armed with their photocopies of Gabriel, and trying to scan every person who left the *Beauregard*. Just as Shamrock had reported, our suspects, who had originally been in coveralls, had removed them and their ski masks as soon as the one who ventured out on deck had been shot. They were mingling with the crowd, and it was pretty impossible to identify them in the rush, but at least twice they were helped by irate and frightened passengers who helpfully pointed out suspects. Nice work. They'd be re-examined in the holding areas.

We also had a woman blackjack dealer point one of the robbers out to us. It was kind of funny, really. She just grabbed his nylon windbreaker, and wouldn't let go. All the way down the ramp.

"Here's one! I've got one here!"

He was afraid to hit her with all the cops about. We scarfed him up and got her into a secure area for a statement.

Still no Gabriel.

I did see Nancy and Shamrock come down a ramp on the other side of the bow from me. They looked all right, but Nancy seemed to be a little wet. I waved. She glared back, and then grinned. One of the additional DCI agents, who'd arrived within the last couple of hours, came running over. He talked to Art and Hester for a second, and then they gave us the news.

The same kid who'd surrendered the stretch van had started to talk. We'd cleared an auditorium in the pavilion, and some DCI and FBI agents were doing the post-arrest interviews there. One of the questions the prisoners were all asked was "And when was the last time you saw Gabriel." They couldn't incriminate themselves no matter what the answer, because they'd all come directly out of the van. They were, as we say, caught in the act. Gabriel's last appearance in itself didn't affect their individual fates at all. Armed robbery was armed robbery. Or, as Sally would have said, piracy was piracy.

Anyway, when he was asked, he said, "Yesterday." The next question was directed at Gabriel's current whereabouts. The answer? "At the bank." So much for name, rank, and serial number.

Hester and Art went to the auditorium, and did the questions. She came out after about two minutes, at pretty close to a dead run. When she got across the street to where I had just been joined by George and Volont, she said, breathing hard, "He says that Gabriel wasn't on the boat. He says Gabriel is at the bank."

The other agent had said that the surviving suspects from the bank had said that Gabriel was on the boat. At first, they'd just thought that the two groups had their stories co-coordinated to confuse the cops. It looked to Hester, though, that both groups thought they were telling the truth.

"That's impossible. If he wasn't in the van, wasn't on the boat, and sure as hell wasn't in the bank . . ." said George, "where the hell is he?"

Our first thought was that we had missed him as they disembarked from the *Beauregard*. Then a state trooper came over, with a paper in his hand. He stood politely by, not wanting to butt in.

"Excuse me, sir?" Directed to me. I was pleased.

"Yeah, what you got?"

"The guy in this picture . . . are you sure he was on the boat?"

"Pardon?"

"Well, just before they went out with the cable, I could swear I saw him leave the parking lot over there in an old, beat-up green Chevy. It was weird, it caught my eye, because he was talking on a cell phone, and, well, he nearly fit the profile for a drug dealer, so I noticed him . . ."

Everybody was listening intently before he was finished.

He indicated the parking lot behind and offset to the left of the pavilion. "Right back there."

Well, sure. Of course. Right in front of us all the time. Well, more behind, actually. Right where he could see into the back windows of the DCI office, and also part of the boat, and part of the bank. He'd been there all along. Had to have been. Complete control, close contact, and concealed by being obvious. Son of a bitch.

We put out a message for anybody who saw a car matching that description to merely report it and give us the location and direction of travel. One of those "Do Not Stop" bulletins. Advisedly so.

The Freiberg officer, who had been assigned to the bridge ramp before the fun started, responded immediately. He gave the same description as the trooper had, and said, ". . . went through here about ten or fifteen minutes ago, headed west or south, depending on where he went at the intersection . . ."

In a perfect world, we would simply have put out a call to block some roads. Unfortunately, all the available assets in N.E. Iowa were either home in bed, or up at Freiberg with us.

"He picked up a hitchhiker, right up here . . ."

What?

We would have wasted time getting to our own vehicles, especially going back through the crowd. We commandeered two state troopers and their cars, and Volont, George, Hester, and I headed up the bridge ramp toward the Freiberg officer.

"Well, yeah," he said. "I was standing here, doing traffic control, and this guy came walking up out of the fog . . . from over that way . . . and he just talked with me for a couple of minutes. Said he was supposed to meet somebody. I told him that I was stopping all traffic into town, but he said they'd be leaving . . ."

"And . . ." said Volont, tightly.

"Well, this old green Chevy came up out of the fog, and the door opened and the driver just yelled, 'Get in, Harv,' and he did. He said, 'Good-bye' and they left." He looked at each of us, trying desperately to help. "They went that way . . ." he said, gesturing.

"What did this 'Harv' look like?" I asked.

I received a pretty good description of Harvey Grossman, Cletus Borglan's hired man.

For somebody whose best-laid plans were turning to shit in his hands, Volont was remarkably self-possessed. He directed the troopers to drive us up the hill to the spot where the Huey had landed, up out of the fog.

It was the fastest 10 mph I'd ever gone. I know the troopers were young, and highly trained drivers, and all that, but I for one couldn't see beyond the hood of our car.

When we got about halfway up the bluff, we emerged into blinding sunlight. It was just like climbing above the cloud layer in an airplane. It was so bright, in comparison, it almost hurt.

We covered the remaining mile to the Huey's location at about 100 mph.

I'd expected, I guess, that the TAC team members assigned to the Huey would have stayed with her. Of course not. They'd quite properly arranged to be transported to the bank area, via State Patrol, because that was where they were needed. Well, needed then. I really wished they were here now.

I was wondering just where we were headed. So, too, was Hester.

"So, you think we just fly and look out the windows for a car?" She said this as we took notice of the enormous traffic jam in the single lane leading down toward Freiberg and the fog. All traffic was still being stopped.

Volont put down his cell phone. "They just pulled into Grossman's farm," he said.

"What?"

Volont looked surprised. "You didn't think we'd pulled our surveillance just because you caught a couple of agents, did you?"

Actually, I had. If he hadn't, that meant that he knew about the tractors in the field that night about as soon as I had. Among other things.

"Get in, Houseman," he said. "You hold the arrest warrant. I think you ought to serve it."

Volont, Hester, George, and I. That was it.

"You serious?" I asked, as I hauled myself into the dark green helicopter.

He was. He told the pilot to take us where instructed, and then to immediately return for some of the TAC team. He said that there was a "high probability" that we'd need assistance, so to bring them as fast as possible.

Right. Like that would be fast enough.

The pilot had a map of the county, and I indicated Grossman's farm. "The people we want are there, so far, and they're armed. Like he said, we gotta hurry . . ."

"Hang on, troops," he said, over the intercom. "We're gonna haul ass, here . . ."

The term fit. We went up, the nose came down slightly, and we were off. Fast. I leaned forward, and saw the airspeed indicator hovering around 110 knots. 120 mph. Cool. It was about fifteen road miles to Grossman's, maybe thirteen air miles. Six or seven minutes.

Volont's cell phone apparently didn't work in the chopper. He put it away with a scowl, and began to brief us in a loud voice.

"They plan to flee," he shouted, "in a private plane. It flew in late last night!"

I stared at him. Of course.

"Houseman just missed seeing the plane," he shouted. "But he did see them grooming a runway for it!"

Damn. Damn. Of all the possibilities, smoothing the lumps and ridges to make a runway just hadn't occurred to me. But now that he had said it, it was so damned obvious.

"Harvey Grossman's a pilot. He's apparently with Gabriel. We have to stop them before they leave! It gets too complicated if they take off!"

No kidding. But it had the advantage that they'd be out of my jurisdiction in a hurry. I kept my thoughts to myself.

"I have no idea where they might be headed!"

Sure he didn't.

"Here we are! Put us over by the big shed . . ."

I looked out, and saw the Grossmans' house about two miles away. As we swooped in, and I hung on for dear life, I saw an old green Chevy near the house, but no plane. Gone? Already?

Then I saw the nose of a propeller-driven small plane, blue and white, as we went by the open machine shed and settled to the ground.

Thirty

We left the Huey as fast as we could, slipping in the damp snow, and I swear that helicopter was starting to lift off before I was out the door. The downwash was enormous, and we were pelted with chunks of snow, bits of mud and straw, and tiny lumps of cow manure. Then it was gone, and I found myself running toward the cover of a tractor with a scoop bucket attached to the front. I slid to a stop behind the comforting disk of the big rear wheel. I stopped, snuggled up against the tire. The shed with the aircraft was just about straight ahead of me, with a barn to my left, and the house on a little rise to my right. None of them more than 100 feet away.

The sound of my running, and of the departing helicopter, had stopped at the same time, and it became very quiet in the yard. The only thing I could hear was my own breathing. I cautiously looked to my left, and saw George crouched behind a corner of the barn about fifty feet from me, with Volont behind a couple of rusted old 55 gallon drums between George and the airplane. I looked to my right, and saw Hester was on one knee behind a woodpile. About thirty feet from my position. So far, so good. I did notice, though, than none of us had anything but a handgun. Not good.

"Carl!" I saw George frantically gesturing toward the inside of the shed containing the airplane. "On the ground, to the left . . ."

I cautiously peered around the edge of the tractor tire, expecting to see a man with a gun. Or a bazooka. Or a tank emerging . . .

Instead, I saw nothing in the dark recesses except the plane. The sunlight on the snow was making things so bright the inside of the impromptu hangar was like a black pit.

"What? I don't see anything . . ."

"To the left of the building," he said. "On the ground!"

I looked again. Ah. Oh, my. Grossman had apparently used the space between the shed and the barn as a place to push the snow out of his yard and driveway. He'd left a small space on either side of the ten-foot-high pile, wide enough to permit someone to walk between the buildings. There was a black snowmobile boot, and a dark blue snowmobile-suited leg visible on the far side of the pile. It was very still.

"Yeah?" I said.

"Surveillance. They got down here to keep them out of the plane . . ." He looked awfully grim.

As he spoke, Volont rose from his position behind the rusted drums, and ran straight toward the pile and the motionless leg.

One shot, but so suddenly loud that I jumped. I don't know where it went, but Volont covered the last ten feet in the air, and hit the side of the shed with a loud *thump*. I thought he'd been hit, until he got up, knelt over the figure, and then scrambled frantically up the snow pile, tumbling down the other side and out of my line of sight. As he did, there was a burst of fire, and the side of the shed where he had just been erupted with small holes, bits of metal, and dust.

I caught what I thought was a muzzle flash from inside the shed. It seemed to come from near the tail of the plane, but it was very hard to tell. No handgun, though. No, sir. Automatic rifle.

I could imagine the surveillance man moving slowly between the shed and the pile, and shots coming through the corrugated steel of the shed and cutting him down. Never had a chance. I glanced toward Hester, and saw that she was looking toward the house. I could only see an edge of the upper floor and part of the roof from my vantage point.

"Hester . . ." She turned toward me. "You got something in the house?"

She shook her head. "Gotta be there, though."

Of course. The shooter inside the shed couldn't see anybody moving in the narrow space between the shed and the pile. But somebody in the house sure could.

Well, now we knew where. It then became a question of how many. And, given the capabilities of Gabriel, I thought it would be very nice to know who was where.

Since the tractor I had picked as my refuge had a large glazed cab with a pair of frozen coveralls obscuring my view, and since the bucket and engine stood a good eight feet above the ground, I had a dilemma. If I looked at the shed and airplane from the rear of the tractor, I wasn't able to see the house. If I looked at the house, I wasn't able to see the shed. Furthermore, it occurred to me that, if I moved toward the front of the tractor in order to see the house again, the lower half of my body was completely exposed to whoever was in the shed. Well, I had to find out who was where. On both sides. I'd now lost sight of Volont, and assumed that there was at least one other member of the surveillance team somewhere . . .

"George . . ." Sort of came out in a very energetic whisper.

He looked toward me.

"How many people from the surveillance team . . . ?"

He held up two fingers.

"Where . . . ?"

He shook his head.

I took a deep breath. Well, maybe I could at least locate Gabriel. "Jacob Nieuhauser!" I hollered, generally toward the shed.

Silence. I repeated myself. With an addition. "Deputy sheriff! We have a warrant for your arrest! Surrender!"

Total silence. I tried again. Nothing. I was thinking about

reinforcements, and stalling until they arrived. I figured that it had taken us about ten minutes to get to the farm via helicopter. That meant that, if things went completely without a hitch, we could expect the chopper back about twenty minutes after it had left us. And with it, some of the TAC team. At least fifteen minutes from now, and probably thirty, knowing how things usually went.

I looked to my right, toward Hester. She was looking toward the house. "Hey, Gorse!" She looked around. "Cell phone?" I mouthed.

"What?"

I made a "talking on the phone" gesture, and then held out my hand. She fumbled inside her jacket, and then produced her phone. She squared herself facing me, concentrated for a second, and then tossed it toward me, underhand.

Unfortunately, it landed just on my side of the front tractor tire. About fifteen feet from me, and twelve of those feet were completely exposed to whoever was in the shed.

Hester stared at the phone, and then looked up. She appeared to start to say a word that began with an f, from the way her lower lip curled under her teeth.

Well, now. I thought about it for a few seconds. Most of the time, if you're in a rush, you screw up. Calm and deliberate actions usually succeed. Right. With that in mind, I holstered my sidearm, and almost literally threw myself at that damned phone. I slipped as I reached for it, caught myself with my left hand, went down on one knee, grabbed the phone, and hurled myself back toward the safety of the huge rear tire.

Panting, I became aware that there hadn't been a shot fired. Even better.

Still breathing hard, I dialed the Sheriff's Department. They answered on the second ring.

"This is . . . Houseman . . . here. I need . . . Grossman's phone number . . . really fast . . ."

I dialed the Grossman house. I was betting that Linda was in the house, and that Harvey and Gabriel were in the shed. I felt that I would be able to convince Linda to give up, or at least to not make it worse for herself by taking shots at us, or signaling to the men in the shed.

"Hello?" Such a little voice.

"Uh, uh, Carrie?" Carrie. I'd forgotten about Carrie.

"Yes."

"Hi. This is Deputy Houseman. Remember me?"

"Yes. You're the one behind the tractor, aren't you?"

"Yes, I am." Oh, Lord. "Carrie, can I speak with your mom?"

"She's not here, Deputy Houseman." A little voice, but so very serious.

"Oh, that's too bad. Uh, do you know where she is, Carrie?"

"In the shed with my dad." Her voice quavered just a bit. "Are you going to hurt them?"

"I sure don't want to, Carrie." I didn't want them to hurt me, either. "Uh . . . is there somebody else there in the shed with them, too?"

There was a pause. "No."

No? In there with Carrie? "Are you alone in the house, Carrie?"

"Yes."

Well, that was sort of a relief. She was effectively out of the way for any activity. But the crucial question was "Where's the other man, Carrie?"

There was a longer pause. "I shouldn't tell you. But I can see him. Can't you? He's by the snow pile."

Oh, hell, I thought. That's Volont.

"I think that man came with us in the helicopter, Carrie . . ."

"No, it's Mr. Gabriel. I can see him. He's *with* that man who came with you. See? Here they come . . . I better go now . . ." And she hung up.

"See?" "See?" I looked toward the edge of the snow pile where Volont had disappeared. A moment later, Volont and Gabriel emerged. Together. Sort of. Except Volont had his hands clasped behind his head. As they moved out a bit more, I could see that Gabriel was, as usual, doing things right. None of this gun to the hostage's head business. No, not him. Gabriel was about three feet behind Volont, with a handgun pointed at the agent's back. No way Volont was going to be able to try for the gun without being shot. None. Just too much distance between them.

They came just about to the front edge of the shed, and stopped.

Hester saw them, too. "Carl . . . They've got Volont . . ."

"I see . . ."

George, way over to my left, couldn't see either Volont or Gabriel because of the edge of the barn.

"What? What . . . ?"

"Gabriel's got your boss," I said. "Between the buildings . . ."

George scooted out from behind the pile of drums, and ran as hard as he could for the barn. He slipped once, but made the concrete apron leading to the main door. He pressed himself against the side of the barn, and held his gun down at his side. From where he was, the people in the shed couldn't see him unless they came forward from the shadows. They had to have known he'd broken cover and headed for the barn, though. I pointed my handgun around the edge of my faithful tractor tire, and took aim at the general area where one of the Grossmans would have to be if they were to get a shot at George.

"Hester?" As quietly as I could, and still have her hear me. Pretty loud.

"Yeah . . . ?"

"Hester, the little Grossman girl is alone in the house. She answered the phone. Both parents are in the shed with the plane."

You never have to tell Hester twice. Ever. She popped her head up for a second, got her bearings, and then began to move quickly and apparently effortlessly to her right, into the cover provided by the house. The last I saw of her, she was disappearing around the corner, heading for the backyard.

"Drop your guns!" Gabriel. Nobody moved.

"I said, 'Drop your guns'! If you do, nobody will get hurt."

I doubted that. The dead surveillance agent had pretty well gotten me past that point. It did occur to me that, with George concealed from the line of sight of the bad guys, and Hester slipping around the back of the house, I was the only one to do any talking for the good guys.

"Nobody will get hurt if you put yours down," I shouted. Brilliant. But I couldn't really think of anything else to say.

"Deputy Houseman? Is that you?" Gabriel sounded almost happy.

"Yes!"

"Are you still insured with Lloyds of London?" he boomed.

"Probably not!"

"You can't bluff this one, Houseman! Drop your guns!"

Well, of course we couldn't. No way. The thing was, time was really on our side, now. The helicopter would be coming back soon, with the cavalry. Once they landed and got into position, what with George and Hester flanking the bad guys, and me blocking the front . . . endgame.

It began to occur to me that me blocking the front was the only catch. They knew about George heading toward the barn, but they had to think Hester was still out front with me. Their obvious move was to take out the people blocking the front. Get in the plane. Taxi straight out of the shed, and just take off.

I began to feel there was a neon arrow pointing to the ass end of my tractor.

Stall. I had to stall.

"It's all over!" I shouted. "Don't get any more people hurt or killed! Surrender!"

I keep forgetting. "Surrender" to your average criminal has a lot less stigma than "surrender" does to a career military man.

"No!" He paused. "Take him out!"

What?

Somebody in the shed, I assumed Harvey Grossman, let loose with a rifle on full auto, and pretty much emptied a magazine toward me and the woodpile where Hester had been. I could see, even as I started to duck back, that some of the slugs tore into the ground between the front and rear of the tractor. Most seemed to strike the cab and the huge rear tires and rims. I was showered with tiny bits of glass, wood splinters, and sprayed with a thick liquid. For a second, I thought the viscous stuff was blood, until I realized that most farmers filled the tractor tires with oil instead of air.

I waited what seemed like forever before I screwed my courage up and hollered around the tire again.

"There's no more reason to go on with this! Give it up!" How many ways are there to say "surrender" without saying "surrender"?

At least this time, nobody shot.

"If you don't come out with your hands up," hollered Gabriel, "I'm going to shoot our boy Volont!"

Where was that damned helicopter? I couldn't think of anything else to say, and until it arrived, Gabriel had the upper hand.

"Like I said, 'Give it up!' " Stalling, stalling . . .

"Harvey, start up the plane!" Gabriel stepped forward with Volont, toward the opening to the shed. They stopped, so close to the front of the barn that Volont, a few feet in ahead of Gabriel, saw George. He only glanced at him, and then looked steadfastly over in my direction. Control.

There was a little commotion inside the shed, near the plane. I more sensed it than actually saw anything. But a few seconds later, Linda Grossman emerged, hesitant, with a gun in her hand. "I'm going to the house!" she yelled. "We're taking my daughter!"

I saw Gabriel's lips move, but didn't hear what he said. Linda stepped slowly into the yard area, obviously afraid of being shot any second. She was concentrating mostly on the house, and began to move more quickly the closer she got.

Shit. Now we'd have Carrie in the plane as well. No chance at all. Gabriel was just about home-free.

Just as Linda Grossman got to the porch door, she turned, looking toward Gabriel. That's when she spotted George. That's also when she screamed, and started to bring up her gun. Things happened very, very fast after that. In the space of two seconds . . .

Hester stepped out of the porch door of the Grossman house and slammed into Linda, pitching her to the ground.

Carrie stood in the door, and screamed, "Mommy!"

Gabriel knocked Volont down, and stepped toward Linda Grossman, bringing his gun around toward Hester.

I fired two rounds at Gabriel, and missed. He shifted his aim toward me.

And George stepped out from the side of the barn, and fired once. There was a flash of pinkish halo around Gabriel's head, in the bright sunlight. He went to his knees, and pitched forward, facedown into the mud and snow. It was freaky, seeing him do that and make no attempt to break his fall. He was dead before he hit.

Hester, firmly pressing Linda Grossman's head into the snow with her knee, pointed her gun into the shed. "Come out, now!"

I stepped around the tire as I saw Harvey Grossman emerge from the shadows. His hands were in the air. I advanced slowly toward him, pointed my gun at his chest. "You're under arrest!"

In the silence that followed, Volont expressed his gratitude to George. "You fucking idiot! I needed him alive!"

If George had decided to shoot again, I wouldn't have stopped him. In the distance, I could hear the *wop*, *wop* of Huey rotor blades. Closer, I could hear Carrie crying and screaming at Hester.

"Don't hurt my mommy, you . . . you damn cop!"

Epilogue

As far as the *Beauregard* goes, there was some truly great TV coverage, with her being pulled to shore by the two diesel locomotives. Endless interviews with the "survivors." A great print article by Nancy, with exclusive photos by Shamrock. The two of them covered the entire event, with a little help from their friends. If they ever were really angry at me, it didn't last too long. They sent me a tin of cookies with a note. WE FORGIVE YOU. JUST DON'T LET IT HAPPEN AGAIN. It was signed NANCY & SHAMROCK.

I'll tell you, they got some *great* photos of Adams and me at the stretch van.

ATF had a bomb team search the *General Beauregard* just as soon as the last person came off the boat. There were no more bombs. The marine engineers told us that, if the railroad yard diesels hadn't been ready when they were, we likely would have lost the boat, and most of the passengers. Points to Lamar on that one.

At any rate, Cletus got two years for conspiracy. A plea bargain. He claimed he'd been duped. I sort of think that he was. Well, with a lot of his own effort.

Blitek was charged with attempted murder, but skated on a plea of insanity. Honest. I couldn't believe it. As far as I'm concerned, he was inept and fearful, not suicidal. But the prosecutor said we wouldn't be able to prove who he was trying to kill, since he hadn't actually killed or hit anybody. My argument was that we couldn't prove he was suicidal, since he was still alive. Prosecutors have no sense of humor. I'm told that all Blitek does at the Mental Health Institute is argue politics with the doctors.

Freddie, the poor devil who started the whole thing off by missing his cousins, got a five-year suspended sentence for burglary. One of the few plea bargains I agree with. And I know Fred. We'll probably get him for burglary again someday. He won't be able to help it.

Freddie's aunt, the mother of the murdered Colsons, came to see me. She wanted to know what the man was doing in the house, when he killed her sons. Why he was there in the first place. I finally told her that he was a burglar, too, but a much more dangerous one than her sons.

The best news, from an evidentiary point of view, was that we finally had access to the real fingerprints for Gabriel. We were able to match them as far back as an ejected rifle cartridge found at the Stritch farm where the photographer was shot. Finally closed that case.

Both Harvey and Linda Grossman told us that Gabriel had, indeed, killed the two boys at the farm. He had thought they were cops, and never changed his mind. Harvey's in prison, doing an armed robbery stretch for the boat business, time plus fifteen years for having the handgun in his possession. He was, it turned out, a convicted felon. Federal. Volont had been onto him from the start, and made sure Gabriel was able to recruit him. Seemed kind of unfair to me. After all, he never would have been there in the first place if it weren't for Volont. Linda got a twenty-year suspended sentence. Her daughter, Carrie, was the main reason for that.

I never told anybody what Volont told me about the devices Gabriel wanted to buy. But I watch the news every night, waiting. Somebody, after all, has probably purchased them by now.

Volont said that, when he was at the body of the first surveillance agent, he could hear somebody say, "He's where?" inside the shed. Turned out that Carrie was on the phone to her dad, telling everybody where we were. That's why he jumped over the snow pile. When he did, he just about landed on the second surveillance agent's dead body. Gabriel had apparently killed him just before we got there. As Volont was checking the body, Gabriel was behind him. Must have been quite a surprise.

Oh, one more thing. George told me that Volont was really mad at him. Kept making the claim that he could have gotten the gun away from Gabriel, and it wasn't necessary for George to shoot at all. Right. The thing was that, this way, we all damned well knew where Gabriel was now. For the first time.

The thing that bothered me most, though, was the hurt look on Hester's face when Carrie was yelling at her. She deserves so much better than that.